I0819169

TED BELL'S
WARMONGER

TITLES BY TED BELL

THE ALEX HAWKE SERIES

Ted Bell's Warmonger (by Ryan Steck)

Ted Bell's Monarch (by Ryan Steck)

Sea Hawke

Dragonfire

Overkill

Patriot

Warriors

Phantom

Warlord

Tsar

Spy

Pirate

Assassin

Hawke

NOVELLAS

White Death

What Comes Around

Crash Dive

YOUNG ADULT NOVELS

The Time Pirate

Nick of Time

TED BELL'S
WARMONGER

RYAN STECK

BERKLEY
NEW YORK

BERKLEY
An imprint of Penguin Random House LLC
1745 Broadway, New York, NY 10019
penguinrandomhouse.com

Book design by George Towne

Library of Congress Cataloging-in-Publication Data

Names: Steck, Ryan author
Title: Ted Bell's Warmonger / Ryan Steck.
Other titles: Warmonger
Description: New York: Berkley, 2026. | Series: An Alex Hawke novel
Identifiers: LCCN 2025032885 (print) | LCCN 2025032886 (ebook) |
ISBN 9780593817261 hardcover | ISBN 9780593817278 ebook
Subjects: LCGFT: Fiction | Spy fiction | Thrillers (Fiction) | Novels
Classification: LCC PS3619.T4325 T45 2026 (print) | LCC PS3619.T4325 (ebook)
LC record available at https://lccn.loc.gov/2025032885
LC ebook record available at https://lccn.loc.gov/2025032886

Printed in the United States of America
1st Printing

The authorized representative in the EU for product safety and compliance is Penguin Random House Ireland, Morrison Chambers, 32 Nassau Street, Dublin D02 YH68, Ireland, https://eu-contact.penguin.ie.

For Theodora Byrd Carver.
Oh, what a blessing you are.
And what a special name you carry forward, Teddy.
And for my dear friend Byrdie Bell.

TED BELL'S
WARMONGER

ONE

ISTANBUL, TURKEY

Though it wasn't perhaps what he was best known for, it was certainly no secret that Lord Alexander Hawke knew how to make an entrance.

His Lancia D24—custom-built in 1953 and driven to victory in the 1954 Mille Miglia by Alberto Ascari—roared down the cobbled Bab-ı Ali Caddesi, negotiating a maze of minor streets through Sultanahmet Square before coming to an abrupt and quite dramatic halt at the Imperial Gate, entrance to the historic Topkapı Palace. He idled there, slowly advancing down the queue of attendees, occasionally revving the 3,284-cubic-centimeter, 265-horsepower V6 engine as if to say, *"Still here, old chap,"* until at last it was his turn to hand the reins of his mechanical steed over to a waiting valet.

Hawke stepped out, the midnight blue of his bespoke Tom Ford tuxedo accentuating his athletic frame, looking every inch the aristocrat that he, in fact, was. He stood just north of six feet tall, with a thick mane of unruly black hair that was deliberately at odds with the rest of his immaculate appearance. As he made way for the valet, he allowed himself a wry smile. "Mind you, don't scratch the paint, old boy," he said. "It's older than both of us."

The nervous valet just stared back, goggle-eyed, as Hawke swept past him and joined the line filing through the security checkpoint leading into the complex.

Built in 1459 under Sultan Mehmed II—or Mehmed the Conqueror as he was known to history—the sprawling complex known as Topkapı Palace had, for nearly four centuries, been the stage for crucial state affairs, with viziers and foreign dignitaries gathered beneath its soaring dome. Though now a museum celebrating the fallen grandeur of the Ottoman Empire, the palace nevertheless retained a regal aura, especially tonight, as it played host to some of the most powerful figures in the Western world: ambassadors, military leaders, and, of course, spies.

The NATO strategic alliance summit had been held in Istanbul to address the ongoing conflict in Eastern Europe and growing fears that Russia's adventure in the Ukraine might lead to an all-out conflict with NATO member nations that had once been part of another fallen empire: the Soviet Union. The Republic of Turkey, a NATO member nation since 1952, straddling the line between Europe and the Middle East, had been chosen to host the summit, and this final soiree put on by Turkey's minister of national defense, Amir al-Fulan, celebrated the close of the event. One last chance for the attendees to come together and, theoretically at least, reinforce their mutual commitment to the alliance.

Hawke detested formal events. Found them unimaginably tedious. The only thing that could be said for them was that the champagne usually flowed in copious amounts—though, given a choice, Hawke would have preferred a tot of Goslings Black Seal rum in some grimy outlaw dive bar on a Caribbean waterfront. The company was usually better, and something about it appealed to his pirate blood. He was, in fact, a direct descendant of the notorious buccaneer Richard Hawke, known as "Blackhawke," and had inherited more from his ancestor than just an affinity for grog.

But Hawke wasn't here for the champagne.

He had attended the summit in his role as the CEO of Hawke Industries, an internationally recognized defense contractor whose participation in bolstering NATO's defenses against Russia's growing aggression was a given. The ongoing war in Ukraine had created an unparalleled opportunity for NATO member nations to "sell" many of their aging war machines to Kyiv and replace them with new, state-of-the-art technologies, many of which were produced by Hawke's subsidiary companies, so he had a vested interest in not only knowing how his wares would be used in days to come but also what the next generation of warfare might look like. Yet this too was merely a cover. Alex Hawke wasn't just another billionaire businessman, and he wasn't at the summit to rub elbows with the rich and powerful.

He was here to hunt.

TWO

I*t would appear that there's a warmonger, Alex,"* Sir David Trulove had told Hawke less than a fortnight previously. *"A bloody fucking nasty man causing all kinds of ruckus around the world."*

As the head of the Secret Intelligence Service, the United Kingdom's spy agency—sometimes referred to as MI6—it was Trulove's business to know about all the nasty men causing ruckuses around the world, and as Trulove's most intrepid and audacious secret agent, it was Hawke's business to be told about them.

Despite his successes in the private sector—he was now the fifth wealthiest person in the United Kingdom—Hawke was constitutionally incapable of sitting still. Like his distant pirate ancestor, when adventure called, he answered, first as a Royal Navy aviator, flying Harriers and other fighter-interceptor aircraft into combat, then as an elite commando in the Special Boat Service. He now used his wealth and the access it afforded him to conduct and execute clandestine missions on His Majesty's Secret Service.

"*We don't know much about him, to be quite frank,"* Trulove had continued, *"but, you see, he's making demands of the king, and, well, Charles trusts nobody but you to handle this."*

Alex, already craving a new adventure, had not needed much convincing. *"A warmonger, you say. Well, Trulove, then it sounds like we had better get moving rather quickly, don't you think?"*

The next day, in Trulove's private study on the fourth floor of 85 Albert Embankment, Vauxhall Cross—the modern ziggurat-style structure known variously as Babylon on Thames, Legoland, and HQ of the Secret Intelligence Service—Gwendolyn "Pippa" Guinness, a deputy chief of the Service and Trulove's number two, had laid out exactly how little was actually known about the Warmonger.

"He's an enigma," she had told Hawke. *"We don't know who he is or where he's from. All we have are rumors hinting at his influence. He's rather like Moriarty in the Sherlock Holmes stories: a mastermind working behind the scenes, manipulating events."*

It was a reference Hawke's best friend, former Scotland Yard chief inspector and Holmes aficionado Ambrose Congreve, would have appreciated.

"'The Napoleon of Crime,'" Hawke had murmured, recalling how Conan Doyle described Holmes's archnemesis.

"Only the Warmonger is the Napoleon of war."

"I rather thought Napoleon was the Napoleon of war," Hawke had remarked. *"I daresay, Pip, for a bloody intelligence service, you don't seem to have much in the way of bloody intelligence."*

"That's why you're here, Alex. You're C's bloodhound, and he wants you to run the Warmonger to ground." C was the official designation used by every chief of the SIS.

"Even a bloodhound needs a sniff."

Pippa's wry smile had told Hawke that she had been waiting for just such a prompt. *"We have received credible intelligence indicating that the Warmonger will be putting in a personal appearance at the upcoming NATO strategic alliance summit in Istanbul."*

"A personal appearance, you say?"

"It's the opinion of the Eastern European Section that the Warmonger may be a highly placed government official from one of the NATO member nations, possibly one of the former Soviet states, working as a saboteur to undermine the alliance on Putin's behalf. That's just conjecture, but it's a place to start looking."

THREE

Eschewing the offer of a ride in one of the electric trolleys shuttling attendees back and forth across the grounds, Hawke proceeded on foot, strolling through the First Courtyard, the wide, open expanse of manicured gardens and ancient trees that separated the outer and inner walls of the Topkapı Palace. His stroll brought him to the Gate of Salutation, with its two iconic towers standing watch on either side of the entrance. Hawke did not fail to notice the soldiers stationed in the turrets, gazing vigilantly down upon the crowd. Beyond the gate, he entered the more intimate environs of the Second Courtyard, a vast rectangle enclosed by various palace buildings: the Imperial Hall, the Treasury, the Audience Hall, and the kitchens. Elegant lighting illuminated the garden paths, casting soft, amber hues over the old stone buildings of the palace complex.

Inside the magnificently domed Imperial Hall, the atmosphere was thick with decadence and intrigue. Brilliant blue and emerald tiles adorned the walls, shimmering in the glow from the golden lamps that lined the space. Each tile told a story: scenes of paradise, intricate floral patterns, and verses from the Quran, all perfectly preserved from a time when sultans ruled these very halls. A raised dais stood at the far end of the room, where once the sultan would sit, flanked by advisors and warriors, receiving ambassadors and enemies alike. Tonight it served as the stage for a quartet playing Ottoman classical music on ney flutes and tambours, their haunting melodies mixing with the gentle murmur of conversation.

The rich scent of saffron and spices drifted from long banquet tables, where silver trays gleamed with delicacies. Waiters floated amidst the throng, balancing trays loaded with glasses of champagne and, as a concession to the Muslim faith to which many of the host nation's attendees at least nominally adhered, tall glasses of *sharbat*, a sweet, spiced drink of honey and fruit.

Hawke helped himself to a flute of champagne and ventured out into the midst of the gathering. The crowd—an assortment of diplomats, high-ranking military officers, and plus-ones—parted instinctively as if sensing that someone important was in their midst. Yet it wasn't his aristocratic lineage or prodigious fortune that commanded their attention. It was the way he moved: with the confident, almost predatory gait of a man who was equally at ease on the battlefield or in the boardroom. Alex Hawke resembled nothing so much as a lion sauntering lazily through his pride, seemingly indifferent to the wary gazes of lesser beasts and yet poised and ready to pounce. Counterintuitively, his natural charisma concealed his true purpose, for while he could not help but be noticed, those who observed him often failed to realize that he was also watching them.

Over the course of the four-day-long conference, Hawke had observed dozens of mid-level functionaries as well as members of his own cohort, wealthy defense contractors and arms dealers, warmongers in the literal sense—merchants trafficking in the means to make war—but not necessarily the Warmonger. Now, in the less structured environment of a mixer, he was curious to see who would gravitate toward whom, who came together to whisper, who exchanged discreet nods or glances. In this more relaxed setting, with the barriers down and alliances—both secret and strategic—being made with a casual clink of champagne glasses, perhaps the Warmonger would reveal himself.

Many of the VIPs who had addressed the summit were conspicuously absent. Having so many senior world leaders in one place would have made a very tempting target for terrorists. Consequently, most attendees of the soiree represented lower-tier figures—men and, yes, a few women, whose names and faces were not well-known outside the insular world of international diplomacy but who nonetheless did most of the heavy lifting.

Hawke spotted General Markus Schroeder, the imposing commander of NATO's Eastern European defense forces, in an apparently heated conversation with Ambassador Leena Valge, Estonia's envoy to NATO. General Osman Gul, rumored to be next in line for the post of Turkish national defense minister, hovered near the buffet while the current minister, Amir al-Fulan, was chatting up Alain Devereaux, a notorious French arms dealer.

Then he noticed another familiar face and felt an unexpected flush of excitement. Commander Savannah Stone, Royal Navy—adjutant to the senior British commander in NATO, General Sir Richard West—was someone who had not escaped his notice during the summit, and not merely for professional reasons. Tall, blond, and striking in her navy service dress uniform, she managed a delicate balance between authority and elegance. Now, however, attired in a sleek royal blue evening gown that hugged her spectacular figure, with her hair freed from the strict regulation bun, falling in soft waves to frame her angular face, the balance tipped.

When she caught him looking and flashed a dazzling smile, Hawke inclined his head in an appreciative nod, then looked away. He wasn't a free man, and he wasn't here to play. In any case, Savannah Stone was not someone to trifle with.

All of a sudden, Hawke's senses went to full alert. His instincts, which had more than once awakened him to unexpected danger, were sounding an alarm. He had noticed something—noticed it without really noticing—and now, like the missile warning systems in the jet fighters he had once piloted, his subconscious was pinging like crazy.

He did another slow scan of the hall, searching for the cause of his premonition, and locked in on a figure lingering at the edge of the hall, a man of average height and build, with sharp, angular features and short-cropped dark hair peppered with gray. Hawke did not recognize the man, and while this was not in itself unusual—there were more than five hundred names on the guest list—there was something about this man—the unease in his stance, the sharpness in his gaze as he surreptitiously scanned the room, much as Hawke himself was doing—that seemed to validate Hawke's subconscious alert.

Hawke was not the only one hunting tonight.

There might have been a perfectly reasonable explanation for the man's heightened vigilance. He could have been a plainclothes security agent or even an intelligence operative from one of the other NATO member nations, like Hawke, quietly hunting the elusive Warmonger. But Hawke's instincts said otherwise.

Careful not to look directly at his target, Hawke began moving toward the man, weaving fluidly through the crowd, exchanging pleasantries with military leaders and diplomats, as he closed in on the . . .

Damn it, where the devil did he go?

Hawke surveyed the area where the man had been only moments before, broadening his search in ever-expanding arcs until he spotted someone that he thought might be his quarry, passing through one of the exterior entrances leading back out into the Second Courtyard. The man's face was turned away, but the hair and build looked right, and the conspicuous bulge in the man's dinner jacket, which looked suspiciously like the print of a concealed firearm in a kidney holster, removed any lingering doubt.

Abandoning his pretense of nonchalance, Hawke crossed the hall at a brisk walk, reaching the ornate doorway a mere five seconds after the man's exit. He burst out into the open and spotted the man moving swiftly along the edge of the building, keeping close to the outer walls of the Imperial Council Hall. He was moving fast—too fast for someone who was just taking a leisurely stroll to get some fresh air. No, this man had a purpose, and it wasn't sightseeing.

Hawke followed quickly, almost at a run, the sound of his steps on the cobblestone path lost in the lively murmur emanating from the building behind him.

The man had turned onto a path veering north, across the courtyard, and toward another section of the palace. Hawke was rapidly closing the gap, but as the pursuit moved deeper into the wooded courtyard and away from the hall, his footfalls were no longer masked by the sounds of the festivities. Hawke saw the man's shoulders tense, and while he did not look back, Hawke knew that the man had sensed his presence. He took a few more steps, then veered to the right, leaving the path and disappearing behind one of the ancient trees.

Not good.

Figuring that his quarry was either going to spring out and challenge him with gun drawn or remain in hiding, waiting to spring an ambush, Hawke—who, as a student of warfare, followed the admonition of American general George Patton's *When in doubt, ATTACK!*—immediately turned off the path, ducking behind the nearest tree trunk. Rather than play a waiting game, however, he kept going, stepping around the tree, weaving through the boughs in a flanking maneuver that would, he hoped, catch his target looking the other way.

It worked.

Mere seconds after ducking into the woods, Hawke spotted the other man crouching behind a tree, facing the path and, more importantly, facing away from Hawke. At the last possible instant, he seemed once more to sense Hawke's presence, spinning around, pistol in hand, to cover his six o'clock, but by then it was already too late.

Hawke caught the man's wrist, thrusting the arm up and away and giving it a savage twist that put the man on his knees, the pistol falling from suddenly nerveless fingers. The suddenness and ferocity of Hawke's attack overwhelmed the man, but only momentarily. Rather than make a futile attempt to wrest free of Hawke's grip, the man rotated his body into the hold, easing the pressure on his joints and giving him enough leverage to slip out of the wrist lock. Then, just as quickly, he went on the attack. Hawke barely had time to brace himself as the man launched a punch at his ribs and just managed to turn his body so that the strike mostly glanced off him. The force of the blow nevertheless rattled him.

Quick as a cat, the man shifted, attempting to grab hold of Hawke's jacket collar, clearly aiming to throw him off-balance and take him down. Hawke, who regularly trained with Roger Gracie at his London jujitsu academy, realized what the man was attempting and snapped his knee up into the man's gut, momentarily disrupting the rhythm of the fight. Still, the man's technique confirmed Hawke's original impression that this was more than just a common thug; he was a professional.

The man staggered back but regained his footing almost instantly, launching a barrage of rapid punches, which Hawke was hard-pressed to either dodge or block.

All right, that's just about enough of that, thought Hawke.

When the man threw his next punch, Hawke let it sail past his head, catching the arm and pulling the man toward him, using his foe's momentum to whip him around in a spinning throw. The man hit the ground hard with Hawke riding him down, locking the arm in a submission hold. The man struggled, trying to break free, but this time he had no leverage and no room to maneuver. Hawke gave the arm another twist, and a howl of frustration and pain tore from the man's lips.

"There, now," Hawke said, "let's have a little chat, shall we?"

The man managed to snarl something through his torment. The outburst wasn't in English, and although Hawke was no polyglot, he recognized both the language—Russian—and the particularly vulgar oath. He pushed his hold another inch, cutting off any further imprecations.

"Let's leave my mother out of this," he growled, easing off just a little. "Now, let's try again. In English this time. I'm sure they taught you it in SVR or whatever outfit you're working for. What the bloody hell are you doing here?"

Anticipating that the man was gathering steam for another show of defiance, Hawke preemptively increased the pressure of his hold. "Need I remind you to keep a civil tongue?"

"Nyet," gasped the man.

"There, now, see? We can talk this out like gentlemen. So let me ask you again: Why are you here?"

"Security."

Hawke glanced down at the discarded pistol, a Makarov. The compact semiauto was once the standard-issue sidearm of the Soviet bloc military and remained a favorite of spies. "Hmm. Protecting the hors d'oeuvres, is that it? Let's try again. The *truth* this time. Who are you working for? Putin?"

The man remained silent, his jaw tight, eyes flashing with anger.

"Someone else?" On impulse, Hawke threw out another name. "The Warmonger, perhaps?"

At the mention of the nom de guerre, the man tensed, just for a fraction of a second, but it was enough.

"Ah," said Hawke, unable to entirely hide his satisfaction. "Now we're getting somewhere. Let's have it, then. Who is he? Who is the bloody Warmonger?"

But before the man could answer—or, more likely, refuse to answer—a series of loud but very distinctive popping sounds shattered the relative quiet: the unmistakable reports of automatic rifles.

Judging by the volume and intensity of the discharges, quite a few of them.

Despite the pain Hawke was inflicting, his captive laughed aloud. "You want to know who is Warmonger?" he sneered. "Why don't you go ask him yourself?"

FOUR

Hawke narrowed his eyes at the struggling man. "Don't mind if I do," he said, and then delivered a savage blow to the base of the man's neck.

As satisfying as it was to watch the man crumple senseless beneath him, Hawke reeled under the weight of the revelation. When Pippa Guinness had told him that the Warmonger would be putting in an appearance at the summit, the last thing he expected was a frontal assault.

And yet, why not? Based on what little they knew of the Warmonger and his aims, weakening NATO seemed to be a priority goal. What better way to discredit the alliance than to strike at the very heart of its leadership, demonstrating, if only symbolically, that NATO could not even protect itself?

The question is, Alex, old boy, what are you going to do about it?

What indeed?

He cocked his head to the side, trying to fix the location of the shooters, then glanced down at the unconscious form of the Warmonger's agent—an advance scout or inside man, no doubt sent in to open the gates for the main force.

He scooped up the little Makarov, swiped down the safety, and press checked to ensure that it was ready for use. A standard Makarov held a single-stack eight-round magazine.

Eight bullets to take on an unknown number of hostiles.

Well, it's a start.

He considered searching the man for spare magazines, but the intensifying crackle of gunfire made the decision for him. The reports were multiplying, echoing in the courtyard like approaching thunder, but he could tell that it was coming from several different places all at once. It wasn't a single skirmish but a coordinated assault. The loudest reports, and logically the closest, were coming from behind him, from the direction of the Imperial Council Hall, which meant that at least some of the attackers were on the verge of overrunning the reception.

Hawke's first impulse was to rush into the fray, but he knew better. A headlong charge into a firefight would do no one any good, least of all himself.

Stay hidden. Work out the situation. Then act.

He judged the attacking force to be no less than a dozen men and perhaps as many as two dozen—long odds, even for Alexander Hawke, but not insurmountable with the element of surprise on his side. If he could find isolated groups of two or three, pick them off, and acquire their weapons and equipment, he could winnow the enemy force down to a more manageable size.

Holding the Makarov ready, he stole through the woods, moving back the way he'd come until he was able to get a look at the entrance to the hall. A pall of smoke hung over the cobblestone pavement, and through it he could see black-clad figures dropping down from the roof, swarming into the ornate entrance.

Too late, thought Hawke. *Damn it.*

So this was the Warmonger's plan: to seize control of the Imperial Council Hall, take key NATO leaders hostage, and then negotiate for their safe return. The audacity of it surprised Hawke. Situations like this rarely ended well for the hostage takers, never mind the hostages. Bottled up inside the hall, the attackers would have only so much leverage, and the clock would be working against them. Brutality against the hostages would only deepen the resolve of the authorities to attempt a rescue, and while there would inevitably be friendly casualties, the Warmonger's force would be annihilated.

Hawke's concerns were more immediate, however. He was in a position to nip this thing in the bud, as it were, to disrupt the enemy and keep them off-balance, and to do that he needed to get inside the hall without drawing attention to himself.

His brain went into overdrive, running through counterattack scenarios with the speed and efficiency of a chess computer. He searched the surrounding area, looking for enemy sentries or snipers who might be covering the entrance. The courtyard—at least what he could see of it—was clear, but he spotted a dark silhouette on the balcony of the Tower of Justice, which jutted up from the roof over the Imperial Council Hall. He spotted a second man perched in front of the domes of the adjacent treasury building and a third stationed atop the porch of the Audience Hall to the north. All of them were well beyond the useful range of the Makarov. Taking them out was the only way he'd have a shot at getting inside without being turned into target practice, but he wasn't going to be able to do it from where he was.

He would need to take the fight to them.

Hawke fell back into the trees, moving away from the hall and across the courtyard toward the eastern edge of the complex and the long structure that had, in the time of the Ottoman Empire, served as the palace kitchen. After a quick check to ensure that there were no snipers posted atop it, he shinnied up one of the columns supporting the porch roof and heaved himself up onto the gently sloping overhang.

He lay there for a few seconds, waiting for any indication that his ascent had attracted unwanted attention, then crawled up the slope until he was beyond the roofline, concealed amidst the maze of enormous chimneys that had once vented smoke from the sultan's cookeries. Using the stacks for cover, he made his way along the length of the roof until he reached the corner where it joined the roof of the Audience Hall. He crouched there for a moment, fixing the location of the nearest sniper, more than a hundred feet away. The man's attention appeared to be fixed on the courtyard below, but Hawke knew that could change in a heartbeat if the man sensed his presence. So, instead of rushing him, Hawke moved out to the farthest edge of the roof, keeping the roofline between himself and the gunman until he was directly behind the man. Crawling forward soundlessly, watching the man's back for even a hint of awareness, Hawke closed the remaining distance and then, quick as a viper, struck.

One down.

The takedown yielded an unexpected bonus in the form of the sniper's rifle—a Russian-made SV-98 equipped with a bipod, a telescopic sight, and, more importantly, a suppressor—and Hawke did not hesitate to make use of it. Getting down into a prone firing position, he braced the stock of the weapon against his shoulder, put his eye to the glass, and quickly found the sniper atop the treasury roof. At such close range—about sixty yards—there was little chance of missing, even with an unfamiliar weapon. Hawke centered the aiming reticle on the unsuspecting sniper's forehead, took a breath, let it out, and squeezed the trigger.

Two down.

He quickly worked the bolt to eject the spent brass and advance another round into the firing chamber, then swiveled the rifle until he found the shooter lurking on the tower balcony. Hawke had been a little worried that the sound of the shot would give him away, but the suppressor did its job, muffling the report to nothing more than a loud *click.* The man on the tower remained oblivious. Hawke lined up his shot and fired.

Three.

He continued scanning the walls and rooftops, checking for any hostiles that he might have missed. Finding none, he pushed away from the rifle—it would be of little use in the close-quarters combat that he would soon face—and started moving along the rooftops toward the entrance to the Council Hall.

Then everything changed.

FIVE

Hawke froze and threw himself flat on the roof as below him several of the dark-clad figures he'd seen going into the Imperial Council Hall emerged from it, dragging some of the attendees along with them. There were six hostages in all—among them, the ambassadors from Latvia, Lithuania, and Estonia, as well as the Turkish defense minister and . . .

Rage suffused Hawke when he recognized the sixth hostage, Commander Savannah Stone, who was being savagely dragged out of the hall by two of the gunmen. Her hair was disheveled, her gown torn, and her feet bare, but even now she continued to resist.

Hawke had to fight the urge to leap down and throttle her captors with his own bare hands.

The assaulters—more than a dozen in number, all armed with compact submachine guns—moved purposefully, roughly hustling their captives down the path leading back to the Gate of Salutation.

Hawke's pulse quickened as he processed this new development. The Warmonger's men weren't just hijacking the gala and taking hostages en masse. They had come with a specific target list, and now that they had them, they were leaving, taking the hostages with them.

This is no standard hostage situation, thought Hawke. *It's a bloody abduction.*

Hawke's mind raced through his options, none of which were good.

There were too many hostiles, too many hostages, and too many unknown variables. Charging in now would be suicide. While Hawke had no fear of death and quite preferred to go out fighting when his number was up, he knew that striking now would almost assuredly doom the hostages to a similar fate.

His mind raced again.

There's no winning play to be had.

But he had to do something. If they made it through the gate and left the palace grounds, those hostages would be as good as gone.

The gate!

It was the only way in or out of the palace. If Hawke could reach it before they did, maybe he could cut them off or at least throw a wrench into the works. Buy some time for the Turkish authorities to mount a response.

Leaping up, Hawke dashed along a long section of wall separating the courtyard from the old stables. If any of the Warmonger's men happened to look up, they could not help but see him, but that was a chance he would have to take. The Gate of Salutation was not even a hundred yards ahead. If he could just get there before—

A loud crack, like a hammer striking the roof tiles, sounded behind him.

What the hell?

Another crack sounded. It was louder . . . closer.

A bullet.

Sniper!

The realization hit just as the next shot smacked into the roof tiles inches from his left foot. Hawke's body moved before his mind could process it, veering away, trying to zigzag on the narrow roof even as he searched for the hidden shooter.

He's in one of the towers, Hawke thought, gripping the Makarov and searching the dark turret openings on the two octagonal towers that flanked the gate ahead.

But which one?

The sniper's weapon was suppressed, probably another SV-98, so there would be no muzzle flash or telltale report to give away his location.

Before the next round came, Hawke squeezed off two quick shots in the general direction of the towers, not expecting to hit anything but merely to give the sniper something to worry about. Then he dropped flat, rolled to the edge of the roof, and dropped down into the courtyard below. He hit the pavement and rolled, executing a parachutist's fall to avoid injury, and came up in a crouch with the Makarov still clenched in his hand. Through the scattered trees fifty yards away, he could see the procession of hostiles and hostages moving up the path. Now fully alerted to the fact that he was in pursuit, they had quickened their pace and were nearly at the gate.

The Warmonger's men were moving efficiently, hustling the captives toward the exit. Hawke knew that he had already missed his chance to get ahead of them and block their way, but there was still a chance to stop them or at the very least slow them down. He rose from his crouch and started forward, but before he could significantly close the gap, two of the gunmen at the rear of the procession turned toward him and leveled their weapons at him. Hawke dove behind the nearest tree a heartbeat before the muzzles of their weapons spat fire.

Rounds tore into the trunk, stripping bark and foliage, filling the air around him with smoke and splinters. Undeterred, Hawke leapt from behind the tree and sprinted for another, this one even closer to the gate, reaching its shelter before the two gunmen could shift their aim. Hawke guessed the men would recognize what he was doing—a standard infantry tactic for advancing while under fire—so instead of bounding forward again he edged out from behind the tree until he put eyes on one of the gunmen. Foolishly, the man was standing in the open, trusting his sub-gun to protect him. Hawke drew attention to this fatal error with a well-placed round from the Makarov.

As the gunman staggered back, collapsing onto the cobblestones, the second gunman snapped his head toward his fallen comrade and opened fire in a wild, desperate burst. Hawke fell back behind the tree trunk, throwing himself flat as more splinters and bullets whizzed over his head, but as soon as the other man's weapon went silent, he rolled out from behind cover and fired twice. The gunman, who was frantically trying to slot a fresh magazine into his weapon, panicked, ducking in place and fumbling the mag exchange.

Hawke smiled.

Amateur.

Capitalizing on the unexpected lucky break, Hawke took steady aim and fired again, putting a round between the shooter's eyes.

But in the brief moment it had taken for Hawke to deal with the rear guard, the rest of the Warmonger's attack force had succeeded in ushering the hostages through the gate. Hawke, leading with the Makarov, passed into the archway, expecting at any moment to be met with a fresh storm of gunfire. Instead, when he emerged from the gate, he saw two of the electric trolleys that had been ferrying guests across the First Courtyard rolling noiselessly, bearing all of the hostages and most of the gunmen. A third trolley sat nearby, with two of the hostiles aboard, waiting, no doubt, to pick up their comrades—the ones Hawke had just taken out.

One of the pair spotted him, shouted a warning, and tried to bring his rifle up, but the other man, sitting in the driver's seat, reacted faster, stomping down on the go pedal. The trolley jerked into motion, the electric engine whirring as it quickly accelerated away even as the first man's finger tightened on the trigger. The wild burst peppered the wall behind Hawke, who calmly stood his ground and returned fire.

The first shot from the Makarov struck the shooter's shoulder, spinning him sideways. The second caught him in the chest. He spilled from the open vehicle and tumbled onto the cobblestones. The driver didn't look back but kept the pedal to the floor, racing to join up with the rest of his comrades.

Hawke immediately gave chase, sprinting after the trolley, the soles of his patent leather John Lobb oxfords pounding against the stone. The hum of the vehicle's electric motor grew louder as it continued to accelerate, but Hawke, holding nothing back, slowly began to close the gap. At top speed, the shuttle moved slower than his running pace, but whereas the motorized vehicle could sustain that pace indefinitely, Hawke was already feeling the burn.

Pushing through it, he dug deep, found an untapped reserve, and tapped it, pouring on a burst of speed that brought him even with the rear of the trolley. He grasped the frame just as his leg muscles hit their threshold and was abruptly yanked off his feet. He hung there for a moment, the soles of his oxfords bouncing over the cobblestones as he was dragged along, then pulled himself up one-handed until he got his feet onto the floor of the trolley.

The driver, possibly feeling the jolt of Hawke's boarding, glanced back and then, seeing that he now had an unwanted passenger, took his foot off the pedal and stomped on the brake.

It was the wrong move. The sudden deceleration threw Hawke forward, catapulting him over the seats and toward the front of the trolley, putting him within easy reach of the unlucky driver. Before the man could put a hand on his sub-gun, Hawke swiped the butt of the Makarov across the base of his skull.

After helping himself to the man's weapon—a PP-19 Vityaz submachine gun—and shoving him out onto the pavement, Hawke settled into the driver's seat, gripped the steering wheel, and pressed down on the go pedal. The trolley began moving, sluggish at first but steadily picking up speed until it was going as fast as it could. Unfortunately, in the brief moment it had taken him to commandeer the vehicle, the trolleys bearing the hostages away had moved ahead by more than a hundred yards and were nearing the Imperial Gate, beyond which they would be unconstrained by the palace walls. Hawke muttered an oath under his breath when, for a moment, both vehicles barreled through the security checkpoint, not even slowing.

As his trolley reached the gate a few seconds later, a knot of dread twisted Hawke's gut. Bodies lay scattered around the wreckage of the security checkpoint, Turkish police and military personnel draped lifeless over their weapons. The smell of gun smoke still lingered in the air, and bullet casings glittered like metallic confetti on the stone path. The security forces had been obliterated before they even had a chance to respond. Hawke glanced at the faces of the fallen as he sped past, their uniforms soaked in dark patches of blood. There had been no hesitation, no mercy. Just death.

"Bloody hell," he muttered, knuckles white on the steering wheel.

Every aspect of the attack had been meticulously planned: timing, targets, and even their escape route.

He emerged from the gate and into the sprawling, open plaza where he'd dropped off the Lancia and, for a moment, had no idea where the other trolleys had gone. The towering walls of the palace loomed behind him, but ahead was nothing but a sea of space and scattered clusters of people, frozen in the aftermath of the attack, some staring in shock, others hurriedly fleeing.

He scanned the plaza, eyes darting left and right. Where the hell had they gone?

He needed a sign—anything. He drove out across the pavement until he spied a group of onlookers, wide-eyed and traumatized by what they had just witnessed.

"Which way?" he barked, not bothering to slow down.

None of them answered, and a few of them cowered as if fearful of his wrath, but he noticed one of them looking to the left in the direction of one of the roads leading out of the plaza. Hawke didn't need any more than that. He cranked the wheel hard, veering left, the trolley skidding slightly as its wheels squealed on the pavement.

Trying to navigate the narrow street was like threading a needle. Rows of parked luxury vehicles lined both sides, opulent cars gleaming under the faint glow of streetlamps. No doubt the Lancia was among them, but while it would have been a far better vehicle for hot pursuit, there simply wasn't time to track it down. He squeezed the steering wheel and pushed the pedal harder, as if by so doing he might eke out a few more miles per hour.

It didn't work.

The street followed the edge of the outer wall for a short stretch, then veered away to the right, dipping downward and curving around in a wide bend that took him out from under the shadow of the palace. The route ducked beneath an overpass, a dimly lit tunnel that momentarily swallowed him in gloom, then emerged on the other side, eventually coming to an intersection with an unrestricted view of the Sea of Marmara, just a couple hundred feet away. And there, just at the rocky shore, were the two trolleys he had been chasing, parked at the water's edge, the dark figures of hostiles and hostages silhouetted against the glimmer of reflected moonlight, moving, it appeared, out into the water.

Hawke's pulse quickened. The kidnappers had reached their escape point, and the hostages were surely about to be loaded onto waiting boats. Once they were on the water, they'd vanish into the Bosphorus and be halfway to the Black Sea before he could even make a call for help.

He had only seconds to reach them.

And then what?

Would he take them on, one man against an army?

Of course I will, he thought grimly. *What bloody choice do I have?*

SIX

Hawke silently urged the trolley as he crossed the remaining distance, barreling through a major thoroughfare without even bothering to check for cross traffic, and bounced the trolley over the curb and onto the gently sloping, rocky shore.

As he topped the crest, he saw a pair of large Zodiac-style RIBs—rigid inflatable boats. One of them was just starting to motor away from the shore, carrying several of the gunmen and three of the hostages—Savannah Stone, Hawke had seen, among that number. The other boat, which held the remaining hostages, had been driven up onto the rocks to facilitate boarding. With that task evidently complete, two of the gunmen were pushing against the bow, trying to shove the craft back away from shore.

Hawke, seeing his last opportunity to interdict their slipping away, steered the trolley toward the boat. The uneven surface slowed the vehicle's momentum considerably, but he was still moving at a good clip when the front end of the trolley slammed into the two unsuspecting men, crushing them against the Zodiac. At the instant of impact, Hawke launched himself from the trolley and leapt for the boat, flinging his arms over the inflated gunwale even as the collision jolted the RIB off the rocks and sent it shooting out into the sea. His legs splashed down into the water, his toes briefly dragging on the sloped bank as it fell away beneath him. He hung there for a moment, all too aware of his vulnerable position, then began kicking his legs furiously to propel himself up onto the gunwale.

His first attempt brought him up high enough to glimpse the occupants of the boat. The impact from the trolley collision had knocked everyone off their respective perches, but the gunmen were already beginning to regain their balance and restore control over the situation.

Hawke kicked again, sustaining the effort and pulling himself farther up by sheer force of will, inch by inch, until his upper torso was resting atop the gunwale. That was when he saw one of the gunmen looking back at him, eyes going wide with the realization that someone was attempting to board the RIB and that he should probably be doing something about it.

Bloody hell.

With a mighty heave, Hawke pulled himself the rest of the way into the boat, flopping down onto the deck even as the gunman started bringing his weapon to bear on him.

Then something completely unexpected happened. The gunman suddenly pitched backward, as if yanked by an invisible hand. As he fell, the muzzle of his submachine gun swung up and the burst of gunfire from an inadvertent trigger pull shot harmlessly skyward.

Never one to let such an opportunity pass him by, Hawke darted forward, seizing the gun with one hand, keeping it aimed skyward, and delivering a knife hand jab to the gunman's unprotected throat. It was only then that he saw what had caused the man's unexpected fall.

The hostages, realizing that someone was trying to help them and bolstered by the resultant adrenaline surge, had shaken off the torpor of captivity and seized the moment, turning on their somewhat disoriented captors. They were still outnumbered and definitely outgunned, but they were no longer going to go quietly.

Wresting control of the sub-gun from the gasping man beneath him, Hawke's first thought was to start shooting, but with the hostages and gunman clustered together in the close confines of the RIB, there was no way to shoot the latter without endangering the former. He would have to do this the old-fashioned way, hand to hand, just like his pirate ancestor of old.

He threw himself into the fray, swinging the PP-19 like a club, smashing the skull of one of the men presently menacing the Turkish defense minister, Amir al-Fulan, freeing the senior military leader to deal with the other on a more equal footing.

Hawke pivoted just in time to avoid a wild punch from another attacker, who was now fully aware of the rapidly shifting odds. Hawke dodged the man's next punch and then jammed the gun into the man's ribs like a battering ram. The hostile gasped as the wind was knocked out of him. Hawke followed up with another swipe of the PP-19 that knocked the man clean out of the boat.

The sound of a struggle behind him made Hawke whirl around just in time to see al-Fulan grappling with the remaining captor. Despite his age, the Turkish defense minister fought with surprising vigor, delivering a solid punch to the man's jaw, stunning him momentarily. But it wasn't enough to end the fight.

Hawke sprang forward, swinging his weapon at the attacker's temple. The blow landed with a sickening *thud*, the man's knees buckling as he fell hard against the side of the boat. For good measure, Hawke grabbed the collar of the man's tactical vest and heaved him over the side. Borne down by the weight of his gear, the unconscious man disappeared into the depths and did not resurface.

With the last of the captors dispatched, Hawke quickly checked on the hostages. They appeared shaken but alive and in surprisingly good spirits, their chains of fear broken by the unexpected act of deliverance.

"Hang on, all," he called out to them as he climbed over the thwarts and took the helm, engaging the idling twin Yamaha F250 outboards. He gave the throttle a nudge and the boat began moving forward. A few seconds later the rigid fiberglass hull scraped onto the rocks once more.

"Right," said Hawke cheerily. "Everyone ashore."

The hostages stared at him blankly for a moment but then seemed to understand and clambered over the gunwale to splash ashore. Amir al-Fulan, however, lingered. "And what will *you* do, Lord Hawke?"

Hawke was not surprised at all to be recognized. "Well, I'm going after them," he said almost casually. "Now, off you go. Chop, chop."

"I shall go with you."

Hawke shook his head. "Absolutely not," he replied, the firmness in his voice leaving no room for debate. "I didn't go to all the trouble of rescuing you just to have you get yourself killed playing the hero. Besides, I work better alone."

The last bit was only partly true.

While it was true that there was a note in Hawke's personnel file that read "Does not play well with others," he also understood that war was a numbers game. And while he would have dearly loved to have someone like his old pal Stokely Jones Jr. or his friend Tom Quick backing him up, Amir and his fellow hostages were an unknown quantity. Hawke's friends were highly trained and seasoned warriors. Stoke was a veteran New York City detective and a Navy SEAL, and Quick had been an instructor at the US Army Sniper School. More to the point, Hawke had fought alongside them, knew their capabilities, and trusted them implicitly. While Amir and the others had acquitted themselves well by seizing the opportunity to turn the tables on their captors, that didn't mean Hawke was ready to entrust his life to them.

Amir looked as if he might argue but then nodded, reluctantly acknowledging Hawke's reasoning, and then climbed over the side to join the others.

As soon as he was clear, Hawke reversed the outboards, backing the RIB away until he was far enough out to turn the boat around and head off in pursuit of the other Zodiac. The hostage takers had at least a minute's head start, and in the dark of night, with no running lights, their RIB was effectively invisible, but its settling wake *was* visible, pointing the way like a giant arrow. Hawke pushed the throttle to the stops, the dual Yamaha F250 motors propelling the lightweight craft forward like rocket engines. With no passengers to weigh it down, the boat rode higher and higher until it was practically hydroplaning across the water. Judging by the wind on his face, Hawke guessed he was running at close to fifty knots, and with each passing second the wake trail ahead of him grew more substantial as he closed in on the other RIB, the keel bouncing as it knifed through the disturbed water.

Hawke realized that he now faced the same dilemma as a dog chasing a car: What would he do when he caught up to the other boat?

It wasn't just that he was still outnumbered. Once he overhauled the RIB, he would have to figure out how to kill or otherwise subdue the hostage takers without harming the hostages, likely while still moving at high speed.

He shuffled through scenarios, discarding them just as quickly. Ramming them wasn't an option. If he could pull alongside the other boat, he might be able to leap across, but he couldn't imagine that the hostiles would simply stand by and let him board.

He wondered what his pirate ancestor would have done in his stead.

He needed a distraction, something to divert the attention of the hostage takers long enough for him to get in close and neutralize them. But what?

Then, unexpectedly, the nature of the challenge changed.

Looming directly ahead, a barely visible silhouette against the night sky, was a large yacht running dark, and the wake of the lead Zodiac led directly to it.

Hawke throttled back, keeping his speed in check as he closed the remaining distance. The yacht loomed larger, and soon he could make out the faint glow of red lights on its decks. Red light, with its longer wavelength, was harder to see at a distance and had long been used in combat situations where unfiltered white light might betray a position to the enemy. In that glow, Hawke could make out shadows moving near the yacht's stern. The lead Zodiac had already made its rendezvous and begun transferring its passengers to the yacht.

Though it was difficult to gauge in the darkness, Hawke put the larger vessel at about 140 feet—not a full-on megayacht but still quite impressive. It had three decks stacked like the tiers on a wedding cake gone slightly askew, thrusting skyward, with room enough for a helipad at the top and a swim platform extending from the stern, where the first Zodiac was moored.

That's the Warmonger's boat, he thought, and that realization was quickly followed by another: *He could be aboard right now.*

The Warmonger had thought of everything. From the overwhelming force and lightning quickness of the attack on Topkapı Palace to the meticulously planned escape route to this—a luxurious floating palace that would hide the hostages more effectively than any remote coastal hideaway—the villain had left nothing to chance.

Well, almost nothing.

He hadn't counted on Alex Hawke.

SEVEN

As the twin outboards brought him inexorably closer to the yacht, Hawke settled on a plan. It was audacious, to be sure, maybe even slightly crazed, but that was what made it so bloody brilliant. Like his ancestor, the legendary Blackhawke, he would board and capture the Warmonger's yacht. All he was missing was a dagger clamped between his teeth.

He had cut his speed by more than half but was still moving at a decent clip as the inflatable boat cruised the last hundred yards, angling toward the yacht's tail. He took it as a good sign that nobody was shooting at him. Hopefully, that meant the bad guys thought the approaching RIB was manned by their comrades.

The first boat was still moored to the swim platform at the stern, bobbing lazily in the mostly placid sea. Hawke angled toward it and cut the throttle completely, letting it coast the remaining few yards.

Suddenly a face materialized in the gloom, looking faintly demonic in the red glow. It was a man, dressed in black like the men who had attacked the palace, standing on the swim platform, staring right at him.

So much for the element of surprise, thought Hawke.

But there was nothing menacing in the man's expression. If anything, he looked almost relieved as he watched the inflatable craft close the remaining distance. He was, it seemed, standing by to offer his assistance to the occupants of the arriving boat. This misperception would not last long. Indeed, Hawke saw the exact moment when the man realized something was off about the approaching boat and saw his face change to a look of confusion and then alarm. But those precious seconds were enough to bring Hawke within striking distance. He jammed the throttle forward again, and as the RIB shot ahead, coming alongside its counterpart, Hawke leapt into that boat and then leapfrogged onto the platform, slamming the butt of his machine pistol into the side of the man's head.

As the man slumped to the deck, Hawke dropped into a crouch, waiting for a hostile reception from the other hostage takers.

But nothing happened.

No alarms. No shouting. No shooting.

Now for the tricky bit, he thought.

He moved stealthily up the companionway to the lower deck, straining for any sound of activity above, his PP-19 held at the ready. As he neared the top of the flight, he crouched low to stay hidden as long as possible before stepping onto the deck, ready to meet any threat. But the deck, at least the open part of it, was unoccupied.

Hawke moved like a wraith, stealing along the exterior deck until he reached another companionway leading up to the bridge deck. From this elevated position, he had no trouble finding the lights of Istanbul directly astern, five, maybe six miles away, or so he guessed based on the length of time it had taken him to reach the yacht.

Not far at all.

He crept ahead, stopping just outside the door to the pilothouse, listening to the quiet murmur of voices within.

Russian.

As if there had been any doubt.

He tested the door handle—unlocked—and then threw the door open and swept inside, his PP-19 leading the way. Three men, all in standard shipboard uniforms, sat in the glow of control panels and instrument displays. A fourth, the captain—a thickset man with a grizzled beard—stood behind the helm, speaking in low tones to his first mate. The moment Hawke stepped through the door, all heads turned his way.

For a long moment no one moved. The appearance of this man, this stranger, dressed for a night on the town but wielding a submachine gun, was so incongruous as to defy belief. Then the moment passed. The captain's hand shot toward his belt, reaching for the pistol holstered there. Hawke was faster.

"I wouldn't," Hawke said, his voice calm but deadly, the muzzle of the PP-19 leveled at the captain's chest.

The captain froze, his hand still hovering near the gun. He met Hawke's gaze, saw the resolve there, but nonetheless began calculating. Finally, he raised his hands, taking a slow step back from the helm. "You have no idea who you are fucking with," he said in heavily accented English.

Hawke gave him a half smile. "Well, you're not wrong, old boy. Care to enlighten me?"

The captain returned a confused look. "What?"

"*Who* am I, as you so eloquently put it, fucking with?"

The captain did not answer, and in the long silence that followed, the tension on the bridge thickened, the other crew members glancing nervously at one another. Hawke kept both his weapon and his focus trained on the captain. "Come on, now. I haven't got all bloody night. Who owns this boat?"

The captain narrowed his eyes for a moment but then relented. "Sergei Yevgenyevich Mulmuscovy."

"Mulmuscovy," echoed Hawke. He recognized the name immediately. Mulmuscovy—the Moscow Mule—was a Russian oligarch and the CEO of the Perun Group, a notorious mercenary outfit that had, among other things, supplied cannon fodder for Putin's adventure in the Crimea. His name had come up frequently in reports on the Warmonger's activities, but the analysts at Six had assigned a low probability to him actually *being* the Warmonger. Still, there was no denying that war had made Mulmuscovy obscenely wealthy.

So, was he the Warmonger or merely one of his lieutenants?

"Is he here?"

"Here?"

"Is he aboard?" Hawke hissed.

The captain seemed to consider whether he ought to answer the question, then shook his head. "No. Lucky for you. If he was, you would already be dead, I think."

Hawke couldn't tell if the man was lying. "Hmm. Too bad. I was hoping to have a chat with him. No matter. I'll look him up later. Right now, I want you to bring us about and head toward shore."

The captain stared back at him in disbelief.

"Hop to," Hawke urged. "We haven't got all night."

"You are serious? And if we refuse?"

Hawke glanced meaningfully down at the PP-19. "It's not a request."

The captain folded his arms over his chest. "No. I don't think you will kill us. But if I do this, *he* will."

It was times like this that Hawke wished he had more in common with his pirate ancestors. Blackhawke would not have hesitated to execute the captain on the spot. In fact, he would have deemed it a necessity, as any display of compassion or mercy would have been perceived as weakness. But as ruthless as Alex Hawke could be and often was, he drew the line at cold-blooded murder.

"Right," he said. "I was afraid you might feel that way."

He stepped forward quickly and clubbed the captain with the weapon. As the man sank to the deck, dazed but not completely unconscious, Hawke knelt and relieved him of his sidearm—a Yarygin PYa 9-millimeter semiauto—and then just as quickly stepped back, brandishing the PP-19 one-handed to discourage the rest of the crew from coming to the captain's assistance.

"Everybody out," he said, raising his voice for the first time since entering the pilothouse. The crew returned blank looks, glancing between their captain and Hawke, clearly wondering what to do. Hawke aimed the weapon at the first mate—identifiable by the three stripes on the epaulets of his uniform shirt. "You heard me. Off the bridge. Now."

The man opened his mouth as if to argue but then thought better of it. He stood, said something in Russian to the other two men, then began moving toward the door. The others reluctantly followed.

"Take him with you," Hawke added, gesturing to the writhing form of the captain.

The mate and another crewman came over and helped their groggy superior get his feet under him, then escorted him toward the door Hawke had just come through.

He knew this apparent surrender would be short-lived. As soon as they were through the door, they would regroup, perhaps coordinate with the gunmen who had carried out the attack on the palace, and try to retake the ship. But that would take time, and that was one thing they did not have much of.

Once the bridge was clear, Hawke moved quickly, locking the door behind them, then moved back to the helm station. The console glowed with navigational readouts, radar sweeps, and engine diagnostics. Everything was labeled in Russian, but he didn't need a translation to understand the controls.

The engines were idling, the anchors already weighed, confirming Hawke's earlier suspicion that the Warmonger had been planning to move the yacht the moment the hostages were aboard. He switched off the ship's dynamic positioning system, which the crew had been using to hold station, and pushed the throttles to all-ahead full.

He felt the raw power of the yacht's engines surge through the deck beneath his feet as the vessel lunged forward. The sudden acceleration pushed him back in his chair, the yacht's bow lifting ever so slightly as it picked up speed. Hawke, who was never more at home than when commanding a vessel at sea, experienced a tingle of exhilaration as he gripped the wheel and turned the craft to starboard. The lights of Istanbul came into view off to the right, glittering like a beacon as the yacht swung toward them. When the bow was pointing directly landward, he straightened the rudder. After a quick check to verify that all the other controls were exactly where they needed to be, he stood, stepped back, and then fired a burst from the PP-19 into the helm station.

Shooting the control board would, he knew, have about the same effect on the yacht as smashing the keyboard and monitor display would have on a computer. The important systems would continue to function normally. All he had done was destroy the user interface, but, without that, nobody would be able to change the yacht's course. Not easily. There were other ways to manually alter course or engine speed, and once the crew discovered what he had done, they would no doubt set to work trying to do exactly that. But all of that would take time, during which the yacht would continue its inexorable journey toward shore, where the authorities would no doubt be waiting. At top speed, it would take the yacht ten or fifteen minutes to reach shore, where, absent any interference, it would run aground on the rocky beach, but before that happened, the vessel's collision course would attract the notice of the harbor authorities and the Turkish coast guard, who would quickly move to intercept, especially if they made the connection between the yacht and the attack on the NATO gala. If they were smart, the Warmonger's men would realize that their only hope of salvation lay in boarding the remaining Zodiac and saving their own skins, but Hawke didn't think they would simply abandon Sergei Mulmuscovy's multimillion-dollar yacht. In fact, he was counting on it.

With a final glance toward the bridge door, Hawke turned, leaving the bridge behind and stepping through the narrow passage that led to the captain's quarters. The cabin was as luxurious as he might have expected: rich mahogany paneling, leather-bound chairs, and a bed that looked more suited for a five-star hotel than a maritime vessel. Hawke didn't stop to admire the decor but moved quickly through the cabin, exiting into what appeared to be the crew prep room, with an internal companionway leading down to the main deck. He paused there a moment, listening, and heard the faint sound of voices raised in distress. The bad guys had already figured out that things were not going according to plan.

As he descended the narrow stairwell cautiously, ready to engage or evade as circumstances dictated, the voices grew louder: shouts in Russian, questions and commands. No doubt the gunmen and the crew trying to figure out what to do next. A moment later he heard footsteps pounding up the companionway from belowdecks.

Perfect, thought Hawke.

He ducked through the nearest doorway, found himself in a well-appointed but dark and unoccupied lounge, and waited as the thundering herd ascended the companionway he had just descended. As the sound of footsteps receded, Hawke emerged and descended belowdecks.

The companionway brought him to a corridor running the length of the vessel. Aft, he knew, would take him to the engine room, so he moved forward to the first of a series of closed doors—likely guest cabins or crew quarters. He pressed himself against the wall, listening for any sounds inside. Nothing. But then he heard faint but unmistakable voices coming from farther down the passage. Not frantic but hurried, tense. He followed the sound, bypassing several more cabins, and came to a door that was slightly ajar, just enough for him to peer inside.

Through the gap, Hawke caught sight of two gunmen near the far bulkhead, their weapons trained on a trio of hostages: two Eastern European NATO ambassadors and Savannah Stone, the latter still looking defiant despite the situation.

Setting aside the PP-19 for the more precise Yarygin pistol he'd taken from the captain, Hawke pushed the door open and fired twice, dropping both gunmen with perfectly placed headshots.

The twin reports were deafening in the close confines, so despite Hawke's subsequent exhortations it took the shocked hostages a moment to grasp that they had just been liberated. Savannah was the first to react, leaping to her feet and snatching a PP-19 from the hands of one of her former captors, holding it like she knew exactly what to do with it.

She was, Hawke reminded himself, an American soldier.

Then she turned to him and flashed a smile.

"Lord Hawke," she said, almost shouting to make herself heard. "I was hoping to run into you tonight."

Anyone who knew Hawke well knew that he disdained the use of his noble title, so if it was Savannah's intention to impress him by employing it, she achieved the exact opposite effect, which, given the circumstances, was probably for the best.

"Hmm, quite," he replied coolly. "Rather busy just now, but you're welcome to tag along."

If she was put off by his brusque manner, Savannah gave no indication. "I take it you've got some sort of plan?"

"As a matter of fact, I do. Before I came down here, I put us on a direct course back to Istanbul and locked out the controls. While they're occupied with trying to figure out how to change course, we're going to head back to the inflatable and get out of here."

She considered his answer for a moment, then nodded. "I like it." She gestured toward the door. "Lead the way."

With Savannah and the two NATO ambassadors behind him, Hawke stepped back out into the hallway. They hadn't gone more than a few steps, however, when one of the black-clad gunmen swung out from the door to the aft companionway and opened fire.

"Back!" Hawke shouted, firing one-handed at the gunman even as he used his free hand to sweep Savannah and the others back into the stateroom. Bullets sizzled through the air around them, splintering the walls to either side of the corridor but miraculously failing to find a flesh-and-blood target.

As soon as he was back inside the cabin, Hawke readied himself to lean out and resume firing but found a kneeling Savannah attempting to wriggle past him.

"I'll go low," she said, answering the unasked question. "You go high." Before he could protest, she continued, "On three. One . . . two . . . three!"

As she spoke the final number, she edged out into the corridor and loosed a burst from her captured PP-19. Hawke, realizing that he was failing to keep his end up, followed suit, leaning out over her, firing his own sub-gun.

The response was immediate. The gunman, who was prudently staying mostly behind cover in the companionway, stuck his weapon out and fired blindly, his shots going wide. Hawke tried to target the hand holding the gun, but the man drew back before he could dial his shot in.

This cycle repeated a few more times, broken by longer intervals of silence.

"We aren't going to be able to keep this up much longer," shouted Savannah.

"We don't have to," replied Hawke. "The clock is on our side."

"Do they know that?"

Hawke considered the question. Surely the Warmonger's men must have realized that the yacht was heading toward the city, but in the minutes since he'd left the bridge, he had not felt the vessel turn or slow. He would have expected the crew to, at the very least, shut down the engines.

"You make a good point," he allowed. "What do you suppose they're up to?"

"Whatever it is, it won't be good for us." She brought her eyebrows together in a thoughtful frown. "We've got to make a push. I'll stay low. You cover me."

"Now, just a minute—"

That was as far as he got. Savannah was already gone, moving down the corridor in a sort of duckwalk, the hem of her bright blue dress pulled up to mid-thigh to facilitate movement.

Her legs were rather shapely, Hawke noted absently as he belatedly leaned out to provide the covering fire she had requested.

There was no need for it, however. The enemy shooter did not appear, and a few seconds later, after reaching the door to the companionway, Savannah called back. “All clear. Come on up.”

Though somewhat relieved that Savannah had not come under fire, Hawke felt a vague uneasiness about the lack of any further resistance. He sensed that the Warmonger’s men were up to something, and he didn’t like not knowing what it was.

Hawke stepped cautiously into the corridor, his PP-19 raised and ready to meet any new threat as he moved forward. Savannah remained by the companionway door, standing with a relaxed readiness that belied her earlier bravado.

The lack of further resistance gnawed at him. These men weren’t amateurs; they’d been coordinated. Efficient, even. Now, they were simply . . . gone.

“Something’s not right,” Hawke muttered, more to himself than to her.

“I was thinking the same thing. How do we play this?”

Hawke did not have to consider his reply. “My turn to draw fire,” he said, stepping through the door and mounting the steps. “Try to keep up.”

As he ascended the companionway with no sign of an enemy presence, Hawke’s sense of foreboding continued to deepen. The silence was more unnerving than gunfire. He paused at the top of the flight, listening for a moment, but the only sound to be heard was the thrum of the engines pushing the yacht steadily toward shore.

He emerged from the companionway, swept through the lounge and the dining room, then edged out onto the aft deck. There was no sign of anyone—no gunmen, no crew. Behind the yacht, there was only the frothy white trail of the yacht’s wake, extending like a finger out into the inky darkness of the open sea.

“Where is everyone?” asked Savannah, coming up beside him.

Hawke thought he knew the answer but just shook his head and gestured toward the companionway leading down to the swim platform. "This way."

When they reached the platform, Hawke's suspicion was confirmed. The Zodiac was gone. The Warmonger's men, evidently recognizing the hopelessness of trying to take back control of the boat in the brief time remaining to them, had elected to abandon ship.

"Well," he announced with feigned philosophical indifference. "The good news is that the ship is ours."

"Is there bad news?"

"Hmm. Remember how I said that I put the ship on a direct course for Istanbul and locked out the controls?"

She nodded.

"We've got about ten minutes to figure out how to unlock those controls."

Savannah blinked, trying to grasp what he was saying. "And if we can't?"

"We'll smash into the shore at twenty knots."

She narrowed her eyes at him. "That doesn't sound fun."

"No. We might survive, but it won't be pretty."

She looked out at the frothing wake trailing out behind the yacht. "Can we jump?"

"That wouldn't be my first choice."

Savannah nodded slowly. "Okay. How do we unlock the controls?"

Hawke was ready with an answer. "There should be an emergency cutoff switch in the engine room. It won't bring us to full stop, but once the screws stop turning, we'll begin slowing down. It will take a while, but it should do the trick."

She gestured back to the companionway. "Then what are we waiting for?"

He wasn't actually sure. Some part of him worried that he might be misreading the situation—that the apparent abandonment of the yacht by the Warmonger's men was a ruse, bait for a final trap.

"I'll go below and see what I can do," he said. "The rest of you, see if you can find the life rafts. Just in case we have to ditch."

Savannah and the other two men acknowledged with nods and then headed back up the companionway. Hawke followed, then headed down into the lower deck and made his way back to the engine room. As he reached for the door handle, he held the Yarygin ready.

But the ambush he feared did not materialize. The engine room was unoccupied. Nevertheless, he entered cautiously.

The room was hot, the air thick with the smell of oil and the incessant hum of the twin diesel engines, each the size of a small car, which dominated the enclosure. Thick pipes crisscrossed the ceiling, and bundles of cables snaked along the bulkheads. He moved down the narrow aisle between the diesels toward the main control board but stopped short as he noticed something from the corner of his eye, something that didn't belong.

It was bright orange, the shape and size of a fireplace brick, secured to the port engine fuel supply line with several wraps of aluminum heat tape. Jutting out from the tape was a small digital timer, its liquid-crystal display showing: *2:51.*

2:50...

2:49...

"Bollocks."

EIGHT

Hawke spent a precious five seconds studying the improvised explosive device.

Semtex. About two pounds of it.

Not a lot in terms of raw explosive power, but then, it didn't need to be. Positioned where it was on the fuel supply line, it would not only rip apart the yacht's stern but also trigger a secondary explosion that would blow what was left of the vessel in half.

Evidently, the Warmonger's men had not been content to merely abandon ship; they had decided to scuttle it, taking Hawke and the hostages down with it.

And what am I going to do about it?

2:42 . . .

2:41 . . .

Disarming the bomb might have been as simple as pushing the off switch on the timer, but then again, that might automatically trigger the detonation. It appeared to be a hasty build—plastique, fuse, timer, tape—with no obvious anti-tamper measures. The Warmonger's men hadn't expected anyone to discover their little surprise before it went up.

Thank God for that.

2:38 . . .

Carefully, willing his hands not to tremble, Hawke began peeling at the tape. A knife would have simplified this task, but he didn't have one and he didn't have time to look for one. He was so intently focused on the bomb that he nearly jumped out of his skin when a voice called out from the door.

"More bad news." It was Savannah. "They shot up the life raft canisters. We're not leaving that way. Any luck in— Alex! Is that a—"

"Yes," said Hawke, not looking at her.

2:05 . . .

2:04 . . .

"Well, are you going to do something about it?"

"I *am* doing something," he said, peeling more of the tape away. The timer, which had just ticked past the two-minute mark, was still covered by several wraps of the stuff, as were the wires that connected it to blasting caps buried deep in the block of explosives, but there were only two more wraps holding it against the fuel lines.

"There's no time." Savannah spoke quickly, almost frantic. "We have to jump for it."

"Do that, and the shock wave will turn you to pulp. And if that doesn't finish you, the burning fuel slick will."

One more wrap.

1:49 . . .

"Then what—"

"Would you bloody well shut it?" Hawke snarled.

Savannah fell silent.

He peeled the last wrap of tape from the fuel line and then, holding the Semtex block steady, maintaining its spatial orientation just in case there was some kind of tilt switch attached to the fuse, slowly moved it clear and turned toward the exit.

"Could you get the door?"

Savannah hastened to comply. Hawke, still watching the countdown, moved more deliberately.

1:26 . . .

1:25 . . .

Plenty of time, he told himself, trying not to think about what he was holding in his hands or what would happen when the count got down to zero.

It took him thirty-nine excruciating seconds to ascend the companionway to the main deck and another twenty more to descend down to the swim platform. When he got there, with nearly twenty seconds left on the clock, he threw caution to the wind and pitched the bomb out over the trailing wake.

When or if it detonated, he couldn't say. There was no eruption of white water, no shock wave, or if there was, it was too far behind them to be noticed.

"Thank God," said Savannah, and threw her arms around him, hugging him fiercely. It was not a sensual embrace—or if it was, Hawke chose not to interpret it that way—but rather a gesture of shared relief.

"That was too close," she murmured into his chest.

He chose not to argue that the margin had actually been considerable and simply accepted her gratitude. "We're just lucky that we spotted it . . ." He trailed off, suddenly remembering why he'd gone down to the engine room in the first place. "Damn."

Hawke disentangled himself and sprinted back up to the main deck, racing to the starboard rail. Leaning out for a look ahead, his heart sank when he saw the city lights of Istanbul looming dangerously close, the distinctive skyline of the Old City and the Topkapı Palace drawing nearer by the second.

Close.

Too bloody close.

He spotted the lights of several vessels moving toward them: Turkish Coast Guard, no doubt racing to intercept. He could almost imagine the frantic radio calls—someone on one of those boats, desperately signaling them to heave to.

"What's wrong?" Savannah asked, breathless after having chased him up the companionway.

"We're too bloody close," he said miserably, voicing his previous thought.

"Shut the engines down!"

"It won't matter. We'll still pile up on the rocks."

"Well, there's got to be something you can do."

"There's not," he snapped.

She stared back at him, then shook her head, defiant. "No. I refuse to accept that. We didn't go through all this just to give up now."

He stared back at her, despair gnawing at him. "I'm out of ideas here, Savannah. They don't grow on trees, you know."

"Look, let's shut off the engines anyway. Maybe that way we won't be going as fast when we—"

Hawke stiffened, a glimmer of hope sparking in his mind. There *was* a way.

"No," he breathed. "Just *one* of them."

He gripped her shoulders to command her attention. "Find the others and get them into the lounge. Grab some seat cushions, sit on the deck with your back to a bulkhead, preferably facing aft, and brace for impact."

"Brace for impact." She nodded, understanding the gravity of the situation. "And what are you going to be doing?"

"I'm going to try to turn this beast," said Hawke, then turned and bolted for the engine room.

When he got there, he moved to the control panel and punched the stop button for the starboard engine. The ambient rumble filling the engine room quieted noticeably as one of the diesels fell silent.

Hawke didn't linger there but spun away, heading back to the upper deck. This time he ran all the way forward to the bow, leaning against the rail as he watched the yacht's progress. The boat was still moving forward at an alarming pace, but the effects of having cut the starboard engine were already apparent. With only the port screw still driving the ship, the yacht was veering to starboard, beginning an eastward swing.

The shoreline, with its rocky beaches and centuries-old waterfront structures, still loomed ahead, but the yacht was now starting to veer toward the mouth of the Bosphorus Strait, the narrow passage connecting the Sea of Marmara and the Black Sea and separating Europe and Asia.

Degree by painstaking degree, the bow swung toward the strait, away from the shoreline.

It was going to be close.

"Come on," Hawke growled under his breath, willing the yacht to turn faster.

A few boats floated ominously in their path, lights twinkling like distant stars. One small boat—a fishing skiff—darted out of the way just in time, but another, a two-masted ketch, wasn't so lucky. The yacht struck it broadside, cleaving it in half and grinding the pieces under the hull.

But then they were clear. The asymmetric thrust from just the port engine had done its job. The yacht's bow swung parallel to the shoreline, avoiding the rocks by less than a hundred yards. Now it was gliding past the Golden Horn into the Bosphorus.

With far less urgency than before, Hawke made his way back to the engine room and shut down the port engine.

A sublime silence fell over the yacht.

When Hawke came back up on deck, he saw that the yacht had slowed to a crawl, its latent momentum quickly diminishing in the face of the current flowing out of the Bosphorus. Soon it would be carried back into the Sea of Marmara.

As he leaned against the rail, Hawke allowed himself a rare moment of satisfaction. He'd thwarted the Warmonger's brazen attack, rescued the hostages, uncovered a critical link to the Russian oligarch Sergei Mulmuscovy, and even captured the Russian's yacht.

His pirate ancestor would have been proud.

That said, the job wasn't finished. Not by a long shot. The Warmonger was still out there, lurking in the shadows, plotting his next move.

A voice reached out through the quiet. "There you are."

Hawke turned to see Savannah and the two NATO ambassadors making their way across the deck toward him.

"You did it," she said, her voice full of admiration. "I knew you could."

Hawke allowed himself a smile, but then his expression hardened. "But this isn't over. In fact, it's just getting started."

She regarded him for a long moment. "So, what happens now?"

"Now?" Hawke gazed out across the dark water. "We strike the colors and raise the black flag. This is war, after all."

NINE

THE BARENTS SEA
THREE MONTHS LATER . . .

The submarine lurked like a sleeping leviathan, silent and unseen beneath the frigid waters of the Barents Sea, prowling the edge of Russia's territorial waters, about twenty miles off the coast of the Novaya Zemlya archipelago.

USS *Toledo*—SSN-769, a *Los Angeles*–class fast-attack submarine out of Naval Submarine Base New London in Groton, Connecticut—had been in the region for three weeks of a six-week-long mission gathering intelligence on Russian naval activity in the Arctic. Novaya Zemlya, a desolate, frozen stretch of land at the top of the world that had, during the Cold War, proven valuable only as a test range for Soviet weapon systems, most notably the obscenely powerful fifty-megaton Tsar Bomba—the most powerful explosive device ever built or detonated. Now, with climate change shrinking the polar ice cap, the island chain had taken on new significance as a gateway to control of the Arctic Ocean, but it continued to serve as a proving ground for Russia's most secretive military operations. Every few months the horizon would light up with fire as long-range hypersonic missiles arced over the barren land, disappearing into the Arctic sky. These tests served not only to further sharpen the Russian sword but also to remind the world that Russia held the keys to the Arctic.

The *Toledo*'s control room was a hive of quiet, disciplined activity. It was a tight space meant for work, not comfort. The sonar operators sat hunched over their consoles, wearing heavy headphones with which to hear the sea's faintest whispers. The helmsman and planesman monitored the boat's status, making fine adjustments to keep them at their current position and depth—about four hundred feet beneath the surface and just barely above the seafloor. A large electronic wall chart displayed their position and the surrounding waters. The *Toledo*'s skipper, Lieutenant Commander Michael Harris, stood near the periscope stand, his hands clasped behind his back as he presided over the scene.

Unlike many of his peers in the modern Navy, Harris had built his career the hard way: through relentless hard work and a reputation for getting the job done, no matter the obstacles. Born and raised in a blue-collar family in Charleston, South Carolina, Harris had learned discipline and, more importantly, patience early on courtesy of a stern but loving father who worked as a shipyard welder. Lacking political connections, he had throughout his career remained laser-focused on FitReps—fitness reports—which would determine both his assignments and promotions, and the higher up the ladder he rose, the greater the stakes. He could not afford to fail—not even a little bit. This mission was critical to his reaching the next rung; he needed to bring back something significant, something spectacular.

One of the sonar technicians spoke up. "Conn, Sonar. New contact bearing two-four-zero, designated Sierra-six."

Harris nodded to the fire control officer. "Mark and track it."

On the plotting table, a small blip appeared, representing the new contact. Sierra-6—the sixth Russian vessel to depart the vicinity of Mityushikha Bay on the southwestern corner of Severny Island in half as many hours.

"Conn, Sonar. Sierra-six increasing speed—flank."

The *Toledo*'s executive officer, Lieutenant Commander Nathan Ellis, peered at the sonar display. "They're in a hurry."

Harris hummed an acknowledgment.

Military vessels—*Gorshkov*-class frigates and *Udaloy*-class antisubmarine destroyers—had been moving with unusual haste out of the bay and out into international waters, seemingly with little interest in patrolling the area or looking for interlopers like the *Toledo.*

Something big was happening, and evidently it was happening soon.

"Conn, Sonar. Another contact, bearing three-one-five. Multiple prop signatures. Large surface vessels."

Harris leaned forward, his jaw tight. "Confirm types."

The sonar tech was already filtering through the sounds, identifying the distinct signatures of the engines.

"Affirmative, Conn. Confirming warship signatures. Destroyer class . . . And one *Kirov* class."

Harris raised an eyebrow. The *Kirov* class was a heavy battlecruiser—a dinosaur in terms of modern naval operations—more a symbol of power than a literal projection of it. There was only one *Kirov*-class ship in service, the *Pyotr Velikiy*—Peter the Great—and it was the flagship of the Northern Fleet.

What the hell are they up to?

"All contacts increasing to flank," added the tech.

Flank speed, the maximum possible thrust, varied by class but ranged in the neighborhood of thirty knots.

The Russians were clearing out fast.

He watched with interest as the Russian vessels continued steaming away from the island, heading out to sea, presumably to join the first contacts, which had departed a few hours earlier and had taken up a station more than forty nautical miles away.

"They're clearing the area for something," mused Ellis. "Another missile test?"

"Could be," Harris replied equivocally. His gut, however, told him it was something more.

The departure of the *Pyotr Velikiy* seemed to signal the end of the exodus, and, after forty minutes with no new contacts, Harris's curiosity had risen to a fever pitch. "I want to see what's going on up there. Prepare to rise to periscope depth."

Ellis let out his breath in a low sigh. Rising to periscope depth—breaking through the thermocline—would make them particularly vulnerable to detection. And while the Russians had not given any indication that they even suspected an American sub was lurking nearby, that could change in a heartbeat if they shed the protection of the quiet depths. "Rise to periscope depth, aye."

When all crew stations reported ready, the diving officer called out, "Bring her up to sixty feet."

"Sixty feet, aye," answered the planesman adjusting the submarine's angle.

The ascent was slow, agonizingly so, the quiet broken only by the voice of the planesman calling out incremental depth changes.

"Approaching sixty feet."

"Mark depth, sixty feet."

"Up scope," Harris said, leaning over the periscope stand. He grabbed the handles, adjusted the eyepiece, and began a slow, deliberate sweep of the surface. "Clear the baffles."

"Clear baffles, aye," echoed Ellis, relaying the order to begin a slow turn to cover the sub's sonar blind spot to the rear.

As the periscope panned across the bleak horizon, Harris saw nothing but the cold gray-blue of the Barents Sea. The Russian ships were now well beyond the visible range, but he was more interested in what they had left behind. He continued turning until the land mass of Novaya Zemlya filled the scope.

"Conn, Radio. We're getting some major ELINT. Signals between the fleet and an airborne asset. It's huge, sir."

Harris's pulse quickened. He didn't ask the young submariner to elaborate on what he meant by *huge.* "Can you get a bearing on the airborne contact?"

"Negative, Skipper. Not enough data to triangulate a position. But it's encrypted military."

A sense of urgency clawed at Harris's nerves. Every moment spent near the surface escalated the risk of discovery, but whatever the Russians were up to, it was happening now. He pulled the periscope around once more, angling the view upward into the low cloud cover.

And then, there it was, breaking through a gap in the clouds.

Harris had no difficulty identifying the aircraft. With its sleek, arrow-shaped profile, white underbelly, and boxy jet intakes, it was unmistakable. A Tupolev Tu-160 Blackjack bomber was coming in from the south, following the island crest. As he watched, the bomber's payload bay yawned open, and something dark and ominous fell away from its belly.

"Goddamn," he whispered, pulling away in horror. "Lower scope! Dive! Dive! Get us down—*now*!"

The diving officer slammed the ballast controls, and the *Toledo* tilted downward as they plunged beneath the surface.

"Take us to two hundred feet—make your depth two-zero-zero feet!" Harris tried to maintain a professional calm, but his voice was taut, the urgency breaking through.

"Aye, two hundred feet!" responded the planesman.

"Skip?" asked Ellis. "What did you see?"

Harris blew out his breath. "It's a test all right. A bomb test."

"A bomb?" Ellis swallowed. He did not need to ask for clarification.

For several months, Russian president Vladimir Putin had been threatening to resume nuclear weapons tests, ending a thirty-year-long moratorium, as a way of signaling Russia's readiness to employ the literal nuclear option if the NATO alliance members allowed Ukraine to use weapons supplied by them against targets in Russia.

Now, it seemed, Putin had made good on that threat.

"Passing one hundred feet," the planesman called out.

Not fast enough, thought Harris.

They were about twenty nautical miles from ground zero. Was that far enough to be safe?

The answer to that question was a function of two things: the bomb's yield and their depth.

Thermonuclear bombs came in all shapes and sizes, from tactical warheads designed to obliterate a single target to megaton beasts meant for total devastation. But this wasn't a battlefield detonation—this was a weapon test. More than that, it was a statement, a threat. Putin wasn't likely to use anything small if he was trying to make a point.

"Passing one hundred and fifty feet," the planesman called.

Come on . . . Faster. Harris clenched his fists as the seconds dragged.

"Approaching two hundred feet!"

Suddenly, a gut-wrenching rumble rolled through the deck.

"Conn, Sonar! Massive acoustic event!"

"Brace for—"

The submarine lurched violently to the side as the water surrounding it convulsed. Harris, failing to heed his own advice, was hurled against the periscope stand but somehow managed to wrap his arms around it as the sub was buffeted by the pressure wave. After a few seconds, the stabilizing gyros overcame the turbulence. It took a moment longer for Harris to overcome his disorientation, but he could hear the hull creaking and groaning. Critical alert lights were flashing all over the control room.

"Damage report!" he gasped.

The answer was a long time coming.

"Minor hull stress," said Ellis. "No breaches! We're holding, sir!"

"Casualties?"

Ellis made a slightly strangled sound. "Yeah. I think we've got a few of those." He gazed down at Harris and offered a hand up. "Starting with you."

Harris would later learn that he'd broken an arm and several ribs, but in the grip of an adrenaline surge he felt no pain.

"We should clear out of here," Ellis went on. "Head for the Norwegian Sea . . . someplace where we can get a detailed report out. Washington needs to know about this."

Harris regarded his subordinate for a long moment before answering. "Trust me. They already do."

TEN

ST. PETERSBURG, RUSSIA

Sergei Yevgenyevich Mulmuscovy slouched in the plush leather seats of his Mercedes-Maybach G 650 Landaulet—an armored colossus favored by many of his fellow Russian oligarchs—as it moved quietly through the dark streets of Moscow. The interior of the SUV, hidden away from the outside world behind darkly tinted ballistic-glass windows, was a testament to obscene wealth: quilted ostrich skin leather, hand-stitched by artisans, deep-wood paneling, and soft amber lights that barely illuminated his brooding form. Yet the luxury surrounding him was not enough to loosen the knot of dread in his stomach.

Putin had done it. The fool had actually done it.

The screen of his large high-def television was filled with the image of a nuclear mushroom cloud rising high—more than sixty miles high, if the Kremlin's propaganda machine was to be believed—into the Arctic sky.

"One hundred megatons," crowed a military spokesperson with undisguised pride in a voice-over report. "That is our estimate of the yield. It is the biggest bomb detonation in history, bigger even than the original Tsar Bomba. Now the West will know that we mean business."

Mulmuscovy found the remote and switched off the screen, then took a bottle of Beluga Epicure from the chiller. His hands shook as he decanted some of its contents into a crystal tumbler, inadvertently splashing vodka on the upholstery. Ordinarily, the waste of even a few drops of the precious spirit—the Epicure was a limited run with only a thousand bottles produced, each of which retailed for 650,000 rubles—or the possible damage to the ostrich skin leather would have elicited a torrent of profanity, but today he barely noticed. Without even bothering to return the bottle to the chiller, he downed the tumbler and then poured another.

The ice-cold vodka left a warm trail from gullet to gut, and gradually the sensation spread to his extremities, calming his nerves.

He knew what he had to do.

Sergei Mulmuscovy, the son of a petty criminal from St. Petersburg, had clawed his way out of Russia's underworld through sheer ruthlessness and cunning. His rise to power began in the tumultuous 1990s, in the post-Soviet economic chaos, where he built a modest fortune operating shady construction contracts and running catering deals that supplied government institutions. It was through these ventures that he first crossed paths with Vladimir Putin, then a rising political figure. The two men shared a common vision of restoring Russia's strength through whatever means necessary, and Mulmuscovy became one of Putin's earliest confidants, using his street-honed survival instincts to eliminate rivals and secure lucrative government contracts. Together, they cultivated a network of oligarchs and former KGB operatives, profiting enormously from Russia's shifting political landscape.

His greatest success was the creation of the Perun Group, a private mercenary army that took its name from the Slavic god of war and thunder. Modeled after similar forces like the South African outfit Executive Outcomes and the American Blackwater, but with greater reach and brutality, Perun gained notoriety during the war in Donbas in 2014, where Mulmuscovy's forces helped destabilize the region while securing key strategic objectives for the Kremlin. He became fabulously wealthy, profiting not only from military operations but also from control of natural resources in occupied territories. As the war in Ukraine escalated, so did his influence, with Perun playing a crucial role in Russia's shadow operations across Europe and Africa, while Mulmuscovy consolidated his position as one of Russia's most powerful oligarchs.

Yet, for all that his partnership with Putin had brought him, Mulmuscovy secretly despised the man. To him, the Russian president was a blunt instrument—useful for extending his own global ambitions but also reckless and increasingly unstable.

When would-be tsar Ivan Korsakov had briefly dethroned Putin, consigning him to a lethally radioactive cell in Energetika Prison, Mulmuscovy had been one of a loyal few to stand by Putin, albeit secretly, facilitating his return to control of the Kremlin following Korsakov's demise—not because he believed in Putin, but rather because only through Putin could Mulmuscovy achieve his true ambition: power that extended far beyond the shortsighted reach of Putin's nationalist agenda. He dreamed of controlling entire regions, expanding the influence of Perun Group beyond Russia's borders, and turning it into a global force to rival even the most powerful governments.

But now all of that was in mortal danger. The test of the Tsar II bomb was a signal that Putin was slipping into madness, flirting with nuclear war, and jeopardizing everything Mulmuscovy had worked to achieve. His partnership with Putin had always been transactional, but now it seemed the tool he had so carefully wielded was on the verge of destroying them both.

He took out the encrypted satellite phone, staring at it for a long moment before finally dialing the only number he ever called with it, a number he had not dared use in months.

The call was picked up almost immediately.

"I did not think I would hear from you again after the unfortunate way things ended." The voice was smooth and faintly sardonic, the words in English, the only language they had in common.

"I lost my yacht," Mulmuscovy grumbled, frowning at the memory.

"You're lucky that's all you lost," replied the other man with a chuckle.

He wasn't wrong.

The debacle in Istanbul had left Mulmuscovy, an international fugitive, unable to leave Mother Russia. What should have been a surgical strike had turned into a botched operation, with his fingerprints all over the scalpel. His claim that the assault had been conducted without his authorization or knowledge by "rogue" Perun operators who had commandeered his yacht had been laughable on its face but created just enough uncertainty to allow President Putin to ignore calls by the Western alliance for Mulmuscovy's head. In response to allegations that the action had been carried out on Putin's orders, the Russian president had merely replied: "If I had ordered this attack, it would have succeeded."

In fact, Putin had been completely unaware of Mulmuscovy's plan and its ultimate intent. Had the operation succeeded, things might have been very different in Moscow. Unwittingly, Putin continued to shelter Mulmuscovy, mistakenly believing that his former protégé was still a loyal ally.

Thankfully, the metaphorical fallout from the Istanbul operation hadn't hurt his business, but the literal fallout from Putin's little demonstration threatened to utterly destroy it.

"If I ever get my hands on that English bastard Hawke, I will make him pay," promised Mulmuscovy. "He ruined everything."

"Yes, he did. But I'm sure you didn't call me just to commiserate."

"Are you seeing the news?"

"Everybody is seeing the news, my friend," replied the other man.

"He jeopardizes everything. We must accelerate the timetable."

There was a long silence over the line. Then he heard the other man sigh. "I fear it may already be too late. We cannot undo what he has done. We must allow this to play out and pray that Putin does not make good on his threat."

"He won't."

"How can you be so sure? You know better than anyone how unpredictable he is. With his back to the wall—"

"He won't," insisted Mulmuscovy. "He can't."

"What are you saying, Sergei?"

"The Russian strategic arsenal is a Potemkin village." The words were out before he could call them back. Maybe it was the vodka loosening his tongue, or maybe it was just that this secret, which he had kept for so long, had finally burned its way out. "We want the West to think that we are accelerating production of new weapons. Bigger bombs, faster missiles. But is all an illusion."

Even before the war in Ukraine, the Russian strategic arsenal, the source of so much existential dread in the West, had been little more than a bluff. Decades of neglect and corruption had eroded its actual capacity. Warheads had gone without proper maintenance. Missile silos had been emptied under the guise of modernization, only for the components to be siphoned off and sold to the highest bidder. The proud arsenal of a former superpower had become a rotting relic, propped up only by propaganda.

This was the real reason why Putin's escalation with the Tsar II missile test was so dangerous.

In the event of a nuclear escalation, NATO might realize that Russia's vaunted strategic capabilities were more bluster than bite. Worse yet, if Putin continued pushing the world toward a full-scale confrontation, the truth would come out: there weren't enough functional nuclear warheads in Russia's entire stockpile to light up a city, much less deter a unified Western assault. Mulmuscovy's ambitions of ascending to power in a post-Putin Russia depended on maintaining this illusion of strength. The balance of global power was a precarious game, and the collapse of Russia's nuclear deterrence would shatter the last vestiges of its credibility on the world stage.

"You are being serious?" asked the other man. "Can this be true?"

"It is," replied Mulmuscovy gravely.

"Oh, my. Oh." The man seemed at a loss for words. Then he began laughing. "All this time . . . living in fear . . . and it was all an illusion." He paused a beat. "But surely you still have some functional weapons. Even a few hundred warheads would still be a deterrent."

Mulmuscovy shook his head sadly. "Not enough. When the dogs realize that the bear has no teeth, nothing will stop them from tearing her to shreds."

"No, you are correct, of course."

"Then you understand why we must act now. Before this goes any further, I cannot move against him. He is too well protected. Too popular. Especially now that he has shaken the world."

"Yes. Now, let me think a moment. Hmm. There may be a way . . ." He fell silent for a few seconds. "Yes. I think it might work. Tell me, my friend, do you play chess?"

"No. Chess is for men with soft hands."

"I thought you Russians made the best chess players. No matter. To win at chess, you must know how to use all the pieces on the board—not just the powerful ones. The pawns are just as important as the rooks, the bishops, and the queen. It's not about brute force. It's about manipulation. You must guide the enemy, encourage them to make the moves you want them to make. Make them think they're in control. But all the while you are setting them up for a fall. But, to seize victory, you must take risks. You must be willing to go beyond what's safe." He paused to let his metaphor sink in. "Are you willing to risk everything, Sergei? Sacrifice everything in order to win?"

Mulmuscovy did not like the implication. "Do I have choice?"

"No. You don't."

The Russian sighed. "What is plan?"

"Putin has roared at the world. We will answer with . . . silence."

ELEVEN

LONDON, UNITED KINGDOM

Alex Hawke stared out the window of his private Gulfstream G800 as it parted the veil of clouds to reveal the sprawling urban landscape of London rising up to meet him. His nerves were humming in anticipation of what the day would bring.

Three months, Hawke told himself. *Three bloody months.*

Three months since the NATO summit. Three months since the Warmonger struck the first blow in this new war. Three months since Sergei Mulmuscovy retreated into the welcoming arms of Vladimir Putin. Three months in which he, Alexander Hawke, had done little more than pace the length of the veranda at Teakettle Cottage in Bermuda, waiting for the chance to strike back.

Now the wait was over.

The call to action had been sounded.

He could still see the text message in his mind's eye: Summons to Clarence House. His Majesty requests your presence.

The words had triggered an immediate rush of adrenaline.

It's time.

Anastasia had read it in his eyes. "You're going again, aren't you?"

She wasn't angry, or if she was, she had hidden it well. Her tone was one of resignation and, perhaps, just a little sadness at the realization that this life of quiet mornings and fatherhood, of shared evenings with their son, Alexei, wasn't enough for him. It would never be enough. He could tolerate it for a while, even revel in it—the conquering hero, home from war—but war always called him back.

Maybe the damn nickname is a rather snug fit after all.

Their relationship had been like something from a fairy tale but more grim than anything suitable for Disney. They had first met nearly nine years ago, by chance or fate, on a secluded beach in Bermuda—she a world-renowned artist, he . . . well . . . himself. The connection between them was immediate, electrifying. The chemistry was damn near combustible.

But, as in any fairy tale, there was a long way to go before "happily ever after."

To begin with, Anastasia's father, Count Ivan Ivanovich Korsakov, a descendant of the Russian royal family through Grand Duke Kirill Vladimirovich, a cousin of Tsar Nicholas, had staged a coup in Russia, toppling the government, jailing his rival Vladimir Putin, and declaring himself tsar. His ambitions, however, hadn't stopped at merely ruling Russia. Korsakov had, in fact, devised a global terror plot that would have brought the West to its knees, and he had very nearly succeeded. It had, of course, fallen to Alex Hawke to stop him, and, in doing so, Hawke was forced to destroy Korsakov's airship—believing that Anastasia had perished aboard alongside her father.

Asia—as he had always called her—had reawakened him to a belief in the power of love—something he hadn't felt since the death of his wife, Victoria Sweet, struck down by a sniper's bullet on the steps of their wedding chapel—and so losing Asia was that much more painful. If anything, Asia's death was worse because he had given the order to detonate the explosives that destroyed Korsakov's airship.

Then, three years later, a message arrived, one he would never have dreamed possible. Asia was alive but living under house arrest in Russia with their son, Alexei, a boy he had never known existed, and she needed Hawke to take the boy home.

For the next four years he raised Alexei as a single father, the precocious lad bringing unexpected joy into Hawke's life. And then, miraculously, Asia was freed from her confinement. Retaking her ancestral name—Romanova—she reunited with father and son, and for a time, it looked as though the story might finally have a happy ending.

But "happily ever after" was turning out to be a bloody long time.

Or perhaps, thought Hawke, *not bloody possible at all.*

While there was still love between them—deep, undeniable love—the cracks were beginning to show. Asia had her son and her freedom, and yet . . . it wasn't enough. Not with Hawke's restless spirit pulling him back into danger at every turn. He had tried to stay grounded, to settle into life as a father and partner. But his heart belonged to the thrill of the fight, to the danger and excitement that had defined his existence for so long.

And that was the problem.

Because Hawke was indeed down to his very bones the "Warlord," a storm that was rarely not on the move. He couldn't fully commit—not to Asia, and certainly not to the quiet life she craved and deserved. For her part, she had never asked him to choose between her and the mission, but Hawke knew deep down that sooner or later he would have to or risk losing her, and perhaps his son, forever.

It wasn't an issue of love.

To be certain, Hawke loved them both—Anastasia and Alexei—and he would sooner die than desert them. But he simply wasn't made for the peaceful life.

The Warmonger was still out there, sowing the seeds of chaos. The Russian bear was roaring louder than ever before. A week had passed since Putin's audacious test of the Tsar II bomb, the most powerful thermonuclear weapon ever built, and the world was closer to Armageddon than at any time since the Cuban missile crisis.

And what had Alex Hawke been doing? Cooling his heels in paradise, sipping rum, and having a game of catch with his son while the world teetered on the brink.

But now, finally, at last, the call had been sent.

The calm before the storm was over.

"You are the storm," Alex heard Anastasia's voice say in his head. The words, spoken under the falling snow just moments before they had decided to call off their wedding, had provided a revelation of sorts for Hawke, who, even when he was just a young boy, had always loved storms and prayed that they'd never stop. *"The storm is all you know . . . It's where you thrive. Not in warm shelter but in the chaos of elements you cannot control."*

"A new storm," Hawke whispered to himself.

Before leaving Bermuda, he'd asked his lead mechanic, "Young Ian" Burns, to have a car sent over from Hawkesmoor, the family estate in the Cotswolds.

"Which one, sir?"

Hawke had given this matter some serious consideration. He owned quite a few cars and liked them all for different reasons. He usually preferred the classics, like the Lancia or his very favorite, the Locomotive—his nickname for the elephant's-breath-gray Bentley R Type Continental, which he'd bought from the Fleming estate and which, unfortunately, had gotten a bit banged up a year earlier. Young Ian was still working on the restoration.

"I leave it to your judgment," Hawke had told the mechanic. "Just make sure that whichever one you pick, it's up to the challenge."

"And what challenge would that be?"

Hawke had laughed. "Why, all of them."

Alex was therefore pleased to see one of his most recent acquisitions, a British racing green 2025 BMW M8 Competition Gran Coupe, waiting just off the tarmac. With its 617-horsepower twin-turbo V8 and the ability to hit sixty miles per hour in under three seconds, the M8 was the perfect steed upon which to ride forth on the King's business.

The early morning light reflected off the Thames as he navigated the streets of east London, merging onto the A3211 along the Embankment. The city was stirring to life, but the roads remained clear enough for him to give the M8 a workout. As he approached Trafalgar Square, he spied the imposing towers of Buckingham Palace looming in the distance. His destination, while not so iconic, was just as consequential.

Clarence House, located on the Mall, adjacent to the St. James's Palace, had been built in 1825 for the Duke of Clarence—later King William IV. It had been home to several members of the Royal Family, including the Queen Mother, for nearly fifty years and had, since 2003, been the private residence of then Prince and now King Charles III, who preferred its more intimate, understated elegance to the grandiosity of Buckingham Palace.

Hawke had a unique relationship with King Charles. When his parents had been brutally murdered, orphaning young Alex at the tender age of seven, the Royal Family had opened their hearts and their homes to him. He spent summers at Balmoral Castle, riding and hunting with three generations of the Windsor family. Later, when Hawke had answered his true calling—a life of adventure—he had become a sort of knight-errant on behalf of first Her Majesty Elizabeth II and then, upon his succession, King Charles III. Just a year earlier, when a Scottish secessionist had abducted Charles away from Balmoral, it had been Hawke, with a little help from his closest friends, Sir Ambrose Congreve, formerly of Scotland Yard, and Stokely Jones Jr., who had come to the rescue.

Typically, however, Hawke's work on behalf of the Crown was carried out in a less direct fashion. He usually received his marching orders from the head of the SIS, Sir David Trulove, or "C," as he was officially known. For Charles to personally request his presence—and at his home, no less—was portentous indeed, though, judging by the headlines of the last week, it came as little surprise.

The fate of the world was at stake. Who else was the King to call upon if not his favorite knight-errant?

As Hawke turned down Stable Yard Road and came to the security gate, an officer from the Royalty and Special Protection Unit approached. After a quick glance into the car's interior, the officer offered a polite nod. "You're expected, m'lord. Please proceed."

The gate swung open and Hawke continued down the road to the front of the four-story residence, where he parked the M8. A member of the household staff was already waiting to receive him. "If you'll follow me, sir, His Majesty will see you in his study."

The man led him through the house and then entered the room ahead of him, announcing his arrival. "Your Majesty, Lord Alexander Hawke."

As he entered the room, Hawke hid his displeasure at the formal rigamarole behind a forced smile. He found it all rather tedious, but Charles was the King, after all, and protocols had to be observed. He saw the monarch standing by the window in a somewhat contemplative pose, and then something else caught his attention—or, rather, someone else. The King was not alone in the study.

There was a woman sitting demurely in one of the high-backed reading chairs.

A strikingly beautiful woman.

Hawke managed to keep his attention focused on his host, but from the corner of his eye he appraised the King's other guest.

The first word that came to Hawke's mind was *prim.* Her dark hair pulled back into a tight bun, glasses perched on her nose, and a blouse buttoned high enough to suggest restraint but not modesty. She sat—primly—with a leather portfolio on her lap, looking for all the world like a repressed librarian in an adolescent schoolboy's fantasy.

"Alex," the King said warmly, turning from the window. "It's good to see you again."

Hawke gave a small bow of his head. "Your Majesty."

"How is Anastasia? And Alexei? How old is he now?"

The pleasantries were to be expected, but Hawke found it rather conspicuous that the King had not introduced the woman. "Both are well. Alexei is eight now."

Charles shook his head. "Only eight? He seemed so much older than that the last time I saw him."

"You know how it is with children."

"Wait until you have grandchildren."

Grandchildren? Hawke laughed politely—though, frankly, the thought terrified him. Grandchildren were for *old* people, and he was in no hurry to enter the autumn years.

"I imagine you must be wondering why I've summoned you."

"I think I have some idea, what with the news and all."

"Ah, yes. That." The King pursed his lips. "As the head of state, I am, by constitutional design, bound by strict limits. I can express concern and offer guidance privately to our elected leaders, but when it comes to decisive matters of foreign policy, defense, or even something as catastrophic as this present moment, it is up to Parliament and the Prime Minister to chart our course. My hands, much as they are eager to move, are tied by the very institution I represent."

Hawke needed no reminders of the King's official role in the government of the United Kingdom, nor had he come with the expectation that the King would be sending him forth on an officially sanctioned mission. He wondered if Charles's disclaimer was for the benefit of the as-yet-unintroduced guest.

But if that's the case, why is she here?

"The reason I've called you here," the King went on, "is rather of a more personal nature."

"Personal?" Hawke was now thoroughly mystified.

"I shall endeavor to explain." Charles turned to the woman and extended a hand toward her. "I imagine you're wondering about my other guest. Allow me to introduce Dr. Ariadne Silk. She's a specialist in forensic document examination, employed by the Royal Archivist."

As if that were the cue she had been waiting for, Silk rose and took a step forward, extending her hand. There was something in her eyes—a knowing look that Hawke knew all too well; a seductive look.

Her fingers were warm as they clasped his, lingering for just a fraction longer than necessary.

"Lord Hawke, it's a pleasure to meet you."

"Call me Alex." The response was reflexive, and he found himself regretting it immediately. He neither wanted nor needed any romantic entanglements. He quickly turned his attention back to the King. "You were saying?"

"Dr. Silk," said the King, "let's show Alex what you've found."

"Right away, sir," replied Silk. Her gaze still lingering on Hawke, she placed her portfolio on a side table and took out a yellowed parchment protected in a Mylar sleeve, which she then held out to Hawke. "I think you'll find this of interest, Alex."

Hawke regarded the parchment with a degree of suspicion. The handwritten letters were sprawled across the page in flowing, elegant script, loops, and lines that looked completely alien to his modern eyes. It was barely recognizable as English. He took the document, turning it around, and began reading.

"George, by ye Grace of God, King of Great Brittain, France, and Ireland, Defender of ye Faith, etc.

"King George?"

"George the First," offered Silk. "He reigned from 1714 to 1727."

Hawke resumed reading and quickly came to understand why King Charles had brought this document to his attention.

"Whereas it hath been represented unto Us that Richard John Hawke, late of Our dominion, hath, by force of arms upon ye high seas, engaged in certain unlawful and pyratical activities against ye peace and safety of Our subjects, and ye good Order of Our Realm . . .

"Blackhawke," Hawke murmured.

"Your ancestor, I believe."

"He started as a privateer for the Crown, attacking Spanish merchantmen, but rather enjoyed it too much. After he took a couple of East India Company ships, he was declared an outlaw. He was eventually convicted of the murder of a mutinous crewman and sent to the gallows."

Silk nodded. "You should keep reading."

Hawke did.

". . . and whereas it hath also been demonstrated unto Us, that ye said Richard John Hawke hath, since his unlawful Endeavours, repented for his pyratical misdeeds, and hath rendered faithful Service in ye apprehension of certain notable Offenders against ye Crown . . .

"We, therefore, out of Our most gracious and royal clemency, do hereby grant unto ye said Richard John Hawke, full Pardon of all Crimes and Offences committed upon ye Seas or elsewhere in Our Dominions, before ye date hereof, in so far as such may extend to Pyracy and unlawful Depredations . . ."

The elaborate script seemed to swirl in front of his eyes. Hawke looked up, first at Charles, then at Silk. "This is a Royal pardon."

"Yes," replied Silk, smiling, almost purring. "It is."

"When he was in Newgate Prison awaiting execution, Blackhawke prayed that the King would extend a pardon, honoring the letter of marque authorizing him to raid Spanish treasure ships. His pleas went unanswered. The pardon went to one of his crew who offered sworn testimony against him.

"Accompanying documents indicate that it was King George's intent to pardon Blackhawke because of his earlier service on behalf of the Crown," Silk explained. "He went as far as to write and sign the pardon, but—bowing to pressure from the East India Company—he withheld it until after the judgment was carried out."

"A grave injustice was done to your family," said Charles, in an almost reverent tone. "That document can't undo what was done, but at least you have the satisfaction of knowing that your ancestor's reputation is restored."

Hawke stared at the parchment in his hands, rereading the words inscribed there. It was more than just a pardon; it was the absolution of his family's legacy. Yet, as he continued to read, a different emotion crept in—one he hadn't expected. He looked to Charles, a wry smile tugging at the corner of his mouth. "Haven't you heard? Pirates are all the rage nowadays. Blackhawke's reputation was well deserved, and I think he'd rather be remembered as the terror of the Spanish Main. A man who made his own fate with a cutlass in one hand and a pistol in the other."

The King's eyebrows drew together in a frown. "Perhaps. But I believe we, the living, have a responsibility to our ancestors, whether that means acknowledging their sins or offering redemption."

"Redemption was never his currency." Hawke took another look at the pardon and then handed it back to Silk. "I hope you don't think me ungrateful."

Charles waved the apology away. "You're right, of course. Honor, legacy—these things are delicate, complex, and not always in our control. But righting past wrongs . . . well, it's something I take seriously. As it happens, there is another more recent 'sin' that still haunts the Royal Family. And it's why I've asked you here."

Hawke nodded to the document in Silk's hand. "I thought—"

"That was merely an inducement. Something Dr. Silk came across while looking into the subject at hand." The King gestured to the chairs. "Please, have a seat. And I will tell you the story of *my* family's greatest shame."

TWELVE

History," Charles began, "as you well know, is not always kind. And my family has no shortage of sins to atone for." He paused, letting the words settle. "But there is one sin that has cast a shadow over House of Windsor for generations and which time has not annealed. The betrayal of the Romanovs.

"After Tsar Nicholas II was forced to abdicate the throne following the Russian Revolution in 1917, he and his family were placed under house arrest. Initially, the British government under Prime Minister Lloyd George, at my great-grandfather's urging, offered asylum to his cousin Nicholas and his family. The offer was made in March of that year, but the situation in Britain at the time was quite volatile, with republican and anti-monarchist sentiments rising among the working class. Hosting the Romanovs could have been seen as a destabilizing act. Under that pressure, my great-grandfather George V, deeply conflicted, was convinced to withdraw the offer of asylum in April 1917. The Romanovs were moved to Siberia that summer and eventually to Yekaterinburg, where, in July 1918, they were executed by the Bolsheviks."

He sighed heavily. "I don't think history will ever fully forgive us for turning our backs on them."

"King George couldn't have known that their lives were on the line," countered Hawke. "The Bolsheviks kept them alive for more than a year after the revolution."

Charles pursed his lips together. "Unfortunately, that may not be entirely true. Dr. Silk, please show Alex the letter."

Silk carefully laid the pardon aside and took another document from her portfolio. This one was similar in appearance to the pardon letter—written letters on parchment—but, unlike the latter, it was not in a protective Mylar sheath. When she passed it over to Hawke, he understood why such measures were unnecessary. The document was a color photocopy.

Clarence House, 17 April, 1918
To the Chairman of the All-Russian
Central Executive Committee,
Yakob Sverdlov,

In response to your urgent communiqué regarding the impending fate of my cousin, Nicholas, and his family, I must express my deepest personal sorrow. It weighs heavily upon me that their plight has reached such a state, and I have not ceased in my prayers for their welfare.

Regrettably, circumstances beyond my control compel me to refrain from offering the refuge that I would so earnestly wish to extend. The political climate within my own country, coupled with the demands of this grievous war, preclude any such intervention. While I implore you to consider further clemency, I fear that I must reluctantly bow to the inexorable tide of history that now sweeps over us.

May you, in your wisdom, see fit to mitigate the harshness of their sentence, and may peace soon return to your nation and to the world.

With deepest regret and respect,
George R.
By the Grace of God, King of Great Britain, Ireland, and the British Dominions Beyond the Seas, Emperor of India

Hawke checked the date at the top again.

April 1918.

A full year after the offer of asylum was withdrawn.

He raised his eyes to Charles. "This letter mentions a communiqué."

Dr. Silk provided the answer. "If this letter is authentic, then it would seem that sometime in the spring of 1918, probably around the time that the Tsar and his family were moved back to Yekaterinburg, Yakob Sverdlov, the chairman of the Bolshevik ruling committee, sent a secret message to King George, apparently offering to negotiate terms for the safe passage for the Romanovs."

"An offer which George refused," added Charles gravely. "Knowingly consigning them to their fate."

Hawke took a moment to process what the King was telling him. Through his lineage on Asia's side, his son, Alexei, was a Romanov, which meant, in a roundabout way, this was a family matter. He turned to Silk. "You said '*if* this letter is authentic.' I take it there's some question regarding that."

Silk gazed back at him, blinking slowly like a cat. "I did. And there is."

"Well, forgive me for being so blunt, but isn't it your bloody job to figure that out?" Hawke's unnecessarily brusque response was more a reaction to Silk's come-hither gaze than irritation at her professional lapse.

But Silk appeared unruffled by his manner. "There is no communiqué in the Archive received from Sverdlov or anyone else in the Bolshevik leadership during the weeks prior to the date of this letter, nor is there any record of King George V issuing a reply. Given the subject of this correspondence and the need for secrecy, that's not surprising. However, an entry from his personal diary two days later makes mention of sending his 'most trusted servant' carrying a dispatch of 'grave import to the Crown,' so it is possible that the King did indeed send this letter.

"Ultimately, the only way to determine the authenticity of the document is through a forensic examination, compared to that of the original, which we do not possess."

"Ah. Who does?" Hawke leaned back in his chair, looking once more to the King. "No, don't tell me. The bloody Russians."

Charles seemed reluctant to confirm the supposition, leaving Silk to do so. "The document was found in St. Petersburg, in a cache of old correspondence dating back to the Russian Revolution. We were contacted by a representative of the Kremlin inquiring about how we would like to handle the release of this—"

"Putin is blackmailing you," Hawke said, cutting her off.

Charles gave a humorless smile. "In a manner of speaking. The letter is being offered as a—and here I am quoting—'a token of our good faith, honoring our long tradition of diplomacy.' The subtext is clear enough: Putin is dangling it in front of me, suggesting that if I don't lend my voice to his calls for peace, for NATO to stop arming Ukraine, the letter might be leaked to the press. The public would see it as a betrayal of the Romanovs by the British monarchy—something the monarchy has tried to distance itself from for over a century. It would also undermine our standing in the current conflict. The optics of the British Royal Family being complicit in the murder of our cousins would play right into Putin's hands."

Hawke's eyes narrowed. "Surely, you aren't considering going along with this."

Charles exhaled deeply. "Of course not. I won't be coerced into any course of action. It is unthinkable that I should compromise my principles or the interests of the Crown because of veiled threats from Moscow. Nevertheless, I must deal with this matter discreetly. The Family can ill afford another scandal."

"It will come out no matter what you do. Better to get out ahead of it. Steal his thunder."

"If the letter is authentic, I intend to do exactly that."

"*If* it is authentic," added Silk, stressing the first word.

"And how will you determine that?" asked Hawke.

"Dr. Silk will be traveling to Russia to verify it in person."

"It's already been arranged," added Silk. "I will be meeting with President Putin at his vacation residence in Sochi Tuesday next."

Hawke arched an eyebrow. "You're sending her into Putin's backyard?"

"I'm more than capable of handling myself, Lord Hawke," said Silk with a touch of haughtiness.

"Well, bully for you."

"I have every confidence in Dr. Silk," continued Charles. "Nevertheless, given the delicacy of this situation, never mind the danger, I think it prudent to send someone along to guarantee her safety."

Hawke was in no doubt regarding who that "someone" was. Though he would not have dreamed of refusing—not an order from his king, nor the request of a favor from a friend—this was not the mission he had been expecting. He considered his answer carefully.

"With respect, Majesty, you may recall that Putin put a price on my literal head. Granted, I think he's mostly forgotten about it, but he's not the sort to forgive and forget."

"If anyone can get in and out of Russia without attracting unwanted attention, it's you, Alex."

The King's comment, while offhand, was veering into territory of a classified nature. "Majesty," said Hawke carefully, "I wonder if I might have a word with you in private."

The King seemed unperturbed by the request. "I was about to suggest the very thing. Dr. Silk, would you excuse us for a moment?"

Silk inclined her head, her eyes lingering on Hawke for a second longer than necessary, then gathered her things and made her exit. As soon as the door clicked shut behind her, the King spoke. "Alex, I know this sort of thing isn't exactly in your wheelhouse."

"Charles, you needn't explain yourself. My only concern is whether Dr. Silk is cleared for a discussion touching on operational details."

"Ah, quite right, of course."

"As for what you're asking me to do . . . of course, I'll do it. You have only to ask."

The King returned a grateful smile. "As it happens, there's something else I need from you." He paused and then, lowering his voice to just above a conspiratorial whisper, went on.

"I do want you to ensure Dr. Silk's safety, yes. But if that letter turns out to be authentic"—he hesitated as if weighing his next words carefully—"I want you to steal it."

"Steal it?"

"I won't have Vladimir Putin deciding when and where to release that letter to the world."

"Charles, aren't you at all worried about creating an international incident?"

"Right now the international community has other things to be concerned with."

Hawke rubbed his chin thoughtfully. The King's mission had just gotten a lot more interesting.

"There's one other thing I haven't told you," Charles went on. "You'll recall Dr. Silk made mention of George's 'most trusted servant.'"

"Yes. Poor chap."

A wry smile touched the corners of the King's mouth. "That poor chap was your great-grandfather and namesake, Lord Alexander Hawke."

INTERLUDE—PART ONE

LONDON
APRIL 1918

Normally the drive from Hawkesmoor to London was a pleasure, a chance for Lord Alexander Hawke to enjoy the hum of the engine and the solitude of the open road, but on this day the sojourn brought little joy. Rain had been his constant companion, a steady drumming on the canvas top of the Daimler 45-HP. The country roads were muddy and uneven, requiring a firm grip on the wooden steering wheel as the car jostled and slid. The side curtains, fastened tightly to shield against the rain, nevertheless let in a draft that sucked the warmth from his bones. Yet it was the unexpected summons that weighed heaviest on him, turning his thoughts as gray as the lowering skies under which he drove.

Through the rain-streaked windscreen, the spires and chimneys of London appeared, the rutted dirt and gravel roads giving way to slick, shimmering cobblestones as he entered the city proper. The streets were quiet—it was Sunday, after all—with only the occasional wagon or motorcar trundling by.

Turning in to the Mall, he pulled to a stop before the gates, their gilded patterns dull in the gray drizzle. A uniformed guard stepped forward from his post at the side, his figure blurred behind the fogged curtain. Alexander leaned over and unfastened the nearest side curtain panel, pushing it open just enough to be heard.

"Lord Hawke," he said. "I believe I'm expected."

The guard snapped to attention. "You are indeed, m'lord. Straight ahead."

He waved to another sentry stationed at the gate, and a moment later the massive iron gates were swinging open to admit him.

Alexander closed the curtain and eased the Daimler forward, pulling into the courtyard parking near the entrance. He cut the engine and sat for a moment, listening to the rain tapping softly against the canvas. After a moment, a liveried footman emerged from the building and opened a capacious umbrella, which he carried over to the Daimler, holding it over the car as he opened the door. Alexander got out under the cover of the umbrella, straightened his naval officer's coat, and then strode to the open door, leaving the gray day behind as he entered the warm environs of Buckingham Palace. Once inside, the footman took his coat, then another attendant led him through the familiar hallways, bringing him at last to a pair of tall oak doors, which, after a light knock, he opened.

The room beyond was stately but intimate by the standards of the palace. A fire crackled softly in the hearth, casting a flickering glow over shelves lined with leather-bound volumes and a heavy oak desk strewn with correspondence. Gazing out the window with his back to the door was a stocky figure in a navy blue morning coat.

"Alexander, Lord Hawke, Your Majesty," announced the attendant.

Alexander stepped inside, bowing slightly. "Your Majesty."

The King turned, his face lighting up with the briefest hint of a smile. "Alexander," he said warmly, dismissing Alexander's guide with a shooing gesture. "Come in, come in. Please, let's dispense with the formalities."

Alexander obeyed, stepping further into the room as the footman retreated, closing the door behind him with a quiet click.

Alone now, the King moved toward the hearth, gesturing for

Alexander to take a seat in one of the chairs positioned before it. "How are Catherine and young John?" the King asked, lowering himself into the opposite chair.

"They're well," Alexander replied. "Catherine is grateful to have me home again."

"Two years at sea is a long time," said the King, nodding.

Alexander knew it wasn't the fact of the time spent apart that had weighed on his wife's soul but rather the very real possibility that he might not come back at all, but he kept this to himself. The King needed no reminder of the toll taken by the Great War.

"And the Admiralty?" continued the King. "How are you finding it?"

"A different sort of combat," Alexander said, choosing his words carefully. "Not quite as . . . visceral as hunting U-boats. But just as necessary, of course."

The King leaned back, resting his hands on the arms of his chair. "I daresay Catherine has found her patience tested over the years. Still, I suspect she's quite glad to have you in safer waters." His gaze lingered on Alexander for a moment, his tone turning thoughtful. "Which is why I feel right bloody awful for what I'm about to ask of you."

Alexander shifted forward. "Sire?"

The King exhaled slowly, his gaze drifting to the fire for a moment before he spoke again. "Tell me, Alexander, are you aware of what's going on in Russia right now?"

"Only what I read in the papers."

George nodded, his expression grave. "Then you'll know it's bloody chaos. The Bolsheviks have overthrown the Provisional Government and declared themselves the ruling authority. The country is split apart. Reds against Whites and anyone caught in between is trampled underfoot."

Alexander inclined his head. "It's a grim picture, sire. From what I've read, the Bolsheviks are consolidating their hold on the cities. The White forces are scattered but not broken."

"Indeed," the King said. "And amidst all of this, my cousin Nicholas and his family remain prisoners."

The mention of the Tsar seemed almost an afterthought, but Alexander caught the way the King's voice tightened. He didn't reply immediately, letting the words hang in the air between them.

George pressed on, leaning forward. "I've received word—private communication from the Bolshevik leadership. They have . . . made an overture."

Alexander straightened slightly, his curiosity piqued. "An overture, sire?"

The King met his gaze, his voice low and steady. "A proposal to negotiate terms for the safe passage into exile of Nicholas and his family."

A long silence followed. Alexander was desperate to know what the King's response would be, but he held his tongue. He knew what a painful subject the plight of the Romanovs was to the King. He'd already been compelled once to withdraw Britain's offer of asylum, a decision he privately regretted. Yet, the circumstances that had forced him to deny sanctuary to his relatives had not changed.

For his own part, Alexander believed no effort should be spared to save the Romanovs, if only for the sake of the women and children—innocents caught up in the chaos of revolution. But this was not his burden to bear, and he would not add the weight of his conscience to the King's own.

Finally, the King leaned back and took an envelope from a side table. The wax seal glinted faintly in the firelight. "This is my reply." He paused a beat before adding, "I want you to take it to Moscow, Alexander. *Personally.* I don't trust the Bolshevik courier who delivered Sverdlov's communiqué. There is too much infighting among the Bolsheviks. This letter must reach Yakob Sverdlov without interference, without delay, and without the faintest hint of mistrust."

Alexander felt his pulse quicken. *He's sending me to Moscow?* But he could not refuse a request from his king. "I will ensure the letter is delivered, Majesty."

"This must be kept in strictest secrecy, Alexander. No one can know of this correspondence. That is why I am sending you. There's no one I trust more."

The simple statement, spoken with such conviction, carried more weight than any royal command. "You honor me, sire," Alexander said quietly.

The King's visage darkened. "I've chosen a hell of a way to show it." He shook his head. "This is a perilous task, Alex. Just getting to Moscow will be nigh onto impossible. There will be no guarantees of safe passage. Furthermore, Russia is in chaos. The Bolsheviks are ruthless. If misfortune should befall you . . ." He paused, his frown tightening. "You must understand, the Crown will deny all knowledge of your mission."

Alexander inclined his head. "I understand."

"You will need to provide some reason to explain your time away from the Admiralty. Leave nothing behind—no correspondence, no notes, nothing that could lead anyone to your true destination."

George leaned forward slightly, his tone softening but his words no less firm. "And, Alexander . . . that includes Catherine. For her sake as much as your own, she must remain in the dark."

"Understood, sire. When am I to leave?"

The King straightened slightly, resting his hands on the arms of his chair. "Tomorrow evening, a Royal Navy vessel—the *Scimitar*—will take you across the Channel to Calais. The Bolshevik courier will meet you aboard. Once in France, you'll have to make your own way to Moscow."

Alexander gave a short nod, already thinking about the preparations he would have to make. "That gives me time to return home first and set my affairs in order."

The King inclined his head. "Just so. But remember, you must say nothing of the true nature of your journey."

"Of course, sire."

George rose from his chair, signaling the end of their conversation.

Alexander followed suit, standing tall as the King approached him, reaching up to place a hand on Alexander's shoulder. "You've always served with unwavering loyalty, and I have no doubt you'll see this through."

"I will not fail you, sire."

The King held his gaze for a moment longer, then stepped back, his royal demeanor once more firmly in place. "Godspeed, Alexander."

INTERLUDE—PART TWO

NEAR DOVER, ENGLAND
APRIL 1918

The Daimler jostled and slid along the rutted country road, the mud from the previous day's rain clinging stubbornly to its wheels. Though the skies had cleared, the pale afternoon sun had done little to dry things out. Yet, as treacherous as the road conditions were, Alexander found negotiating them to be a welcome relief from the turmoil in his head. His thoughts were consumed by the memory of his tense parting with Catherine that morning.

"You've only just come back to us, Alex," she had said, her voice low but charged with emotion. "And now you're leaving again? For some inspection in the North Sea?"

Alexander had busied himself fussing with his uniform, avoiding her piercing gaze. "I have my orders, Catherine. You know how these things are."

"Your promotion was supposed to mean the end of you running off to sea. Isn't there someone else who can do this? You've already done your fair share. More than your fair share."

Alexander had straightened, finally meeting her gaze. Her frustration and worry were etched plainly in her expression, and for a moment he softened. "Catherine, I know it's not fair—not to you, not to

John. But this war . . . it's far from over. And until it is, I won't ever feel like I've done enough."

Her brow furrowed, her voice rising slightly. "Enough? You've already done more than most men would dare. Two years at sea, risking your life every day—if that's not enough, Alex, what is?"

He held her gaze, his tone steady but edged with resolve. "It's not about what I've done, Catherine. It's about what's left to do. This bloody war has taken too much from too many. I won't feel right until it's finished, until everyone—every man still out there—has a chance to come home."

Her eyes narrowed, her jaw tightening. "And what about you, Alex? What about us? Do we not count in your reckoning of duty and honor?"

The words struck him like a blow, but he held firm. "You do. More than anything. But you know as well as I do that I can't turn my back on this. I swore an oath, Catherine. To the King, to the men I served with, to this country. That means something. It has to."

Her lips parted as if to argue further, but she hesitated, shaking her head. "You and your bloody sense of honor." She turned away, crossing her arms tightly. "What good is it to us if it gets you killed?"

Alexander took her into his embrace, enfolding her even though her arms remained closed, shutting him out. "It's just an inspection, Catherine," he lied. "I'm sure there'll be no trouble."

The silence that followed was heavy, the tension between them unresolved. Alexander wanted to say more, wanted to explain to her just how important this mission was, that it was the King's business, but knew that would not put her at ease. Instead, he simply said, "I'll come back, Catherine. I promise."

The words—the promise that he did not know if he would be able to keep—haunted him as the Daimler slipped and slid along the muddy roads.

Saying goodbye to his son had been no less painful. In the nursery, John had been playing with a toy ship—a wooden replica of HMS *Culloden*, Alexander's first command. The model was painted a dark gray, its tiny deck guns rendered with impressive detail. The boy had looked up with wide, curious eyes as his father knelt beside him. "Look, Papa," he cried. "I'm going to sink a U-boat, just like you did."

Alexander smiled faintly, resting a hand on his son's shoulder. "Is that so, lad? You'll need a steady hand and sharp eyes for that."

"And courage too. You said it takes courage."

"That it does," Alexander said, his voice softening. "But it's not just about sinking U-boats, John. It's about protecting the men who sail with you, making sure they all come home."

The boy tilted his head, his brow furrowing as he considered this. "Did all your men come home, Papa?"

Alexander hesitated, the innocent question weighing heavily on him. He met John's gaze, seeing nothing but innocence and admiration reflected back at him. "Not all of them," he admitted quietly. "But I did everything I could."

John seemed to ponder this for a moment, then held up the toy ship again. "I'll bring them all home," he declared. "Every one of them."

Alexander's smile widened, a flicker of pride warming his chest. He reached out and ruffled John's hair. "That's my lad. I don't doubt you will."

The boy's resolve melted into a grin, and he returned to sailing the toy ship through an imagined sea. Alexander watched him for a moment longer, his heart heavy. "Listen, my boy. Papa has to go away again."

John looked up sharply, his eyes suddenly wide, his expression cutting Alexander to the quick. He pressed on. "I want you to look after your mother for me while I'm away. Will you do that for me, lad?"

John nodded solemnly, clutching the ship in both hands. "Yes, Papa."

Alexander smiled, ruffling the boy's hair. "That's my lad."

Finally, he rose to his feet, his voice catching slightly as he said, "Goodbye, my boy."

John waved the model of the *Culloden*. "Goodbye, Papa. I'll sink all the U-boats for you."

As he rose to leave, he paused in the doorway, looking back at the small figure engrossed once more in his play.

HMS *Scimitar* was moored at the far end of the dock, her sleek profile cutting an imposing figure against the horizon. A low mist lingered around her hull, blending with the smoke curling from her stacks.

Alexander parked the Daimler near the quay and stepped out, the mud squelching underfoot. A naval officer approached briskly and saluted.

"Admiral Hawke, sir. The *Scimitar* is ready to depart as soon as you're aboard. Captain Greaves will meet with you in his quarters."

Alexander returned the salute with a nod. "Very good, Lieutenant. I'll come aboard at once."

The officer gestured toward the gangplank, stepping aside as Alexander moved forward. He paused at the edge of the dock, his gaze lingering on the water. Catherine's parting words—the last thing she had said to him as he left, the answer to his promise—echoed in his mind: *"I'm worried that one day, Alexander, you won't come back."*

He pushed the thought aside, straightening his coat as he stepped onto the gangplank. The envelope in his inside pocket felt like an anchor, weighing him down. At the top of the gangplank, the boatswain and his mate awaited him, standing at attention. The boatswain raised his whistle, the sharp trill of the pipe cutting through the salt-tinged air as Alexander was formally welcomed aboard.

The sailors nearby paused momentarily in their tasks, standing a little straighter as Alexander passed. The lieutenant who had met him on the quay now stepped forward. "This way, sir."

Alexander followed, ducking slightly as he descended into the cramped interior of the ship. He could feel the vibration of the engines humming through the bulkheads as if the *Scimitar* were champing at the bit, eager to be away.

The captain's quarters were modest but tidy, with a small desk bolted to the floor, a single porthole admitting a sliver of daylight, and a small bed nestled against the bulkhead. Captain Andrew Greaves, who had been sitting at his desk, rose as Alexander entered, his face betraying an unusual mixture of discomfort and formality.

Alexander remembered signing the orders that had given him the *Scimitar*, a decision made with some apprehension due to Greaves's lack of experience but also with the understanding that command was something one could only learn by doing. He would have no shortage of opportunity to gain the requisite experience patrolling the channel.

"Admiral Hawke," Greaves said, saluting stiffly. "Welcome aboard."

As Alexander returned the salute, he noticed someone else in the room with them. A woman.

She sat in one of the two chairs near the desk. Even seated, Alexander could see that she was strikingly beautiful. Her blond hair was swept into a loose chignon, framing a face that might have been sculpted from porcelain. She wore a tailored coat of deep green wool, a hint of lace peeking from beneath the cuffs, and gloves that were removed but neatly folded on the desk beside her.

Alexander blinked, momentarily thrown. Sailors were notoriously superstitious about women aboard ships of war, considering them bad luck, yet here this woman was, poised and entirely at ease. His discomfiture deepened as her sharp blue eyes fixed on him with a faint, knowing smile.

"Captain Greaves," Alexander said, "I didn't realize you made a practice of entertaining civilians aboard your ship."

Greaves cleared his throat, looking as though he'd rather be anywhere else. "Ah, yes, sir. I mean no, sir. Not a practice. This is . . . Allow me to introduce you to Miss . . . er, Madam Natalya Volkova."

Alexander raised an eyebrow. "Volkova? You're the courier."

"I am not courier," replied the woman in clear English with only a trace of an accent. "I am envoy, sent by Central Executive Committee."

"Your pardon, Madam Volkova," said Alexander. "I wasn't expecting—"

"Call me Natalya," she said, interrupting him. "If we are to travel together, calling each other 'sir' and 'madame' will certainly become tiresome."

"Natalya it is. And I am—"

"Lord Hawke. Yes, I know."

"Alexander," he finished.

She cocked her head to the side, looking at him as if for the first time. "Very well. Alexander." She spoke his name slowly as if savoring the consonants.

Captain Greaves returned to his formal demeanor, his hands clasped behind his back. "If we get underway now, Admiral, we can have you in Calais in time for supper." He paused, his gaze shifting briefly to Natalya before quickly returning to Alexander. "You may use my quarters for the duration of the journey, sir. It's more comfortable than anywhere else aboard, and"—he hesitated slightly, his tone tightening—"it will give you some privacy."

Alexander caught the unspoken meaning behind the captain's words. Natalya's presence was as much a disruption as it was a curiosity, and Greaves clearly wanted her kept well away from his crew.

"Very considerate of you, Captain," Alexander replied smoothly, though he allowed a hint of amusement to creep into his tone. He turned toward Natalya. "Does that arrangement suit you?"

Natalya's lips quirked in a faint smile, her eyes gleaming with a mix of amusement and defiance. "Of course. I wouldn't want to be a . . . distraction."

Greaves stiffened slightly but did not acknowledge the comment. Instead, he turned to Alexander. "By your leave, sir?"

"Quite. I'll leave you to it, Captain."

Greaves came to attention and then exited the room, leaving Alexander alone with Natalya. He moved to the desk, where he placed his hands on the back of the captain's chair as he regarded her for a long moment.

"So," he said, breaking the silence, "envoy of the Central Executive Committee. I take it you're more than just a messenger."

She turned fully toward him, her chin lifting slightly. "A messenger delivers words, Alexander. An envoy carries the authority to negotiate." She stepped closer, her sharp blue eyes fixed on his. "I represent the Revolution in this matter. Your king could have saved a great deal of time by simply giving me his answer. I don't know why he chose instead to have you deliver his reply."

"So you know about the subject of the correspondence?"

"I drafted the letter for Comrade Sverdlov myself." Her tone was even, but her eyes were watchful.

"Then I expect you'll be surprised to learn that I have no idea what King George's reply says."

Natalya's brow furrowed, and for the first time her composure wavered. "What do you mean you don't know?"

Alexander tapped the pocket containing the envelope. "The letter is sealed. I wasn't told its contents, nor will I open it. My orders are to place it in Sverdlov's hands."

Her lips pressed into a thin line, and she crossed her arms again, this time more tightly. "That wastes precious time we may not have."

"That's not my concern," Alexander replied evenly. "I have my orders from the King himself."

Natalya rose, turned away as if to pace, then spun back to face him. "Do you not grasp the urgency of this? The White Army threatens Tobolsk, where the Tsar and his family are being kept. If the city falls to them, the Romanovs could end up in the hands of counterrevolutionary forces. That cannot be allowed to happen. If they are not exiled from Russia, Comrade Sverdlov will have no choice but to have them executed to prevent them from becoming a symbol to rally the Whites. With a simple telegram to Moscow, we can begin making the arrangements to get them out of Russia."

"You know as well as I do why this negotiation can't happen over the wire."

"There are codes—"

Alexander raised a hand to cut her off. "I won't open the letter. I don't expect you to like it, Natalya, but I expect you to respect it."

She exhaled sharply, her frustration evident but contained. "I see. Duty above all, is that it?"

"I would think an envoy of the Central Executive Committee would understand the importance of duty."

Her lips curved into a slow smile, one that was both amused and knowing. She stepped closer, her sharp blue eyes catching his and holding them for a moment longer than was necessary. "But when duty prevents us from doing what needs be, we must be . . . flexible."

The way she said the word sent a ripple through him, a warm and wholly unwelcome flush creeping up his neck. He stiffened, his hands tightening behind his back as he fought to steady himself.

"Still," she continued, her gaze lingering on him, her voice softening as her eyes flicked briefly to his lips before returning to his. "As we'll be traveling together, I suppose we'll just have to make the best of it."

For a moment Alexander could only stare at her. Her tone was light, her words innocuous enough, but the way she delivered them left no room for doubt about her meaning. His body certainly received the message.

He knew better than to entertain even a passing fancy. He had a mission to complete. *And a wife, for God's sake.* And yet, here he was, standing in the captain's quarters, his pulse slightly quicker than it had been moments before and feeling . . . entirely too human.

Sending a telegram to Moscow with the King's reply was beginning to sound like a very good idea.

THIRTEEN

HAMILTON, BERMUDA
PRESENT DAY

It was the sort of day that reminded former chief inspector Ambrose Congreve, late of Scotland Yard, why he had come to Bermuda in the first place.

The sun shone golden from an azure sky, dazzling the eye as it was reflected back from the turquoise waters. The air was thick with the heady scent of jasmine and frangipani. Oleanders, in bright bursts of pink and red, lined the roads alongside vibrant purple bougainvillea. It was the sort of day that people imagined when they thought of paradise. Bermuda, thought Congreve, with its idyllic calm and intoxicating beauty, was exactly the kind of place where any sane man, having retired from public service, would want to settle down and while away the days.

Thankfully, Congreve had managed to mostly avoid retirement.

It turned out there was plenty of real work for someone with his unique skill set—his good friend Alex Hawke often described Congreve as *"Scotland Yard's very own demon of deduction"*—even after reaching a career plateau, which in Congreve's case had been the top spot at the Metropolitan Police.

Congreve had always wanted to be a copper, even from a very young age and over his parents' objection. Though hardly what one would describe as a prime physical specimen—he was shorter than average and a bit *round*... though not as round as he had once been—he possessed a razor-sharp intellect—easily the equal of his fictional heroes Sherlock Holmes, Hercule Poirot, and, his personal favorite, Lord Peter Wimsey—and so solved the crimes that others could not. His successes propelled him through the ranks of the Metropolitan Police, making him one of the most respected investigators in the United Kingdom—and the most feared, at least by those in the criminal class. His deductive prowess had led to no shortage of work after stepping aside as commissioner of the Metro Police, and he was frequently called in to consult on some of the trickier cases. His reputation was such that, following the unprecedented and still largely unreported abduction of His Majesty King Charles III, it had been Congreve who had been called in to crack the case, and crack it he did.

With a little help from a friend, of course.

I wonder what in the devil Alex is up to at present, thought Congreve.

One of his most consequential cases, back when he was just a lowly detective inspector, had brought him into the orbit of a young, orphaned lordling named Alexander Hawke, who at the time was being raised by his aged grandfather Lord Hawke at the family pile in the Channel Islands. Congreve had taken a real liking to the teenaged Alex, and when the grandfather had eventually passed on, Congreve and Hawke's family retainer, Pelham Grenville, had taken upon themselves the not-inconsiderable job of overseeing the remainder of the lad's childhood. Subsequently, and despite a nearly twenty-year difference in age, Alex and Ambrose had become the closest of friends, with Congreve often working to support Alex on his missions for the Crown and, occasionally, vice versa.

Alex was even, albeit indirectly, responsible for the fact that Congreve now spent half the year at Ambrose's Bermuda estate, the

Shadowlands—which at one time had been the residence of playwright Noël Coward—along with his lovely wife, Lady Diana Mars. Theoretically, Congreve was supposed to be enjoying his retirement by spending his days painting watercolors and his evenings sipping his favorite rum concoction, the dark 'n' stormy. In reality, however, Ambrose more often than not found himself just waiting for the phone to ring and trouble to call.

Usually, he didn't have to wait long.

On this spectacular day, as fate would have it, Congreve found himself riding in the shotgun seat of a constable's car on his way to a fresh murder. He'd gotten a call earlier that morning from DCI Nigel Calder, asking for his services as a consulting detective.

"It's nothing special," Calder had said. "Routine crime of passion. Most likely the boyfriend. Or maybe a girlfriend. One never knows these days. But, you see, the girl worked at the Home Office, so we want to make sure it's all cricket. No loose ends. Politics, you know."

Congreve did know. But he also knew that no murder victim deserved anything less than justice. So, as the car made a final turn onto King Street, bouncing across a stretch of uneven pavement, and pulled up in front of the Somersby Apartments, Congreve took out his favorite briar, clamped it between his teeth, and emptied his mind of preconceptions.

As was often the case, the mere proximity of tragedy had brought out the neighborhood. The curious peered over the barricades and peeked through their curtains, hoping for a glimpse of something unspeakable. Congreve knew from experience that the murderer might be there, hiding in the crowd, relishing the aftermath of his dark deed, and so paid more than the usual attention to the throng as he made his way to the door, where a uniformed constable stood guard. Congreve acknowledged him with a brief nod before entering the small foyer.

The apartment was tidy if a bit small. His wife would have called it "cozy." The furnishings were an eclectic mix, probably secondhand purchases and castoffs. A brass umbrella stand by the door was shaped like a heron, and framed art—abstract yet strangely appealing—lined the hallway. A faint scent of lavender lingered in the air, possibly from an air freshener or recently used soap. The orderliness of it all made the disturbance in the living room stand out.

The wine bottle was the first thing that caught his eye, sitting on a delicate glass coffee table. Congreve took note of the label: Château Pichon Baron, 2015. Two glasses also occupied the table—one still full, standing upright, and the other tipped over, spilling a dark red puddle. He noted the position of the items, then shifted his gaze to the real focus of attention.

The young woman lay on the floor, her body contorted, her dark hair fanned out like a halo around her head. She was fully dressed, attired in a simple blouse and skirt, neither of which appeared to be out of place. In fact, despite the violence that had been done to her, the surroundings remained surprisingly neat, a dissonance that sparked Congreve's curiosity.

He let his gaze wander over a stack of magazines on the nearby side table: travel guides, mostly, and an open planner with appointments written in a tidy hand. Next to them, a small figurine of a cat sat with its head cocked, playful but frozen in place. These were all little details that likely held no significance in his investigation, but Congreve filed them away for future reference, just in case.

Just then, the sound of footsteps on the carpet intruded into his thoughts. "Chief Inspector Congreve."

He turned to regard the caller: DI Winston Trott. Trott was Bermudian, a diligent and methodical policeman who had worked his way up the ranks in the island's police service, earning his stripes with an unflappable demeanor and a reputation for sticking to the letter of the law. Trott had little patience for the kind of deliberate deductive reasoning Congreve relied on so heavily. He was, in this respect, the epitome of his native culture: pragmatic and grounded. Congreve respected him—even liked him in his own way—but there was no denying that Trott was a touch . . . hidebound. Still, Congreve knew Trott was good at his job. If there was anything to be uncovered through standard police work, Trott would find it. The question was whether that would suffice or if this case would require a descent into the murkier waters of human nature.

"Detective Inspector Trott," Congreve returned enthusiastically. He gestured toward the living room with the stem of the briar. "Tell me why I'm here."

"Looks pretty straightforward t' me," Trott began, his Bermudian accent rounding the vowels just slightly, softening the sharper edges of his words. "The victim's Marian Smith. Twenty-six. Worked at the Home Office, but nothin' unusual there. No high clearance, no special responsibilities."

He gestured at the table. "Bottle of wine, two glasses. Fella comes over, they drink, things go south, and . . . well"—he gestured to the lifeless body with a casual motion—"you see the result."

Trott moved to the edge of the room, pointing out the obvious signs like a tour guide explaining well-known landmarks. "No signs of forced entry. No struggle in the other rooms. Neighbors didn't hear nothin' except a door close round eight. That's about when it would've happened. Likely the killer takin' his leave. Seems clear enough to me."

Congreve listened, taking in the details, but his sharp eyes were already moving over the room with more interest than Trott's summary. "Do you have a suspect?"

Trott scratched his chin. "No suspect as yet. If there's a regular boyfriend, none of the neighbors knew a thin'. Like I said, no forced entry. Could be someone she knew well enough to let in. Could be someone she met just before. But it's a small island, eh? We'll find him. Got the forensics boys comin' soon. We'll dust for prints and collect DNA."

Congreve absently returned the briar to his mouth, puffing thoughtfully even though the pipe was unlit, and moved in for a closer look at the body of Marian Smith.

Her young face was calm, almost unnervingly so, as if she had simply fallen asleep on the floor. The dark line around her neck told a different story. "Strangled," he murmured.

Her clothes—a cream-colored blouse, buttoned up to the top, and a simple black skirt—were neat, not at all disheveled. No broken buttons, no torn fabric. Her fingers lay curled against her side, her manicure neat and intact. Her shoes—a sensible pair of black flats—were still on, as if she had only just come home and certainly hadn't expected the night to end like this.

But then, one never does, does one?

"No indication of a struggle."

"We noticed that," Trott admitted. "We're thinkin' she may have been drugged. Something in the wine. The coroner will be able to tell us."

Congreve straightened and took another look at the wineglasses. There was a distinctive lipstick smudge on the glass that had been tipped over, but no fingerprints were visible on the stems or bowls of either glass.

"Château Pichon Baron, 2015." He raised an eyebrow. "Not the sort of wine you find at the local market, is it?"

Trott gave a small shrug. "Could've been a gift or somethin'. Maybe she bought it for a special occasion."

Congreve shook his head, his gaze fixed on the label. "A very special occasion. A bottle like this would set you back about four hundred dollars. And if I'm not mistaken, you'd have a hard time finding it anywhere on the island."

Trott frowned. "So, you're sayin' . . . the killer brought the wine."

Congreve hummed thoughtfully. "Was she violated?"

"Not as far as we can tell."

"DCI Calder said this was 'a routine crime of passion.'"

Trott nodded. "That's how it looks to me."

"Not much actual *passion*, though."

"Beg pardon?"

"Your theory of the crime is that Miss Smith welcomed her killer—someone with whom she had at least a passing acquaintance—into her home. That person, presumably a man, proceeded to drug her wine and then strangle her to death."

Trott nodded again. "Looks that way."

"Why?"

"Beg pardon?"

"Why kill her that way?" His tone wasn't accusatory, merely contemplative.

Trott furrowed his brow. "That's how it went, ain't it? Knock her out, strangle her after."

"Knocking her out first implies premeditation. If the goal was simply to kill her, drugging seems unnecessary, doesn't it? If it was a spur-of-the-moment crime of passion, the killer would've resorted to violence immediately. But *this*"—Congreve gestured toward the body—"*this* was deliberate. Methodical."

Trott considered the statement. "Maybe he wanted to make sure she wouldn't fight back."

Congreve leaned closer to the body, eyeing the pristine state of her clothing and the complete lack of defensive wounds on her hands. "No sign of a struggle, no damage to her clothes. She's fully dressed, shoes still on. It's too clean."

Trott shifted uncomfortably. "What are you thinkin'?"

Congreve straightened, rising to his full height and stepping back to take in the room once more. "There's no passion in this room, Trott. None at all. This wasn't a lovers' quarrel gone wrong. Whoever did this wanted it to look like a crime of passion, but they've gone through too much trouble to keep things tidy."

Trott frowned, arms crossed over his chest. "So, what's your theory, then?"

Congreve hummed softly, staring down at Marian Smith's peaceful expression. "I haven't one. Too soon for that. We're just getting started.

We know what the killer wants us to believe. Now it's up to us to discover what he *doesn't* want us to believe. But fear not, Detective Inspector. The truth will out."

Trott stared at him for a long moment before nodding slowly. "Right. Well, let's hope we find it sooner rather than later, eh?"

"Indeed, Trott. But the truth, much like the qualities of a fine wine, only emerges over time. We must be patient." He clamped his briar between his teeth and regarded Trott with a gleam in his eye. "And I do so enjoy the chase."

FOURTEEN

LONDON

There was nothing remotely prim about the woman who got out of the taxi and made her way to the front entrance of the stately Mayfair manse.

Dr. Ariadne Silk was dressed to kill.

Gone was the uptight schoolteacher guise she had worn for her meeting with His Majesty and Lord Hawke. In its place was a sleek, clingy crimson velvet cocktail dress with matching clutch and heels, all purchased from Harrods earlier that day. The ensemble looked like it would probably put a crimp in the budget of a mere public servant, but Silk was holding nothing back.

If it had not already been clear in the King's study, she had her sights set on Lord Alexander Hawke. And when the moment was right, she very much intended to pull the trigger.

The only vestige of her earlier persona was the large-framed eyeglasses that, like a mask worn by a comic-book character, seemed to conceal some crucial part of her identity and remained there on her face like a dare. That mask could not hide the look of disappointment in her eyes when the front door opened to reveal an ancient figure in a bespoke black suit.

"Good evening, madam."

"I'm . . . ah, here to see Lord Hawke?" Uncertainty turned what ought to have been a declaration of intent into a question. "I'm Silk . . . Ariadne Silk . . . Dr. Ariadne Silk."

"Of course, madam. You're expected. Please, follow me."

The man turned and began moving into the interior. His gait was steady but unhurried. Despite the appearance of great age—he was, in fact, nearly ninety years old—he did not wheeze or huff. His posture was upright without being rigid, his demeanor cool without a trace of arrogance.

His name was Pelham Grenville, and he had been a loyal retainer of the Hawke family for his entire adult life—he had, in fact, first begun working in the household at the tender age of fifteen—ministering to the needs of three generations of Hawkes. Following the deaths of Alex's parents at the hands of a trio of brutal narcotraffickers in the Caribbean and the later passing of Alex's grandfather, he had been the closest thing to a father in young Alex's life. He had watched Alex grow from a brash young man into the formidable figure he was today, and yet, despite the deep affection they felt for each other, Pelham remained a consummate professional. His love for Alex Hawke was manifest in the meticulous attention he paid to every aspect of managing the household. Service was his sacred duty, something that went beyond mere employment; it was his life's purpose. Indeed, despite the fact that his accrued earnings and investments had left him with a net worth somewhere in the neighborhood of eight figures, retirement was a word best not uttered in his presence.

Silk followed him into the spacious entry hall, her heels clicking against the polished marble floor. Despite her best efforts to command the moment, Pelham's slow, measured presence dominated the space.

He paused just inside the door to the dining room and turned, regarding her with a look that was both assessing and impassive. "M'lord, your guest has arrived."

Silk had doubtless envisioned Hawke himself greeting her at the door and positively melting when he beheld her transformation and now saw a second chance to make her grand entrance. With her head held high, she swept past Pelham and strode seductively into the dining room, where her second surprise of the evening waited.

Hawke, who was sitting rather casually at the table, attired in faded blue jeans and a simple black pullover with the sleeves pushed up to his elbows, looked over at her, but the low, appreciative whistle that greeted her came from the dining room's other occupant—an enormous Black man wearing a garish red aloha shirt that seemed barely able to contain his muscular build.

"Well," he said, "now I feel underdressed."

Silk's eyebrows drew together in a chagrined frown. "I think perhaps I'm the one who's *overdressed.* I thought . . ."

She trailed off, leaving the rest unspoken, knowing full well that Hawke knew exactly what she had *thought.*

When he had called her a few hours after their first meeting at Clarence House, suggesting that they discuss their upcoming sojourn to Russia over dinner at "my place," he had known that she would likely interpret the choice of venue as a signal of more intimate intentions. His actual reason for inviting her into his home was almost exactly the opposite. Meeting in public, even at one of London's exclusive clubs or high-end restaurants, would have guaranteed unwanted attention. His celebrity status ensured that any such outing, especially with someone as striking as Silk, would have been splashed across gossip columns within hours, and that was attention he could ill afford, particularly given the fragile state of his relationship with Asia. The last thing he needed was to complicate things further by fanning the flames of suspicion.

He had also taken a few other precautions to ensure that the dinner would be anything but intimate.

"Dr. Silk," said Hawke, making no effort to hide a mischievous smile, "allow me to introduce my good friend Stokely Jones Jr."

Stoke rose to his full height—a towering six feet five inches—and came around the table to offer his hand. "Call me Stoke," he said with a broad grin.

Silk just gaped at him. "I didn't realize . . ." Again she trailed off, leaving the thought unspoken.

"Stoke is who I call when I need help dealing with, ah, shall we say, *delicate* situations," explained Hawke. His ironic word choice was intentional. *Delicate* was not the sort of word that one would naturally associate with Stokely Jones Jr.

Born and raised on the mean streets of Harlem, Stoke had escaped what would likely have been a short, brutal life selling crack cocaine on a street corner by joining the United States Navy. He signed up for and cruised through BUD/S—Basic Underwater Demolition/SEAL training—earning the fabled "Budweiser," the eagle and trident badge of the Navy SEALs. His natural leadership and tactical prowess soon set him apart even among the elite brotherhood of the SEALs, and on the advice of his mentor, the late, great Richard Marcinko—founder of SEAL Team Six—he attended the University of Southern California on an ROTC scholarship.

It wasn't long at all before his prodigious physique—Stoke was, as Alex often remarked, about the size of your average armoire—brought him to the attention of the athletic director. After completing his degree and earning his reserve commission, he found himself with the enviable problem of having to decide whether to continue pursuing his naval career or take a chance with the NFL draft. He chose the latter and signed with the New York Giants as a defensive lineman, but a late hit in the early minutes of the season opener, a Monday night game against the Denver Broncos, sidelined him for the rest of the game and likely—or so his trainer had told him—the remainder of the season. The next morning, while lying in bed with his knee packed in ice, he watched the Towers fall and realized he'd made the wrong decision. As soon as he was fit to walk again, he called his former commander at the Naval Special Warfare Development Group (DEVGRU)—the new name for SEAL Team Six—and went back to work.

When eventually he climbed as high up the Special Operations ladder as regulations and politics would allow, he retired from the military and returned home to New York to begin his next career as a New York City cop. It was in this capacity that, one fateful night, he tracked a group of gangbangers who had kidnapped a visiting tourist in a bold daylight carjacking to the abandoned building where they were torturing their hostage. When they realized their plot had been foiled, the gangbangers set fire to the building and fled, leaving Stoke to rush in and single-handedly save the life of the young hostage. The hostage's name was Alex Hawke, and from that moment forward the two men became fast friends.

Now retired from law enforcement, Stoke headed up one of Hawke's companies, an outfit called Tactics International, which specialized in the kind of things Stoke had done as a Navy SEAL: hostage rescue, counterespionage, and counterterrorism—or as Stoke liked to say, "kicking ass and blowing shit up."

After concluding his audience with the King, Hawke immediately put a call in to his friend—because if anyone could get him in and, more importantly, *out* of Russia, it was Stoke.

Stoke, who seemed to realize that Silk wasn't going to shake his hand, drew it back, but his grin did not falter. "Alex tells me you all are planning a little trip."

Silk blinked and then shook herself as if waking up from a particularly absurd dream. "Um, yes, that's right."

Sensing the need to steer the evening back on course, Hawke pulled out one of the chairs. "Please, Dr. Silk, won't you have a seat?"

Silk hesitated for a moment, glancing around the room as if reconsidering the entire situation, then summoned up a smile. "Why, thank you . . . Alex," she said, smoothing down her dress and settling into the chair.

"We'll be serving dinner presently," Hawke continued. "Chef Pierre has prepared an appetizer of smoked salmon terrine with a salad of watercress and lemon for an appetizer, followed by duck confit with a truffle jus, served with roasted root vegetables."

As if making casual conversation, Hawke briefly explained that when it had become apparent that his stay in London would be extended, he had flown Pelham—the elderly gentleman she'd only just met—over to see to the household duties. Since Hawke spent most of his time at Teakettle Cottage in Bermuda, he explained further, he did not employ permanent domestic staff at his residences in the UK, but Pelham kept a roster of elite professionals who were available on short notice to step in when required. For this dinner, Pelham had brought in Chef Pierre Laurent, a Cordon Bleu–trained virtuoso with stints at Michelin-starred restaurants in Paris, Tokyo, and New York on his CV.

"In the meantime, let me get you something to drink." Without waiting for her answer, Hawke called after his retreating retainer. "Pelham! Another round, please. And something for Dr. Silk." Then he turned back to her. "What's your poison? Pelham is quite the master mixologist."

Pelham floated back into the room. "Another dark 'n' stormy, m'lord?"

"The very thing," replied Hawke. "And for Dr. Silk . . ." He gave her a sidelong glance. "How about one of your legendary Negronis?"

Silk blinked, pulling herself back from whatever thoughts had momentarily distracted her. "A Negroni sounds wonderful," she replied, a slight smile finally curling her lips, evidently allowing herself to relax.

Pelham, ever the picture of composed efficiency, gave a nod. "At once, m'lord." He then turned to Stokely, who had returned to his chair. "And another Diet Coke for you, sir?"

"You know it, my man."

Pelham, with his characteristic quiet efficiency, moved to the sideboard and went to work. Hawke watched him for a moment before turning his attention back to his guests. "Stoke and I have been working on the logistical challenges of our little jaunt."

"The thing is," said Stoke, "getting in and out of Russia's a whole different ball game these days. Since the start of the Ukraine war, the FSB has developed a nasty habit of arresting foreign visitors on trumped-up charges and then using them as bargaining chips to exchange for Russian spies and gangsters who've been arrested in the US for actual crimes. And that doesn't take into account the fact that Alex here is on Putin's permanent naughty list."

"What Stoke is trying to say is that we're not leaving anything down to luck. Now, Sochi is a bit off the beaten track compared to Moscow, and that will work in our favor, but if Putin is there, we can expect a serious security presence. So here's what we're thinking: we'll fly into Istanbul and then charter a flight to Batumi, in Georgia, just across the Russian border. From there, we can hire local transport to take us discreetly up the coast and into Sochi. Stoke will be standing by with some old friends of ours, just in case things go sideways."

Silk guessed that as much as Hawke would have liked to have Stoke at his side instead of waiting in the wings, the hulking man before her was not exactly an inconspicuous presence. She agreed, even without voicing her position aloud, that he would be far more useful at the head of a quick reaction force—their "old friends," as Hawke had called them, though Silk had done her homework and knew he was talking about the mercenary outfit known as Thunder and Lightning.

Unwilling to let Hawke continue any further with his plan, Silk interrupted. "No, I'm sorry, but this won't do."

Hawke shot her a quizzical look. "Beg pardon?"

She looked down at her fingernails, refusing to meet his gaze. "I can't fly. I won't."

"You won't?" said Hawke.

"I just can't do it. Believe me, I've tried everything. Tranquilizers, hypnotism . . . but nothing works. I go into a complete state of panic." She shook her head. "No planes."

Stoke let out a short laugh. "Well, that would have been nice to know."

Hawke regarded her from under one raised eyebrow. "It's nearly two thousand miles to Sochi. How do you propose to make this journey if not by air?"

"We'll be taking the train," she said smoothly, finally looking up at him. "Actually, I've already made all the arrangements."

"The train? I wasn't aware that Eurail had a line running to Sochi."

"They don't, exactly. We'll have to make a few connections."

Hawke and Stoke exchanged a skeptical look.

"We'll start by taking the Eurostar to Paris," Silk went on, undeterred. "Then a Nightjet sleeper to Vienna. From there, another Nightjet to Bucharest. Then it's on to Bulgaria, where we'll catch the Sofia–Istanbul Express."

Hawke folded his arms. "Istanbul is still a long way from Sochi."

Silk gave a guilty shrug. "From there, it gets a little tricky. We'll need to hire a car for the bit on the Turkish-Armenian border, but after that we can ride to Tbilisi in Georgia. The train between there and Krasnodar will get us into Russia, and from there it's a short hop to Sochi."

Hawke stared at her. "You're having me on."

She shook her head. "Not at all. It's all in the itinerary."

"And exactly how long is all of this going to take?"

"Five days. That's allowing a bit of a cushion for unexpected delays."

"Five bloody days? You're supposed to meet with Putin Tuesday next. In order to get you there, we'd have to leave . . ." He paused, trying to do the math in his head.

"Tomorrow," Silk finished. "We'll catch the eleven o'clock Eurostar at St. Pancras."

Hawke stared back, momentarily struck dumb. Pelham chose that moment to slide an old-fashioned glass full of dark liquor garnished with lime in front of him. The disruption broke the spell. "There's no bloody way I'm spending the better part of a week stuck in a train compartment."

Silk eyed him, wondering if he wanted to add *"especially not with you,"* but he bit his tongue. That nearly made her smile.

Good boy, Mr. Hawke.

Especially not with you.

Stoke, arms crossed, added his own objection. "It's not just the time involved. I won't be able to back you up. You'll be on your own until you get to Russia."

"Exactly," Hawke declared. "It's a logistical nightmare. You don't like flying? Fine. Pop a sedative and get over it. There's no way we're—"

"No," Silk cut him off, her voice unwavering. "I don't fly. Ever. And I'm not going to 'pop a sedative' just to make things more convenient for you. This is my show, and we're going to do it my way."

"You can't seriously expect me to—"

"I do," Silk interrupted again, this time with a firmness that even Hawke couldn't ignore. "Besides, the train really is the best way to cross into Russia without drawing attention. The airports are too closely monitored. This is the only way we get in discreetly. And since you yourself"—Silk waved an arm to Stoke—"noted that Hawke is on Putin's '*naughty* list,' this is the best way in."

She'd been deliberate in her emphasis on the word *naughty* but was careful not to overly sexualize the innuendo. No need to be too forward too quickly. After all, they would soon have five days together.

We'll see what other, naughtier lists you're on, Alex.

Stoke shook his head. "Discreet doesn't mean safe, Doc. You'll be out in the open . . . sitting ducks . . . for the better part of a week."

Silk fixed her gaze on Hawke, her resolve strengthening. "It's already arranged. If you want this mission to succeed, you're going to have to trust me on this. If not . . . Well, then you can explain it to His Majesty."

Hawke looked as if he might swear aloud.

Silk smiled at him, watching his deep blue eyes, imagining the gears turning behind them. If she had to wager a guess, her gut told her that, sitting there now, Alex was battling his every instinct, which no doubt told him that her plan was madness: days of crawling across Europe with no real control over their security and, worse still, stuck in close quarters with her.

But Silk knew that no matter how many scenarios Hawke ran through in his head, in the end he would comply with her demands. And the reasoning was simple.

The King was counting on him.

Of course, there was also the minor historical footnote that put the Hawke family squarely in the middle of one of the British monarchy's darkest decisions—the fact Alex's own great-grandfather might have delivered what effectively amounted to the death warrant for the Russian royal family into the hands of their executioners.

Silk had found the one pressure point that could compel him to go along with her crazy scheme. She continued to watch him, noting a tightening in his chiseled jawline.

Break, Alex. Stop fighting it.

Hawke glanced over at Stoke, who could only offer a helpless shrug.

"Well," said Stoke, "I won't be much good to you while you're on the move, but I can be there for you once you're in Putin's playground."

Hawke let out his breath in a low growl and turned back to Silk. "Fine. We'll do it your way."

That won't be the last time he speaks that very line, Silk thought to herself as a victorious smile tugged at the corners of her lips.

Hawke did not let her savor the victory. "Pelham."

The butler appeared almost instantly.

"Call a taxi for Dr. Silk, please."

A taxi?

Silk blinked in surprise. "What about dinner?"

Hawke faced her again, offering a thin, humorless smile. "Rain check, I'm afraid. I've got to pack, you see. Seems I'm going on a trip tomorrow."

INTERLUDE—PART THREE

THE ENGLISH CHANNEL
APRIL 1918

The *Scimitar* was an hour into the crossing when the attack came.

Alexander felt it first—not a sound but a sudden, subtle shift beneath his feet as the ship executed a sharp turn. A faint vibration followed, humming through the bulkheads.

Natalya, seated across from Alexander, arched an eyebrow. "Is this . . . normal?" she asked, her tone more curious than concerned.

Alexander's response was cut off by the distant, muffled boom of an explosion. It reverberated through the ship, setting the porthole glass quivering. A second later the deck pitched and Alexander had to grab the edge of the desk to keep from being thrown flat.

"Stay here," he barked, surging to his feet.

Natalya started to rise as well. "What's happening?"

Alexander ignored her, yanking open the door, and stepped into the corridor. Almost immediately, the sound of raised voices reached him: urgent commands, clipped and precise, filtering down from the bridge.

"Hard to port! Engines full ahead!"

"Hard to port, aye, sir!"

"Depth charges, stand by!" barked another voice, likely the gunnery officer, directing his men from the aft section.

"Depth charges standing by, sir!" came the more distant reply.

The deck swayed underfoot as the ship began the turn, the pitch of the engines rising through the bulkheads as the *Scimitar* surged forward.

When Alexander stepped out onto the bridge, he found Captain Greaves gripping the chart table for stability and, to all appearances, directing his ship with a confidence Alexander hadn't been sure the younger officer possessed.

"Steady as she goes!" Greaves barked, then spoke into the voice tube. "Report on the hydrophone!"

"Contact holding steady, port aft!" came the tinny reply from the tube. "Estimated depth: ten fathoms!"

Greaves turned his head slightly, acknowledging Alexander's arrival without taking his eyes off the horizon. "Admiral. It seems we're having a bit of excitement. Torpedo launch. Just missed us. We're deploying depth charges to flush the bastard out."

A torpedo in the water could mean only one thing: a German U-boat. It might be a lone hunting wolf or the advance scout of a larger pack. Either way, it was damnable luck. Now the success of his mission—never mind their survival—depended on the *Scimitar*'s speed and maneuverability and on the untested captain's ability to outthink the enemy.

The ship jolted again as another charge detonated, sending a spray of water cascading over the bridge, soaking the lookout station. Alexander stepped closer, bracing himself against the railing, his coat whipping in the wind.

"Have you plotted her course?" he asked.

Greaves nodded curtly. "She's playing coy—every time we turn to engage, she ducks out of range. Bloody cat and mouse."

"Cut speed," Alexander said, his voice firm. "Let her think she's hurt us. That we're an easy target."

Greaves hesitated, his knuckles whitening on the edge of the chart table. "That's risky."

"Riskier to keep playing their game," Alexander countered. "If she surfaces to finish us, she'll be exposed. That's our chance to strike."

For a moment, uncertainty flickered in Greaves's eyes, but then he gave a sharp nod. "Reduce speed to half," he said. "Prepare the guns."

Alexander stepped back, watching as the crew sprang into action. A faint smile touched his lips: Greaves was green, but he had the makings of a fine officer.

The ship began to slow, and Alexander felt the tension rise in the confined space of the bridge. Every man there knew they were dangling themselves as bait to the predator. The minutes, which Alexander measured out with his 1916 silver Omega officer's wristwatch, were heavy with anticipation.

When the torpedo came, it was almost anticlimactic. A shout from the lookout broke the silence: "Wake off the port bow!"

"Ahead full," Greaves barked. "Hard to starboard!"

Alexander's gaze shifted toward the bridge windows, where the horizon stretched in a restless, gray expanse.

"Contact is moving," the hydrophone operator called out. "Shifting to port. Depth increasing."

Greaves leaned over the chart table, calculating quickly. "Launch depth charges. We'll force them to surface. Gunnery, adjust bearings and prepare to fire on my command."

"Aye, sir!" came the gunnery officer's clipped response over the voice tube.

The *Scimitar* pitched slightly beneath Alexander as it turned sharply, her engines roaring at full power. He moved over to the railing for a better look and could see the deck crews carrying out their respective duties, their shouted commands barely audible over the booming of the deck guns and the rumbling churn of the sea.

"U-boat surfacing," came a shout from a gunner's mate. "Port quarter. Six hundred yards."

Alexander turned toward the spot where the gray, rounded shape of a conning tower broke the surface, water cascading down its sides.

"Target confirmed!" the gunnery officer called. "All guns, fire at will!"

The deck guns roared to life, their barrels spitting flame and smoke as shells streaked toward the vulnerable submarine. The first volley splashed harmlessly into the water, but the second struck true, slamming into the base of the conning tower with a resounding impact.

Alexander watched in fascination as the U-boat lurched under the force of the hit. A spray of debris and smoke erupted from its side, followed by a burst of fire. Then the vessel began to list as one of its dive planes shattered, leaving it floundering on the surface.

The destroyer's gunners didn't relent. Another salvo tore through the U-boat's skin, punching holes into its hull. Men spilled from the conning tower, waving white scraps of fabric in frantic surrender.

Then an explosion rocked the U-boat, likely one of her unlaunched torpedoes detonating in its tube. The submarine tilted sharply, its stern rising out of the water before it slipped beneath the waves, leaving only a churning patch of foam and oil in its wake. The spreading slick seemed a fitting reminder that this mission, scarcely begun, would be no quiet passage.

An hour in, and already death had reached for him.

He had no illusions it wouldn't try again.

INTERLUDE—PART FOUR

CALAIS, FRANCE

The motor taxi jolted to a stop, its engine sputtering faintly as the driver took it out of gear, letting it idle as he got out to open the door for his passengers. Alexander, now in civilian attire, got out first, then turned back to offer a hand to Natalya, who hesitated briefly before accepting. As Alexander paid the driver, she regarded the establishment to which they had been delivered with a faint wrinkle of her nose.

"This place looks . . ." She searched for the word, finally settling on "Quaint."

The inn was an unassuming two-story structure tucked away from the bustling main streets near the port. Its whitewashed exterior bore the streaks of salt and soot that came with constant exposure to the sea air, and the swinging sign above the door—bearing the faded image of an anchor—creaked on its iron hinges in the gentle breeze.

"Surely an aristocrat such as yourself would prefer a hotel," she went on.

"Hotels are far too public," Alexander replied, starting up the path leading up to the front door. "I'd prefer to keep a low profile moving forward. Besides, I thought you'd appreciate the . . . what would you lot call it? Working-class charm?"

Her lips quirked into a faint smile. "Ah. You're trying to enlighten me. How considerate."

"Not at all," he said smoothly, opening the door for her. "Just trying to avoid having to listen to you lecture me about bourgeois excess."

Inside, they found a handful of patrons sitting at rough-hewn tables, drinking wine and engaged in quiet conversation.

The space was rustic but clean. Wooden beams darkened by years of smoke stretched across the low ceiling, and the uneven floorboards creaked underfoot. The room smelled of simmering stew and freshly baked bread, mingled with the faint, acrid tang of pipe smoke curling from a man seated near the hearth. A pair of gas lamps mounted on the walls cast a golden light, flickering slightly as a draft followed them inside. To the right, a large stone hearth dominated the room, its fire crackling and spitting embers into the grate.

Behind a counter near the far wall, a stout woman in an apron was polishing wineglasses with a cloth. She straightened as they approached, her sharp gaze appraising them with a practiced eye.

"Bonsoir," Alexander greeted her in polished French. "We require accommodations for the night. Two rooms, if possible."

The woman studied them both for a moment before answering. "Only one room, monsieur. Too many travelers, you see? It cannot be helped."

Alexander frowned, but he gave a curt nod. "One room, then. We'll take it."

The woman gave a sly smile, her gaze lingering on Natalya, then she pulled a key from beneath the counter and slid it toward him. "Upstairs, last door on the left. Supper will be ready soon."

"Merci," Alexander said, pocketing the key. He turned to Natalya, switching to English. "Would you like something to eat?"

She shook her head. "No. The crossing was enough excitement for one day."

"Let's get you settled, then." He grabbed her luggage and nodded to the stairwell. "After you."

She regarded him from beneath a raised eyebrow. “Sharing a room?” she said in French. “And we’ve only just met. How scandalous.”

Alexander chuckled. “You needn’t worry. I’ll come down here and sleep by the hearth.”

“How noble of you, Lord Hawke. Are you protecting my virtue—or are you simply afraid of me?”

“A little of both, I expect.”

They reached the last door on the left, as the innkeeper had directed. Alexander unlocked the door, pushing it open to reveal a modest room. A bed with a simple quilt dominated the space, and a small, slightly warped nightstand held an oil lamp, which Alexander promptly lit. A single chair and a basin on a stand completed the furnishings.

“Cozy,” Natalya said dryly, stepping past him and dropping onto the mattress.

Alexander set her luggage at the foot of the bed. “I’ll leave you to it, then. Good night, Natalya.”

He turned toward the door, but her voice stopped him mid-step. “Oh, for pity’s sake, sit down. Your chivalry is charming but unnecessary—and, if I may be brutally honest, feels rather . . . performative.”

He raised an eyebrow. “Performative? Coming from a revolutionary, that’s rich.”

She smirked. “Touché.”

Alexander allowed himself a grin, then pulled the chair closer and settled into it. “All right, let’s discuss our itinerary. How are we getting to Moscow?”

She regarded him for a moment before answering. “It’s simple enough, really. Tomorrow we’ll take the train to Amiens. From there, we’ll make our way to Saint-Quentin.”

“Saint-Quentin?” Alexander leaned forward, his expression sharpening. “You are aware that Saint-Quentin is on the wrong side of the front.”

“I’ve crossed through occupied France before, Alex,” she said evenly. “It’s not impossible—just . . . delicate. But I know people who can get us to the other side. I know a man who can provide us with forged travel documents that will get us through occupied territory. After that, we'll take the rail line east, through Warsaw and Minsk, until we reach Moscow."

"You make it sound like taking a stroll through Hyde Park."

"There are no completely safe routes to Moscow," she said, her tone matter-of-fact. "But this way is the quickest, and right now time is our greatest enemy. Every hour we delay . . ." Her hands stilled against the quilt.

"What?" Alexander pressed.

Natalya hesitated, then met his gaze. "I fear Comrade Sverdlov may be compelled to make his decision without hearing your king's answer."

He studied her face. "You mean to tell me you care what happens to the Tsar?"

She exhaled sharply, standing abruptly to pace the small room. "Don't misunderstand me, Alex. I am a loyal servant of the Revolution. I believe in its goal of a better future for Russia. The Romanovs are prisoners of the Revolution. Whatever their fate, it will serve the cause. But . . ." She stopped near the window, looking out into the darkened street below. "What harm can they do now? His power is broken. His wife and their children—children, for pity's sake. They're no threat to anyone."

"You do care about them," he said quietly.

Natalya looked at him for a long moment, her expression unreadable. "Many feel as I do. That we are better served by showing restraint—by showing the world that the Revolution is just. If we become executioners, how are we different from the tyrants we overthrew?"

"Surely, if Sverdlov meant to kill the Tsar, he would simply have done it already. He would not have made a second appeal to King George for asylum."

"Comrade Sverdlov will do what he must to hold the government together. If that means appeasing the radicals who call for Romanov blood, he will not refuse." She narrowed her eyes at Alexander. "The secrecy surrounding your king's reply to the appeal concerns me, Alex."

"He has his reasons. If word of these negotiations were to get out, it might embolden the radicals within your government—or, worse, provoke outrage among the British public. The Romanovs may be his cousins, but they're hardly beloved here. Supporting their asylum might be seen as condoning tyranny."

"And what would he call abandoning them? Pragmatism? Diplomacy? He withdrew his offer of sanctuary once, Alex. Do you think the people of Britain forced his hand, or did he simply choose to protect his crown at the expense of his family?"

Alexander's jaw tightened, but he held her gaze. "You're speaking of a man who has carried the weight of the empire through the bloodiest war this world has ever seen. He's not only a king but a father and a husband. Do you think that decision didn't cost him?"

Her eyes narrowed. "So why the secrecy? If he truly intended to save them, why not make his intentions clear? Why not give them hope?"

"Perhaps he doesn't trust your revolutionary comrades any more than I do," Alexander countered. "The Bolsheviks are fractured, by your own admission. If he doubts the integrity of those handling the Romanovs, he'd have every reason to keep his cards close."

"Or perhaps," Natalya said softly, stepping closer to him, her tone laced with quiet intensity, "he knows his answer will condemn them, and he fears the stain it will leave on his legacy."

The accusation struck like a physical blow. "You can't know that."

"Then open the letter."

Alexander's expression hardened. "I won't."

Natalya crossed her arms, her frustration evident. "You're afraid of what it might say."

"I'm not afraid," he replied, his voice clipped. "I'm following my king's orders. The letter is sealed, and it will remain that way until it reaches Sverdlov's hands. That's the end of it."

"You hide behind duty like it's a shield. It isn't, Alex. It's an excuse. You are dooming a family to death and washing your hands of it just as your king is doing. What about your duty to humanity? To your conscience? Is obedience worth the price of your soul?"

The question hung in the air. He could not meet her eyes because, deep down, he knew she was right. Finally, he straightened. "You're tired," he said, his tone softening slightly. "Get some rest. We have a long journey ahead."

He started to turn away again, but her voice made him falter. "Alex, wait."

He turned back, meeting her gaze.

"I'm sorry. I should not have questioned your integrity," she said softly. "You've done nothing to deserve that."

Alexander waved a hand dismissively. "Think nothing of it."

"You don't need to go downstairs."

The words hung in the air between them, bristling like a static charge. Alexander felt the warmth rise unbidden.

"Natalya," he said, his voice low, almost a warning, "I don't think that would be wise."

"Wisdom is overrated," she replied, her lips curving into the faintest of smiles. "We are going into dangerous places together. What is one more risk?"

"Good night, Natalya," he said firmly, reaching for the door. Closing it behind him felt like the hardest thing he had ever done.

Natalya had been wrong about one thing. Duty wasn't his shield. It was his compass.

But tonight it felt more like a chain.

FIFTEEN

HAMILTON, BERMUDA
PRESENT DAY

The air conditioner in DI Trott's office kept the humidity at bay but did little to refresh the two men who sat dejectedly at either side of the detective's desk. It had been a long, draining day, filled with the kind of routine legwork Congreve hadn't done in a good long while.

He idly toyed with his pipe while Trott went through the utterly pointless exercise of transferring information from his notebook to a computerized case file. Pointless because, while the two of them had spent the better part of the day talking to everyone who might have had even the vaguest connection to Marian Smith—her neighbors, co-workers at the Home Office, and a few acquaintances—they were no closer to having a suspect than when Congreve had first arrived at the scene.

Marian Smith had been living in Bermuda for only eight months, and although she wasn't a recluse, she hadn't exactly gone out of her way to put down roots either. Her neighbors described her as polite but distant. At work, she was competent and professional but nothing more—the sort of woman who kept her head down, did her job, and went home at the end of the day. There were no glaring red flags, no suspicious relationships. No one knew of any enemies, and the only thing anyone could say for certain was that she didn't seem the type to court trouble. And yet, despite the hours spent chasing leads and picking through her life, Congreve and Trott were no closer to understanding why someone had ended it. To make matters worse, the forensics team had turned up no useful fingerprints and no DNA.

The crime scene still nagged at Congreve. The incongruities, the pristine condition of the apartment, the bloody wine . . . it all pointed to something more than the routine crime of passion Trott had suggested, but if Marian Smith was as . . . well, frankly *boring* as she seemed to be, why had the killer gone to all the trouble?

Trott snapped his notebook closed and leaned back in his chair, a thoughtful frown creasing his brow. "You think maybe a tourist did it? We got cruise ships dockin' here all the time, plenty of fellas lookin' for a good time. Maybe she met someone at one of the local spots and brought him back to her place. Things got outta hand."

"A tourist?" Congreve rolled the word around his mouth as if tasting it.

Trott nodded. "Yeah. We get thousands of them comin' through every week, and some of them ain't exactly upstandin' citizens, if you take my meaning. And once they're on the island, well, people relax."

Congreve absently tapped the stem of the briar against his knee. "If we're dealing with a visitor, it's possible that they've already left the island."

Trott seemed not to have heard. "We ought to start askin' around the bars and restaurants, show her picture. Maybe someone saw her. Saw them together."

"Hmm, yes. Still, even if she did pick someone up, it doesn't explain the crime scene. No prints, no sign of a struggle, and an expensive bottle of wine you can't even buy locally." He narrowed his eyes at Trott, the wheels finally beginning to turn. "She *knew* him. Not casually. Not just a pickup."

"Someone we talked to, then?"

Congreve stared at his pipe, recalling a line from one of his favorite stories. "'You see, but you do not observe. There is a distinction.'"

Trott stiffened. "What's that, then?"

Congreve, realizing that he had unintentionally given offense, raised his hands in a show of supplication. "Not you, sir. Or rather, not just you. It's something Holmes said. 'A Scandal in Bohemia.' We have been looking at our victim's life . . . *seeing* it . . . but we've overlooked something obvious."

"And what would that be?" retorted Trott.

"We have been going about this as if Miss Smith's life began the moment she arrived on our shores. She had a life before Bermuda. And her killer was a part of it."

"You think it's someone from before she got here? Someone from London?"

"Depend upon it. We need to speak to her friends, old flatmates, anyone she left behind. The answer's there, Trott. And that's where we need to be looking."

Congreve was mildly impressed when the detective inspector reached for the phone on his desk and began dialing. *Now we're getting somewhere*, he thought.

He was only a little disappointed when, after a few seconds' delay, Trott, in a subdued tone, said, "I won't be makin' it home for dinner tonight, love. Sorry 'bout that."

SIXTEEN

Anastasia Romanova's knuckles were bone white on the handle of the palette knife as she pulled it across the canvas, dragging angry strokes of crimson, black, and ochre. She'd been at it for hours, losing herself in the rough textures and angry colors, avoiding the brushes entirely and instead virtually sculpting her subject with the blade, shaping the strong line of his jaw, the shadow under his cheekbones. Her movements were precise but aggressive, as though cutting into the memory of him rather than simply drawing it up. She had painted him so many times before, but this was different. This time, it wouldn't be for public display or something to hang over the fireplace. This was just for her. This was the real Alexander Hawke—*her* Alexander Hawke—haunted, driven, and utterly consumed by his thirst for conflict.

She wiped her hand across her forehead, inadvertently leaving a smear of crimson on her skin like a wound, and then took a step back to behold her creation. It was raw, unfinished, a reflection of how she felt inside.

Damn him for leaving again, she thought.

She attacked the canvas again, dragging the knife through the paint once more, deepening the shadows in his eyes.

She loved him, of course—more than anything—even knowing who and what he really was, how his restless nature and insatiable need for danger would pull him away from her, from their family. Naively, she had believed that, with her and Alexei in his life, he would come to see the appeal of stability, that the roles of father and husband would supersede the lure of adventure, that his desire to be there for them—instead of putting his life on the line again and again—would naturally bring about a change in his priorities. What man, after all, would not want to live to see his son grow into a man? But so far the allure of family life had not quenched Hawke's instinctual inclinations in the least.

She set the palette knife down and looked out through the wide windows at the lights of boats floating in the dark ocean. She knew now how the wives of ancient mariners must have felt as their husbands answered the siren song of their true love, the vast and indifferent sea.

It's always just one more. One more voyage. One more mission. One more favor for the King.

She had asked him how long, and he had thought that she meant, *How long will you be away?*

"Can't say for certain. Not more than a few days, at most, I should think."

But that wasn't what she had really meant. What she wanted to know was: *How long before you realize that Alexei and I will never make you happy?*

How long before you stop pretending you will ever be suited for this life?

The trilling of her mobile phone snapped her out of her dark mood, her immediate thought—*Alex!*

But it wasn't Alex. The number displayed on the screen was unfamiliar, but she knew the country code.

+7

Russia.

Her pulse quickened. She hadn't received a call from Russia in months. Her contacts there had all but fallen silent since her departure, vanishing like ghosts as Russia grew increasingly isolated on the world stage.

Striving to conceal her apprehension, she answered, "Allo?"

There was a long silence on the other end, long enough for her to wonder if the call had been a mistake. Then she heard a voice.

"Bez imen. Znayesh', kto eto?" ("No names. Do you know who this is?")

She did.

The voice belonged to Vasily Markov.

A mid-level official in the Ministry of Internal Affairs, Vasily had been assigned to monitor Anastasia's whereabouts during her long period of house arrest, ensuring her compliance with the restrictions imposed by the FSB. Despite his role as an enforcer of government rules, Vasily had taken pity on Asia, recognizing the injustice of her situation, and over time had become something of a confidant, carefully providing her with small but vital favors—such as facilitating her communications with the outside world and, ultimately, helping to coordinate Alexei's exodus.

A call from Vasily, out of the blue, was reason for concern. The fact that he wished to hide his identity from any possible listening ears was ominous.

"Da," she replied and continued in Russian. "Why are you calling?"

"The man that you love is in great danger. They know that he's coming."

The words hit her like a slap. She did not need to ask who *they* were. But the broader implication staggered her.

Alex is going to Russia?

She knew of his ongoing hunt for the Warmonger and his belief that Sergei Mulmuscovy was, if not the Warmonger himself, then a highly placed lieutenant in his organization. She also knew that even Alex wasn't reckless enough to try to go after Mulmuscovy in Russia.

Her gaze fell upon the portrait: her lover, the very embodiment of violence.

Or is he?

"That is all I can tell you," Vasily went on. "Be careful."

Then he ended the call.

Asia just stared at the phone in her hand, her mind racing. Vasily's voice, so unexpected and yet so familiar, had brought old memories to the fore. Long, cold, gray days in the velvet prison of the Winter Palace. Being under Putin's iron thumb. And now, with those same dangers closing in on Alex, she felt insurmountable dread.

They know he's coming. Alex is walking into a trap.

She thought of calling him. Her finger hovered over his name in her contact list. Warn him that his mission was already compromised. Plead for him to return home and evade the trap.

But, no, he wouldn't listen. He would rattle off some old pearl of military wisdom—*Forewarned is forearmed, and all that*—and then run headlong into the teeth of danger.

No, she thought, setting the phone aside. *I need to go to him.*

She paced the room, weighing her options. Going to Russia would be almost as dangerous for her as it would for Alex. She had friends there, yes, but she also had enemies. Many more of the latter, thanks to her father's ambitions. Nevertheless, Russia was where she would have to go.

She decided what she needed first and foremost was a base of operations. A place where she could monitor the situation, gather information, and, when the time came, cross the border.

Somewhere secure, where she wouldn't be recognized right away. Somewhere . . .

Somewhere mobile.

"Pelham . . ." She started to call out, then caught herself. Pelham was gone. Alex had whisked him off to London to oversee his affairs at the house in Mayfair. She growled in irritation, more at her own helplessness than at the aged retainer's absence. She'd become far too reliant on other people to do things for her.

Wiping the paint from her hands, she left the studio and made her way to the front room, where Teakettle Cottage's only connection to the outside world—aside from individual mobile devices—was kept: the telephone.

Early on in his occupation of the cottage—which had been converted from an old sugar mill sometime around the turn of the last century—Alex had gotten the strange notion in his head to preserve the rustic atmosphere of the place, eschewing modern conveniences like televisions, computers, and Wi-Fi, and while he had gradually relaxed some of his prohibitions against modernity, he had not upgraded the old Bakelite housephone, which sat in pride of place on the monkeywood bar. Asia wasn't interested in the phone, however, but rather the old, leather-bound address book that sat next to it. It contained all the phone numbers that any sane person living in the twenty-first century would have stored on their mobile.

She flipped through the pages until she found the listing she was looking for and then punched the number into her own device. The call rang three times before Alex's head of security, Tom Quick, picked up. The delay from the aptly named former sniper instructor, who always answered promptly, made her wonder if she had caught him sleeping. It was just past dusk in Bermuda, but she had no idea where Quick was, which was part of the reason for her call.

There was no trace of drowsiness in the voice that came over the line. "Good evening, ma'am."

"Tommy, good evening. I am wondering: Where is the *Blackhawke* right now?"

Quick's position in Alex's organization was not limited to the decks of the fortified megayacht, but with the destruction of Alex's *other* battle-ready yacht—the *Sea Hawke*, which had gone down in the Southern Ocean several months earlier—it was where he spent most of his time. *Sea Hawke*'s replacement, a three-hundred-foot behemoth that would eventually be christened the *War Hawke*, was still under construction at the venerable Lürssen shipyard in Lemwerder, Germany, and wouldn't be ready for at least another year.

"She's right here, ma'am. London, that is. Shipshape and at your service. Thinking of taking a little cruise?"

Asia smiled. "Yes, Tommy. I am."

SEVENTEEN

BRUSSELS, BELGIUM

The headquarters of the North Atlantic Treaty Organization was a monument to the alliance that ultimately won the Cold War. The sprawling structure, completed in 2017 at a cost north of a billion euros, reflected the organization's evolution from a post–World War II pact of Western nations into a global force for stability and collective defense. Built to house representatives from its now thirty-two member states, the headquarters was a complex of glass, steel, and stone—a definite upgrade from the hastily assembled postwar offices where the alliance had first taken shape.

Viewed from above, the eight wings of the complex, which fanned out from a central spine, resembled nothing less than interlocking fingers, symbolizing the unity of the organization, a physical representation of NATO's mandate—sovereign nations bound together, prepared to fight as one.

The building itself occupied 254,000 square meters and housed over 4,000 employees. Inside its labyrinth of hallways and high-tech conference rooms, diplomats and military officials worked side by side, hammering out policies, discussing global threats, and fine-tuning the strategies needed to confront a world that had grown even more dangerous in the decades since NATO's inception.

Despite the modernity of its headquarters building, the organization's purpose had remained remarkably consistent: collective defense. An attack on one was an attack on all.

It was this guiding principle that had kept the alliance strong through decades of Soviet aggression, Balkan unrest, the war on terror, and, most recently, the creeping shadow of unchecked Russian aggression.

And now, with the test detonation of the Tsar II bomb, that aggression had reached a fever pitch.

The mood inside NATO headquarters was one of apprehension, frustration, and thinly veiled dread. An emergency planning session had been called, bringing together senior leaders from the member nations for the first time since the ill-fated summit in Istanbul.

They had assembled in the Meeting Room, a circular chamber designed to evoke both a sense of equality and unity. Small flag placards from each member state were arranged on the wall above the entrance. A round table, with a single seat for each nation, circled the center of the room, where stood the lectern from which the gathering could be addressed. Much like King Arthur's Round Table, the arrangement symbolized that no one nation was above another: all had an equal voice. Theoretically, at least. Much like the characters in George Orwell's classic *Animal Farm*: "All animals are equal, but some are more equal than others."

Commander Savannah Stone sat in the gallery, right behind the place designated for the British delegation. Sir Marcus Godfrey, the United Kingdom's Secretary of Defence, occupied the seat reserved for Britain. Godfrey was a well-known figure, whose sharp intellect and keen strategic mind were often masked by his unassuming appearance. An older man with neatly combed silver hair and the bearing of a lifelong civil servant, he had spent years in defense and intelligence roles. Although less publicly outspoken than some of his colleagues, he was tough, pragmatic, and unafraid to speak his mind when the situation required. Savannah could see how heavily the weight of responsibility rested on his shoulders.

This was not just another geopolitical summit. The world was on the brink of thermonuclear Armageddon.

"Let's not beat around the bush," Godfrey said, his voice measured but firm. "The detonation of the Tsar II bomb changes everything. Putin may be ruthless, but he isn't irrational. He's sending a message, and what we have to decide now is how we're going to answer it."

Several representatives exchanged uneasy glances, none wanting to be the first to respond. Finally, the French Defense Minister spoke up, voicing the concerns of some in Western Europe. "With respect, Secretary Godfrey, this escalation is a consequence of our continued overreach in Ukraine. The question we should be asking is not how we retaliate but whether we need to reconsider our involvement. NATO was not formed to defend nonmember states, and we are risking a global catastrophe over a conflict that, at its core, is beyond our mandate."

A murmur of agreement rippled among some of the European representatives, but Godfrey's eyes narrowed slightly, his expression growing steely.

"So you're suggesting we pull out? That we leave Ukraine to fend for itself?"

The French minister hesitated but did not back down. "What I am saying is that we need to rethink our strategy. We are being pulled toward a nuclear confrontation. My people are asking if the potential destruction of Paris is too high a price for supporting Ukraine."

Savannah scanned the faces of the other delegates, noting the mixed reactions. The German representative gave a slight nod, and the Italian delegate looked visibly torn.

Then a voice cut through the room, clear and forceful. "If NATO will not stand against Russia, then Turkey will."

It was a face Savannah knew well: General Osman Gul, Chief of the General Staff of the Turkish Armed Forces, a man widely seen as a rising power within Turkey's political-military landscape. Gul, upright and unflinching, spoke with a conviction that silenced the room. His dark gaze swept across the table, daring anyone to challenge him. "We are not afraid of Putin, nor will we be intimidated by his theatrics. If necessary, Turkey will act alone."

Savannah felt a chill at Gul's words. Since the attack on the Topkapı Palace summit—an attack believed to have been backed by the Kremlin—Turkey had adopted an increasingly aggressive stance toward Russia, even threatening to close access to the Black Sea. But this bold declaration hinted at something beyond mere posturing.

Godfrey raised an eyebrow, studying Gul carefully before addressing the room once more. "The United Kingdom remains resolute in its support of NATO's stance on Ukraine. Putin's show of force only solidifies our commitment to the alliance. But let us be clear: this is not merely a matter of Ukraine. It is about the future of Europe and indeed the integrity of NATO itself. We must stand together or risk facing this threat alone."

Savannah noticed several delegates nodding in agreement, the earlier dissent softening in the face of Godfrey's statement.

"And as for your suggestion," Godfrey continued, fixing the French Defense Minister with a cool stare, "with respect, this extends beyond Ukraine. If we allow Russia to dictate terms here, it won't stop at Kyiv. Europe itself is at stake."

As Godfrey argued for NATO solidarity, Savannah glanced over at Gul. He met her gaze, his expression unreadable, and she quickly looked away, pretending to focus again on the ongoing discussion. But a lingering unease persisted.

What sort of game is the Turk playing?

EIGHTEEN

EN ROUTE TO PARIS

Alex Hawke stared out the window of the Eurostar as it slipped through the rolling countryside of southern England, heading toward the Channel Tunnel. The high-speed train hummed beneath him, but the soft, constant vibration did little to ease his foul humor.

Most of it could be put down to his choice—or rather lack of choice—of traveling companions. The mere thought of spending the better part of a week in close quarters with a woman who made no secret of her desire for him was simply exhausting. Even now, seated across from her in the first-class cabin, he could feel the weight of her hungry stare.

There was once a time, and not too terribly long ago, when Hawke would have enjoyed such attention. Not so many years back, taking a woman like Ariadne into his bed would have been part of the fun, a simple and no doubt pleasurable distraction from the dangers of his work.

But things had changed.

He had changed.

Hawke's playboy days were now behind him. Even before Asia had reentered his life, he had begun to understand the futility of such hedonistic pursuits and was haunted by their emptiness. In fact, despite his reputation as a Casanova, he had always been something of a serial monogamist. Deep down, he was, after all, a romantic.

Oh, there had been flings, to be sure. Nights of passion with nothing remotely resembling a deep connection, and that, if he was being honest with himself, he deeply regretted. Some more than others. His one-night stand with Pippa Guinness all those years ago now hovered over their professional relationship like a dark cloud.

And not the kind of dark 'n' stormy that he enjoyed.

But deep down, no matter how uncomfortable it made him, there was no denying the fact that Hawke wanted to love, and he desperately wanted to *be* loved.

So, what are you doing here? You've got a perfectly good woman at home and a son, for God's sake, and yet here you are, flirting—almost literally—with danger?

The thought, which had snuck up from behind like an assassin, shook him, leaving him unsettled. He loathed introspection. As he often told his good friend Ambrose Congreve, *"Deep down, I'm really a very shallow person."*

But that was merely a lie to deflect.

What Alex Hawke put down to a lack of depth was really just his armor. He was far more complicated than he wanted anyone, especially himself, to believe. His refusal to settle down with Anastasia, despite the deep bond they shared and their commitment to raising Alexei together, was only a symptom of a deeper problem—one he refused to admit to. It wasn't just his restlessness or his thrill-seeking nature that kept him from fully committing. It was the old wound, a scar from his childhood that he had never allowed to fully heal.

The loss of his parents in that brutal attack in the Caribbean had left more than just a void; it had shaped the man he became. From that moment on, he had built walls around himself—walls of steel and adventure, walls that kept him on the move, from mission to mission, never fully allowing anyone inside.

Hawke glanced across the compartment at Silk. She had traded her crimson cocktail dress and heels for charcoal wool trousers, a high-neck cashmere jumper in a soft dove gray, and low-heeled black ankle boots. Her hair, which had been so meticulously styled for the post-poned dinner in London, was now pulled back into a sleek, effortless ponytail. The only constant was the ever-present, oversize spectacles through which she peered down at the book she had brought along: *The Last Days of the Romanovs: Tragedy at Ekaterinburg* by Helen Rappaport.

Realizing that she had caught his eye, she smiled—a slow, knowing smile that made it clear she had no intention of letting up. And why would she? He was, after all, the great Alex Hawke . . . the man who could have anyone but wanted no one.

Well, why not, then? he thought. *It doesn't mean anything. And if it doesn't mean anything, then it doesn't mean anything.*

He looked away, determined not to play her game. Instead, he settled back in his seat, pretending to focus on the landscape as the train began its descent into the tunnel under the English Channel. Silk was a complication he didn't need, especially given the mission ahead. He was supposed to keep her safe and secure the original copy of King George's letter, not get entangled in a doomed affair.

The Eurostar brought them to Paris in just over two hours. As they disembarked at Gare du Nord, Hawke checked his watch, mentally calculating the waiting time before their connection to Vienna. They had about an hour to kill, and that gave him just enough time to stretch his legs and mentally prepare for what would be one of the longest legs of the trip: a thirteen-hour overnight journey on the Nightjet.

The train itself was sleek and modern, and—more important to Hawke—it was private. Silk, in a rare display of discretion, had booked them individual deluxe sleeper cabins. After hours of being uncomfortably close to her, he welcomed the chance to be alone with his thoughts.

Silk, however, had other ideas.

As he was about to enter the compartment, she called out to him. "Oh, Alex."

He turned his head to regard her.

"I believe you extended me a . . . what was the term you used? 'Rain check'?" she said, her voice light but teasing. "Hope I used that correctly. Had to look it up. For dinner? I'd like to cash it in."

Hawke narrowed his eyes at her. "There's no restaurant car. Only room service."

Silk's smile widened. "Perfect. Your place or mine?"

"Wouldn't you rather wait until we're somewhere more . . ." He trailed off, not sure where he was going with it.

"We have to eat," she said coyly. "And you do owe me." She held his gaze for a long moment. "My place, then. Say . . . seven?"

"Fine," he sighed. As much as he valued his privacy, avoiding Silk for the entire trip wasn't practical. Better to just get it over with.

"See you then." Clearly pleased with herself, she slipped past him to the door of her cabin with an effortless sway in her step, letting her body rub across his.

Hawke watched her go with a scowl and then entered his own cabin, closing the door behind him. The cabin was small but functional, with a single bed made up for the night, a small table, and a washbasin tucked into the corner.

He stowed his luggage and then flopped down on the bed, stretching out and trying to think about anything, anything at all, except Ariadne Silk.

INTERLUDE—PART FIVE

AMIENS, FRANCE
APRIL 1918

Although only eighty miles separated Calais from Amiens, the journey felt more like a long descent into hell.

The first indication that this would be no ordinary rail journey came when Alexander and Natalya boarded the train car and found it crowded with soldiers on their way to the front, many of them—judging by their youth and wide-eyed stares—for the first time. There were, in fact, hardly any civilians aboard at all.

Having spent his part of the war at sea, Alexander's only knowledge of the state of the war on the Continent came from news reports and the odd military dispatch that crossed his desk, so he was completely unprepared for what he beheld as the train pushed south.

The change in the landscape was nothing short of shocking. Pastoral calm gave way to devastation with startling abruptness. The tidy patchwork of green and gold fields melted into a wasteland of mud and ash. Fields were pockmarked with raw blast craters, some filled with stagnant water that reflected the gray sky. Blackened tree stumps, the remnants of orchards and woods scorched by artillery fire, jutted from the ground like broken teeth.

Even the air seemed to change, growing thick with the acrid tang of smoke and decay. The rhythmic sound of the train's wheels on the rails was broken by the distant rumble of guns, a low, ceaseless growl that grew louder with each passing mile.

They passed the remains of villages, their names unmarked because there was no need: no one lived in them anymore. Crumbling walls and skeletal chimneys stood as silent sentinels over rubble-strewn streets. No children played here; no faces appeared in the shattered windows.

Dark columns of smoke rose from the horizon, smudging the sky like charcoal strokes. Occasionally, flashes of light punctuated the gloom: artillery fire or an exploding shell followed seconds later by the distant echo of its impact.

Natalya, who sat across from Alexander, was uncharacteristically quiet, her sharp gaze fixed on what lay outside the window. Alexander, too, found himself leaning forward, scanning the horizon as though expecting danger to materialize from the smoke. It was not, he had been told, outside the realm of possibility that German artillery would target the train.

He had seen his share of battle, but nothing like this. It was as though they were crossing the threshold into another world—a world where no rules of civility or nature applied.

It was no longer the France he knew. It was the land of war.

By the time the train reached Amiens, the distant thunder of guns had grown to an almost constant roar, punctuated now and then by the sharper cracks of explosions closer at hand. The station was swarming with soldiers—British, French, and a smattering of others—standing in huddled groups, their voices blending into a low cacophony of orders, laughter, and weary complaints. The activity was relentless: supply crates were unloaded from trains; carts piled high with ammunition rolled by; couriers darted through the chaos, clutching orders bound for the front; stretcher-bearers carried the wounded to the platform to be loaded aboard the next train out.

"Follow me," said Natalya, her tone brisk but not unkind. "Where we are going isn't far, but this isn't a place to linger."

Alexander fell in step behind her as they left the station, weaving through the crush of soldiers and supply wagons. The city itself was little more than a military camp. Uniformed men marched in tight columns, their boots pounding against the cobblestones. Lorries rumbled by, piled high with crates of ammunition or medical supplies, their engines grumbling above the din. Alexander noticed more than one officer giving him a curious glance and was painfully aware of how conspicuously out of place he looked in his tailored suit.

The farther they moved from the station, the more apparent the scars of war became. Many buildings had been hastily patched with timber and sheets of tin, their original facades crumbled under the weight of German shells. Here and there, civilians moved about, their expressions grim and purposeful. Women with baskets darted in and out of bomb-damaged shops, and old men with hunched shoulders pushed handcarts laden with whatever goods could still be found.

Natalya kept her pace quick but steady, her eyes flicking to every alley and doorway they passed.

"The house is near the cathedral," she murmured over her shoulder.

Alexander cast a glance upward. The spires of Amiens Cathedral loomed over the city. He could see where shrapnel had gouged the ancient stone, but even in its damaged state the building retained a kind of defiant grace.

A side street led them to a row of narrow houses, their shutters drawn tight against the chill. Natalya slowed as they approached a nondescript doorway, its paint peeling and the brass knocker dulled by time. She glanced up and down the street, then knocked twice, paused, and knocked again.

After a long moment the door creaked open, revealing a gaunt, dark-haired man with sharp cheekbones and a wiry build.

"Natalya?"

He said more, but it was in Russian, which Alexander did not understand, then the man's eyes flicked to Alexander.

"May we come in, Viktor?" she replied, speaking in French.

The man, Viktor, hesitated, his gaze lingering on Alexander. "Who is this?"

"I will tell you what I can," Natalya said evenly. "But not out here."

Viktor continued to stare at Alexander with naked suspicion but after a moment gave a curt nod and stepped back, opening the door wider.

The interior was dimly lit, the curtains drawn tight. Papers and maps covered a small wooden table in the corner, while a battered sofa and two mismatched chairs completed the sparse furnishings. Viktor closed the door behind them, sliding a heavy bolt into place before turning to face them.

"Why have you come, Natalya?" he asked, his tone tinged with suspicion. "And who is this man?"

Alexander had to fight the urge to answer for himself. Viktor was Natalya's contact, and she knew best how to deal with him.

"This is Sasha," she said, gesturing to Alexander. Her unilateral decision to withhold his name told Alexander that his instincts about letting Natalya take the lead were spot-on.

"He is traveling with me. That's all you need to know. We need to get to the other side."

Viktor's eyes narrowed. "That is no small matter."

"I understand the risks," Natalya replied evenly. "Is Jean-Pierre still making the run across the frontier?"

A shadow passed over Viktor's face. "Jean-Pierre is dead."

Natalya's expression betrayed no more than a flicker of emotion. "I'm sorry to hear that." She hesitated, then pressed on. "Has anyone taken over his business?"

Viktor frowned, his gaze shifting to Alexander before returning to Natalya. "There is someone. A man named Luc. But it will cost you. Especially after what happened to Jean-Pierre."

"Please make the arrangements."

"When?"

"Tonight if possible."

Viktor gave a humorless laugh. "That will cost you even more."

"Just make it happen, Viktor. We will also need documents to get us through to Minsk. We will travel as representatives of the Red Cross surveying the impact of the war to the east."

Viktor shook his head. "Natalya, this is madness. There are other ways to reach Minsk. Safer ways."

She shook her head. "We don't have the luxury of time. We must reach Moscow as soon as possible."

"Why, Natalya?" He glanced at Alexander again. "What is so important that you would risk your life needlessly?"

Natalya's expression hardened, her tone cold and deliberate. "My reasons are not your concern, Viktor. Your duty is to make the arrangements, not to question them."

For a moment Viktor held her gaze, his mouth tightening. Then he exhaled sharply, muttering something under his breath in Russian before returning to French. "Very well. I'll need some time to prepare your papers and make the arrangements with Luc." He turned for the door. "It's best if you stay here. Get some rest. It will be a long night for you."

As the door closed behind him, Alexander turned to Natalya. "'Sasha'?"

"Sasha is the Russian diminutive form of Alexander." She arched an eyebrow. "You don't like it?"

"I'm not sure how to feel about you having a pet name for me," he said dryly. "Should I start calling you something equally endearing? How about Talia? No, I've a better idea: I shall call you Natty."

"Sasha and Natty? Sounds like name for music hall duet."

Alexander smiled. "Well, we are taking our show on the road. Perhaps we'll play the Bolshoi?"

"I think we are not ready for the Bolshoi," she said with a laugh. "Very well. You may call me 'Natty,' but, please, not in front of Viktor."

Alexander's smile faded slightly as the tone shifted. "Speaking of Viktor . . . can we trust him?"

Natalya looked away, her expression thoughtful. "Viktor is loyal servant of the Revolution. But trust?" She shrugged lightly. "In my world, Sasha, trust is a luxury, not a necessity."

"Your world? As an envoy? Or would *spy* be a better word for it?"

She ignored the question. "Viktor will do this for me. That is enough."

The afternoon sun cast long shadows over the ruined countryside as Viktor's cart bumped and jostled along a narrow dirt track. Alexander and Natalya rode in the back, sharing the space with a substantial stack of firewood that Viktor would be delivering to the soldiers manning a remote section of the trenches near Péronne. The distant rumble of artillery was a near-constant presence now. Occasionally a sharper crack would rise above the din, marking a closer explosion.

A few hours' ride brought them to a derelict farmhouse. "Luc will meet you here at midnight," said Viktor. He handed Natalya a satchel. "Your papers are in here, along with some food."

"Thank you, Viktor."

"Natalya . . ." Viktor glanced briefly over at Alexander, then back to Natalya. "This is a very bad idea. There are other ways to get back to Moscow."

"I told you already, Viktor. There's no time for that."

The man hesitated, his sharp gaze flitting between her and Alexander. "Then I will only tell you to be careful."

She placed a hand on his arm, her expression softening. "Thank you, comrade."

Viktor gave her a curt nod, then climbed back onto the cart. With a final glance at the pair, he clicked his tongue, urging the horse into motion. The cart trundled away, leaving Alexander and Natalya standing alone amidst the ruins.

Alexander gave the farmhouse a dubious glance. The roof was partially caved in, and one of the walls leaned precariously inward. The glassless windows gaped like empty eye sockets. The interior was as grim as the exterior: rotting timbers, broken plaster—and the faint stench of damp and decay lingered in the air. There was nothing resembling furniture, only heaps of moldering fabric and broken wood.

They stepped inside, careful to avoid the debris scattered across the floor. "Well, this makes the inn in Calais look like the Ritz," remarked Alexander.

Natalya smiled. "At least you won't have to spend the night on the hearth."

"I would almost rather. We'll have to do without a fire tonight." He sighed. "Let's try to get some rest. Like Viktor said, it's going to be a long night. We'll take turns. Two hours, I should think. I'll keep first watch."

Natalya offered no argument. She settled onto the floor, using her coat as a pillow. "Wake me when it's my turn."

Alexander leaned back against the wall, his thoughts drifting as dusk fell over the farmstead. For a while, the only sounds were the occasional rustle of wind through the broken windows and the distant rumble of artillery.

Natalya's breathing slowed as she drifted off, her face softening in sleep. In the fading glow of twilight, Alexander studied her in repose. There was something about her composure, even in the face of such danger, that unsettled him as much as it impressed him. When he was certain that she would not stir, he went over to her, shrugged out of his coat, and spread it over her like a blanket.

He returned to his spot by the wall, noting the time on his Omega in the last vestiges of daylight filtering through the broken windows. Night deepened, and as the farmhouse sank into near-total darkness, it became almost impossible to see the white face of his wristwatch. He did not want to risk striking a match and possibly revealing their presence, so he simply let the minutes tick by. He had no real intention of rousing Natalya for the prescribed watch shift. Nevertheless, after what was probably only about two and a half hours, he heard her voice in the darkness.

"Sasha, you were supposed to wake me."

"You looked far too comfortable, Natty. I couldn't bring myself to disturb you."

He could just barely see her silhouette moving in the darkness, sitting up, stretching like a cat. "As much as I appreciate your chivalry, dear Sasha, we agreed upon two hours. I need to know that you will keep your word."

Though her tone was playful, he sensed an underlying seriousness to the complaint. "Quite right. Please forgive me. Performative chivalry has become something of a habit."

He heard a faint hum of disapproval and then felt something soft press into his chest. "Here is your coat."

He took it, somewhat reluctantly, wanting her to keep it as she would doubtless feel the night's chill more than he, but knowing she would only see the offer as a further provocation.

"You'll rest properly?" she pressed, her tone light but with genuine concern threaded beneath.

"I'll lie down," he allowed, stretching out across the hard floor. "What happens after that remains to be seen."

"Very well. *I* will wake you in two hours."

He rolled his coat into a makeshift pillow and settled his head upon it. The scent of Natalya's perfume, so subtle that he had never even noticed it before, now filled his nostrils and, inexplicably, sent a flush of heat through him that was all the more noticeable in the cold.

He knew he would not sleep, especially not now, but nonetheless closed his eyes to perpetuate the illusion of taking his rest.

They passed the rest of the night in this fashion, standing watch and feigning sleep in two-hour increments, until at the stroke of midnight they heard a voice calling in a stage whisper from the farmhouse's door. "Hallo?"

Alexander, who had been on watch, was on his feet in an instant, but it was Natalya who answered. "Who is it?"

"Luc."

"How do we know it's really you?"

"Who else would it be?" the man replied in French.

A chuckle came from beyond the doorway. "Ah, careful and clever. I like that. Very well—your friend Viktor said to tell you that Jean-Pierre couldn't make it on account of being dead. Now, shall we begin our journey, or do you want to keep playing this charming game?"

Satisfied with the recognition code, Alexander and Natalya moved outside. Luc was little more than a silhouette in the darkness, but he nevertheless swept off his hat with an exaggerated flourish. "Bonsoir. So, you are the fools who need to cross No Man's Land?"

"That would be us," Alexander said, his tone dry.

"Then it's your lucky night. I know a way across, but I'll warn you now: it's no walk in the park. You'll do exactly as I say, step where I tell you to step, or you'll end up like poor Jean-Pierre."

"Understood," said Alexander. "What's the plan?"

"The plan is simplicity itself: we walk. East of here, there's an orchard . . . There *was* an orchard. It's too far from the trenches to be patrolled, so both sides laid mines to do the job for them. Fortunately, I know a safe path through."

"Mines?" Alexander was immediately wary. He had lost many close friends to floating sea mines. Land mines, he knew, were far more insidious and brutal, blowing off legs and leaving the wounded to die of blood loss. Still, a minefield would be easier to deal with than German patrols, provided Luc really did know how to get through.

"Don't worry. I have made the crossing many times. But now you understand why I say 'Step where I tell you'?"

"Yes, we understand," said Natalya impatiently.

Luc bent over and picked up two satchels, handing one each to Alexander and Natalya. Alexander took his, finding it heavier than expected.

"What, pray tell, are these?" asked Alexander.

"Cigarettes, mostly. A few bottles of brandy. Small comforts that those on the other side will pay dearly for."

"So we're pack mules for a smuggler now?"

"This is the part of the price we must pay," explained Natalya. She hefted her bag onto her shoulder, then turned to Luc. "Now, shall we go?"

"Follow me."

They moved out with Luc leading the way and Alexander and Natalya close behind. The night was frigid and eerily quiet, save for the far-off thunder of artillery and the occasional rustle of wind through the barren landscape. The moon hung low in the sky, its pale light offering just enough illumination to see the outlines of the ruined terrain.

Luc moved with confident ease as he led them away from the farmhouse through the cratered debris field that had once been pasturage. Alexander was constantly looking around, searching the darkness, his senses on high alert. Natalya kept pace without a word, her silence as tense as his own.

After more than an hour of walking, they came to a rusted barbed wire fence. The wire hung slack in places, its posts leaning drunkenly, but it remained an unmistakable warning. Beyond it, the orchard—now a blackened wasteland—loomed, its twisted remains barely recognizable as trees.

Luc crouched by the wire, pulling a pair of heavy gloves from his coat pocket. He whispered over his shoulder, his voice barely audible. "Follow exactly where I step. Not an inch to the left or right. Understand?"

Alexander nodded, his throat dry. Natalya murmured her assent.

Luc reached for the barbed wire and carefully lifted a sagging section, motioning for them to duck underneath. Alexander went first, feeling the wire dragging along his coat as he crawled under it. Natalya slipped through without even touching it. Then the two of them stood there stock-still, waiting for Luc to show them where to step.

When he joined them, Luc stared out into the darkness for nearly a full minute as if looking for some familiar landmark to orient himself. Then he stood and took a cautious step forward, planting his boot firmly before lifting the other. "Follow," he said without looking back.

Alexander took a deep breath and stepped forward, his eyes fixed on Luc's feet. Stepping forward almost as soon as Luc's foot left the earth. Traveling so close to each other, Alexander knew, might prove disastrous if any of them happened to trigger a land mine, since the resulting spray of shrapnel might wound or kill all of them, but in the darkness it was the only way to guarantee treading in Luc's footsteps.

The silence was suffocating. Even the distant guns seemed to have paused, leaving nothing but the sound of his own breathing and the faint crunch of soil underfoot. A bead of sweat slid down his temple despite the cold, and he felt his pulse hammering in his ears.

Luc paused every few steps, turning his head slightly to ensure they were keeping up, his sharp eyes catching the faint glint of starlight. At one point he crouched again, brushing aside a layer of dirt to reveal a jagged fragment of metal buried just beneath the surface: a mine casing, corroded but still deadly. He motioned for them to skirt carefully around it, his finger pressed to his lips in a silent command for caution.

They crept onward, step by agonizing step. Alexander's shirt was soaked with perspiration, and only the constant exertion of movement kept it from freezing to his skin. The satchel containing Luc's contraband seemed to grow heavier by the minute. He felt the tension in his muscles increase, every nerve alight with the anticipation of a misstep, of an explosion that would shatter the fragile quiet and end everything in an instant.

When they finally reached another fence marking the far edge of the minefield, Luc stopped and straightened, exhaling softly. He turned to them with a faint smirk, his voice a whisper that barely carried. "See? That was not so bad."

Alexander had to fight the urge to say something unchristian. His legs were leaden. His back ached from the weight of his pack. Still, being clear of the threat of being blown to smithereens was a welcome relief. He glanced over at Natalya just as she lowered her satchel to the ground, rolling her shoulders to ease the strain.

"No time for that," said Luc. "We must keep moving."

"For God's sake, man," said Alexander. "We're spent. Give us five minutes."

"No. It is much too dangerous to remain here. We are still close to the frontier, and there are patrols. We must keep moving."

Natalya gave a weary sigh but reached down for the pack. Alexander caught hold of it first. "I'll take it for you."

She held on to it. "Enough of your chivalry, Sasha."

"It's not chivalry, Natty. It's practicality. We'll be able to move faster if you're not carrying a load. It just makes sense. I can carry more. What is it your comrades are always saying? 'From each according to his ability, to each according to his needs'?"

"You're going to quote Marx to me? What's next, a worker's cap?"

"If it gets us to Moscow, I'll do whatever it takes." He tugged the strap from her grip and hoisted it onto his shoulder. "Now, let's get moving."

Alexander felt the weight of the second pack acutely but soldiered on in silence. Complaining wouldn't lighten the load, and it certainly wouldn't get them where they needed to go.

Luc proceeded cautiously, often pausing to listen for any sound that might betray the presence of German soldiers. Finally, after the better part of an hour, their journey brought them to the remains of an old barn. As soon as they were inside, Luc struck the flint on a small carbide lamp. After so many hours spent in deep darkness, the initial flare of ignition seemed as bright as the sun, but Luc quickly adjusted the flame to a faint orange glow that barely illuminated the barn's interior.

Alexander now saw that the barn was as abandoned as the farmhouse on the other side of the frontier where they had waited for Luc. There were no animals sheltering inside the barn, no hay in the loft.

Scattered debris littered the ground. The air was damp and heavy, carrying the smell of rot and mildew.

"Now you can rest," said Luc, breaking the long silence. He gestured to a refuse pile in one corner of the barn. "Put them over there."

Alexander deposited the satchels as directed, groaning aloud as he gratefully lowered them to the ground. Luc knelt there and began meticulously removing the trash to reveal a tarp stretched out on the ground and anchored at the corners to stakes pounded into the earth. He untied one corner of the tarp and flipped it back, uncovering a shallow hole just large enough to conceal the satchels. He placed both within and secured the tarp over the hole.

"Clever," remarked Alexander as Luc began reconstructing the refuse pile. "I take it you have an accomplice who will collect the goods and sell them."

"The brother of Jean-Pierre," Luc said, scattering dirt over the tarp to further conceal the cache. He rose and dusted off his hands. "This is where we part company, my friends. We're far enough from the trenches now that you can continue your journey safely. Or at least as safely as anyone can in occupied territory. There is a road just past the ridge behind this barn that will lead you to a village called Ham. It is about eight kilometers to the east. In the town square, ask for a man named Mathieu. He has a cart and may be persuaded to take you on to Saint-Quentin, if that is your wish. However, I would recommend that you wait here until first light to continue on your way."

Alexander shot a glance at his Omega, noting that it was about half past four. Dawn wouldn't be more than a couple of hours off. The exertion of their long trek had kept the night's chill at bay, but now that they weren't moving, he was starting to feel the cold. He knew it would only get colder until after sunrise, but while he didn't much like the idea of sitting idle in the cold for another two hours, he knew that Luc's advice was sound. The Germans would no doubt be keeping a close watch on the roads, and anyone traveling them at night was liable to be shot on sight as a spy.

He extended a hand to the smuggler. "Thank you, Luc. We'd never have made it this far without you."

Luc gave a small, dismissive shrug. "It is what you paid me to do."

Natalya stepped closer, her voice soft. "Even so, you've risked much. Thank you."

Luc's expression softened. "Good luck, my friends. You will need it."

With that, he closed the valve on the carbide lamp, plunging them into near-total darkness, and then slipped out into the night.

"Well, now we wait," said Alexander, more to break up the uncomfortable silence than anything else. "Shouldn't be more than a couple of hours."

"It is going to get colder," said Natalya.

"Hmm, quite. We'll need to keep moving so we don't freeze. Some calisthenics should do the trick."

"Are you going to do press-ups and star jumps for the next two hours?" She moved closer to him, slipping her arms under his coat and around his waist, pressing her body against his. "In Russia, we have better ways to keep warm on cold nights."

Alexander suddenly felt very warm indeed.

NINETEEN

HAMILTON, BERMUDA
PRESENT DAY

Ambrose Congreve carried himself with an almost carefree air as he strolled into Hamilton's police headquarters dressed in a crisp, lightweight linen suit the color of pale sand, with his unlit briar pipe extending jauntily from the corner of his mouth. Anyone seeing him likely wouldn't have guessed that his mind was on murder . . . that is, not unless they knew him.

He had risen early, not because it was his habit but because the unsolved mystery energized him more than any caffeinated concoction could. When his wife, the lovely Lady Diana Mars, commented on the uncharacteristic rapacity with which he broke his fast—full English, hold the black pudding—he replied, "Just topping off the petrol tank, my love." He further broke with his customary abhorrence of anything remotely resembling physical exercise by embarking on a vigorous stroll through the gardens of the Shadowlands, out to the edge of the property and back, his well-fueled brain buzzing in anticipation of solving the murder of Miss Marian Smith.

Detective Inspector Trott was already at his desk, papers spread out in neat piles before him. He looked up as Congreve entered, regarding the consulting detective with eyes that were slightly bloodshot from the strain of too many hours spent staring at a screen. The two of them had worked late into the evening of the previous day, extending their investigation to include the victim's activities and associates in London prior to her move to Bermuda, scouring her social media accounts for any connections that hadn't been documented through official channels. Inquiries had been sent to former employers and landlords, requesting more information—information that, Congreve surmised, now lay on Trott's desk in the form of hard copy.

"Good morning, Detective Inspector," said Congreve cheerily as he took a seat opposite the policeman. "Shall we get down to the business of solving this crime?"

"Good morning, Chief Inspector," replied Trott with considerably less enthusiasm.

"I see that the seeds we cast upon the wind have borne fruit."

Trott required a moment to decipher the statement, then glanced down at the stacks of paper. "I'd say that remains to be seen."

"Nonsense," retorted Congreve, grabbing one of the stacks and holding it up as if displaying a winning lottery ticket. "The answer is here, Trott. We just need to winnow the chaff."

He turned the paper around and scanned its contents, which, he now saw, was an application for a flat rental. His eyes rolled down the page, which included personal references and prior rental history, and frowned, his enthusiasm ebbing a bit. Winnowing would prove to be a tedious process—good old-fashioned police work. Still, he felt confident that somewhere in that pile of chaff, he would find the . . . the . . .

He groped for the right metaphor.

A kernel of truth?

That was a bit underwhelming.

A golden nugget! That was much better, though it would require recontextualizing the search. Panning for gold, then, just like a prospector on the Klondike, methodically sluicing away the gravel and sand to find the golden nugget of truth.

He raised his eyes to Trott again and managed an almost sincere smile. "Let's begin, shall we?"

They spent the next few hours making phone calls, running down Marian Smith's former acquaintances. Because her next of kin had not yet been notified of the death, they had to tread carefully, especially with Miss Smith's closer acquaintances, who, quite naturally, wondered if something had happened to her.

"Just a routine matter," Congreve had lied, and then, depending on whether he felt he had established rapport, he would either explain it away as a background check on behalf of the Home Office or admit that Miss Smith had reported someone stalking her, and, oh, by the way, do you know anyone who might have taken a particular interest in her when she lived there in London?

It was all for naught. All chaff and no kernels. All sand and gravel but no nuggets. But then, that was to be expected, wasn't it? If it were an easy thing, Trott would have found the killer already.

Then, around noon, he hit the mother lode.

He had been going down a list of Miss Smith's roommates during her university days at Newnham College. Newnham was one of the more prestigious all-female institutions at Cambridge. Founded in the late nineteenth century, Newnham had a long history of producing exceptional women—leaders in the arts, sciences, and politics. It wasn't hard to imagine Miss Smith as part of a tight-knit circle of ambitious young women, their days spent in lecture halls, their evenings filled with discussions that stretched long into the night. For a woman like Marian Smith, who had been in Bermuda for only a short time and had few local connections, the women she had matriculated with at Newnham would likely be lifelong confidantes. Or so he had assumed. The first two names on the list, however, had provided little background, but the third woman, a Miss Lila Goddard, had indicated that Marian and the prior roommate, Samantha Knowles—the next name on Congreve's list, as luck would have it—had been very close. Congreve thanked Miss Goddard for her time and then proceeded to call the number provided for Miss Knowles.

The line rang. It rang again. And again. Congreve expected it to go to voicemail and was preparing to deliver his standard message requesting a call back when someone picked up and a tentative male voice came across the line. "Hello?"

"Ah, yes, may I speak with Samantha Knowles, please?"

There was a brief pause, then: "May I ask who's calling?"

"Chief Inspector Ambrose Congreve," he said, using his most officious tone and conspicuously failing to mention his status as a retiree.

"Chief Inspector?" The tone of the caller changed. Congreve could almost imagine the person at the other end of the line snapping to attention. "This is Constable Rigby, Metropolitan Police. I'm afraid Miss Knowles won't be able to come to the phone."

Congreve's brow furrowed. "And why might that be, Constable?"

"Sir, I'm sorry to say it, but she's deceased. I'm calling from the scene."

"Deceased, you say?" Congreve felt his pulse quicken. "What's the cause?"

From behind his desk, Trott looked up, eyebrows raised. Congreve met his gaze and nodded gravely.

"Well, I'm not sure as I can say—" He broke off, and Congreve heard a brief shuffling sound across the line, then a new voice came through, more composed. "Chief Inspector Congreve, Detective Inspector Carter. I'm overseeing the investigation here."

"Inspector Carter," Congreve said, his tone steady. "Tell me what happened."

"It's early, but the scene suggests a domestic incident," Carter explained. "It looks like she was strangled. No sign of forced entry or a struggle, so she most likely knew her assailant. A boyfriend, I'm guessing. Looks like things started off right enough, but then . . ."

"Describe the scene to me," urged Congreve. "In detail, please."

"Ah, well, the body is in the dining room. There's a bottle of wine and two glasses, one of them full, the other half drunk."

"What's the vintage?"

"Sir?"

"The wine. What does it say on the label?"

There was a long pause, then Carter came back with the answer. "It's in French. I can't quite—"

"Is it Château Pichon Baron?"

"Uh . . . yeah, that's it."

Congreve took a breath and then let it out slowly before continuing. "Detective Inspector, I'm in Bermuda, investigating a murder nearly identical to what you've just described—same method, same bloody wine. And the victim here was a confidante of your victim."

There was another long pause as Carter absorbed the information. "Are you saying what I think you're saying?"

"If you think I'm saying that we may have a serial killer on our hands, then yes. That's exactly what I'm saying."

TWENTY

EN ROUTE TO VIENNA

When Silk had first proposed the idea of a long train journey across Europe, Hawke's mind had immediately conjured up images from films like *Murder on the Orient Express* and *From Russia with Love*: elegant dining cars, champagne in crystal flutes, luxurious sleeper cabins decorated in velvet and mahogany . . .

And, of course, intrigue and danger.

He had pictured the romance of it all, the adventure of speeding across the continent in old-world style. But the Nightjet was a different beast entirely. It was efficient and practical and had almost no aesthetic appeal.

In any other situation he might have lamented the lack of refinement, but now, given the circumstances, it felt like a small mercy. There was no polished grandeur here, no atmosphere to fuel the seduction that Ariadne Silk clearly intended. If this had been the Orient Express, with its intimate dinner settings and candlelit carriages, he might have been in real trouble. As it was, the stark, no-nonsense nature of the Nightjet was the equivalent of a cold shower—a reminder that this was a mission, not some romantic European getaway.

He lay stretched out on the narrow bed, one arm draped across his forehead, gazing out the window as the French countryside streaked by, the sky above darkening with the onset of dusk. He'd brought along a book, a thriller by the late Nelson DeMille, but was in no mood to read. What he was in the mood for was a tot of Goslings Black Seal, but, alas, the best that the Nightjet's room service could offer was a premixed Jim Beam and Coca-Cola in an aluminum can or a premixed Malfy gin and tonic in a glass bottle. He cursed himself for not having had the foresight to bring along a flask.

When the hand of his stainless steel black-dial Rolex GMT-Master informed him that the dreaded dinner hour had arrived, he rose, splashed some water on his face, and regarded himself in the mirror. Although he was still on the better side of forty, there were a few wisps of gray just beginning to show at his temples—a sprinkle of salt in his pepper. His face and forehead bore the hard lines—and not a few scars—testifying to a life lived on the edge.

Old enough to care, he mused, *but too young to know better.*

Hawke made a conscious decision not to dress for dinner. This wasn't a dinner party; it was an obligation. A necessary evil. He kept telling himself that as he stepped out into the hall, moved down to the door to Ariadne Silk's cabin, and knocked lightly.

Silk *had* dressed for dinner, exchanging her travel clothes for a black dress that clung to her shapely figure without being overly revealing. Her dark hair was down, loose around her shoulders, and the faintest hint of a musky floral perfume hung about her—not overpowering by any means but strong enough to force a hairline crack in his resolve.

"Alex," she said, her voice soft, inviting. "Won't you come in?"

Said the spider to the fly, he thought. *Do be careful, old boy.*

Hawke hesitated for just a moment before stepping inside. The cabin was small, but she had somehow managed to make it feel cozy, intimate even. Two plates of paprika chicken with egg noodles—one of two entrée choices from the room service menu—were arranged on the small table, along with two single-serve bottles of Aperol Spritz. The configuration of the sleeping car was such that the two of them would have to sit side by side rather than across from each other, and Silk took the initiative of sliding across to the seat closest to the wall. Hawke settled in next to her, feeling the warmth of her body, breathing in her scent, his heart and mind screaming at him to resist, while his body responded in a very different way.

Silk picked up her bottled cocktail and raised it in a casual toast. "To rain checks."

Hawke swallowed but took up his bottle, clinked it against hers, and took a sip. The bittersweet aperitif would not have been his first choice, but it was palatable enough. Silk seemed to savor the taste for a long moment, then turned to face him. "Do I make you uncomfortable, Alex?"

Hawke would have choked on his drink had he not already swallowed it. The directness of her question both surprised and discomfited. He considered denying it, brushing the question off with one of a flirtatious quip, but for some reason he felt compelled to answer with the truth.

"As a matter of fact," he said, meeting her gaze directly, "you bloody well do."

She eyed him playfully. "Why is that?"

"Because I know what you're up to," he replied, his voice level. "And it's a terrible idea."

Silk tilted her head, a feigned innocence glinting in her eyes. "What exactly do you think I'm trying to do?"

He chose his words carefully. "You're trying to get close to me. Too close. Given what we're doing . . . where we're going . . . that's a dangerous place to be. For both of us. In this business, you don't mix business with pleasure. Not if you want to stay alive."

It was the truth, but not the whole truth. Were Anastasia not in his life, he most certainly would have answered differently.

"Do you really think it's going to be dangerous?" asked Silk. "Putin needs us to verify the letter from King George. He gains nothing by taking us hostage or . . ." She didn't finish the sentence, as if unwilling to verbalize direr possibilities, and instead scooped up a forkful of noodles.

"If I know Putin . . . and as it happens, I do . . . this business with that letter is a feint. Something to distract us from what he's really up to."

Silk's fork hovered in front of her mouth. "You *know* Vladimir Putin? Personally?"

Hawke took a bite of his dinner, chewing and swallowing before giving his answer. The noodle dish fell well short of gourmet fare but wasn't the worst thing he'd ever eaten. "I do," he said. "He saved my life once."

She looked at him sideways. "I heard you tell the King that he put a price on your head. What happened?"

Hawke thought back to the night he'd spent at the notorious Energetika Prison, a Russian penal facility built on top of a nuclear waste dump. Putin, at the time a political prisoner following the coup staged by Count Ivan Korsakov, had used his underworld contacts to have the bed in his prison cell lined with lead sheeting to protect him from the deadly radioactivity, and Putin, in turn, had extended that protection to Hawke, doubtless saving him from a horrible death. Hawke had indirectly returned the favor by killing Korsakov, thus paving the way for Putin's return to power. For a time, Hawke had even considered him a . . . well, *friend* wasn't the right word, but more than just an acquaintance. However, Putin's quest for world domination had strained that relationship beyond the breaking point. Time and time again, Hawke, as an agent of the Crown, had been obliged to stop Putin's mad schemes, and Putin, in turn, had offered a million-dollar bounty to anyone who could bring him Hawke's head on a platter.

"The short answer is that he's completely mad," replied Hawke. "A mad genius. He wants power, plain and simple. And he doesn't care what it costs. He'd burn the world down if it meant sitting on the ashes as its king."

"So you think we might be walking into a trap?" There was a note of apprehension in her voice.

"If I didn't think that way, I'd probably be dead a hundred times over."

"I never realized . . ." She trailed off, and then suddenly her hand was on his forearm. "Tell me that we're going to make it through this, Alex. Promise me."

Hawke's breath caught in his throat. He felt the heat of her touch on his arm, a tingle of electricity surging into and through him. "There are no guarantees. I can only promise that I will do everything in my power to keep you safe."

Silk's gaze lingered on him, her fingers moving, tracing small, deliberate circles against his skin. She let out a nervous laugh. "I never really thought we'd be in actual danger. It sort of puts everything in perspective, doesn't it?"

"How so?"

Silk's fingers stilled for a moment, her gaze softening as she considered his question. Then, with her free hand, she reached up and removed her eyeglasses, setting them aside and staring directly into his eyes.

The effect was startling. It was not that the glasses somehow made her less lovely and their removal had transformed her into a creature of irresistible beauty. Rather, it was something more symbolic: the removal of a barrier, the lowering of her defenses. Hawke felt his heart stutter in his chest.

"It makes you realize what's important," she said. "When you know that you might die tomorrow, it makes you realize how precious every moment is." Her tone had lowered almost to a whisper. "When you think of it that way, it would be a shame to pass up a chance at . . ." She hesitated, sliding her hand further up his arm. "Happiness."

Some part of him recognized the audacity of her attempted seduction, while another part grasped eagerly at the underlying premise.

After all, why not?

Her hand continued moving higher up his arm, caressing his biceps, her gaze holding his, expectant, and his body responded. Her scent swirled about his head like a fog of opium smoke. Past and future vanished in a haze of immediacy.

Nothing mattered but this moment.

Here . . . now . . .

Her.

The urgency of his need was a raging torrent, sweeping over him, carrying him along, almost drowning out every other consideration.

Almost.

Happiness.

The word flashed through his mind like a beacon, cutting through the fog. What Silk was offering wasn't a chance at happiness. It was a distraction. A moment of pleasure, and thereafter another regret he would take with him to the grave.

He groped for a memory of Anastasia's face, grasping it like a lifeline.

Silk's hand slid still further up his arm, her touch almost burning through the fabric of his shirt, but instead of pulling him in deeper, it startled him with the realization of just how close he had come to the precipice.

He let out a slow breath, steadying himself. "I think it's best if I retire for the night."

Silk blinked, her hand pausing in mid-motion as the unspoken invitation hung in the air between them, unanswered. She tilted her head, studying him. For a moment he wondered if she might push further and wondered if he would be able to say no.

Then she gave an embarrassed laugh, covering her mouth with her hand, and reached for her glasses, sliding them back into place, raising the barrier once more. Her cheeks flushed a delicate shade of pink. "Oh, my. I'm so sorry. You must think I'm terrible."

Her coyness was insincere, her apology as calculated as the rest of her actions, and yet Hawke felt himself being sucked in again. He stood up awkwardly, trying to conceal just how effective her overtures had been. "It's been a long day. I think we're both a bit tired."

"Tired," she repeated softly, as though tasting the word, the eyes behind the lenses flickering with something unreadable. "You're right, of course. Perhaps I got a bit carried away."

Hawke felt some of his equilibrium restored. "Thank you for a lovely evening," he said, turning away. "I'll just see myself out."

He grasped the door handle, opened it, and stepped out into the hall. Before he could close it between them, however, Silk was there.

"Oh, Alex?"

He paused but didn't look back. "Yes?"

"Rain check?" She gave a nervous titter. "Did I get that right?"

"Good night, Ariadne," he said, and pulled the door shut firmly behind him.

A moment later Hawke slipped into his cabin, closing the door with more force than intended, and sagged against it, letting out a long, slow breath as the emotional wave he had been riding finally crashed down upon him. His pulse was racing, his skin still tingling where Silk's hand had touched him.

He'd barely said no—barely held himself back from letting it go too far. His resolve felt thin, frayed, and he knew, with sickening certainty, that if she had pressed just a little harder, asked just one more time, he would not have been able to refuse her.

"Damn it all," he whispered. "I need a bloody drink."

He stood there, eyes closed, clinging to the idea that he had made the right decision, but temptation lingered like an aftertaste. His body ached with unfulfilled desire, and the emotional battle to keep it in check had left him drained.

Then the thing he dreaded most happened: a knock at his door.

His heart lurched in his chest.

The rational self—Dr. Freud's superego, the angel perched on one shoulder—begged him to ignore it, while the devil id demanded he answer. Every fiber of his physical being tingled with anticipation.

He turned slowly, his hand already reaching for the knob.

What would he say?

He didn't know, but he couldn't stop himself. His fingers wrapped around the cold metal, and he pulled the door open.

It wasn't Silk.

A hulking figure in a leather trench coat loomed in the doorway. Hawke had barely a moment to register the man's face before a gleam of steel flashed in his peripheral vision.

TWENTY-ONE

The attack itself was a blur. The blade stabbed forward like a laser-guided missile, locked on, arrowing straight at Hawke's unprotected throat.

Instinct, honed over years of training and combat, took over.

Hawke's first reaction wasn't to leap or duck. Instead, his right hand shot out, catching the assassin's wrist mid-thrust, turning the knife just enough to prevent a killing blow. Even so, the blade grazed his collar, snagging the fabric and pulling the edge dangerously close to the side of his neck.

Time seemed to freeze as Hawke stared deep into the eyes of his attacker. They were cold, calculating, and dead inside. This was someone for whom taking the life of another person was no more consequential than swatting a fly. He was a professional.

An assassin.

But who had sent him? Putin? The Warmonger? Or had one of his many other enemies decided now was the time to collect on old debts?

Who was a question that could wait. All that mattered at the moment was survival.

The assassin recovered with unexpected quickness, planting his forefoot, shifting and pulling the knife arm free from Hawke's grip, but with the element of surprise no longer a factor, the next move was Hawke's. He lashed out with his foot, connecting with the man's knee in a vicious kick that sent the attacker staggering back through the doorframe. But before Hawke could follow up, the man was moving again, heaving himself inside the cramped space, slashing the air before him with the blade to both intimidate and drive Hawke back until there was nowhere for him to go. Hawke's mind raced, calculating the dimensions, the limitations, the angles of attack, as he watched the blade in his peripheral vision, keeping his focus on the man's eyes, looking for the subtle cues that would telegraph his next attack.

Unfortunately, the knife gave the advantage to the assassin.

When Hawke had trained with the Special Boat Service, one of his close-quarters battle instructors told him, "In a knife fight, expect to get cut." While using one's forearm to deflect or stop a slash was better than letting the blade inside your defenses, there was no acceptable place on the body to be cut or stabbed. A sliced tendon could end a fight almost as quickly as a thrust through the heart. But as the blade wielder drove him back against the wall, Hawke knew if he couldn't find something to use as a shield, he would have to sacrifice flesh and blood in order to save his skin.

At the apex of each slash, the fleeting pause before the blade reversed to cut back the other way allowed Hawke to identify the weapon: a Melita-K Karatele. The distinctive six-and-a-half-inch-long, double-edged, leaf-shaped blade, with a deep blood groove running down the center, was a favorite of the Spetsnaz—Russian special forces—which, oddly enough, did little to illuminate the mystery of the assassin's affiliation.

He saw the man's dead eyes shift ever so slightly downward, fixing on his lower torso. A memory of a similar struggle flashed through Hawke's mind: another blade-wielding assassin named Smith had once gotten through Hawke's defenses and literally gutted him, leaving him for dead.

Not this bloody time.

Hawke looked around frantically for something to use to deflect the blade, but anything solid enough to be of use was bolted down. His suitcase was out of reach. There was a stack of towels near the basin . . . Was there time to wrap one of them around his forearm for an added layer of protection? Then his gaze lit on a Nelson DeMille novel, its title blazing in red block print like a twisted prophecy.

The blade angled again, the assassin's aim shifting toward Hawke's midsection, intent on opening him up. Hawke snatched the novel from the table, swinging it up just as the knife slashed toward him.

He felt the collision shudder up his arm. The razor-sharp edge sliced into the hard chipboard cover and bound paper but got no deeper than half an inch before the force behind the slash was spent.

The assassin recovered quickly, but so did Hawke, and as the assassin drove the point straight at him, trying to ram the blade past his pitiful defenses, Hawke took the novel in both hands, opening it as he brought it up, and then slammed it shut with the knife caught between the pages like a bookmark.

The man grunted, struggling to wrench his weapon free for another attack, but Hawke moved faster. With the book held firmly shut, he pivoted into the assassin's reach, driving his shoulder into the man's sternum, and in the same motion twisted the book and the blade trapped inside it, tearing the knife from the assassin's grip. Then, before his assailant could recover, Hawke drove an elbow into his throat. The man stumbled back, gasping for breath, but Hawke wasn't done. Tossing the book aside, he leapt at the man, wrapping one arm around his throat and locking him up in a choke hold.

The assassin, realizing what was happening, tried to struggle free but was unable to draw breath past his crushed windpipe, and with Hawke's forearm and biceps squeezing against his carotid arteries, cutting off the flow of blood to his brain, his odds of escaping were slim.

Or they would have been if not for one thing that Hawke had not taken into account.

The assassin had a partner.

TWENTY-TWO

Hawke heard the muted snap of a pistol shot, the sound of which was almost swallowed by the surrounding rumble of the train. No earsplitting crack—just the mechanical click of the slide blowing back and cycling forward, followed almost instantaneously by the sharp *thunk* of the bullet embedding itself in the wooden panel almost directly behind him. The unmistakable acrid scent of burnt gunpowder filled the compartment.

A miss, but too bloody close for comfort.

He reacted without thinking, again letting his instincts guide him as he twisted around so that the nearly unconscious body of the first assassin was between him and the man standing in the doorway of the compartment, aiming a pistol directly at him.

The pistol snapped again, but this time there was no sound of the round hitting something solid. Instead, Hawke felt a shudder pass through the body of his first assailant. The bullet had indeed found a flesh-and-blood target all right, just not the one intended.

The eyes of the gunman widened in alarm as he realized his mistake, giving Hawke one more precious moment in which to consider how best to meet this new threat.

He glanced at the fallen book, with the combat knife still caught between its pages, lying on the floor just a few feet away and, without releasing his choke hold, leaned sideways, grabbed the novel with his free hand, and hurled it at the gunman.

As the makeshift missile flew through the air, the knife and book separated. The book clipped the assassin's shoulder, bouncing off with little effect, but the heavier blade hit lower, connecting squarely with the suppressed pistol, then caroming away to strike the man in the chest. The hilt slammed into the gunman's breastbone, the force behind the throw insufficient to do any real damage, but the man nevertheless sprang back in surprise, dropping the pistol and clutching his now-empty gun hand to his chest in a primal response to injury. Bright drops of blood, like a rain of rubies, fell around him.

Surprise flickered across the man's face, morphing into something more like dismay at the realization that he was now unarmed. Hawke seized the moment, thrusting the now-unmoving first assassin away and launching himself at the gunman. Still off-balance, his weapon gone, the latter staggered into the corridor, out of Hawke's reach; then, evidently realizing that he had lost any advantage, he spun on his heel and took off running.

Hawke's leap took him through the doorway and into the corridor. He scooped up the fallen pistol—a Makarov equipped with a suppressor that more than doubled its length—and brought it up quickly, sighting on the back of the retreating assassin. His instincts screamed at him to take the shot, kill the man who had tried to kill him, but no: he needed this man alive . . .

You need him to find out who sent him, Hawke told himself.

At the far end of the car, the man reached the exit door and passed through.

Damn it.

Lowering the pistol, Hawke gave chase.

Reaching the end of the car, he stepped into the accordion-like vestibule that connected the carriages. The noise of the train's wheels clattering along the rails was louder here, the wind whipping through small gaps around the pleated walls, which shifted slightly as the train moved along the tracks. The floor swayed beneath him, but the flexible walls and deck protected him from both the elements and any risk of falling between the cars. Hawke grabbed the cold metal handle of the door to the next carriage, yanked it open, and swept inside, wary of an ambush.

He found himself in another sleeper car and spotted the assassin, still running, approaching the far end of the corridor, leaving a long trail of bright red drops on the floor. Hawke kept going.

The next door opened into a couchette car, a more economical option for travelers, consisting of shared compartments with four to six padded bunks arranged along the walls and equipped with basic bedding, which could be folded up into seats during daylight hours. A few of the compartments had their privacy curtains drawn, but many more were open, the passengers receiving their food service deliveries from train attendants. The assassin barreled through their midst, jostling attendants and passengers alike, leaving a trail of shocked expressions and scattered food trays in his wake. Hawke deftly wove through the resulting mayhem, the passengers and attendants shrinking back at the sight of the pistol in his hand.

Ahead, the assassin reached the far end of the car, slammed into the door leading out of the couchette car, and stumbled through. Hawke was there within seconds, hastening through the articulated passage and into another sleeper car.

The corridor stretched ahead of him, empty.

Hawke skidded to a stop. Something wasn't right. The fleeing assassin could not possibly have traversed the corridor to the next carriage in the brief interval that he had been out of Hawke's view. So where was he? Had he forced his way inside one of the private cabins, hoping to hide out?

Hawke dropped his gaze to the deck, looking for the telltale trail of blood drops. That was when he became aware of a shrill, persistent wail. It had barely registered at first, so focused was he on the chase, but as the fog of war cleared, the noise seemed to grow louder, more insistent.

An alarm.

He looked around for the source and realized that the window almost immediately to his right was marked as an emergency exit. And there, on its handle, was a smear of red.

Hawke could not fathom what might have possessed the assassin to leave the relative safety of the train's interior. In the great wide open, between urban centers, the Nightjet trains cruised along somewhere in the neighborhood of 140 miles per hour. Jumping from a train at that speed was certain death. Russian operatives—and there was little doubt in Hawke's mind that the assassins could be classified as such—were not suicidal.

So, what did the man hope to accomplish by exiting through the window?

A moment later Hawke felt a slight but unmistakable shift in his center of gravity. The train was slowing.

A soft chime sounded, and then a calm but firm voice issued from an unseen speaker:

"Mesdames et messieurs, en raison d'une alarme d'urgence, nous ralentissons le train pour une inspection. Merci de rester dans vos cabines." There was a brief pause, then the same voice spoke again, this time in English. "Ladies and gentlemen, due to an emergency alarm, the train is slowing down for inspection. Please remain in your compartments."

Hawke's eyes narrowed. The crew was aware of the alarm and likely believed it was a simple malfunction, but until they could be certain that no passengers were at risk, they would decelerate, possibly even bringing the train to a complete stop.

Now Hawke understood the assassin's plan. He wasn't going to leap from the train at full speed. He would wait until it slowed enough for him to safely drop onto the tracks and disappear into the French countryside.

Well, that's just not going to happen.

Hawke yanked the emergency exit window open, and a gust of wind blasted into the cabin. Cold air whipped through the narrow space, slapping against his face as the train's velocity surged through the open window. Squinting against the chilly blast, Hawke thrust his head out into the night. He half expected to see the assassin hanging on just below the window, clinging to the side of the train as it slowed, but there was no sign of the man. Given the ferocious wind, it would have required superhuman strength to hold on even for a few seconds, and the assassin would surely have realized this when he made his escape bid.

There was really only one place for him to take refuge.

The roof.

Hawke shoved the silenced Makarov into his belt and then grabbed the edge of the window frame with both hands. The cold metal stung his bare skin, and as he pushed head and shoulders through the opening, the wind tore at him, pressing against him, threatening to rip him away from the safety of the train. His legs were still inside the car, anchoring him in place, but to reach the rooftop, he would have to sacrifice that connection. Risk everything. One wrong move—one slip—and he would become a bloody smear along the track bed.

Everything told Hawke not to pursue.

But what else could he do? The train was slowing, and the assassin would escape if he didn't commit. He gritted his teeth, thrust his doubts aside, and went for it, heaving himself through. The wind buffeted him, trying to peel him away as he wedged his knees against the window frame and reached up to grab the lip of the roof. His fingers found the cold metal, slick from condensation and the evening chill, but he held firm. Then, when his feet were on the window frame, he flexed his legs and propelled himself upward.

The blast of wind nearly took him, sweeping his legs and lower torso sideways in an arc, but he clung tenaciously to the thin metal lip and swung up onto the aerodynamically curved expanse of aluminum that was the roof of the train car. As he landed, he pressed himself flat, spreading his arms and legs out to get as much contact with the surface as possible. The metal was ice-cold underneath him, the wind an arctic blast ripping across his back. For a moment, all he could do was hold on, amazed to still be alive but afraid to move lest even the slightest adjustment break the tenuous adhesion holding him in place.

Then he risked raising his head, peering through slitted eyelids, and began looking for the assassin . . .

. . . and saw a flash of movement in the darkness. The sole of a boot hurtling toward him.

There was no time to think. Reflexes took over. Hawke jerked his head to the side but wasn't quick enough. The edge of the assassin's foot grazed his temple, sending a sharp jolt of pain through his skull. The blow was glancing, but it was enough to disorient him.

The assassin kicked again, this time aiming at the hand that still gripped the narrow lip at the edge of the roof. Hawke let go, barely managing to get his fingers out of the way before the man's heel shot past, and felt himself starting to slip. Desperate, he slapped his palms flat against the metal, willing them to stick like gecko feet—and, miraculously, they did.

His slide had taken him beyond the reach of the assassin's kicks, but he could sense the man shifting position, trying to get close enough for another try. Hawke thought about going for the pistol from his belt but just as quickly rejected the idea. Even if he could get the weapon and fire it—a big *if*, given the circumstances—he needed the assassin alive.

The assassin kicked again, harder this time, a solid hit to Hawke's forearm, and then, just like that, Hawke was sliding backward, the wind peeling him from his precarious perch. He felt a surge of panic as the cold aluminum slipped away beneath him. He slapped his palms down again—pressed the soles of his shoes against the metal—but nothing worked. He kept sliding and then felt the hard surface fall away as first his legs and then the rest of him shot out over the back end of the train car.

Then, mercifully, his fall was arrested as he landed atop the accordion pleats of the vestibule connecting the train cars. He grabbed onto the ridges, clutching at them desperately, even though he was now in a much better position than he had been in moments ago.

But the assassin wasn't finished with him. Hawke saw the man repositioning himself, scuttling along the top of the roof toward him, intent on ending the fight. Ending his *life*.

The man moved deliberately, staying low to avoid the full force of the wind. He wasn't going to risk anything reckless—not on this unforgiving surface. As Hawke watched, unable to go on the offensive, the assassin slid down onto the vestibule and then got in a seated position with his feet pointing in Hawke's direction. His plan was clear. He was going to literally kick Hawke off the train.

Hawke gripped the metal ribs of the vestibule tightly, bracing for the inevitable attack. The kick was low, aimed at his right hand. At the last instant, Hawke slid his fingers to the side, evading the boot sole, which struck the metal frame instead. Then, before the man could draw back his leg for another strike, Hawke let go and dropped his arm around the extended foot, trapping it against his own body.

For a moment, neither man moved. The assassin, realizing his mistake, tried to pull his leg free. Hawke tightened his grip, both on the assassin's foot and the metal rib of the vestibule.

He knew the train had slowed considerably and could feel it in the relenting wind. How fast were they moving now? Seventy miles an hour? Still too fast, but if he could just hold the assassin a little while longer . . . Thirty more seconds . . . a minute, maybe . . . and he might have a chance to end this without getting them both killed.

The assassin, however, had no intention of complying. The man began to panic and then started kicking wildly, trying to push himself away from Hawke, and inadvertently shifted his weight too far to the side.

"Don't do it!" Hawke shouted, but his warning came too late. The assassin had already fallen over the side and was now dragging Hawke along with him.

There was only one thing Hawke could do.

He let go.

Less than a second later the assassin's scream was swallowed by the wind and his body was claimed by the darkness.

INTERLUDE—PART SIX

EN ROUTE TO MINSK, BELARUSIAN PEOPLE'S REPUBLIC
APRIL 1918

The next four days were spent in a perpetual state of anxious tedium, confronting one life-threatening challenge after another.

The first test came at the German checkpoint as they rounded a bend in the road on the way to the village Luc had mentioned. The German soldiers eyed the two foot-travelers warily as they approached, and while their Red Cross documents, meticulously forged by Viktor, seemed to pass initial scrutiny, Alexander felt the officer's eyes linger on him a moment too long.

"Sind Sie Schweizer?" ("Are you Swiss?"), the officer asked, his tone skeptical.

"Geboren in Zürich" ("Born in Zurich"), Natalya said smoothly in flawless German, before gesturing at Alexander. *"Mein Kollege kommt aus Genf. Sein Deutsch ist schlecht—er spricht hauptsächlich Französisch."* ("My colleague is from Geneva. His German is poor—he speaks mostly French.")

Alexander, who understood only a smattering of German, gave a half-hearted shrug and what he hoped was a suitably sheepish expression. He forced himself to remain still as the officer inspected his papers, his pulse hammering in his ears.

Finally, the soldier gave a grunt of disinterest and waved them through. In Ham, they found Mathieu and hired him to take them on to Saint-Quentin, where they were able to board a train to Cologne. They endured countless document checks and the inscrutable stare of soldiers manning checkpoints as they moved deeper into German-controlled territory. Each stop along the way led to another nerve-racking inspection of their forged documents.

The inspections became less rigorous once they crossed into Germany, but Alexander did not allow himself to lapse into complacency. Crammed into crowded carriages, shoulder to shoulder with German soldiers and wary civilians, they were always one errant glance away from being unmasked.

There was little opportunity for them to explore the connection forged in those fleeting hours back in the barn, where they had held each other for warmth against the night's chill. The cramped train compartments, the wary eyes of soldiers, and the relentless push forward left no space for whispered conversations, much less lingering touches.

Alexander knew he should be grateful to be spared the temptation, but instead he felt only anguish, a gnawing ache at what was being denied him. Every fleeting glance from Natalya, every subtle brush of her hand as they passed through crowded stations, sent a thrill of longing through him. And he knew, as only a man can know, that she felt it too. He told himself it was merely the intensity of their shared peril drawing them closer, but with every mile they traveled, it became harder to believe.

Once beyond Warsaw, their journey turned rougher. Eastern Poland and the Belarusian People's Republic had seen more than their share of conflict during the war, caught between German and Russian forces during the earlier campaigns of the Eastern Front. Now, with the recently signed Treaty of Brest-Litovsk, the Belarusian People's Republic lay in a precarious state. The treaty had ceded control of the region to Germany, but the lines of occupation were tenuous at best as the Bolsheviks worked to consolidate their hold on the territories beyond. As always, it was the local population that suffered, enduring the privations of military occupation and the uncertainties of political upheaval.

Train service in the Belarusian People's Republic was unreliable at best, with locomotives often commandeered for military use or delayed by damaged infrastructure. At one point Alexander and Natalya found themselves stranded at a small rural station and were obliged to hire a farmer to drive them the rest of the way to Minsk in his horse-drawn wagon.

It was nearly dusk when the farmer halted his cart near a narrow bridge over the Svislach River on the outskirts of the city.

"This is as far as he will go," Natalya said, translating his Russian and nodding to the military checkpoint manned by German soldiers.

The farmer rolled away back down the road, and Alexander and Natalya went up to the checkpoint and presented their travel-worn Red Cross credentials.

Minsk bore the unmistakable scars of recent conflict.

As they made their way into the city, Alexander could not help but be struck by the randomness of the destruction. Unlike the uniform devastation of the countryside, the damage here bore the hallmarks of artillery's capricious hand. Entire streets seemed untouched, their buildings standing with shutters intact and laundry lines swaying in the breeze. Yet, a single block over, rubble spilled onto the cobblestones, broken walls standing as grim monuments to the indiscriminate chaos of war. A church steeple leaned precariously over the street, its bell cracked and silent, while a nearby tenement building showed only spiderweb fractures in its masonry.

They were within sight of the train station—like every other one they had visited, a focus of military activity—when a voice called out from an alley.

"Natalya!"

Alexander's blood turned to ice. At no time since leaving Calais had he felt so exposed. They had been careful—meticulously so. Traveling under aliases, speaking only when necessary, avoiding unnecessary attention. He instinctively stepped closer to her, one hand out as if to shield her. But then, to his further astonishment, Natalya turned toward the alley, her head cocked to the side in confusion. "Viktor? What on earth are you doing here?"

A figure emerged from the shadows of the alley, stepping out just far enough for Alexander to confirm Natalya's identification of her comrade.

Alarm gave way to confusion. *Viktor? Here?*

"How are you here, Viktor?" Natalya pressed. "How did you overtake us?"

It was not the question foremost in Alexander's mind. He was more concerned with *why.*

Viktor's answer, when it came, was in Russian, but then he switched to French. "We must talk. But not out in the open. Please, follow me."

Natalya threw a questioning glance at Alexander, who shook his head. His instincts told him that something was very wrong about this. But, much to his consternation, she turned and headed into the alley. Alexander breathed a curse and then went after her.

Viktor moved deeper into the alley, where the fading twilight could not reach, before turning to address Natalya. "After you left, I wired Moscow to inquire about your mission."

"You had no cause to do that," countered Natalya angrily.

Viktor ignored her. "Comrade Dzerzhinsky was very curious to know why you intended to travel through occupied France when your mission was to negotiate with the British king for the lives of the Tsar and his family. He made inquiries and learned who it is that accompanies you."

The name hit Alexander like a shot. He had read of Felix Dzerzhinsky—the man known as "Iron Felix"—in naval intelligence reports. Ruthless even by revolutionary standards, Dzerzhinsky had been a key figure in the Bolsheviks' rise to power, and now, as head of the Cheka—the new Russian secret police and spy agency—he wielded terror as a weapon to root out enemies of the Revolution. Viktor's affiliation with the Cheka explained how he had managed to reach Minsk ahead of them. The resources at the Cheka's disposal—couriers, commandeered transport, informants—would have allowed him to move faster and more effectively than they could ever hope to.

"You've overstepped your authority," said Natalya. "And you are interfering with the business of the Revolution."

Viktor shook his head. "I was sent by the Revolution—Iron Felix himself—to intercept you and take possession of the letter with the King's reply."

"I'll hand the letter, with the seal intact, to Yakob Sverdlov in Moscow," declared Alexander. "Until then, it stays with me."

"Ah, he speaks." Viktor stared at Alexander for a long moment, then turned to Natalya. "You must convince him to give us the letter. If you cannot, I will."

"I don't take orders from Iron Felix," declared Natalya. "The letter stays with Sasha"—she shook her head—"with Lord Hawke—"

"*Lord* Hawke? You choose loyalty to a British aristocrat over the Revolution?"

"Don't speak to me of the Revolution," she hissed. "Dzerzhinsky is thinking only of himself. How he can use this letter to his own advantage."

Viktor's expression darkened. "Be careful, Natalya. It is unwise to defy Comrade Dzerzhinsky." His gaze shifted to Alexander. "Give me the letter."

Alexander folded his arms over his chest. "The letter stays with me until we reach Moscow."

Viktor's face hardened, and then, with the swiftness of a striking adder, he drew a knife from under his coat.

Natalya gasped, her voice sharp with alarm. "Viktor, no!"

But Viktor was already moving, thrusting the blade at Alexander's chest. Alexander just managed to twist away, feeling the point of the knife snag the heavy fabric of his coat. Before Viktor could draw back for another strike, Alexander seized his wrist and began twisting his arm. Viktor let out a wail of pain as his fingers involuntarily opened, the knife hilt slipping from his grasp to clatter on the cobblestones.

But Viktor wasn't beaten. Unable to wrestle free of Alexander's iron grip, he leaned into his opponent and tried to drive his knee into Alexander's groin. He missed his target but landed a painful blow to Alexander's thigh. The impact caused them both to fall back against a wall and loosened Alexander's grip just enough to ease the pressure on Viktor's captured arm, which in turn allowed him to throw a punch at Alexander's face. The punch landed, and Alexander saw a flash of stars, but he had taken much harder hits learning pugilism at Eton and Dartmouth and knew how to shrug them off. With his right hand still clamped on Viktor's wrist, he countered with a left jab.

Viktor grunted as Alexander's fist hammered into his ribs but recovered quickly, clawing at Alexander's face with his free hand. His attack was wild, unskilled, but nonetheless effective, forcing Alexander to flinch away and giving Viktor an opening to sweep Alexander's legs out from under him. Alexander felt his footing give way, and they went down together, crashing onto the hard stone.

The impact drove the air from Alexander's lungs, but he clung to Viktor's arm, twisting it further and forcing another anguished cry from the Chekist. Viktor's free hand groped along the ground, his fingers seeking the fallen knife, which gleamed faintly a few feet away.

Realizing Viktor's intent, Alexander rolled over on top of his foe, pinning the man's torso beneath his own, and landed another blow—this one square to Viktor's jaw. The force of it sent Viktor's head snapping back against the ground. He slumped, momentarily dazed.

Alexander seized the moment to flip Viktor over and then wrapped an arm around the man's neck and squeezed. Viktor, realizing what Alexander meant to do, began thrashing and bucking, clawing frantically at Alexander's arm to loosen the choke hold, but Alexander did not relent. After only a few moments, the fight went out of Viktor, and he slumped unconscious. Alexander held on a moment longer, his heart pounding and his breath coming in sharp bursts. Then, just as he was about to release his hold, Natalya crouched down beside him and began thrusting the fallen knife into Viktor's chest, stabbing him half a dozen times in the space of a single heartbeat.

The suddenness of her attack shocked Alexander, and he reflexively scrabbled backward as if afraid that he might be her next target.

"Natalya," he gasped, barely able to find his voice. "What have you done?"

She was still hunched over Viktor, her hands on the hilt of the knife now buried deep in the Chekist's torso, her shoulders rising and falling as she struggled to get her breathing under control.

"What had to be done," she finally managed to say. She wiped the blood on her hands on Viktor's trouser leg, then looked back at Alexander. "This is not time for your chivalry, Sasha. If we had let him live, he would have immediately reported to Dzerzhinsky. We would have been caught before the next train stopped."

Alexander knew she was right, but that didn't erase the horror of what he had just witnessed. He had killed before, sent perhaps hundreds of men to a watery grave with a spoken order, but this was different. This was up close and personal.

And Natalya had done it.

He finally exhaled, the tension draining from his shoulders. "You're right, of course," he said, his voice low. "I just—" He stopped, searching for words. "This can't have been easy for you."

Natalya's composure faltered for a moment, her expression softening. "No," she admitted. "It wasn't."

Alexander stood, extended a hand to lift her up, and then put his arms around her. She stiffened at first, then leaned into him, her hands clutching the lapels of his coat. As he held her, it occurred to him that, in killing Viktor, Natalya had made a choice to put Alexander's mission ahead of her duty to the Revolution.

And that was no small thing.

TWENTY-THREE

LONDON
PRESENT DAY

Congreve's arrival at New Scotland Yard felt like a homecoming, even if the building itself wasn't the one he'd spent most of his career working from.

This new address on the Victoria Embankment—a stone-fronted structure in the Stripped Classical style overlooking the Thames and looking at the London Eye . . . well, right in the eye—was, at first glance, quite a step down from the twenty-story rectangular prism at 10 Broadway where Congreve had worked his way up through the ranks, eventually presiding over the entire service. That impressive tower was gone now, razed to make way for a new development, while the police service, a slimmed-down, more efficient version of itself, moved to a smaller building better suited to the evolving needs of a twenty-first-century police force.

However, one thing remained unchanged.

It was still, and always would be, Scotland Yard.

The name had been part of London's policing heritage for nearly two centuries and had come to refer not just to a location but to the institution of policing itself. The roots of Scotland Yard went back to 1829, when Sir Robert Peel, then Home Secretary, created the Metropolitan

Police Service through the Metropolitan Police Act. Peel's vision was revolutionary: a centrally organized, professional, and uniformed police force whose main function was to prevent crime rather than merely just react to it. His new uniformed police officers were called "Bobbies" or "Peelers" in his honor. The headquarters for this new endeavor was a converted residence at 4 Whitehall Place, which backed onto a street called Great Scotland Yard. The name stuck, and when, in 1888, the force moved into its new headquarters on the Victoria Embankment—actually next door to the current location—the building was officially christened "New Scotland Yard." In 1967, the name followed the force to its next location in the gleaming mirrored tower at 10 Broadway and subsequently went back to the Victoria Embankment fifty years later.

Congreve had visited the new location many times on official business in the years since his retirement, so he did not need to be shown the way to the offices housing the Homicide and Major Crime Command—HMCC. The young constable who had picked him up from Heathrow, however, seemed to think he needed an escort befitting his celebrity status, and Congreve was too tired to raise a fuss.

Following his bombshell revelation that the two murders, though separated by a vast distance, might be connected, Congreve had been going nonstop. Since the Metropolitan Police had considerably more resources at their disposal, the decision was made to transfer jurisdiction to Scotland Yard, and Congreve was invited there to consult.

Diana, ever his partner in more ways than one, had insisted on accompanying him. "It's not often that I get to watch that magnificent mind of yours at work," she'd said with a mischievous smile as she began packing for the trip. "Besides, someone needs to remind you to take your meals. You do tend to forget those important little details when you're on a case."

As he could not disagree, he had left off trying to talk her out of going.

They had spent much of the transatlantic flight poring over the case documents. Congreve had brought hard copies—everything he could fit into his carry-on—and spread the files across the fold-down tray between them. But whereas he meticulously cataloged the details—the lack of forced entry, the precision of the strangulations, the locked door at each scene—Diana turned her attention to the subtler human elements.

She had pointed to one of the crime scene photographs showing a pair of wineglasses, one still half full. "You've looked at this a hundred times, haven't you?" she asked, tapping the image.

Congreve had glanced at it briefly. "No need." He tapped a finger to his temple. "You will remember, my dear. I have a photographic memory."

She had flipped the photograph over. "Then tell me what you see."

Congreve had smiled around his unlit briar pipe. "Two wineglasses. One full, one half empty. Positioned carefully on the coffee table. A bottle of very expensive Château Pichon Baron, the label facing away. It's all very neat. Too neat. Classic staging. It's meant to suggest intimacy—a shared moment between the victim and their killer. But that's all it is: a lie."

Diana had studied him for a moment, then lifted a corner of the photograph, peeking at it like a poker player checking their hole card. "Are you certain of that?"

"Of course. There's no evidence that the victim drank from either glass. No fingerprints left behind. It's theater. A deception. The killer's way of muddying the waters, steering us down the wrong path."

She had tilted her head to the side thoughtfully. "Then why stage it at all? If the goal is to mislead, why go to the trouble? Why not simply leave no trace?"

Congreve had frowned. "A clever killer knows the absence of evidence can raise its own suspicions. Staging an intimate scene like this one creates a plausible narrative. It gives the police a false direction to pursue."

"Then why this narrative? Why the expensive wine? Why the implication of closeness? What's he trying to say?"

Congreve was inclined to dismiss her line of reasoning. The staging was a diversion; he was certain of that. Nevertheless, he valued his wife's insights. "What do *you* suppose he's trying to say?"

She had laughed her delightful laugh. "Why, Ambrose, I have no idea. I'm not . . . what is it Alex likes to call you? Scotland Yard's 'weapon of mass deduction.' But mark my words. This"—she tapped the photograph—"this is a window into the killer's soul. When you figure out why he leaves this . . . this signature, you'll be that much closer to solving the case."

Congreve had shaken his head slowly, admiration and frustration warring within him. "You're maddeningly good at this, you know."

"Only because you taught me well," she had teased. "Now, promise me you won't stay at the office too late tonight. Heart's Ease Cottage is such a lonely place when you're not there."

He had pondered over her insights during the balance of the flight. *"A window into the killer's soul."* She was right, of course, but, for the moment, the blinds were drawn. He could only hope that the detectives in London would shed some light on the subject. When the plane landed at Heathrow. Diana went on ahead to the cottage in Hampstead Heath while Congreve proceeded directly to New Scotland Yard. Now, as the constable escorting him chatted cheerfully about his past accomplishments, Congreve's mind was far away, turning over Diana's observations.

In the HMCC office, he was met by Detective Chief Inspector Gerald Whitaker. Back when Congreve had been running the show, Whitaker had been a young DI. Now he was leading the MIT—Major Investigative Team—assigned to investigate both murders.

"Good to see you again, Chief Inspector," Whitaker said. "Wish it were under better circumstances."

"In our line, the circumstances rarely are," replied Congreve, accepting Whitaker's handshake. He looked over the DCI's shoulder to the large smart board on the wall—a digital version of an old-fashioned "murder board"—where crime scene photos and other evidence were displayed on several large high-def screens. "I see you've been busy."

Whitaker nodded. "Not much to show for it yet, I'm afraid." He gestured to the screens. "Two victims, both strangled, both without a hint of struggle or forced entry. You know about Ms. Smith in Bermuda. And here we have Samantha Knowles. Worked in an art gallery. She was strangled, just like your victim. Her body was found in her flat, door locked from the inside. No witnesses, no sign of anyone coming or going. Nothing useful from CCTV cameras in the neighborhood. The killer walked in and out without anyone noticing."

Congreve gave a thoughtful hum. "Sounds like we're looking for a bloody ghost."

"We're interviewing family and known associates as a matter of routine, but we're focusing our attention on people the two women might have had in common."

"Exactly what I would have done," said Congreve. "And has this effort produced any leads?"

"As you know, both women attended Newnham College, so they had quite a few mutual acquaintances there. We're in the process of talking to those women, trying to refine the list." Whitaker pursed his lips for a moment. "There is one other . . . avenue we're exploring."

Congreve raised an eyebrow. "Well, spit it out, man."

"We ran the details of both murders—particularly the method—against the database, looking for any known patterns. You know how it goes: cross-referencing similar cases to see if anything flags up. At first, nothing. But then, once we dug deeper into the MO—the precise nature of the strangulations, no sign of forced entry or struggle—it triggered a hit."

"Go on."

Whitaker gestured to a screen at the far end of the wall, which was cycling through case reports that appeared to have nothing to do with Marian Smith or Samantha Knowles. "The computer flagged several cases—high-profile murders—with similar characteristics. Not just here, mind you, but in multiple countries. Moscow, Berlin, even as far as Buenos Aires. Always strangulation, clean, quiet, no struggle. And no evidence left behind. The murders have been attributed to a contract killer who goes by the name 'Silence.'"

Congreve gave the other man a hard stare. "Why on earth would a contract killer go after these two young women?"

Whitaker spread his hands. "I'll admit, it's a bit of a reach at first blush. Silence usually goes after high-value targets: politicians, CEOs, intelligence officers. These two don't exactly fit the profile."

Congreve hummed. "How certain are we that Silence is behind these murders?"

"When we look at the incidents separately . . . not very. Strangulation isn't exactly uncommon. But once we linked the two cases—same MO, no forced entry, no signs of struggle—the probability that Silence is the killer increases significantly. The precision, the lack of traceable evidence—it's textbook Silence. Whoever did this knew exactly what they were doing. If it isn't Silence, it's someone trying very hard to copy the method."

Congreve took out his pipe, idly puffing on the stem even though the bowl was empty, as he considered this latest wrinkle. After a moment he spoke. "Let's assume that Silence is responsible. Our victims don't fit the usual target profile. Which means . . ." He paused, his brow furrowed in thought.

Whitaker remained silent, sensing Congreve was on the verge of a breakthrough.

Congreve's eyes suddenly sharpened. "You are familiar, no doubt, with the quote from Conan Doyle: 'When you have eliminated the impossible, whatever remains, however improbable, must be the truth.'"

Whitaker nodded. "Sherlock Holmes."

"'The Sign of the Four.'" Congreve hmm'd. "If we accept that Silence is the killer, then the idea that these women were of little importance in some grand scheme is impossible. They were chosen quite deliberately, and when we determine what it is that made them so important, we will have our killer."

"Maybe these women were part of something—or knew someone—important and didn't even realize it."

Congreve's eyes narrowed as he studied the faces of the victims. "Or perhaps the killer wasn't targeting them . . . directly."

"You think they were collateral?" Whitaker asked.

"It's possible," Congreve muttered. "If we knew what connected them, we might have a better idea of what this assassin is really after."

"We're already interviewing friends and family of the victims—"

"We shall have to interview them all again," declared Congreve. "But this time we shall have different questions for them."

At that moment a young detective clutching a notepad hurried over to them. "Sorry to interrupt, sirs," he said, nodding to Whitaker, "but I think we've found something."

Whitaker straightened. "Go on."

"Both victims had another mutual acquaintance—a college friend who stayed in close touch with both of them."

"Aha!" cried Congreve. "Now we're getting somewhere."

"Do you suspect her?" asked Whitaker.

"If she is not our suspect, then she might very well be our next victim. Either way, we need to bring her in."

"That may be a bit of a problem," said the young detective. "She's out of the country on business." Then, as if confiding a secret, added, "For the Crown."

Congreve's eyebrows shot up. "For the Crown, you say?"

"Yes, sir. She works for the Royal Archivist. Some sort of expert on historical documents. Her name is . . ." He consulted his notepad and then looked at both men. "Dr. Ariadne Silk."

TWENTY-FOUR

ANKARA, TURKEY

The NATO planning session had ended, predictably, without any clear results. Government representatives had returned home to consult with their administrations, leaving NATO's military attachés in Brussels spinning their wheels, awaiting guidance. Commander Savannah Stone, however, wasn't one to sit idly by—not with the fate of the world on the line.

Osman Gul's threat to act unilaterally against Russia stayed with her long after the politicians had departed. The Turkish general's words had been calculated, laced with just enough menace to unsettle even the seasoned NATO members. But was he simply rattling his saber, or was his country actively preparing for war? The question gnawed at her, refusing to let go.

For someone in Gul's position, a bellicose public image wasn't unusual. Yet, challenging Russia so openly—especially when it had the potential to escalate into a global conflict—was playing with fire. If Turkey was genuinely preparing to confront Russia, the ripple effects would almost certainly prove disastrous. Either NATO would be dragged into a conflict that could very well escalate to a nuclear showdown or—and this was the scenario Savannah feared most—the alliance would fracture, handing Vladimir Putin the victory he coveted.

Savannah felt she needed to determine whether Gul's rhetoric was just bluster or if Turkey had indeed started preparing for a military escalation. Her instincts told her not to dismiss the general's comments lightly, but she needed more than just a hunch. She needed solid intel—something concrete to confirm whether Gul was posturing or if there were real movements behind the scenes. That meant reaching out to people with inside knowledge of Turkey's military plans.

She began by heading directly to the British embassy in Ankara to speak with Daniel Hughes, officially listed as the embassy's political liaison but, unofficially, the local chief of station for MI6. Savannah had coordinated with Hughes after the attack on the NATO summit in Istanbul and knew that if anyone had their finger on the pulse of what was unfolding within the Turkish military, it was him.

"So," Hughes began, settling back in his chair with a faint smirk, "I take it you're here because of General Gul's little display at the planning session."

"You heard?"

"Oh, trust me. Everyone heard. You're not the first to come to me wondering if he's gone completely mad."

"Well, has he?"

Hughes took a moment, then replied, "It's posturing, or at least that's what he wants NATO to believe. Western European nations have been bending over backwards to appease Putin. This gives Turkey a chance to score points on the international stage, to look like the one NATO member who won't back down. Then, when NATO inevitably realizes Putin isn't going anywhere, Turkey comes out looking strong and decisive."

"So, in your opinion, it's nothing to be concerned about?"

Hughes gave her a sharp, appraising look, then leaned forward to open his desk drawer. A moment later he emerged holding a bottle of the Macallan and two tumblers. Pouring a generous measure into each glass, he pushed one across to Savannah.

It was early for a drink, but she accepted it without comment, recognizing what it symbolized. The gesture meant this was no longer an official briefing but an off-the-record conversation, a chat between two professionals who could speak a bit more freely.

This was how things were done in MI6 these days: cautiously, with plausible deniability. Since the intelligence missteps leading to the Iraq War, the British intelligence community had become warier, with many at Vauxhall Cross adopting an attitude of calculated restraint.

"Turkish politics can be . . ." Hughes paused, searching for the right words. "Well, to be blunt, byzantine. Layers upon layers of obfuscation, all designed to hide what's really going on. You never truly know who's pulling the strings."

Savannah narrowed her gaze. "So, are you suggesting Gul's gone rogue?"

Hughes lifted his glass to the light as if inspecting the contents. "Gul's been playing this game for years. He enjoys testing limits, seeing how far he can push before someone pushes back. Right now he seems to have Erdoğan's full backing, but if this gamble backfires, he'll be on his own, left out in the cold."

"So, why risk it? Surely, he understands the stakes."

Hughes took a slow sip of his Scotch, savoring it. "The thing about Gul is that he didn't get to where he is by playing it safe. He's been maneuvering for ages, especially since the 2016 coup attempt."

Savannah barely remembered the short-lived coup of 2016. In a single night, a faction within the Turkish military had tried to overthrow President Recep Tayyip Erdoğan. Government forces swiftly crushed the movement, followed by a sweeping purge targeting suspected coup participants and thousands of others accused of sympathizing with the rebels, consolidating Erdoğan's power.

"When the rest of the military fractured," Hughes continued, "Gul threw his full support behind Erdoğan. That loyalty earned him a great deal of influence. Erdoğan needed someone reliable to rebuild the military from the ground up, and Gul seized the opportunity. Since then he's managed to consolidate power, modernize the armed forces, and cultivate loyalty among the high-ranking officers. Officially, the military answers to Erdoğan, but in practice Gul runs the show."

Savannah digested this, her mind racing. "So, are you saying Gul's angling for another coup?"

Hughes shrugged, his expression inscrutable. "Erdoğan's aware of Gul's ambitions, but he can't afford to get rid of him—not yet. And so far Gul hasn't crossed any lines."

"Until now," Savannah murmured.

Hughes nodded. "Until now. Gul's playing poker with high stakes—not just with Russia but with NATO as well. He's all in, betting with Erdoğan's chips, and he needs both NATO's backing and Putin to back down. If either side calls his bluff . . ." He spread his hands.

Savannah pondered this for a moment. "And what if . . ." She hesitated, almost afraid to put her thoughts into words. "What if he's not bluffing?"

Hughes cocked his head. "You mean, do I think Gul would go head-to-head with Russia without NATO's support?"

Savannah took a slow, deep breath. "Yes."

Hughes blew out a long sigh. "Let's just say Turkish-Russian relations are complicated. They've fought over everything from the Black Sea to the Balkans and the Caucasus. During the Syrian conflict, they found common ground against the Kurds, but that doesn't erase centuries of rivalry. Since the Ukraine war began, Turkey's economic ties with Russia have actually grown. Turkish companies are replacing Western firms that pulled out due to sanctions, and trade between the two nations is booming, especially in energy. Russian tourism brings billions into Turkey's economy each year, and Turkey relies heavily on Russian gas. Gul knows all of that. He also knows what's at stake if he pushes Putin too hard."

Savannah tapped her glass, mulling it over. "But does he truly believe he could win a war against Russia, even without NATO?"

Hughes looked thoughtful. "The Russian military's stretched thin, and Ukraine's fought them to a standstill. But let's not forget, they've had plenty of Western support. Putin's show of force with the Tsar II bomb wasn't just bluster."

Savannah nodded. "The real question is, Does General Gul understand that?"

Hughes spread his hands. "That, Commander, is something you'd have to ask Gul."

Savannah downed her Scotch in a single gulp and set the glass down with a resolute nod. "You know, I think I just might."

TWENTY-FIVE

PARIS, FRANCE

As Winston Churchill famously said—and Alex Hawke was fond of repeating—"Nothing in life is so exhilarating as to be shot at without result." But when the exhilaration of not dying finally began to ebb, Hawke felt a very different emotion rising—anger.

His ire was not directed at the now-deceased assassins—if anything, he felt a measure of gratitude toward them for being so poor at their job—nor at the as-yet-unidentified entity who had sent them. He would find out who that entity was and respond in kind, but that was a matter of principle. Indignation, righteous or otherwise, was not a factor.

No, mostly he was angry at himself.

Angry for having let himself be put in such a vulnerable position. Angry for having allowed Ariadne Silk to dictate the method of travel. Angrier still for having been caught off guard.

But anger, like a bullet, was of little value if not used purposefully. And so, after the dust finally settled and the interviews with the responding police officers were finished and all the passengers aboard the Nightjet were conveyed back to Paris "out of an abundance of caution," Hawke put his anger to work.

After returning to Paris, Hawke and Silk spent the better part of the evening in a police station, where he was obliged to recount in detail how the attack had proceeded. Hawke's wealth and status, though generally advantageous, proved to be a double-edged sword. On one hand, he was treated with a degree of deference, his story taken seriously from the outset. On the other, the police remained exceptionally cautious about his continued safety. Unaware of Hawke's status as a secret agent working on behalf of the Crown, the gendarmes surmised that the assassins were likely Russian gangsters—violent, highly skilled, and possibly tied to international crime syndicates—targeting him for reasons as yet unclear.

Finally, around midnight, they were released, though because the incident remained unresolved, they had been obliged to be available for further questioning should the need arise. Wanting a secure and comfortable place to regroup, Hawke booked the Suite Vendôme at the Ritz Paris. The unparalleled views of Place Vendôme held absolutely no appeal for him. All he cared about was the fact that Ritz was known for discretion, and the suite had two rooms. Once they'd settled in, Hawke had given Stokely Jones a call.

While Hawke had been occupied with the cross-country train journey with Silk, Stoke had been busy establishing Hawke's plan B—a quick-reaction force that would be prepositioned on a yacht in the Black Sea, ready to intervene if things went sideways in Sochi. Ideally, Hawke would have preferred to use the *Blackhawke*, but since it was docked in London, Stoke had opted to charter the *Flying Fox*, a 136-meter luxury megayacht currently available in Istanbul. With dual helipads, an advanced security system, and a range of anti-intrusion measures, the *Flying Fox* was perfectly suited for covert operations in the Black Sea. Stoke was already aboard the yacht, awaiting the arrival of Thunder and Lightning, the mercenary outfit comprising special operations veterans who had worked with Hawke and Stoke on numerous operations. The hired guns were en route to Istanbul from Fort Whoop Ass, their headquarters in Martinique, but covertly transporting their arsenal and all the other specialized equipment they might need if the shit hit the fan would take a couple more days, which would still leave them plenty of time to get to where they needed to be. Neither Hawke nor Stoke had anticipated that danger would rear its ugly head with the journey barely begun.

"I need you here, Stoke," he had told his old friend.

"I'm already on my way to the airport," Stoke had replied. "Should be there by morning. Now, tell me what happened."

"Plenty of time for that when you get here. Right now, I just need someone to watch my back while I figure out how to get to Sochi in one piece."

"Got it, boss. See you in a bit."

Sleep continued to elude Hawke after the call, as did clarity. He had a bottle of Goslings Black Seal sent up, but the rum did little to dull his nerves. His mind continued to race with unanswered questions.

Who had sent the assassins? And why had they struck now, on French soil, when he and Silk were just a few days away from actually entering the lion's . . . or rather the bear's den? Why not let them reach Russian soil and then simply make them disappear?

Something didn't add up.

His first thought was that the whole business with the Romanov letter had been bait for a trap. But that didn't make sense because Putin couldn't have known that King Charles would send Hawke along as Silk's protector. Or could he? The Russian president might have known about the role that Hawke's ancestor had played in the tragic episode and anticipated the King's decision to involve him.

But, again, why spring the trap prematurely?

He spent the remainder of the night lying on his back, trying and failing to get a few hours' sleep, and instead staring blankly up at the ceiling of his darkened room. He sorted through what he knew and what he could only surmise, arranging and rearranging the information like a deck of playing cards and wishing his friend Congreve were there to help him sort it all out. He even considered giving the detective a call but, owing to the lateness of the hour, decided against it. He would have to puzzle this one out by himself.

When the faint glow of dawn began to creep over the top of the window blinds, Hawke admitted to the futility of trying to sleep and instead ventured out to the suite's kitchenette to use the Nespresso machine. Perversely, the caffeine did not have the desired effect of energizing him. Quite the opposite: he felt the weight of exhaustion bearing down on him. Silk had yet to emerge from her room, and as near as he could tell, she had not awakened, so instead of brewing a second cup or ordering breakfast from room service, he decided to give sleep another try. But no sooner was he back in bed when a text message arrived on his mobile phone: Stoke was in the lobby. With a weary sigh, Hawke pulled on a pair of denim jeans and his favorite T-shirt—a gift from Tommy Quick, which bore the logo of the US Army Sniper School and the legend YOU CAN RUN BUT YOU WILL JUST DIE TIRED—and headed down to greet his friend.

Just the sight of Stoke, as big and solid as a granite monolith, filled Hawke with immeasurable relief. He clasped Stoke's hand in a quick, firm handshake and gestured toward the elevator bank. Stoke fell into step beside him, his keen eyes taking in Hawke's worn expression. They stepped into the waiting elevator, and as the doors slid shut, Stoke cast a sidelong glance at his friend.

"So," Stoke said casually, though his tone held a hint of curiosity, "you and the lady historian . . . anything going on there?"

Hawke kept his gaze fixed ahead, unfazed. "No." And then he added, muttering, "Not that it's any of your bloody business."

Stoke chuckled. "Just doing my due diligence, partner. Last thing we need right now is a"—he paused as if searching for the right word—"distraction."

"You don't need to worry on that score."

"Because I'd understand if . . . you know, with you and Anastasia being on a break and all."

"We're not on a break. And even if we were . . ." He left the rest unsaid, knowing that if he said too much more, Stoke's bullshit detector might start beeping. Thankfully, the lift chimed, signaling their arrival, giving him the perfect opportunity to let the matter drop.

Silk's bedroom door remained closed, and Hawke saw no reason to disturb her. He brewed two more cups of coffee and then quickly recounted the events of the previous night.

Stoke nodded. "You thinking Putin sent them? He still wants your head, you know."

Hawke shook his head, but it was more a gesture of uncertainty than a denial. "It could be Putin's doing or someone who wants to collect that bounty. Right now I want to focus on how we're going to get to Sochi."

Stoke took a slow sip of his coffee, weighing the situation. "Has it occurred to you that this whole thing might be a setup? I mean, you're literally going to the house of the man who put that bounty on your head."

"I've thought about that, but Putin couldn't have known that Charles would send me along with Silk."

Stoke's skepticism remained evident. "And what do you think he'll do when you turn up on his doorstep? Ole Vlad isn't the sort of guy to let bygones be bygones."

Hawke allowed himself a tight smile. "I don't think he'll kill me . . . at least not right away. He likes to brag. Always has. And now he's got two aces in his hand: the Tsar II bomb and the Romanov letter. He'll get a lot more mileage out of that by letting me leave Russia than he will by simply settling a score."

"And if you're wrong?"

Hawke shrugged. "Then I'll be counting on you and the boys from T and L to swoop in and save the day."

Stoke grunted in reluctant agreement, but he didn't look convinced. "Still sounds like a suicide mission to me, but it's your funeral."

Just then, Ariadne Silk emerged from her room, looking effortlessly glamorous in a hotel robe, her hair tousled and her expression somewhere between intrigued and wary behind the lenses of her spectacles. "Oh," she said, leaning against the counter in the kitchenette and striking a demur pose. "I didn't realize we had company."

Hawke pretended to ignore her, studying his coffee cup with sudden intensity, but Stoke flashed a big grin. "After what happened last night, my boy Alex here decided it was time to call in the big dog."

Silk's expression tightened a little at the mention of the previous evening's events. Then she turned her gaze back to Hawke. "You're up early. Or did you even sleep?"

"We're working out the best way to get to Sochi. I think it goes without saying that we won't be taking the train."

Silk's eyes narrowed slightly in what he took to be a pained expression. "I suppose you'll want to fly the rest of the way."

Hawke's gaze hardened as he set down his coffee cup. "We tried it your way, Ariadne. Took the train, stayed out of the sky, and it nearly got me killed. Now we're going to do it my way."

Silk's face tightened, her voice softening but firm. "Alex, it's not that simple. Flying"—she hesitated—"it's not something I can just 'get over.'"

"I understand," he replied, his voice a little sharper than he intended. "But if you want to reach Sochi by next Tuesday, you're going to have to find a way to do just that. We were on a razor-thin margin as it was. Never mind that we've also got enemy agents hunting us. Hunting me. Traveling by rail is an unacceptable risk. And for what? Peace of mind?"

Silk swallowed, her resolve nowhere near what it had been two days previously when she'd first proposed the train journey, but she remained defiant. "I know it sounds unreasonable, but this . . . this phobia. It isn't something I can just switch off. Don't you think I would if I could?"

Stoke, who'd been watching the exchange with a steady, thoughtful gaze, cut in, his tone balanced and diplomatic. "Listen, I've been giving this some thought. There is a way to get there. It'll be tight, but it can be done."

Hawke regarded his friend. "Go on, Stoke. I'm listening."

"We drive to Italy . . . a little place down south called Bari. It's a long haul—about a thousand miles—but we can do it in about fifteen hours if we're lucky with traffic. We drive in shifts, stop only when we have to, and hit Bari just in time to catch the midnight ferry across the Adriatic. That'll give us a few hours to rest. Once we dock in Greece, it's an eight-hour drive straight across to Istanbul, where we can meet up with the *Flying Fox* and go the rest of the way in style. I know it's a lot of time behind the wheel, but we can take turns driving. Minimal exposure and no air travel."

Hawke turned to Silk, who was nodding gratefully, then shot a look at his watch. "Bari by midnight," he sighed. "Well, I guess we should get going."

TWENTY-SIX

KONYA, TURKEY

As the transport plane carrying Commander Savannah Stone banked over Konya Air Base on final approach to the dual-use airport, she got a good look at the hardened aircraft shelters, hangars, and barracks that extended well beyond the civilian terminal. The base, situated on the plains of central Anatolia, was home to the Turkish Air Force's 3rd Air Wing. Konya was a cornerstone of Turkey's military infrastructure and a key NATO outpost, hosting joint exercises and rapid-response operations.

After leaving the embassy, Savannah had made a call to the Turkish Ministry of Defense, hoping to arrange an audience with General Gul, but had been told that he was at Konya, overseeing a readiness exercise: Would she like to meet with him there? Savannah thought that sounded like an excellent idea and, using her NATO credentials, had secured a seat on the next transport headed to Konya.

She was met on the tarmac by one of General Osman Gul's aides, a young officer with a crisp salute who drove her through the secure gates and deeper into the military section of the base. They passed a line of F-16 fighter jets—part of Turkey's contribution to NATO air operations—and a sprawling maintenance hangar where technicians worked on everything from surveillance drones to refueling tankers.

Farther out, on the infantry training grounds, she saw units of airborne infantry engaged in rigorous drills. The training might have been routine, but then again, after what Gul had said in Brussels, it might have signified something more.

Her driver brought her to a range on which a mock city had been erected for training in urban combat techniques. Simulated gunfire echoed from the sand-colored buildings, and a pall of smoke hung in the air overhead. Groups of Turkish soldiers moved streets in tactical formations, pausing to engage the enemy with rifles equipped with blank-fire adapters and MILES (multiple integrated laser engagement system) transmitters. The OPFOR "opposing forces" soldiers were clad in fatigues similar to Russian military uniforms, their red armbands signaling the roles they played.

Her escort parked his sedan near the base of a raised platform set just outside the perimeter of the training range and led her up the stairs to meet General Osman Gul. Gul stood with a small entourage, binoculars pressed to his eyes as he observed the current evolution. His face remained impassive as he watched the action, occasionally murmuring to one of his aides or offering an approving nod.

Savannah waited until the evolution ended to make her presence known. As Gul lowered his binoculars, she stepped forward crisply, coming to attention, and offered a respectful salute. She held it, waiting for the Turkish general to acknowledge her presence.

Gul gazed at her for a long moment, his expression inscrutable, then returned the salute with an almost casual indifference. "Colonel Stone. What a pleasant surprise." He smiled cryptically. "I trust you've fully recovered from your ordeal in Istanbul."

Savannah met his gaze, her expression as steady as his. "It was quite the party. Thank you for agreeing to meet with me."

"Of course. Now, to what do I owe the pleasure?"

"I was in Brussels for the recent planning session," she began, her tone calm but direct. "Your comments there made quite an impression."

"Did they?" Gul's face was impassive, though a glimmer of satisfaction flitted through his eyes.

Savannah kept her expression neutral, weighing her words carefully, aware of the thin diplomatic line she was walking. A misstep, or even the perception of provocation, could have serious repercussions—not only for herself but for the delicate balance of NATO's relations with Turkey. But she also recalled what Hughes had told her about the man—how he liked to test the limits—and knew she had to convey that same unflinching resolve. "You spoke about Turkey's willingness to act—unilaterally if necessary—against Russia. That's bound to get attention."

Gul tilted his head, a faint smirk breaking through his otherwise unreadable expression. "Turkey has always been ready to protect itself, Colonel Stone. We would prefer to have NATO at our side—but if not . . ." He let the implication hang in the air, his eyes sharp, studying her reaction.

"So what you said in Brussels . . . that's the position of your government?"

Gul's smile did not falter. "Of course. As a soldier, it is not my role to set our foreign policy objectives but rather to execute them."

"So President Erdoğan would support you acting independently if NATO doesn't reach a consensus?" she pressed.

"President Erdoğan values the safety and strength of his country. He expects us, his military, to be vigilant and prepared, ready to meet any threat, whether or not NATO chooses to stand with us."

It was, conspicuously, a nonanswer, but Savannah sensed that she wasn't going to get anything more definitive. His noncommittal responses were as good as an admission that Turkey's military actions might not align entirely with NATO's wishes, but whether he was pursuing Erdoğan's agenda or his own remained unclear.

"Thank you for your time, General. I look forward to seeing how Turkey's commitment to regional stability continues to unfold."

"As do I, Commander Stone." Gul's smile remained inscrutable. "We are privileged to live in interesting times, are we not?"

The comment felt like an ominous prophecy.

By way of an answer, she came to attention, saluted, and then turned away. Her gut told her there was more to uncover, and with NATO's fragile unity hanging in the balance, she couldn't afford to ignore that instinct.

So when she got back to the waiting staff car, she took out her mobile and sent a text message to Daniel Hughes, asking for a favor.

TWENTY-SEVEN

FRANCE, EN ROUTE TO ISTANBUL

The narrow streets of Paris soon gave way to winding country roads as Hawke, Stoke, and Silk ventured south in Stoke's rented Range Rover. It was the perfect vehicle for the journey, affording comfort for the long hours they would spend on the road and sufficient horsepower not only to handle the Alpine traverse that lay ahead of them but also to outrun any trouble that came their way.

They followed the Autoroute du Soleil into the verdant heart of Burgundy. The highway cut through France's renowned wine country, where vineyards blanketed the hills in tidy rows and rustic stone houses dotted the gentle landscape. The rolling hills gave way to the kind of pastoral scenery that seemed lifted from a painting: fields of green winter wheat swaying in the breeze, framed by low stone walls and patches of forest. Yet, despite the serenity of the picturesque environment and the luxury of the SUV's interior, the drive was far from a relaxing experience. Both Hawke and Stoke were on high alert, even when not driving, scanning the road ahead and the mirrors behind, watching for tails and wary of ambushes at every turn. Danger had found them once already, and even though this route was a last-minute change of plan, Hawke was determined not to be caught off guard again.

About half an hour after they passed through the little town of Mâcon, an hour or so north of Lyon, the chime of a mobile phone notification broke through the quiet. Silk, looking slightly embarrassed, produced the offending device from her handbag, glanced at it with a slight furrowing of her brow, and then accepted the call.

"Hello?" A pause, and then: "This is she."

Hawke, glancing over from the driver's seat, caught the slightest flicker of surprise on her face before she composed herself. "Oh . . . Chief Inspector. What can I do for you?"

Chief Inspector? Hawke's ears perked up. Why was a policeman calling Silk?

There was an even longer pause, during which time Silk's expression became increasingly grave. "Oh, my," she said at length. "That's . . . that's terrible."

Hawke's curiosity was now burning but he resisted the impulse to interject himself into her conversation and kept his focus on the road ahead, and the party on the other end of the line resumed speaking at length.

"I see," she replied eventually, adopting a reassuring tone. "I appreciate the warning, Chief Inspector, but you see, I already am in rather capable hands." She glanced over at Hawke and smiled, then nodded in response to whatever was being said. "As a matter of fact, my valiant protector is none other than Lord Alexander Hawke."

The mention of Hawke's name triggered a response over the line that was audible even to Hawke's ear. Silk, surprised at the caller's exuberance, moved the phone away from her ear, then glanced over at Hawke again. "I'll put him on."

She tapped the screen of the mobile and then said, "Go ahead, Chief Inspector."

A familiar voice boomed out, "Alex, my boy. Is it really you?"

"Constable?" This nickname was something of an old joke between Hawke and Congreve, a joke that the latter did not find particularly amusing. "How the devil are you, old chap?"

"Fine as frog's fur, my boy."

"And your better half? How's Diana?"

"She's well, Alex. In fact, she's come with me to London."

"London? I thought you were spending the rest of the season at Shadowlands."

"That was my intention, but duty, as they say, called. We've moved back into Heart's Ease Cottage until this business is wrapped up."

Heart's Ease Cottage was Congreve's residence in Hampstead Heath, a quaint brick-and-mortar structure bequeathed to him by his dear aunt Augusta, who had lovingly restored both the house and gardens after it was nearly bombed into extinction during the Blitz.

"I must say, Alex," Congreve went on, "it's a bit of a shock to find you there with Dr. Silk."

"We're on the King's business. Doing a favor for him."

"Quite right. Quite right. Say no more."

There was another long, uncomfortable silence, so Hawke prompted, "I say, Ambrose, what's going on? Is something the matter?"

"A bit of nasty business, I'm afraid. It seems that your lady friend is being targeted by a contract killer—an elusive blackguard that goes by the nom de guerre of Silence. Lethal reputation, and we've not a bloody clue who he is or what he looks like."

Hawke winced a little at the flagrant use of the term *lady friend* but did not address it. "Contract killer, you say? As it happens, we've already had a spot of trouble. Just last night, in fact. A pair of Russian assassins came after us. Or, rather, after me."

"Russians, you say?"

"Rather unpleasant blokes. One of them tried to fillet me. I was actually thinking about ringing you up and having you look into it. I'd like to know who sent them so I can return the favor."

"Russians," Congreve murmured, his curiosity clearly aroused. "Interesting. Silence does have a reputation for working independently, and his preferred modus operandi is strangulation."

"That's assuming your contract killer had anything to do with what happened last night," said Hawke. "Those Russians had all the subtlety of a demolition team. Not exactly what one would expect from someone calling himself 'Silence.'"

"Quite," murmured Congreve before lapsing into another thoughtful pause.

From the back seat, Stoke chimed in. "What makes you think this Silence dude is targeting the doc?"

"Stokely Jones?" exclaimed Congreve. "Is that you?"

"Live and in living color," rumbled Stoke with a chuckle but then became deadly serious again. "Now, why do you think this killer is targeting Dr. Silk?"

"Ah, well, that's the unfortunate bit," Congreve admitted, his voice taking on a more somber tone. "Two of her close associates were found murdered."

From the corner of his eye, Hawke saw Silk's face go pale, her expression visibly alarmed. "My God," she whispered. "Who?"

"I'm sorry to be the one to tell you," began Congreve. "The victims are Marian Smith and Samantha Knowles."

Silk let out a low wail, then pressed her hand to her lips as to stifle any further display of grief.

Almost without thinking, Hawke reached over and took her hand in his, giving it a squeeze. The warmth of her fingers felt strangely vulnerable against his own, soft yet steady. She looked up at him, a flicker of surprise mingling with something else in her eyes—gratitude, perhaps, or a relief she hadn't expected to feel. He held her gaze for a moment, saying nothing, then gave a reassuring nod.

"Suffice it to say," Congreve went on, "the methods employed by the killer were consistent with those of Silence, and since both women were friends of Dr. Silk, we thought perhaps she might be next on his list."

"Do you know who this killer is?" Hawke asked.

"We've made some progress. We started by assuming the killer flew from Bermuda, where the first victim resided, to London, where the second lived, and furthermore that the flight occurred in the narrow window of time between the murders. By cross-referencing passenger manifests for all flights connecting the two destinations within that window, we've managed to narrow the list to about seventy possible suspects. It's not conclusive yet, but it's a start."

"But we're talking about a hit man here," Stoke said. "Not a serial killer. Why would a hit man go after the lady doc here? And why start with her friends?"

"That is the question," Congreve agreed. "I suspect it may have something to do with this Royal errand she's on."

Hawke blinked, feeling vaguely foolish for not having worked this out for himself. It was obvious, really. Why else would a top-tier assassin be gunning for Silk? This wasn't about personal vendettas or petty revenge. This was about her mission for the King. *Their* mission.

"It would appear that someone does not want you to succeed," Congreve was saying.

Well, that's bloody obvious, thought Hawke, his ire directed inwardly. But who stood to gain by preventing them from reaching their destination?

As if reading his mind, Congreve continued: "It might help us identify the villain behind the plot if I knew a little more about the nature of your mission."

Hawke hesitated. He trusted Congreve with his life but wasn't at all comfortable with the idea of discussing the particulars of the mission over an open line. "I'm afraid I'm not at liberty to share that information. Even with you, old chap. But I'm sure Charles would be more than happy to bring you up to speed."

Congreve gave a thoughtful hum. "When you said you were on the King's business, I didn't realize you meant it literally. Very well. Getting past the palace gatekeepers may take some doing, but I shall manage as needs must."

"If anyone can, it's you," replied Hawke.

"I shall endeavor to determine who is behind these killings," Congreve went on. "But in the meantime, stay on your guard. Having Silence hunting you is nothing to take lightly. If he is targeting Dr. Silk, he may already have left London."

"I'll keep both eyes open," Hawke assured him, and ended the call.

"Well, that's a damn mess," Stoke muttered. "As if we didn't have enough to worry about. You think Putin's behind all this?"

Hawke shook his head, keeping his gaze on the road. "Putin needs us to succeed. If Ariadne can't authenticate that letter, he's got nothing to hold over the King's head."

"Unless the letter's just bait to draw you into the open."

"But then, why send a contract killer after Ariadne?" Hawke glanced over at Silk, who still seemed to be in a state of mild shock after the call with Congreve. "And why target her friends?" he added in a low voice.

Stoke grunted. "So if it's not him, then who?"

Hawke's brow furrowed as he considered the question. "Someone who stands to gain by keeping her from getting a look at that letter. God knows Putin has made more than his share of enemies."

"He's not exactly running a fan club in the Kremlin these days."

"True enough. But he's got even more enemies outside Russia. Think about it: What if it's the Ukrainians? If they got wind of this and believe that Charles may withdraw his support for continued aid in exchange for that letter, that would be reason enough to try and stop us."

"So what you're saying is we're playing Russian roulette and we don't even know who loaded the gun. Or how many bullets are in the chamber."

Hawke shrugged. "Story of our lives, old boy."

From Lyon, they followed A43 into the Alps to the eight-mile-long Fréjus Road Tunnel and the border crossing into Italy. As they neared the tunnel entrance, the landscape changed dramatically, the gentle hills giving way to jagged, towering peaks blanketed in snow. Emerging on the Italian side, they found themselves amid the terraced vineyards and stone villages of the Aosta Valley. The highway cut through vast stretches of farmland, with rows of cypress trees lining the road and fields of corn, sunflowers, and wheat extending as far as the eye could see. By the time they reached Bologna, the sun had set, and the sky was deepening into twilight shades of purple. They pushed onward, moving past fields now cloaked in shadow.

Little was said during the journey. There was nothing to be gained by further speculation about the forces arrayed against them or the dangers that might lie ahead, so Hawke and Stokely kept their eyes on the road—one of them always behind the wheel, the other in the back, watching their six. That nothing consequential occurred did not prompt them to relax their vigil. If anything, the uneventfulness only heightened their anxiety.

Finally, with midnight approaching, they reached the coast and beheld the black expanse of the Adriatic Sea. They joined the queue of cars inching their way aboard the waiting ferry, and once the Range Rover was parked on the lower deck alongside other vehicles, they made their way to the private cabin they would share for the ten-hour crossing. Yet, even there, they did not allow themselves to rest easy. If their unknown enemy had divined their plans, Silence or some other assassin might already be aboard the ferry, waiting for a quiet moment to strike.

Hawke and Stoke spent the night alternating between fitful naps and periods of watchful vigilance. They took turns patrolling the dimly lit decks, looking for any activity that might presage a repeat of the events aboard the Nightjet. But all was quiet. Aside from the ferry's crew, everyone appeared to have retired for the night. Ariadne Silk, confident in Hawke's determination to protect her, enjoyed a deep, untroubled sleep. She awoke to sunlight streaming in through the cabin's portholes, refreshed and blissfully unaware of how her traveling companions had spent the night.

They disembarked in Igoumenitsa and resumed road travel along the Egnatia Odos, a route that stretched across northern Greece, through the rugged Epirus highlands and into Thessaly, the region renowned for the centuries-old monasteries perched high on the rocky spires of Meteora. The route led them on through the vineyards and olive groves of Macedonia, with cloud-shrouded Mount Olympus, the home of the ancient Greek gods, visible in the distance before eventually turning southward near the Turkish border. Entering European Istanbul felt momentous, but although the end of the journey was almost in sight, Hawke fought the urge to celebrate prematurely. They skirted the western suburbs and passed near the ancient walls of Constantinople until finally reaching the docks on the Marmara coast, where a launch waited to ferry them to the *Flying Fox.*

The yacht lay at anchor just beyond the harbor's edge. Her silvery-blue hull and towering superstructure lit up like a shimmering palace rising from the dark waters. Built in 2019 by Lürssen—the very shipyard where *War Hawke* was presently under construction—*Flying Fox* had cost an estimated $400 million to construct. Over four hundred feet in length, with dual helipads—currently occupied by a pair of Eurocopter EC145s—the yacht was equipped with advanced navigation and surveillance systems, making it a perfect base of operations for covert missions. Floating gracefully on the Sea of Marmara, it was as much a fortress as it was a floating masterpiece of engineering.

Gazing out at it, Hawke could not help but feel a sense of déjà vu.

"Now, that," Stoke said, looking out across the water, "is how I prefer to travel."

"You and me both, Stoke," replied Hawke wearily. He felt as if the long road trip and the enforced state of heightened awareness had aged him by a decade. Yet he knew the most treacherous part of this odyssey was still to come. "Have our friends completed their preparations?" he asked, referring to Thunder and Lightning.

"Loaded for bear and ready to rumble. You want to talk to 'em about what you're gonna need when we get to Sochi?"

"It can wait. As soon as we're aboard, tell the captain to weigh anchor and set sail."

"Will do, boss. What about you? What are you going to do?"

Hawke managed a faint smile. "I'm going to sleep for a week."

TWENTY-EIGHT

EN ROUTE TO SOCHI

Hawke actually only slept for ten hours, but it was enough to recharge his batteries. He awoke to a glorious day, the *Flying Fox* underway and well into the crossing of the Black Sea. He began the day with a truncated version of his Royal Navy workout, the calisthenic routine helping to work the last kinks out of joints and muscles that had been mostly static for the better part of three days. Then he showered, dressed, and made his way from his stateroom to the main salon.

He found Stoke already there, lounging in a chair, a cup of coffee in one hand and a croissant in the other. He was not alone. Two other figures were seated at the table with him, tucking into plates of eggs, smoked salmon, and fresh fruit. They were Thunder and Lightning, the founding members—or plank owners, to use a bit of Navy SEAL jargon—of the eponymous mercenary outfit that Hawke often called on when faced with a situation that required a little extra muscle. Both men were former Navy SEALs, as were many of the men who worked under them, and both had served with Stoke during the early years of the Global War on Terror.

Thunder was a tall, full-blooded Comanche named Charlie Rainwater, though his close acquaintances employed his old call sign,

"Boomer," a nickname he'd earned because of his demolitions expertise. He had copper skin, long black hair that was tied back in a ponytail, and a set of dark, piercing eyes. He was, rather unselfconsciously, attired only in buckskin trousers. His sartorial choice wasn't just an affectation: Boomer lived by the traditions of his ancestors.

And his tracking skills were legendary.

Thunder's counterpart, Lightning, a rowdy, ruddy Irishman named Fitzhugh "Fitz" McCoy, was typically more verbose than his taciturn friend, but today he seemed more interested in his repast, offering only a nod of acknowledgment, which Hawke dutifully returned.

Stoke greeted Hawke with a grin. "Morning, boss. Sleep well? Or were you dreaming about the lovely Dr. Silk?"

"I won't dignify that comment," Hawke replied, pouring himself a coffee. He took a sip, then said, "However, since you've raised the subject, where is our erstwhile VIP passenger?"

Stoke smirked, nodding toward the deck just aft of the salon. "Out there. Giving us all something to talk about."

Hawke glanced in the indicated direction and spied Silk stretched out on a chaise longue, wearing a bikini that left little to the imagination.

Boomer didn't look up from his plate, but Fitz raised his eyes and grinned. "Ah, now, there's a woman who knows how to make her point without saying a word. She's not sunbathing for her health, if you catch me."

Hawke shot him a withering stare. "She's not 'making a point,' Fitz. And this isn't a holiday."

Fitz's grin widened. "Yeah, well, does *she* know that?"

Stoke chuckled. "You're barking up the wrong tree, Fitz. Our boy here doesn't mix business with pleasure."

Fitz shrugged. "All I'm saying is you'd be the type, wouldn't you, Skipper? Always had a way with the ladies, if memory serves."

Stoke shook his head. "Fancha is all the woman I can handle at my tender age. Besides, that lady out there isn't looking for just anyone.

There's only one man on this boat she's got eyes for. It ain't me, and before that grin gets any wider, it sure as all hell ain't you."

Fitz returned his gaze to Hawke. "Well, isn't that convenient for our lordship here? Must be nice, having a goddess sunning herself just for you."

Boomer finally spoke, his tone measured. "She yours?"

"No," replied Hawke, acidly enunciating his reply. "She's not mine. In fact, I reckon she doesn't belong to anyone."

Boomer grunted as if this answer had failed to impress him.

"That lady's got a PhD in keeping people on edge," Stoke volunteered. "And judging by the reaction she's getting, I'd say it's working."

Hawke shot Stoke a look. "She's the primary. We're just here to make sure she accomplishes her objective."

"There are objectives, and then there are *objectives*," retorted Fitz.

"Well, my objective is to finish the mission," declared Hawke. "End of story."

Fitz shoved his plate aside, his expression suddenly serious. "Right, then. Let's talk about the mission."

He rose from the table to retrieve a large-screened tablet computer. After a few swipes, he brought up a satellite photo of a large estate and then placed the device on the tabletop.

"Skipper tells me this is where you're going. Bocharov Ruchey."

"Putin's holiday residence in Sochi," said Hawke, nodding. "That's where he's going to meet with Dr. Silk to examine a certain historical document. I'll be accompanying her."

"This isn't just a vacation home, Hawke. It's a fortress. Security is airtight. Armed guards, perimeter patrols, electronic surveillance. If you go in there and get into trouble, there's no guarantee that we'll be able to pull your ass out of the fire."

"I've no doubt you'll be up to the task," replied Hawke. "On that subject, what are our assets, exactly?"

"We've got sixteen operators aboard, including Boomer and me." He glanced over at Stoke. "You know most of 'em, Skipper."

Stoke nodded.

"As for gear, we packed light. Suppressed carbines, sidearms, NVGs, and comms rigs for everyone."

"How are you fixed for demo?" asked Stoke.

"We brought along enough C-4 to turn that compound into a parking lot if it comes to that. Don't know what use it will be, but Boomer insisted."

The tall Comanche warrior gave a slight nod, his expression inscrutable.

"And transport?" asked Hawke.

"You probably saw the birds when you came aboard."

"The EC145s," Hawke said with an approving nod.

"Each one can carry up to eight operators, not counting crew, and they're kitted out with our gear. We've got our own pilots. They came over from the Night Stalkers, so they've flown in worse situations than we're likely to see in Sochi."

The Night Stalkers, Hawke knew, referred to the 160th Special Operations Aviation Regiment. Renowned for their ability to operate under the most extreme conditions, the Night Stalkers were the go-to aviation asset for high-stakes operations like the raid on Osama bin Laden's compound.

"We've rigged hardpoints for machine guns. Didn't bring any heavy ordnance—figured subtlety would be more important for this mission. Still, if things go pear-shaped, they can lay down enough fire to keep the enemy's head down while we exfil."

Stoke leaned forward. "Sorry, math was never my strong suit, but if those birds can carry a total of sixteen, and that's the size of your assault element . . . where are Alex and the lady doc going to sit if you have to go in after them?"

"We'll make it work," Fitz assured, though his tone did not inspire confidence.

"What about getting in there? Those birds ain't exactly stealth machines."

"It's a risk," Fitz admitted, "but it also means we'll be quick. We come in hot, grab you, and get out before they can mount a proper response."

"What about Silk?" Stoke interjected. "You do remember she hates flying, right?"

Hawke returned a wry smile. "If it comes to it, I'll knock her out myself and carry her aboard."

"That's romantic."

Hawke nodded, then frowned. "Using the helicopters to exfil makes sense, but I don't want you charging in like the Light Brigade. This needs to be surgical."

Fitz threw up his hands. "Surgical? You want *surgical*, then give me a bloody scalpel and an operating room"—he jabbed a finger at the satellite photo on the tablet—"because there's not a lot to work with here."

Hawke remained calm. "You've done more with less. Figure it out."

Fitz leaned back in his chair, running a hand through his short red blond hair. "Sure. Let me just conjure up a magic carpet while I'm at it."

Boomer broke his silence, his deep voice carrying weight. "We'll figure it out."

Fitz let out a slow breath, his irritation giving way to grudging acceptance. "Right. We'll think of something."

"Make it good," said Hawke. "You've got until tomorrow night."

TWENTY-NINE

Hawke leaned back against the edge of the table in the *Flying Fox*'s salon, contemplating the contents of the tall glass in his hand. It was his third dark 'n' stormy . . . or was it his fourth?

Probably his fourth, judging by the fact that he'd lost track . . . and he was feeling pleasantly numb.

Ambrose Congreve had turned him on to the cocktail—Goslings Black Seal rum, ginger beer, and just a bit of lime—and while he usually preferred his rum straight up, the additional ingredients were useful for moderating his alcohol intake. With less than twenty-four hours to go before venturing into the bear's den, pleasantly numb was where he wanted to be.

Completely blotto might get him killed.

"Got nerves about tomorrow," said Stoke. It wasn't a question.

"Wouldn't you?" Hawke replied, not looking over at his friend, who was sprawled in a leather chair.

Stoke laughed. "I think you're plumb crazy for even thinking about doing this. Putin's just as likely to ice you on the spot as open the door for you. And if he catches on to your little switcheroo . . . let's just say I don't think you'll live long enough to push the panic button."

To carry out his true mission, the one secretly given to him by the King—namely, to destroy the letter if it proved to be authentic—Hawke and Charles had come up with a plan to steal the letter right under Putin's nose. The switch would hinge on a moment of subtle misdirection, a skill Hawke had honed over the years in operations requiring finesse rather than brute force. Once Silk authenticated the letter, Hawke would ask to examine it closely—a reasonable request from someone tasked with ensuring its authenticity on behalf of the King. In that moment, he would perform a bit of sleight of hand, swapping the genuine document with a meticulously prepared forgery Charles had entrusted to him before their departure.

The forgery, painstakingly crafted by experts at the Royal Archives—without Silk's knowledge, since she could not be counted on not to betray the plan through some subtle tell—was indistinguishable from the original in every detail except for the fact that the parchment upon which it was written would contain radioactive isotopes not present when the real letter would have been written—a sure indication of a forgery. If all went according to plan, Putin would leave the meeting none the wiser, believing he still possessed the damning document, while Hawke spirited it away.

Of course, that was assuming everything went according to plan—which, in Hawke's experience, it rarely did.

"I've got my orders, old boy. If the letter's authentic, Charles doesn't want to take the chance that it might find its way out into the world. And he has no intention of bowing to Putin's demands. Stealing it and swapping it with the forgery is the only way to remove the threat."

"And Silk doesn't know."

"No," Hawke admitted. "As far as she knows, we're just there to authenticate it. Reading her in about the switch would only complicate things."

Stoke nodded slowly. "Yeah, keeping her out of the loop makes sense. She's already under enough pressure trying to keep herself together, what with that hit man on her case."

Hawke exhaled, relieved to have Stoke's agreement. "Exactly. She doesn't need to carry that weight. If she focuses on authenticating the letter and nothing else, she'll perform better."

"Still, she's gotta be feeling it. I mean, you and me, we're used to having a target on our backs. She's not."

Hawke waved a dismissive hand. "That's out of our hands. Right now, the best chance we have of eliminating the threat is to accomplish the mission. Maybe if we can take that letter out of play, there won't be any reason to come after her. Best-case scenario, Ariadne declares the letter a fake and this whole thing just blows away."

If Stoke noticed his familiar use of Silk's given name, he declined to comment. "Has it occurred to you that if that happens, Putin won't have any reason to let you walk out of there?"

"It has. Why do you think I've brought T and L along as an insurance policy?"

"I just hope you know what you're doing, boss. This isn't like slipping a wallet from a tourist in Trafalgar Square. We're talking about a Russian stronghold and one of the most paranoid men on earth."

Stoke took a sip of his Diet Coke. "I'll give Boomer and Fitz this," he said, his tone lighter now. "They've got confidence in spades. Whatever harebrained scheme they've cooked up, they seem to think it'll work like a charm."

Indeed, the mercenaries had spent the balance of the day doing weapons drills and rehearsing various scenarios on the *Fox*'s spacious decks and, despite Fitz's earlier reservations, seemed amped for action.

"I'd trust them with my life," Hawke declared. "Hell, I *am* trusting them with my life."

Stoke raised his soda can. "To the plan not blowing up in our faces."

Hawke raised his glass in return, drained the contents, and then stood, setting his empty glass down on the table. "I'm calling it a night, Stoke. Big day tomorrow."

"Sure thing, boss," Stoke said, stretching his legs out in front of him. "I'll stay up a bit longer. Maybe give Fancha a call. She should be getting up right about now."

Hawke nodded absently at Stoke's comment, but the mention of Fancha pierced through the comfortable haze of rum and camaraderie, dredging up emotions that Hawke had so far managed to suppress.

The softening of Stoke's tone when he spoke of his wife reminded Hawke of the life his friend returned to when the missions were over. A life filled with warmth and certainty.

Stoke was deeply, undeniably lucky. Fancha was the kind of woman who could light up a room with her presence and anchor a man through any storm. She adored Stoke with a passion that seemed almost unfair, and he, in turn, was completely devoted to her. They had a bond that even the long stretches of separation couldn't weaken.

Hawke exhaled softly and turned toward the door. "Good night, Stoke."

"'Night, boss," Stoke replied, already looking down at his mobile phone.

Hawke made his way down the corridor, his steps heavier than they should have been. Whether it was the rum or the weight of his thoughts, who could say?

Stoke had Fancha. Congreve had Diana. And he?

He had Anastasia.

Or could have her. All that remained was for him to "take the plunge," as Congreve so often urged. So, why hadn't he? And why wasn't he calling her, the way Stoke was calling Fancha right now, to tell her how much he missed her? How he couldn't wait to see her when this bloody business was done.

It wasn't because he didn't love her. On the contrary, he loved her fiercely—so much so that the depth of it unsettled him. Love wasn't the problem.

He was.

For reasons he couldn't explain but were no doubt linked to his traumatic childhood and the many years he'd spent learning to detach from . . . everyone . . . Hawke just wasn't built to give Asia the life she deserved. A life with a partner who could be present, truly present, rather than rushing headlong into danger, leaving her to wonder if this mission would be the one that killed him. How could he promise her stability when his heart still craved the thrill of the hunt, the surge of adrenaline that came with every high-stakes gamble?

The vulnerability she awakened in him was as exhilarating as it was terrifying. She made him want things he'd long told himself were impossible: a home, a family, a future that wasn't always on the brink of collapse. Yet the very thought of embracing that life felt like stepping into a cage, trading the freedom he thrived on for walls he couldn't bear.

He'd postponed their wedding for the sake of duty. One last mission for the Crown: seek out and destroy the Warmonger. But deep down he knew the delay wasn't just about one mission. It was about the unspoken truth neither of them wanted to acknowledge.

They were drifting apart.

No, that wasn't quite right. They weren't drifting. He was pushing her away. He could tell himself it was for her own good, but Hawke knew it was a lie. He wasn't protecting her. He was protecting himself from the fear of disappointing her.

From the fear of proving that love alone wasn't enough.

Their relationship was already in limbo. They lived together for Alexei's sake, raising the boy with as much warmth and teamwork as they could muster. There were still moments of connection, echoes of the passion that had once burned in both their hearts, but those moments were fleeting, undermined by the growing distance between them.

And now, on the eve of a mission that could very well be his last, Hawke hadn't even called her. Why? To spare her the worry? Or because he feared what she might say?

Tomorrow, he would meet with Vladimir Putin and gamble his life on a sleight-of-hand trick that could go catastrophically wrong. If it did—if that was how his story ended—would Anastasia even mourn him? Or would she feel a sense of quiet relief that the waiting, the uncertainty, was finally over?

Hawke shook his head, trying to banish the dark musings. Whatever pleasant numbness the rum had granted was losing its effect. Now he just felt morose. Introspective. And he loathed introspection.

He realized that he had arrived at his stateroom door. He reached out for the handle but paused, his hand hovering there as indecision reared its head.

I'll call her, he thought. *I'll tell her—*

"Alex?"

He whirled around to find Silk standing a few steps away, wrapped in a thin robe that clung suggestively to her figure. Her dark hair fell loose about her shoulders. Her arms were crossed under her breasts, subtly raising them up as if presenting them for inspection. Her eyes, gazing out through those damned spectacles, were unreadable.

"Ariadne," he said, straightening. "Shouldn't you be getting some rest? Big day tomorrow, remember?"

She smiled coyly. "I could say the same to you."

Hawke felt the electric hum of arousal surging through his body.

No, damn it. You don't need this right now.

"You're right," he said decisively. "We should both turn in. Good night, Ariadne."

Then he opened the door to the stateroom, went inside, closed it firmly behind him, and went right to bed.

Except, he didn't.

He didn't do any of that.

He just stood there, staring at her, unable to move.

She took a step toward him, her bare feet making no sound on the plush carpet. She was so close now that she had to tilt her head back to look up at him, so close that if he took a deep breath, his chest would brush against hers. Her scent enveloped him.

"Alex," she whispered, "I need you."

He knew what he should do, but that part of him that might have been able to resist seduction was still pleasantly numb.

Yet, it wasn't the rum, not really; it was everything. The ominous responsibility of the mission. The tangled, fraying threads of his relationship with Anastasia.

The way Ariadne Silk was looking at him right now.

"I need you."

"Ariadne," he said quietly, as if speaking her name aloud might break the spell, tether him to reality.

It didn't.

Without a word, he reached behind him, turned the handle of his stateroom door, let it swing open, and then pulled her inside.

Except, he didn't do that either.

He might have. God only knew how desperately he wanted to.

But that brief moment of hesitation cost him his chance . . . or, one might argue, saved him. Because before he could act on the almost primal instinct sublimating all rational thought, a voice reached out to him like a lifeline.

"You good, boss?"

Hawke looked away from Silk, down the hall to where Stokely had just appeared, a can of Diet Coke in one hand, a mobile phone in the other, presumably on his way to his own stateroom.

And just like that, the spell was broken.

Hawke coughed to clear his throat, then called back. "Um, yes, Stoke. All good here. Thank you."

"All right," replied Stoke, the customary good humor strangely absent from his tone. "I'll leave you to it, then."

The comment, benign though it was, stung like a slap in the face. Embarrassment flared, hot and immediate, putting a swift end to the desire that had only moments before ruled him.

As Stoke disappeared into his cabin, Hawke turned back to Silk. Her face still registered longing, but the eyes behind the lenses of her glasses were flat and unreadable and held no power over him.

"Well," she said at length, "I should get some sleep."

Then she turned and walked back to her stateroom door. Hawke watched her retreat, his emotions a tangled storm of regret, relief, and shame. When he finally stepped into his own room and closed the door behind him, it was with the sinking realization that he had almost crossed a line he wouldn't have been able to uncross.

And for what? To dull his loneliness for a fleeting moment? To fill a void he had created by his own choices?

No, I'm not that man anymore, Hawke told himself.

He was even starting to believe it.

Alex dropped heavily onto the bed and rubbed a hand over his face, the heat of embarrassment still burning in his cheeks. If she tried again . . . if, in ten minutes, or twenty, or an hour, she knocked on his door, he would not let her in. He would not let it happen.

Not with her. Not now.

Not ever.

I'm not that man anymore, he repeated to himself.

Asia's face came to him then, unbidden but not unwelcome. He wondered what she was doing right now. Was she there at Teakettle Cottage, painting, or perhaps playing with Alexei? She was his anchor, the one constant in a life spent chasing shadows and running toward danger. She deserved better than him.

I'll call her, he thought again, and reached for his mobile, but then hesitated. What would he even say to her?

"Hello, darling. Just thinking about you . . . Well, actually, funny story this, I was just about to cheat on you. Thank goodness Stoke showed up and cut through whatever trance the woman held over me . . ."

He grimaced, feeling faintly nauseated.

"Hi, love. Just wanted to tell you I'm walking into the lion's den tomorrow. If I don't make it out, well . . . sorry for everything."

Unable to find the right words, Hawke lay back on the bed, shut his eyes, and let out a slow breath, trying to will all the thoughts away. Tomorrow would bring its share of new problems. Tonight he just needed quiet.

Or at least the illusion of it.

He lay there, silent and still, letting the weight of it all press him deeper into the darkness.

As he drifted off to sleep, though he never did call her, it was Anastasia's face that he saw in his dreams.

INTERLUDE—PART SEVEN

EN ROUTE TO MOSCOW, SOVIET RUSSIA
APRIL 1918

Alexander and Natalya left Minsk aboard a steerage-class car, packed shoulder to shoulder with refugees fleeing the German occupation established with the Treaty of Brest-Litovsk. While the agreement had ostensibly brought peace to the region, tensions lingered, and the passengers seemed keenly aware of the fragile line between safety and danger. Alexander and Natalya kept to themselves, avoiding eye contact and speaking to each other only when absolutely necessary.

The forged documents provided by Viktor continued to serve them well at the checkpoints and inspections along the way, but every uniformed figure who entered the car—whether German or Soviet Russian—set their nerves on edge, as did the possibility that any of the other passengers might be Cheka agents sent to intercept them and the letter Alexander carried.

The train crawled eastward, crossing into Russian-controlled territory without incident but with an air of palpable unease. Armed border guards patrolled the aisles, scrutinizing and questioning passengers seemingly chosen at random, but as the train pressed on toward

Smolensk and passengers began disembarking at smaller stations along the way, the oppressive tension began to ease.

After Smolensk, the atmosphere shifted noticeably. The train became less crowded, the passengers more subdued, and the specter of immediate danger seemed to recede. For the first time since their departure from Minsk, Alexander and Natalya found themselves with a small measure of privacy, huddled together in the corner of their car, and Alexander was finally able to ask the question that had been burning in his mind for the better part of three days.

"Did you know Viktor was Cheka?"

Natalya gave him a wounded look. "Yes," she admitted quietly, and then, after a pause, went on, "But I did not think he would report our contact to Iron Felix."

"If Dzerzhinsky was willing to send Viktor after us, do you think he'll send someone else?"

"I have no doubt," she replied grimly. "He'll do whatever it takes to intercept that letter. He has eyes everywhere: agents at the station, informants in the streets."

"The damned letter," Alexander sighed.

"Sasha, I know your sense of duty won't allow you to open it. But you must see how that puts us at a disadvantage. Our only hope of outmaneuvering Dzerzhinsky is to open the letter and send the King's answer to Sverdlov by wire."

"And what if . . ." Alexander faltered. "What if our worst fears are true? What if the King truly intends to abandon the Romanovs?"

Natalya reached out and took his hand. "You are only the messenger, Sasha."

"Damn it, Natty. I'm not the messenger. I'm the bloody executioner."

She squeezed his hand. "Sasha, don't do this to yourself. You didn't ask for this mission, and you didn't write that letter. Whatever it says, you are not responsible for the consequences."

Alexander looked away, his jaw tightening. "Not responsible? Their fate will be sealed when I hand that letter over to Sverdlov."

Natalya hesitated, her sharp eyes searching his face. "Then . . . don't."

Alexander's brows drew together. "Don't? Natty, I told you. I—"

"Yes, yes, I know. You have your orders. Your duty. It's twisting you in knots, Sasha. But what if there's another way?"

"Another way?"

"Sverdlov doesn't know what the letter says. What if we were to . . . delay the delivery? I could wire and tell him that King George has agreed to the offer of asylum and sent you to act as an escort. An envoy of the British crown sent to accompany them to Vladivostok."

Alexander stared at her for a long moment. "You want me to lie."

"Sasha, I'm offering you an alternative. Once the Romanovs are on British soil, it will be much harder for your king to refuse sanctuary."

"But a lie, Natty."

She let go of his hand and leaned back, folding her arms over her chest. "Yes. A lie. A lie that will save lives. When all is said and done, your King may even thank you for it." She softened and then gave a wry smile. "Who knows? Perhaps that is exactly what the letter instructs you to do."

Alexander considered the suggestion. "Would Sverdlov believe it?"

"Of course. He's expecting me to give him the answer. Sverdlov isn't Dzerzhinsky. He's pragmatic and concerned with appearances. He *wants* to be rid of the Romanov problem."

"How . . . and I'm not saying I approve of this madness . . . how would we go about this?"

Natalya leaned forward. "When we reach Moscow, I will send a coded telegram to Sverdlov explaining what I just told you and inform him that we are traveling to Tobolsk as envoys to escort the family to Vladivostok, where they will board a British vessel. Then you and I will continue on to Siberia. The Tsar and his family have been under house arrest at the governor's mansion in Tobolsk for months now, under the supervision of Comrade Avdeev and a contingent of the Red Guard."

"This Avdeev—he'll accept us at face value?"

"He'll have his orders from Sverdlov by the time we arrive," Natalya replied. "And Sverdlov will believe the King's offer of asylum is genuine. He wants the Romanovs out of Russia as much as anyone. Exiling them under the guise of diplomacy saves him the trouble of deciding their fate. To him, this arrangement is far better than risking the Romanovs becoming martyrs. We'll likely be accompanied by the Red Guard as far as Vladivostok, but they will follow the orders of Comrade Sverdlov."

"What about the Chekists?"

"Once I send the wire, Dzerzhinsky will have no cause to interfere with us." She took his hand again. "This can work, Sasha."

Alexander looked away, gazing out the window at the Russian countryside rolling by. Natalya's plan, as audacious as it was, offered hope—a chance to save the Romanovs and to preserve the legacy of good King George.

But it would also require him to refuse his King's orders.

He reached into his coat and touched the letter.

What was written on it? A promise of asylum? Or a death warrant?

He leaned back, closing his eyes and exhaling sharply. *Damn the letter.*

He turned back to Natalya. "Let's do it. Let's save them."

The station at the terminus of the rail line connecting Smolensk and Moscow was, coincidentally, called Aleksandrovsky Vokzal—Alexander Station—named for Emperor Alexander I, who ruled the Russian Empire from 1801 until his death in 1825. During his reign, Russia fought alongside Britain against Napoleon, then briefly switched sides to form an alliance with Napoleon before ultimately standing against the Corsican during the latter's disastrous invasion attempt in 1812. Alexander Hawke did not know if sharing a name with his point of entry in Moscow boded good or ill. No doubt the victorious Bolsheviks would in due time change it, but for the present the name endured, a vestige of a vanished era clinging stubbornly to relevance in a city now transformed by revolution.

A product of imperial ambition, recently modernized, the sprawling edifice still bore the elegance of its neoclassical design. The pale stone facade gleamed faintly under a thin layer of soot, the inevitable consequence of Moscow's coal-burning locomotives. Its arched windows shone intact in the golden light of the late afternoon, though faint smudges betrayed months of wartime neglect. Red banners hung from the facade where the double-headed eagle had once been displayed, a stark reminder of the city's new reality.

As the train drew to a halt, Alexander joined the flow of disembarking passengers, his head slightly bowed, surreptitiously scanning the crowd, looking for anyone paying them a little too much attention. Natalya was right behind him, staying close and following the advice she had given him mere moments before.

"Iron Felix will have eyes here, Sasha. Keep your head down and don't make eye contact."

"What if we're spotted?"

"I don't think they'll move against us out in the open. That is not their way. We only have to reach the telegraph office."

They joined the flow of disembarking passengers, moving purposefully but without haste into the station. The interior was grand but not ostentatious, with wide, echoing corridors and high ceilings supported by elegant columns.

At the far end of the main hall, they passed by a small courtyard lined with benches, a few occupied by sleeping forms—weary travelers or refugees with nowhere else to go. Potted plants—likely meant to lend the area a touch of life—dotted the space, their leaves dusty and wilting from neglect.

They found the telegraph office just a short distance down the corridor. It consisted of a small lobby with a long counter where patrons could write their brief messages on cards and then pass them over to one of the clerks, who would, in turn, hand them off to the telegraphers. A handful of boys—runners with armbands marking them as couriers—loitered by the door, ready to deliver messages to their intended recipients.

Natalya had composed her coded missive on the train and so needed only to copy it onto the official form. As she approached the counter, Alexander did another quick check for possible spying eyes, and, finding none, leaned close to Natalya. "I'll be over there," he said, nodding in the direction of the courtyard.

She looked up, mildly alarmed. "We should stay together, Sasha."

He shook his head. "There's something I've got to do. Won't be a moment."

He didn't wait for her reply but hastened over to the courtyard, ducking behind one of the larger shrubs, where he took out the King's letter. The sealed envelope, tucked inside an oilcloth pouch, had not left his inner pocket since he'd changed into civilian clothes aboard the *Scimitar*.

He removed the envelope from the pouch and held it in his hand. Sealed with the wax stamp of King George, it had become more than a mere letter—inked words on parchment. It had become a sort of holy talisman. A quest artifact that he had borne faithfully across Europe. A quest that he was now abandoning.

Which made the letter a liability. If they were captured by the Cheka—and with Dzerzhinsky's agents likely hunting them, that was a very real possibility—the letter would not only give Dzerzhinsky a strategic advantage but quite likely expose Natalya's ruse. That could not be allowed to happen, which meant Alexander now had one last duty to perform.

He knelt down and placed the letter on the soil in the planter, then took a matchbook from his pocket. His hands trembled—not from fear, but from the gravity of what he was about to do.

He struck the match, its head flaring with a tiny burst of light and heat. He turned the stick, cultivating the flame, and then lowered it to the corner of the letter. The wax seal on the envelope caught the reflection of firelight, glinting mockingly.

He hesitated.

What if their plan failed? What if Sverdlov refused to believe Natalya's ploy or demanded some proof of the King's will? Burning the letter would mean severing the one tangible tie to the mission for which he'd crossed half of Europe.

The match burned down to his fingers, and he hissed, shaking it out. Then a new idea struck him. If he couldn't destroy it, he could at least hide it—somewhere no one would think to look. Somewhere he could retrieve it later if necessary.

He shoved the letter back into the oilcloth pouch and then, after a quick glance to ensure that no one was observing him, dug into the soft soil of the planter with his fingers. The earth was dry and crumbled easily, permitting him to scoop out a hollow along the edge. He slid the pouch into it and then covered it with dirt, patting it down until it looked undisturbed. His task accomplished, he dusted his hands off and then eased out from behind the plant just in time to see Natalya headed his way.

"What were you doing back there?"

He shrugged. "Burning that damned letter."

The lie left a bad taste in his mouth, but it was better, he reasoned, for only one of them to know where the letter was hidden.

Her expression changed from suspicion to relief. "Good." She glanced back toward the telegraph office. "I've sent the message. If Iron Felix tries to interfere with us now, he will have to answer to Comrade Sverdlov."

"And now?"

"Now, we take the tram to Yaroslavsky station, where we will book passage to Siberia."

Alexander gestured forward. "Lead on, Natty."

He fell in beside her, walking briskly through the station, and for the first time in weeks he felt an unfamiliar lightness settle over him. The burden of the letter and the dire possibilities it contained no longer weighed him down. As they made their way out of the station and joined the queue waiting for the electric tram, his thoughts turned to the path ahead, not the secret left behind.

THIRTY

LONDON

The 1962 Morgan Plus 4 drophead coupe purred contentedly as it cruised through London traffic, heading northward along Whitehall with Chief Inspector Ambrose Congreve at the helm.

The roadster, an audacious canary yellow, turned heads wherever it went, and Congreve relished the attention. In truth, the roadster, dubbed the "Peril" by Congreve, was more than a car; it was a symbol of his transformation, an impulsive purchase made not long after he met the lovely Lady Diana Mars—the woman who, against all odds, had won his heart. And he, her hand. Meeting Diana and falling in love with her had awakened something in him, a spirit of daring that ran completely counter to his logical nature, and the roadster itself had become emblematic of that transformation, a tangible manifestation of his choice to live boldly.

The late spring evening was cool and clear. The last rays of sun painted the city in shades of amber and rose as Congreve left Victoria Embankment behind, crossing the Thames at Waterloo Bridge. The river shimmered like a ribbon of gold beneath the iconic silhouettes of St. Paul's Cathedral and the London Eye. He navigated through the bustling streets of Bloomsbury, passing Russell Square and the British

Museum before heading north along the quieter residential avenues of Camden, eventually taking the second exit onto Charing Cross Road.

Crossing Euston Road, the scenery subtly changed. The towering glass and steel of the city center gave way to tree-lined streets and Victorian terraces as he entered Camden. Each turn brought him closer to Heart's Ease Cottage, his sanctuary in Hampstead Heath, and with it a life he still sometimes couldn't believe was his.

When he had considered himself a confirmed bachelor, Congreve always focused on intellectual pursuits rather than emotional ones. He could not have imagined a life more content than spending his evenings with only the company of a dusty leather-bound first edition of Conan Doyle and a glass of fine port. Marriage was not on the horizon, not because he disliked the idea but because he'd never thought himself capable of the kind of passion it required. He was too logical for it, too restrained, too . . . practical, he supposed. And yet he'd been wrong—profoundly so.

Though he loathed Shakespeare, there was a line from *Much Ado About Nothing* that summed him up perfectly: "When I said I would die a bachelor," quoth Benedick, the cynical romantic, "I did not think I should live till I were married."

Diana had swept into his life like a summer storm, rearranging all his well-considered assumptions about his life, present and future, and now he couldn't for the life of him remember why he had ever been opposed to the institution.

As he neared Hampstead, the city's rough edges seemed to soften a bit. The air seemed fresher, as though he'd crossed an invisible threshold between worlds, and the anticipation of reaching home buoyed him along. Yet, despite the promise of refuge and tranquility waiting for him at Heart's Ease, the weight of the unresolved investigation into the Silence murders felt like an anchor pulling him down.

In many ways it had become an almost routine investigation now, and that in itself was a source of frustration for Congreve, as it required nothing from his highly logical, intuitive mind. The digital bloodhounds at Scotland Yard were on the hunt, sniffing about in search of a scent trail, tracing the passenger manifests of the flights leaving Bermuda and arriving in London within the prescribed time frame, eliminating possible suspects, winnowing the list down in hopes of finally putting a face and a name to the infamous contract killer. They narrowed the list to a few dozen names and likely would soon have it down to just one. Yet, Congreve's cursory glance at the list revealed senior citizens, families, a pair of identical twin sisters from Poland, but no one he would consider a high-probability candidate.

No . . . that wasn't quite right. Something about the Polish sisters had tripped his detector. It wasn't anything about their background. Swimsuit models or some such nonsense who had probably come over for a photo shoot. What had struck him as odd was the fact that they had stayed in Bermuda for less than twenty-four hours. What sane person would go to all the bother of traveling to paradise and then turn around and leave the next day?

Hardly damning evidence, but it was unusual, and he was obliged to follow up on it. Fortunately, they had not left London, so he would have a chance to pay them a visit in person on the morrow, right before his audience with the King, where he hoped to learn exactly what secrets Dr. Ariadne Silk was carrying.

Yet, for all the semblance of progress, Congreve remained anxious. Time was not on their side. The killer might already have left London and might now be closing in on his next victim, Silk, and her loyal protector, Alex Hawke. And while Congreve did not doubt for a second that his good friend was more than capable of dealing with whatever the villain might throw at him, the uncertainty of the situation nagged at him.

He squeezed the steering wheel, trying to leave his worries behind like so much dust on the road and focus on happier things, like the person waiting for him at Heart's Ease Cottage. He thought about their first meeting when he and his good friend, the late Ross Sutherland, had paid her a visit at Brixden House, her ancestral manse in Gloucestershire, during the investigation of a criminal espionage case. She was peripherally involved—a witness rather than a suspect—but she possessed information critical to the case. Sutherland did most of the talking because Congreve, despite his years of experience in interrogation, found himself utterly undone by her beauty. Diana had swept into the room with an effortless grace, her auburn hair catching the light and her sharp, intelligent eyes alight with curiosity. She'd smiled—an easy, genuine smile that somehow made the grand drawing room feel smaller, more intimate—and Congreve had been reduced to the level of a tongue-tied schoolboy, fumbling over the simplest utterance. Nevertheless, by some miracle, Diana was struck by Cupid's arrow. Despite the fact that he was no prime physical specimen—somewhat . . . round, rather than athletic, with a perpetual baby face—she saw past his awkwardness and spied something precious in him . . . something that, even now, he couldn't quite fathom.

And the rest, as they say, was history.

Thinking of that happy day helped him bring everything into perspective. It wasn't that he put aside his concerns about the case. Rather, he was now looking forward to sharing the details with Diana. Unlike many police spouses, Mrs. Congreve did not insist that her husband leave his work at the office. From the beginning, Diana had been fascinated by the way his mind worked and, in her own way, through probing questions, helped him arrive at conclusions that might have otherwise eluded him. She was already very interested in the pursuit of the killer named Silence, and he was curious to see what she might have to say about the Polish sisters.

The Peril finally reached the edge of Hampstead Heath, and after a few minutes the gated entrance to Heart's Ease Cottage came into view. He hit the remote control to open the gate and then continued down the cobbled drive to the coach house, where he parked the Peril and then simply sat for a moment, embracing the air of calm and serenity. The evening air was scented with the faint aroma of lavender and freshly cut grass, and all was quiet.

Too quiet.

A strange foreboding crept over him. He gazed across the lawn to the main cottage, expecting the bright red front door to open and Diana to emerge, arms open to embrace him.

But the door remained closed.

Swallowing down his apprehension, he got out of the car and strode quickly up to the front of the cottage.

"Diana?" he called, throwing the door open. He set his keys on the table in the foyer and shrugged off his coat. "Darling, I'm home."

No answer.

His apprehension multiplied.

You're being an old ninny, he told himself. *She's probably in the garden, tending the dahlias.*

But something about the quiet gnawed at him. He moved through the house, calling her name again as he entered the great room.

On the low table near the fireplace was a bottle of red wine and two glasses. One of the glasses was half full, as if someone had just been drinking from it.

Diana did not drink.

"Diana?" he cried, dread bursting from his heart like magma.

The only answer he received was silence.

THIRTY-ONE

OFF THE COAST OF SOCHI

The *Flying Fox*'s tender moved smoothly through the dark waters, its hull gliding over the faint chop of the Black Sea. At forty feet in length, the sleek, custom-designed craft was a fitting companion to the opulence of its mother vessel. Built by the renowned Scandinavian manufacturer Windy Boats, the tender boasted a lightweight carbon fiber hull reinforced with Kevlar. The enclosed cabin featured premium leather seating for up to twelve passengers, teak flooring, and a small wet bar stocked with refreshments, but Hawke had chosen to stay outside on the foredeck lounge, where he could feel the cool night air against his face and keep an eye on the shore ahead.

Behind them, the yacht was a ghostly silhouette against the horizon, its lights reduced to a faint glimmer in the distance.

He shifted slightly on the built-in seat, his hand brushing the front of his dinner jacket. The forgery, produced by the Royal Archives, lay flat in a concealed inner pocket under his left lapel, designed to remain unnoticed during the sort of routine security frisk he expected from Putin's gatekeepers. The counterfeit document felt heavier than it ought to have, a tangible reminder of the gamble he was about to take. If everything went as planned, the blackmail threat would be neutralized, and he and Silk would depart with Putin none the wiser.

But if it didn't . . . well, Hawke didn't want to bloody think about that.

He glanced over at Silk, seated near the bow, her profile illuminated by the tender's running lights. She wore a tailored navy pantsuit beneath a designer trench coat, the ensemble striking a balance between elegance and professionalism. She looked every bit the poised academic she'd been at their first meeting at the Duke of Clarence's house, right down to the leather portfolio now resting on her lap, yet there was an edge to her demeanor—apprehension, no doubt, concerning the imminent meeting with one of the most powerful and dangerous men on earth.

Just the sight of her stirred a complex stew of emotions in Hawke. The memory of the previous night lingered—of what had *almost* happened and what actually had—and left a bittersweet aftertaste. He had refused her, though not without difficulty and a little help from Stokely, but now, as he studied her quiet composure, he felt equal measures of relief and regret.

Silk, for her part, appeared focused on the distant shore, her thoughts unreadable. Was she running through the plan again, bracing herself for an uncertain reception? Or was she, too, replaying the events of the previous night, imagining a different outcome?

Hawke couldn't tell, and he wasn't sure he wanted to know.

He let his gaze drift back to the approaching shoreline. A line of dim lights marked the edge of the harbor, and beyond that the crest of the Caucasus rose up like the spine of some great beast—Russia rising to devour them.

"Lovely night," Silk murmured, breaking the silence.

"I'll reserve judgment on that," Hawke replied nonchalantly.

She turned slightly, the boat's lights outlining her profile. "I suppose this is just another day at the office for you?"

Hawke chuckled. "As my American friends would say, this is not my first rodeo."

Her gaze lingered on him for a moment before drifting back to the horizon. "It's mine." She hesitated, then added quietly, "And I don't know if I'm ready for this."

It was quite a departure from the bravado she had exhibited in the King's study when the mission was first proposed. How did she put it? *"I'm more than capable of handling myself . . ."*

Talk, as the saying went, was cheap.

"Second thoughts?"

"No," she said quickly, her voice firm but her eyes betraying a flicker of doubt. "Just . . . thoughts. If this goes wrong—"

Hawke cut her off gently. "It's not going to go wrong. And if it does, you've got me. And the best damn backup team money can buy."

The corners of her lips twitched, but the smile didn't quite reach her eyes. "I suppose that should make me feel better."

"It should. But if it doesn't, just focus on doing what you came here to do. Get in there, authenticate the letter—or, better, prove that it's a forgery—and leave the rest to me."

She nodded slowly, her hands resting in her lap, though her fingers curled slightly as if bracing herself. "You make it sound so simple."

"It is," Hawke replied, though his tone betrayed his own apprehension. Against his better judgment, he put a hand on her arm. "Trust me."

Ahead, the lights of the Sochi Grand Marina glimmered like a diamond tiara against the darkened coastline. Designed to cater to the whims of the ultra-wealthy, the marina was a monument to opulence, a glimmering jewel on the Black Sea, with modern, pristine facilities, high-end boutiques, and fine-dining establishments, all within steps of the water. But the war in Ukraine had cast its shadow across the sea, diminishing the marina's gilded allure. While the superyachts still glided into their berths, the atmosphere of heightened security and the growing presence of military vessels in the Black Sea served as stark reminders that even luxury could not insulate its patrons from the ripples of global conflict.

Hawke's attention shifted to the boat's helm as the tender's captain slowed their approach, expertly maneuvering the craft toward a reserved slip near the customshouse. The tender's bow thrusters activated briefly, nudging the vessel perfectly alongside the dock, which inexplicably appeared to be deserted. Hawke rose from his seat, straightening his jacket as the tender's crew secured the craft. He glanced back at Silk, who sat composed but alert, her dark eyes scanning the marina. When the captain cut the engines, the stillness settled around them like a fog.

Hawke stepped onto the dock first, then offered his hand to Silk, assisting her with the transition.

"Now what?" she asked, glancing around nervously.

Her question was answered when three men stepped from the shadows near the customshouse and began moving purposefully toward them. They were attired in tailored suits, but the cut and fit of the garments couldn't mask the underlying brutishness of the wearers. Their broad shoulders, thick necks, and cold, dead eyes projected nothing less than unrestrained menace. Professional yet palpably hostile, they were no strangers to bloodshed—cut from the same cloth as the assassins Hawke had encountered on the train. He wondered if the men knew who he was or, more importantly, if they knew about the million-dollar bounty their boss had put on his head.

The tallest of the trio, a man with a scar tracing the line of his jaw, gestured back toward the customshouse. "This way."

He spoke English, but his accent was so thick, it took Hawke a moment to realize it.

Without waiting for a response, the men flanked Hawke and Silk, urging them along. Hawke exchanged a brief glance with Silk, his expression unreadable, before falling into step. The night air was cool and carried the faint tang of salt, but it did little to cut the tension that hung thick as they rounded the darkened customshouse and continued toward a black SUV—a Mercedes-AMG 63 with blacked-out windows—waiting on the far side.

When they reached the vehicle, Scar-Jaw turned to Hawke, assessing him coldly. "You have weapons?"

"My reputation precedes me, is that it?" said Hawke with a sardonic smile. "Of course I don't have weapons. Do you think I'm stupid?"

The man's lips twitched—not quite a smirk, but close. "Stupid men sometimes think they are clever."

With that, he raised a handheld metal-detecting wand and gestured for Hawke to lift his arms. Hawke complied, keeping his expression neutral as the device traced deliberately up and down his sides, over his chest, and across his back. The wand emitted only faint beeps as it passed over his cuff links. Scar-Jaw grunted, satisfied, and repeated the process with Silk, who stood stiffly but said nothing.

With that task completed, he gestured to the waiting vehicle. "Get in."

Hawke placed a hand lightly on Silk's arm, guiding her toward the open door, and then followed her into the dark, leather-scented interior. The door shut behind them with a decisive thud, sealing them inside.

Almost immediately, the Mercedes shot away from the marina like a missile, the driver attacking the road with a level of aggression that bordered on alarming. The tires shrieked as the vehicle whipped around sharp curves, the centrifugal force pressing Hawke and Silk alternately into their seats and against each other. The SUV's windows were so darkly tinted that even outside light had trouble getting through. But Hawke knew from studying satellite photos that Putin's summer palace was situated in the hills above the city, less than five miles inland from the marina; he also knew that the approach would be anything but direct—an uphill route that twisted and turned sharply through the densely packed neighborhoods of Sochi's wealthiest district. The residence itself sat at the crest of a wooded incline, and the winding road leading there was narrow and steep, with switchbacks that would be nothing short of nightmare-inducing at their current speed. Hawke suspected their driver would nevertheless make the attempt and braced himself for the sudden shifts he knew were coming. Beside him, Silk gripped the armrest with one hand and clutched her portfolio with the other.

"Can't see much from back here," she murmured, her voice breaking the long, unenforced silence. "Almost as though they don't want us to."

"Yes. Volodya likes to keep people in the dark."

"'Volodya'?"

"It's what Putin's friends call him. What I used to call him back when we were . . . well, not exactly friends, but not enemies either."

She turned toward him, her interest piqued. "You said he saved your life."

Hawke gave a thoughtful hum. "During Korsakov's little coup. The Count didn't take kindly to my meddling, and I ended up in one of his lovely accommodations. Energetika Prison. That's where I met Volodya. He was a guest there too. We had a common enemy back then. He helped me survive, and I helped him, indirectly, retake the Kremlin."

"How did you become enemies?"

"He became obsessed with restoring Russia's glory, rebuilding the empire. Volodya has a way of making you believe that he's the lesser evil, the pragmatic choice. But fundamentally he just wants power. He doesn't tolerate opposition and keeps a running tab of grudges."

"And you're on that list."

"Somewhere near the top, I imagine."

The SUV took a sharp turn, causing Silk to steady herself against the armrest. "And now we're willingly going to see him where he lives. Even though he wants to kill you."

"That's the job," Hawke said simply, though the edge in his voice suggested it was anything but simple. "But he's nothing if not pragmatic. He'll recognize that I'm worth more to him alive right now, at least until this business about the Romanov letter is resolved."

"Do you think he's capable of letting bygones be bygones?"

"I think Volodya only forgives if it suits him. And he never forgets."

THIRTY-TWO

They drove on for another twenty minutes; then, almost abruptly, the wild ride ended as the Mercedes slowed almost to a full stop, made a sharp right-hand turn, and proceeded forward at a more sedate pace.

Hawke allowed himself a quick mental inventory of his assets: the forged letter in its hidden pocket, the discreet GPS tracker in his left cuff link, and, most importantly, the knowledge that Thunder and Lightning would be standing by, ready to move if things went sideways.

A few minutes later they came to a complete halt and, after what seemed like an interminable delay, the door opened and Scar-Jaw appeared, framed in the doorway.

"Get out," he said, his lips curling into a contemptuous sneer.

"Don't mind if I do," replied Hawke evenly.

He slid out from the vehicle. All around him, the grounds were shrouded in darkness. The shapes of structures and trees were hinted at only by their faint silhouette against the night sky. There were no lamps, no illuminated windows, nothing to break the enveloping darkness. Even the outline of the main building was barely discernible, its angular silhouette merging with the night sky. The lack of light wasn't an oversight but a calculated strategy, shrouding the presidential palace in a veil of darkness.

Hawke turned and offered his hand to Silk. She took it, letting him draw her out, and then held on as they followed their escorts up a narrow, gravel-lined path. The crunch of their footsteps was the only sound, sharp and distinct in the quiet. The security men moved ahead, leading them toward the vague outline of a heavy double door that loomed in the shadows like a portal to the unknown. Scar-Jaw stepped forward to pull it open.

What lay beyond was a void—pitch-black and impenetrable. No light spilled from within to reveal the space they were about to enter. The darkness seemed alive, swallowing sound and motion.

Scar-Jaw urged them forward with only a gesture, as if the gloom had deprived him of his surliness. Stifling his apprehension, Hawke guided Silk over the threshold and into the void. His wariness deepened when Scar-Jaw and the others followed them in and then pulled the doors closed behind them.

Almost immediately, the darkness began to recede. Light emanating from recessed fixtures began to rise, illuminating their surroundings gradually so as not to blind them. The entryway came into focus: a high-ceilinged, austere space with smooth stone walls, a polished floor, and another set of closed double doors at the far end. It felt more like an air lock than an entry foyer.

Scar-Jaw pushed forward and threw the inner doors open, then stood there, gesturing for Hawke and Silk to proceed. They stepped through into a luxuriously appointed great room, paneled with dark, polished wood, segmented by ornate columns with gilded accents. A massive crystal chandelier hung from the vaulted ceiling, its light refracting faintly on the smooth, inlaid marble floor. Heavy velvet drapes in deep crimson and gold embroidery framed what looked like a series of tall windows, which a second glance revealed to actually be enormous high-definition video screens displaying a real-time view of the world outside. Leather armchairs and low tables were arranged about the perimeter, and at the far end stood a fireplace with an elaborately carved mantel.

"Looks like the lair of a proper Bond villain," Hawke murmured.

They were not alone in the hall. In addition to Scar-Jaw and the other two men who had accompanied them from the marina, there were four more men, all but one of whom looked to have been turned out from the same basic mold. The outlier looked no less thuggish but appeared to be older than the others by at least a score of years.

At first glance Hawke dismissed the men as just another layer of Putin's security detail: hulking, humorless enforcers from the FSB or some other state security outfit. But when he gave the older man a second look, meeting his steely gaze, he felt a jolt of recognition. He had seen the man's picture before in countless MI6 briefings following the attack on the NATO reception in Istanbul.

It was Sergei Yevgenyevich Mulmuscovy, the oligarch known as the Moscow Mule, founder and CEO of the mercenary army known as Perun Group, a close confidant to Putin . . . and the man voted most likely to be the Warmonger.

Mulmuscovy regarded him for a long moment, smiling without humor. "Lord Alexander Hawke," he said, his voice a low rumble that carried easily across the room. "I've been looking forward to meeting you." His gaze hardened. "You owe me a boat."

Hawke returned a sardonic smile. "From what I've heard, it was your own men . . . mutineers, in fact, who commandeered your yacht. Good help is so hard to find. You should thank me, actually. They were going to scuttle her. I saved your little boat and handed it over to the proper authorities. If you want it back, you'll have to take the matter up with them. You'll understand if they're reluctant to give up their prize. You have a reputation as something of a . . . warmonger."

Mulmuscovy's expression remained frozen, unreadable. Then, leaving the bait on the hook, he made a dismissive gesture. "This way."

He turned and strode toward a door on the far side of the hall. Silk cast a worried glance over at Hawke, an unspoken question for which the only answer Hawke had was a shrug.

They fell into step behind Mulmuscovy, but the security detail, curiously, stayed behind.

Mulmuscovy led them down a flight of stairs that, Hawke realized, could only lead to a subterranean level—a fortified bunker, perhaps, where Putin could feel safe from the reach of Ukrainian drones and missiles. But if that was the purpose of the underground construction, it was not reflected in the decor. The stairwell and the hallway into which it opened were, just like the great room, decorated in classic fashion. The Russian brought them to a closed door, which he opened, and then stood back, indicating that they should enter.

The room beyond was smaller than Hawke had expected, a much more intimate setting than the great hall but no less luxurious. Paneled walls lined with bookshelves filled with leather-bound tomes gave the space a scholarly air. At the far end, a polished desk sat in front of a marble fireplace.

Standing beside it was Vladimir Putin.

Hawke broke the silence first. “Hello, Volodya. It’s been a while.”

Putin’s lips curled into a derisive smile. “Alex. They told me you were coming, but I didn’t believe it was true. I didn’t think you had the balls.”

“You haven’t changed a bit, Volodya. Still underestimating me, are you? Hmm, with all our *history*, I would have thought you’d have learned that lesson by now.”

Putin regarded him for a long moment. “No, I think *you* are the one who underestimates *me*.” He turned to Mulmuscovy and extended his hand. “Give me your gun.”

The words were delivered so calmly that it took a moment for their meaning to register. Without hesitation, Mulmuscovy drew a compact Makarov pistol from a low-profile holster concealed under his suit jacket and brought it over to Putin.

“Really? After I’ve come all this way?” Hawke tried to keep his tone light—tried not to reveal his spiking anxiety. He had been so certain that Putin would set aside his grudge in the name of self-interest; had he actually *overestimated* his old nemesis? “Don’t you want to have a drink first? Catch up? I hear you’ve been rather busy.”

"All I want," said Putin, leveling the gun at Hawke, "is to hear you begging for your life."

Hawke held his gaze steady. "Sorry to disappoint, old chap. Not going to happen."

Putin stared back for a long moment, doubtless looking for a tell, some hint that Hawke's resolve would fail. Finally he shrugged. "Then I shall have to settle for simply listening to you die."

His finger began to tighten on the trigger.

He's bluffing, thought Hawke. *He won't*. . .

THIRTY-THREE

Suddenly, Silk was standing between him and the gun.

"Stop this!" she cried, with far less trepidation than Hawke would have expected.

"Move the bitch out of the way," said Putin in an oddly calm voice.

But Silk did not move. "If you so much as scratch him, you can forget about any concessions from the Crown. I'll report that the letter is fake, no matter how authentic it is."

Putin's eyes narrowed, his finger still poised on the trigger as he studied Silk, seemingly testing her resolve. Then, with a hint of a smile, he thumbed the safety on and lowered the pistol, setting it down on the desktop.

"Business first, then," he said, sounding faintly amused. "Sergei, get our friends something to drink. Let's make them feel . . . welcome."

Mulmuscovy moved without comment, stepping to a sideboard lined with crystal decanters and ornate glasses. Hawke continued to regard Putin but watched the oligarch from the corner of one eye as he produced a bottle of clear liquid, decanting some of the contents into three tumblers.

Putin meanwhile turned his attention to Silk. He snatched a brown folder off the desk and held it up. "I believe this is what you came for," he said, and then tossed it to her with an air of supreme indifference.

She caught the folder out of the air with an almost frantic look, as if he had just lobbed over a bottle of nitroglycerine, and held it at arm's length for a moment before finally drawing it in and opening it. She took a steadying breath, then turned back the flap to reveal a sheet of aged, yellowing paper—the original from which the copy Hawke had seen at Clarence House had been made.

Silk studied it for a long moment before raising her eyes to Putin. "I'll need an idea of the document's provenance."

"It is an interesting story," he said, turning his attention back to Hawke. "I think you will especially enjoy it, Alex. It was found in the Lubyanka Building archives, buried among the personal papers of Felix Dzerzhinsky himself. You know of him, of course—Iron Felix, founder of the Cheka, predecessor to the KGB?

"The letter was in the possession of a spy who was captured by the Bolsheviks during the Revolution and sent to Lubyanka Prison. A certain Lord Alexander Hawke—your great-grandfather, I believe." Putin narrowed his eyes at Hawke. "But of course, you knew that, didn't you? That's why you're here, daring my wrath in the name of family honor. Did you realize that your ancestor was a part of this treacherous chapter in history?"

"It may have come up," replied Hawke equivocally.

Putin nodded slowly. "I'm told he died there many, many years later."

"And it just suddenly turned up now, huh? After all these years?"

"Who can say?" said Putin with a shrug. "Perhaps it was found many years ago. Something like this?" He gestured toward the document in Silk's hands. "You hold on to it for a . . . how do you say it? A rainy day?"

Mulmuscovy chose that moment to bring over a tray of drinks. He placed an empty glass and an opened bottle of Sanpellegrino on the desk for Putin—a well-known teetotaler—and then set two rocks glasses, frosted from the chill of the clear liquid they contained, on a side table closer to the two visitors. He took the remaining tumbler for himself and returned to his earlier station near the fireplace.

Hawke picked up one of the glasses and held it up as if inspecting the contents. "A last drink for the condemned man?"

Putin waved the question away. "Please. We both know I wasn't going to shoot you. Not here, in my private sanctuary." He pointed to the ornate floor covering on which Hawke now stood, a stunning production, red and gold woven into elaborate geometric patterns. "That is a vintage Bokhara rug—late eighteenth century. Do you know how difficult it is to get bloodstains out of wool?" He waved again. "I can have you killed any time I wish. This is much more entertaining."

"Lord Hawke was an emissary from King George carrying a communiqué to the Bolshevik leadership," said Silk. "Why was he arrested and treated as a spy?"

Putin glanced over, his expression inscrutable. "Who can say? The Bolsheviks were not known for their transparency, even with one another. There were rival factions within the party even then. Perhaps they suspected him of duplicity. Perhaps they simply needed a scapegoat. The Revolution was not kind to outsiders, particularly those with noble titles."

Silk nodded slowly, her focus returning to the document. She placed the open folder on the desk. "It appears to be authentic. But of course we would expect nothing less of an expert forgery. I'll need to take samples back to London for definitive testing. Paper, ink, and the wax seal."

Putin waved a hand dismissively. "Take what you need. It will only confirm what I've told you."

Hawke knew he wouldn't get a better opportunity to make the switch. He stepped forward quickly. "May I have a look?"

Silk hesitated, glancing at Putin, who nodded once, almost lazily. "By all means. I'm sure you must feel a personal connection."

Hawke advanced, stepping around Silk, who had not yielded her position, and set his untasted tumbler of vodka down on the edge of the desktop, mere inches from the folder and, Hawke noted, within easy reach of Mulmuscovy's Makarov. Putin evidently did not consider him to be a threat.

"Please don't touch it," Silk cautioned. "The oils in your fingerprints will stain the parchment."

"I'll be careful," Hawke assured her. And then, as if to counterpoint the assertion, his reaching hand brushed against the tumbler, knocking it off the desk and onto the antique rug.

"Blyad!" cried Putin, his attention snapping downward as liquor splashed across the intricate patterns.

In that instant, with the attention of everyone present diverted, Hawke slipped the counterfeit letter from his jacket lining, placed it over the original, and then drew the latter back, stuffing it none too carefully into the now-vacant pocket. Then, he knelt, picking up the fallen glass as if doing so might reverse the damage done. "Terribly sorry, old chap. I'm a bloody mess. Damned nerves got the best of me, you know."

Putin seethed at him. "Do you have any idea what that rug is worth?"

"I'll cover the cleaning costs, of course. Just send me the bill." With the empty glass now in hand, he rose to his feet, surreptitiously checking to make sure that neither Silk nor Mulmuscovy had noticed his performance.

Silk's expression was unreadable. If she had seen him make the switch, she gave no hint. The oligarch, still holding station by the fireplace, seemed completely oblivious. "You are lucky it was vodka," he said with a mild chuckle. "It will evaporate without causing any damage."

Hawke let out his breath in a slow sigh.

Mission accomplished, he thought. *Now all that's left is—*

What happened next caught him completely off guard. Before he knew what was happening, Silk had seized the pistol off the desktop, thumbed off the safety, and taken aim at the Russian president.

"Ariadne?" Hawke gasped, momentarily lost for words. "What the bloody hell are you doing?"

"What you should have done a long time ago," she replied coolly, without even a trace of her earlier anxiety. Her focus never wavered from Putin.

Putin regarded her with a look of pure venom. “Assassin,” he said, his voice low and sharp as a scalpel. “If you put that gun down now, I just might let you live out the rest of your natural life in my old cell in Energetika Prison.”

“And if I don’t?” Silk asked, her voice wry, almost casual.

“Then my friend Sergei will make you beg to die.”

Mulmuscovy, however, did not second the threat but remained mute and motionless at his station by the fireplace as if curious to see how the drama would play out.

Silk’s expression didn’t change. She shook her head slowly, a faint smirk playing at the corner of her lips. “I don’t think so,” she said, and then pulled the trigger.

THIRTY-FOUR

The sound of the shot was deafening in the enclosed space. A red starburst appeared right above the bridge of the Russian president's nose. His head snapped backward, his body toppling like a felled tree to crash down on his priceless rug.

Behind them, Mulmuscovy gasped and then bolted for the door, reaching it before either Hawke or Silk could even think about trying to stop him. Hawke barely noticed. He just stared down at the unmoving figure, struggling to process what had just happened.

Silk calmly turned to him. "Here. You might need this," she said, and tossed the pistol to him. His reflexes were half a second slow. The Makarov thumped against his chest and started to fall before he caught it clumsily.

"What . . ." It was all he could manage to say.

"You're not the only one on His Majesty's Secret Service," said Silk cryptically. "Now, maybe we should think about getting out of here."

Hawke's grip tightened around the pistol as he tried to make sense of what Silk had just said.

"You're not the only one on His Majesty's Secret Service."

His mind raced, but there was no time to dwell. They were deep in enemy territory, and Silk had just committed an act of war.

She moved toward the door, her manner icily calm. "Are you coming? Or would you prefer waiting around to explain this to Mulmuscovy and his merry band of psychopaths?"

That snapped Hawke into motion. He crossed the room and followed her out into the corridor. Silk was already making her way toward the stairwell, moving quickly but carefully, checking corners and doorways with the sort of tactical awareness that he suspected wasn't taught at archivist school.

"You're not the only one on His Majesty's Secret Service."

"MI6 sent you to kill him?" Hawke whispered.

Silk shot him a sharp glance over her shoulder. "You're quick. But this isn't the time for a debrief."

Hawke was tempted to challenge that position. He desperately needed to understand what was happening. If Silk was MI6, why hadn't he been read in on the operation? And what would the fallout be for Britain? For the whole world?

Vladimir Putin was gone—removed from the board in one swift, irreversible act.

Would his death plunge Russia into chaos, a power vacuum filled by opportunistic warlords like Mulmuscovy? Or would his absence finally signal a shift, a chance for new leadership to step back from the brink to which Putin's relentless aggression had brought not only Russia but the entire world?

Hawke wondered if he would live long enough to have his questions answered.

As they reached the top of the stairwell, Silk held up a hand, signaling him to stop. She cracked the door open, peering through the narrow gap. Then, with a muttered curse, she pulled back. "They're waiting for us."

Hawke leaned forward just far enough to glimpse several members of the security detail, positioned facing the stairwell, their weapons drawn and their expressions grim. He shook his head. "This was a hell of a plan," he muttered, then gave Silk an accusing look. "If you'd included me in . . . whatever the hell this was . . . maybe I could have helped come up with a better one."

Silk didn't flinch, her focus still on the door. "If I had included you, you probably wouldn't have gone through with it."

Hawke frowned, his voice sharpening. "You think I'd balk at taking out a monster like Putin?"

She turned to face him fully for the first time, her expression calm but unyielding. "Putin had a hold over you, whether you're willing to admit it or not. Your shared history and sense of obligation. You likely would have tried to justify sparing him. But this needed to be done, no matter the cost."

The accusation hit harder than he would have expected, and Hawke had no rebuttal. The awful truth was that Silk was right. How many times had he spared Volodya's life, even when the man's assassins had come after him, threatened his son, and killed the people he loved? He should have made exterminating Putin his number one priority, but instead he had equivocated and, in so doing, allowed the dictator to bring the world to the brink of war.

And now Silk had done what he had not been able to bring himself to do.

But still, Putin was a head of state. Political assassination was strictly prohibited. He could not imagine Sir David Trulove, or anyone else in the government, sanctioning such a course of action.

The sound of low voices outside the door snapped him back into the moment. His hand drifted to his cuff link, which contained both a GPS tracker and the panic button that would summon Thunder and Lightning. One press, and they would be on their way.

But it would take time for the mercenaries to reach them—too much time. Even in the best-case scenario, they'd have to hold out long enough for the team to breach the compound, and with Mulmuscovy's men already positioned to trap them, that was a fantasy. The stairwell was the proverbial barrel, and he and Silk were the fish at the bottom of it.

"We have to wave the white flag," he said quietly, the words bitter on his tongue. "It's the only way we're getting out of this alive."

To his surprise, Silk didn't argue. She glanced at him, her expression unreadable, and then gave a short, almost imperceptible nod. "I agree," she said evenly. "We're not going to be able to fight through them."

Hawke frowned. He'd expected resistance to the idea of surrender. After all, why else had she given him the Makarov if not to shoot their way out? But she seemed oddly at peace with his decision, almost as if she'd anticipated it.

As if eavesdropping on their conversation, Mulmuscovy called out from beyond the door. "You can't escape. But if you turn yourselves over, I promise you will live long enough to stand trial."

"Trial," Hawke muttered. "How uncommonly civil of him."

Silk didn't reply. Her attention remained fixed on the stairwell door. Hawke couldn't shake the feeling that she wasn't nearly as concerned as she ought to have been. Her calm acceptance felt wrong—too deliberate. But then, what did he really know about her? Everything she had shown him was an act. Everything he thought he knew about her was a lie.

Now wasn't the time to interrogate her motives, Hawke told himself. Returning his attention to the door, he called out, "Looks like you've got us dead to rights, old boy. I'm going to toss out the gun."

Without waiting for an acknowledgment, he placed the pistol on the floor and gave it a shove, sending it sliding through the narrowly opened door and out into the great room.

"A wise decision," said Mulmuscovy. "Now, if you would be so kind, please come out with your hands raised."

Hawke exchanged another glance with Silk, who answered with a slight nod. Then he pushed the door open and stepped out with his hands in the air. All six members of the security detail stood at a remove of about ten yards, handguns trained on them, with the oligarch standing just behind them. Two of the men holstered their weapons and advanced on Hawke and Silk, roughly wrestling their hands behind their backs, securing them with cable ties, which were pulled so tight that Hawke could feel the plastic edges biting into the skin of his wrists. The men then shoved them forward toward Mulmuscovy, who watched with a faintly amused look.

"Well, well," he said, sounding almost smug. "British secret agent Alexander Hawke has just assassinated President Putin. What will the world say when they learn of this?"

"Probably that I did them all a favor," Hawke replied, not bothering to correct the oligarch regarding who had *actually* pulled the trigger.

"You are more right than you know." There was a triumphant gleam in the oligarch's eyes, and it occurred to Hawke that Mulmuscovy was not the least bit upset about Putin's demise. *Almost as if* . . .

He glanced over at Silk, a new suspicion forming.

"Alas," Mulmuscovy went on, "you will not be around to enjoy their accolades."

"Ah, so that bit about the trial . . . that was just you having us on. I should have known better than to take a Russian at his word."

Mulmuscovy shrugged. "Whether you have a trial or not is of no concern to me. I will hand you over to the FSB. They will decide your fate." He narrowed his eyes at Hawke, appraising him. "You are thinking that your friends on the yacht are going to come to the rescue."

Hawke managed, barely, to keep his expression neutral.

Now, how the bloody hell did he know about that?

Mulmuscovy nodded as if Hawke's nonreaction was an affirmative. "I want to show you something. Come over here." He gestured to one of the high-def "windows," which showed the lights of Sochi in the foreground and the vast expanse of the Black Sea beyond, and began moving toward it. One of Hawke's captors grabbed his biceps, propelling him forward.

Mulmuscovy nodded toward the distant horizon, where a few pinpoints of light marked the location of boats on the water. "Which one is yours? Can you tell?"

Hawke remained stone-faced.

The Russian gave an odd smile. "Maybe we can do something to . . . illuminate it." He reached into a pocket and took out a mobile phone, thumbed the screen a few times, and then spoke into it. Something in Russian, short and sharp. *"Gotovy?"* ("Ready?")

Hawke felt a cold knot form in his stomach. Mulmuscovy glanced over at him, his smile widening. "Watch closely, Alex," he said in English, and then uttered one more word in his native tongue. *"Pusk!"* ("Start!")

For a moment, nothing changed in the dark tableau. Then a faint flicker appeared out near the horizon—small, barely noticeable, but unmistakable. Just as quickly as it appeared, it was gone—a fleeting will-o'-the-wisp.

Thirty seconds ticked by with agonizing slowness.

A minute.

"Wait for it," crooned Mulmuscovy.

Suddenly another, much brighter flash lit up the dark water like a supernova.

Hawke did not need to be told what he had just witnessed, but Mulmuscovy told him nevertheless. "That," the Russian said with undisguised delight, "was your yacht having an unfortunate encounter with a Kalibr cruise missile launched from the *Admiral Essen*." He slipped his phone back into his pocket. "Now we are even."

Hawke felt his guts twist at the senseless act of violence. Not just the destruction of the yacht but the staggering loss of life. He forced the emotion down, refusing to give the oligarch even a sliver of satisfaction. "Well," he muttered, "I guess I won't be getting my deposit back."

THIRTY-FIVE

Despite his outward display of cool triumph, Sergei Mulmuscovy was profoundly unsettled.

The world as he had known it had just changed utterly. Vladimir Putin, the man who had imposed his iron will on Russia for more than a quarter of a century, was dead at the hands of an assassin, and it was not altogether certain what the future would look like.

First things first.

He turned to his chief lieutenant, Yuri Borodin—the man Alex Hawke had dubbed "Scar-Jaw." "Take them to the airport," Mulmuscovy said. "I want them on a plane to Moscow within the hour. We must move quickly before the word gets out."

Borodin nodded stiffly and then turned to the other men, all of whom immediately complied without having to be told twice. The men were all members of Mulmuscovy's personal guard, his *urody*—bastards. Like many of the foot soldiers in the Perun Group—Mulmuscovy's private mercenary force—the Bastards had been recruited from Russia's prisons, but unlike the rank and file, the cannon fodder, the Bastards were unique. They were predators of the first order, handpicked not just for their capacity for violence but for their utter lack of conscience. Pulled from places like Black Dolphin, White Swan, and Energetika, these were men whose crimes had made them legends in the Russian penal system—serial killers and sadists.

Once selected, candidates were subjected to a training program so brutal, it made the prison environment seem like a stay at a resort. Beatings were routine, not as punishment but as a tool to strip away weakness. Failure wasn't corrected; it was eliminated. Washouts became live prey in training exercises. The survivors emerged as something closer to weapons than men, their loyalty absolute, honed to a razor's edge. They were so efficient, so dependable, that when Mulmuscovy was tasked with assigning Putin's personal security detail, he chose them without hesitation.

Not that it did him much good, Mulmuscovy thought grimly.

He watched as Borodin and his men herded the captive assassins out the door and off to meet their fate, his thoughts already shifting to what would have to happen next. The most important thing now was to shape the narrative. Truth would matter far less than perception in the hours to come. The first version of events to reach the ears of the Kremlin, the media, and the people would be the one that stuck, and Mulmuscovy intended to ensure it was his.

He turned and descended the staircase leading to the study. The smell of gunpowder lingered in the air, a subtle reminder, if one was needed, that what he had witnessed earlier, impossible though it seemed, had not been a dream. The unmoving form of Vladimir Putin sprawled across his precious Bokhara rug confirmed it. Mulmuscovy moved to stand over his fallen president.

"I am sorry it ended like this, Volodya," he murmured. "But you reached too far."

His eyes moved to the desk, where the glass of sparkling water Putin had left untouched still stood, an absurdly mundane detail in the tableau of death.

"You made them look at us too closely," he went on. "The bear must remain ferocious in the eyes of the world, even if she is starving and toothless. That was the illusion we built together. But you . . . you couldn't stop yourself. You pushed too far, and now you've brought us to this."

Putin, of course, had no answer.

Mulmuscovy sighed, then drew out his phone, this time entering a different number. The call connected almost instantly, and he spoke without a preamble. "It's done."

THIRTY-SIX

Mulmuscovy's thugs marched Hawke and Silk through the now-dark entry foyer and out into the cool night. Hawke kept his eyes on the ground, not out of submission but to hide the storm raging in his head.

The situation had gone wildly out of control, and he was struggling to keep up. Silk an assassin working for MI6? Putin, dead? The *Flying Fox* and everyone aboard her blown all to hell?

How did I get this so wrong?

Hawke realized he'd been playing the wrong game from the start, looking for duplicity in all the wrong places. Looking for the trap when he was already in it.

He glanced over at Silk, hoping to find illumination, some hint of explanation in her expression, but she showed only the same unsettling calm she'd shown since putting a bullet in Putin's skull, her face unreadable, her gaze fixed straight ahead. Not defeated, not defiant—just . . . satisfied?

If she really was MI6, why hadn't he been told? Why the elaborate charade with the Romanov letter?

Or was that part real? Had Putin, with his blackmail scheme, unthinkingly created the opportunity for MI6 to send an assassin into his inner sanctum?

Hawke could imagine Sir David playing that sort of three-dimensional chess game, treating his assets—even Hawke himself—as pawns on the board, but why leave him in the dark as to the true motive? Why bring him along at all?

His jaw tightened as an earlier thought resurfaced, unwelcome but impossible to ignore: *Unless MI6 had nothing to do with this . . .*

Unless she's working for someone else.

He looked away, forcing himself to focus on the ground ahead while scanning the surrounding area as discreetly as possible. It didn't matter who Silk was working for. What mattered was getting out of this mess alive.

He was braced between two of Mulmuscovy's thugs, as was Silk. Scar-Jaw was in the lead, almost to the waiting Mercedes, which was already idling, evidently started remotely. A sixth man brought up the rear.

Six against one, he mused. Or maybe against two, depending on whether he could count on Silk to join in. Not impossible odds.

The men would be overconfident, trusting in their superior numbers and physical strength to overcome any show of resistance. He could use that against them.

Hawke tested the cable ties binding his wrists. They were tight—so tight that his fingers were already going numb—but he could make that work to his advantage.

They were just a few steps away from the Mercedes. Scar-Jaw had already opened the rear door so that his comrades could shove the captives inside.

Never a better time than now.

He changed his stance subtly, resisting his captors just a little, slowing his steps just enough to force them to exert slightly more effort. Scar-Jaw was just a pace ahead, facing them as he held the rear door open wide. The man holding Hawke's right biceps thrust him toward the opening.

Now!

In one explosive motion, Hawke used his captor's energy to propel himself forward but twisted his body, redirecting his momentum toward Scar-Jaw, driving his forehead into the man's face. The big man let out a strangled grunt and staggered backward, slamming into the closed front door.

Hawke didn't stop. He twisted his body again, breaking the grip of his two captors. Then he raised his arms up behind his back as high as they would go and brought them down sharply against his backside, exerting outward pressure at the instant of impact. The cable ties broke apart with a satisfying snap, and just like that his hands were free.

Scar-Jaw was already recovering, shaking his head to clear it, inadvertently flinging gobs of dark blood from his mashed nose, but Hawke didn't give him a chance to launch a counterattack. Leaping forward, he landed an uppercut to the man's chin and then in the same motion grabbed hold of his collar and slammed his head into the front window hard enough to send spiderweb cracks radiating through the ballistic glass. As the lead thug slumped senseless, Hawke darted a hand into the man's jacket, coming up with his sidearm. His thumb instinctively searched the unfamiliar weapon for a safety. There wasn't one. That meant it was probably a GSh-18 or something very similar to a Glock, with no manual safety to fumble with.

And that meant it was ready to use.

He whipped around to face the two men who had, just moments before, been holding his arms. They were already reacting to his unexpected escape bid but had not yet fully grasped his intent. If they had, they would have come up with guns drawn. They didn't. He did.

Hawke took the first man out with a point-blank headshot, but the second man lunged, closing with him before Hawke could shift his aim. Hawke barely had time to brace himself as the thug slammed into him, trying to wrest the weapon from his grip. Hawke didn't fight him but instead drove his knee into the man's gut. The thug staggered but didn't fall, his hands still fighting for control of the pistol. Hawke kneed him again, then wrenched both his hands and the pistol free and swiped the latter across the side of the man's temple, dropping him in his tracks.

Hawke spun toward the others in the group just in time to see the man who had been bringing up the rear drawing a weapon while the pair escorting Silk were trying to drag her out of the line of fire.

Too many bloody moving pieces, thought Hawke.

He decided saving Silk was the immediate priority. The surviving thugs could use her for leverage against him, compel him to surrender a second time. So, ignoring the gunman, he dropped to one knee and fired a quick shot at one of her captors. He had to aim wide to avoid hitting her, and so instead of killing him, the bullet struck the man in the thigh. He did not cry out, but the shock of the wound caused his grip on Silk to weaken just enough for her to wrench herself free from his grasp. The sudden motion caused her to fall forward, which gave Hawke a wide-open shot at the other man holding her.

He took it.

At almost the same instant, a bullet slammed into the side panel of the Mercedes with a metallic thud, missing him by mere inches. He rolled forward, coming up in a crouch, and returned fire, forcing the gunman to dive for cover. Hawke didn't follow him but pivoted toward Silk, who was on the ground, her hands still bound, awkwardly kicking her way backward as the man Hawke had only wounded hobbled toward her.

Hawke surged toward them, closing the distance in a few long strides, and before the man could react, he brought the pistol down in a sharp arc, cracking the butt into the man's temple, dropping him in the gravel.

"Ariadne! Get up!"

She stared up at him, the eyes behind her lenses luminous in the darkness, and for a moment Hawke didn't think she was going to move. Then the moment passed and she half rolled into a kneeling position and got her feet under her.

Just then the remaining gunman leaned out from behind cover and fired. His shot was wilder than it had any right to be. Hawke and Silk were in the open, fully exposed, but somehow he missed. Hawke, who was a believer in the axiom *Never interrupt your enemy when he is making a mistake*, took full advantage, returning fire and forcing the man to pull back again.

But he wasn't about to trade shots with the man all night. Keeping low, with the pistol extended, he grabbed Silk with his free hand and half dragged her toward the Mercedes.

"Get in!" he snapped, pushing her toward the open rear compartment. She hesitated for only a moment before complying, kneeling in and then scooting forward until she was clear. Hawke slammed the door shut and then bent over Scar-Jaw, patting him down until he found the key fob, then pulled open the door and climbed in. As soon as the door was shut, he jammed down on the lock button, sealing them inside and the bad guys out.

"Hold on!" Hawke shouted, throwing the transmission into gear and slamming his foot onto the accelerator. The tires spun for a moment, slipping and throwing out a spray of gravel before catching purchase, and then the G-Class surged forward. Hawke twisted the steering wheel hard to the right, sending the Mercedes into a tight arc that flung Silk across the rear compartment, eliciting a cry of dismay.

Outside, the surviving members of Mulmuscovy's security detail were leaping out of the way of the onrushing juggernaut. A few shots were fired, but the rounds thumped harmlessly off the ballistic glass.

Hawke steered onto the driveway, straightened the wheel, and put the pedal to the floor. The faint outline of the winding road was barely visible in the darkness. Hawke hesitated, weighing the risk of turning on the headlamps, and then reached for the switch.

The lights blazed to life, instantly revealing the road ahead. The surrounding trees cast long, twisting shadows, their branches clawing at the edges of the light. The decision to reveal their position wasn't one he had made lightly. Running dark would confound any pursuit, but navigating the narrow, unfamiliar driveway at high speed without visibility was a surefire way to end up wrapped around one of those trees.

The driveway curved sharply to the left, and Hawke cranked the wheel to match, the SUV's bulk leaning heavily into the turn. The headlamps swung with the motion, revealing the next obstacle: a massive steel gate set on a sliding track, stretching between two concrete posts, reinforced to stop anything short of a tank from getting in.

"Bollocks," he muttered.

Most gates of this sort were meant to keep people out, not prevent them from leaving, and were equipped with a proximity sensor to open them with the approach of a vehicle. Evidently, this one was not, or if it was, someone had remotely disabled it to stop them from leaving. The barrier, now just a few vehicle lengths ahead, did not budge.

Hawke made a snap decision, really the only one he could. Stopping wasn't an option. He kept the accelerator pressed to the floor, aimed the front end at the exact center of the gate, and braced himself for the impact. He hoped the tactical modifications to the G-Class included disabling the airbags. If not, he was going to get a very rude surprise, but there was no time to second-guess his decision.

Let's hope they didn't put as much thought into keeping people from getting out, he thought grimly, and then shouted, "Hold on!"

Suddenly the Mercedes's collision warning system erupted in protest. A flashing red triangle lit up the dashboard, and a shrill alarm filled the cabin, warning him: "Brake."

Hawke ignored the computerized panic, along with every self-protective instinct, and kept the pedal pressed to the floor. An instant later the SUV rammed the gate with a bone-jarring crunch. He tensed, bracing for the airbags to explode in his face—but nothing happened. The reinforced SUV plowed ahead, and the aftermarket bull bars absorbed much of the impact, protecting the vehicle's engine compartment as the steel barrier was ripped from its track and pushed forward ahead of it.

The gate screeched along the pavement, throwing out a shower of bright yellow sparks. Hawke eased off the accelerator, tapping the brakes for a moment, slowing just enough to let the mangled gate fall away. As soon as it did, clattering to the asphalt, he accelerated again, sending the vehicle up and over its battered remains.

Directly ahead, the driveway ended at a T-junction with the main road. Hawke slammed on the brakes, eliciting a cry from Silk in the back seat. He ignored her, trying to recall the route they had used when arriving. There had been a hard right turn . . .

He cranked the wheel to the left and jammed the accelerator down again. The AMG G 63's powerful engine responded instantly, propelling them forward.

Only then did he spare a glance in the rearview mirror. There were no lights visible, but he knew better than to believe they were safe. Mulmuscovy's men would come after them. And before long all of Russia would be hunting them.

They had made it out of the frying pan, but the fire was surely coming.

THIRTY-SEVEN

As soon as the Mercedes was rolling down the main thoroughfare, Hawke eased off the accelerator and allowed himself a moment to take stock. The surrounding hills were dotted with palatial mansions, their grand facades lit up as if to advertise the obscene wealth of their owners.

The road itself was quiet but not deserted, with cars and SUVs zipping by. He checked his speed again, trying to match the flow of traffic so as not to attract any unwanted attention.

"If you're done playing banger racing," Silk called out acidly, "perhaps you'd be so kind as to pull over and cut me loose."

Hawke glanced over his shoulder and saw Silk glaring at him through her eyeglasses. She had managed to raise herself into one of the seats, but with her hands still bound behind her back she was forced to lean forward awkwardly.

"Sorry, can't stop just now," Hawke replied, returning his attention to the road. "We're not out of the woods yet."

"Out of the woods?" she shot back. "Do you even know where you're going?"

"Not exactly," Hawke admitted. "I'm trying to get us back down to the waterfront. Maybe we can steal a boat."

"And go where, exactly? In case you've forgotten, he just blew your boat to smithereens."

Hawke set his jaw. "I haven't forgotten," he said in a subdued voice.

She was silent for a moment, then said, "I'm sorry."

He shook his head, dismissing her condolences. "There'll be time for that later. We don't need the yacht. If we can find a boat, we can head south along the coast. Georgia is only about thirty miles south."

Silk pondered this in silence for a moment. "So our only real problem is trying to get back to the marina."

"That, and the fact that pretty soon the whole bloody country is going to be after us."

Silk did not respond to this. Hawke remained focused on the road ahead, searching for anything that might provide a clue about the route back to the marina. He almost failed to notice the sound of Silk shifting position, drawing in a breath, and then—

A cry of pain tore through the SUV's quiet interior. Hawke started, then craned his head around to find Silk freed from her bonds and massaging the chafed skin of her wrists.

"I see you didn't need me to stop after all," he remarked.

"No. But I'd really rather you had." She rubbed her wrists a moment longer, then, without waiting for an invitation, climbed forward into the passenger seat. When she had settled in, she began examining the center console screen.

"Now I'll just see if I can find a way to make myself useful." She tapped the display, bringing up a menu interface. The display showed Cyrillic letters, which Silk evidently had no difficulty reading. Hawke cast a sidelong glance at her as she navigated the menus with apparent ease.

"You read Russian? That must come in handy when you're reviewing historic documents."

She ignored the dig, focusing on her task. "Ahh, here we go."

The screen now displayed a detailed top-down satnav map of the surrounding area, with their present location marked by a blue dot with an arrow showing the direction of travel. Silk studied it for a moment, then said, "Keep going straight for another kilometer. There's a junction where you can turn left. That should get us on the best route to the marina."

"Left?" Something about that sounded wrong to him. His mental map had the shoreline on their right side. Still, roads didn't always follow straight lines.

A flicker of light in the rearview mirror caught his eye. He studied it for a moment, picking out the headlights of a vehicle behind them rapidly closing the distance.

"Damn," he muttered. "Company's coming."

Silk twisted in her seat to glance out the rear window. "I see two of them coming up fast."

By way of an answer, Hawke depressed the accelerator, sending the G-Class surging ahead. He watched the numbers on the digital speedometer tick steadily upward: 78 . . . 80 . . . 85.

Measured in kilometers per hour, it wasn't a breakneck speed by any means, but much faster than he should be going on a winding residential road. But even with his increased acceleration, the trailing vehicles were still closing, their headlights filling his mirrors.

"They'll have the advantage," Silk was saying. "They know these roads better than we do."

"No kidding." Hawke tightened his grip on the wheel. "Just keep giving me the directions."

She looked back at the satnav. "Junction ahead in about five hundred meters. Left turn."

He saw the junction coming up, a gap in the rows of palatial homes and manicured hedgerows. But before he could maneuver, the pursuing SUV drew dangerously close, its driver clearly intent on trying to run them off the road. An urgent warning chime sounded, the dashboard glowing amber as the collision system detected the approaching vehicle. The pursuer was close now, no more than a car length behind.

"Hang on!" Hawke snapped, gritting his teeth as the pursuing vehicle clipped the back bumper of the G-Class with a bone-rattling jolt.

The SUV fishtailed, its rear end threatening to break loose on the curve. He wrestled with the wheel, managing to keep it straight, but the sudden impact threw Silk forward in her seat.

"Left, Alex!" she shouted, bracing herself against the dashboard.

"Not happening," Hawke growled as the junction flashed past. He leaned into the next bend, the tires shrieking on the macadam, the heavy G-Class tilting precariously as he tried to make up for lost time. The pursuing vehicles were relentless, closing the gap once more. The next warning chime from the proximity sensors seemed somehow sharper, more insistent, as if scolding him for letting the enemy get so close a second time.

Another shuddering impact rocked them as one of the pursuing vehicles rammed the rear quarter panel. This time the G-Class tilted sharply, the tires screaming against the pavement. Hawke yanked the wheel, correcting the trajectory just in time to avoid plowing into a row of parked cars on the shoulder. Meanwhile, the second vehicle—which he now saw was an almost identical G-Class—shot past to get ahead of them.

"They're going to box us in!" Silk warned.

"Not if I can help it," Hawke snapped. But despite his bravado, he was not immediately sure how he was going to prevent them from doing exactly that. His mind raced, trying to come up with alternatives. The road ahead curved sharply, hemmed in by stone retaining walls and wrought iron fencing, but offered no obvious escape routes.

Then he spied a narrow gap in the fence ahead—a driveway leading up to yet another grand estate—and yanked the wheel hard to the right, sending the G-Class careening off the main road and up the slight incline. Silk yelped as the vehicle bounced violently, the tires grinding over a pristine brick driveway before shooting out onto the manicured lawn.

"What the hell are you doing?" Silk demanded, bracing herself once more.

"Improvising," Hawke shouted as they plowed through an ornamental hedge. Branches clawed at the windows, the suspension groaned under the abuse, but the G-Class was unstoppable.

Behind them, the trailing SUV seemed to hesitate for a split second before following, threading through the same gap in the fence. Hawke caught sight of them in the rearview mirror, their headlights bouncing wildly as they struggled to match his unorthodox route.

Directly ahead, the sprawling estate's lawn came into view: ornamental fountains, tennis courts, and decorative stone walls, all brilliantly illuminated by floodlights.

Silk's eyes went wide. "Please tell me you're not going to—"

"Afraid we have no other choice," Hawke replied. He veered sharply to avoid a marble gazebo, the G-Class tearing up swathes of perfectly tended grass and throwing out rooster tails of sod as it hurtled toward the next obstacle: a low concrete wall separating the yard from the neighboring property.

Hawke didn't hesitate. He gunned the engine and sent the G-Class racing forward, smashing through the barrier. The wall crumbled under the impact, sending cinder blocks flying as they burst into the next yard and found themselves in a poolside paradise.

Hawke fought for control as concrete rubble shifted under the tires, sending them skidding across the deck toward the infinity pool. The G-Class slid dangerously close to the water's edge before finding traction again. He steered away from the pool, scattering deck chairs before them, and veered onto another section of perfect lawn.

Behind them, the pursuing SUV was just charging into the breach they had created, but the driver evidently misjudged his position, coming too close to the pool. He slammed on the brakes, but it was too late: the vehicle slid sideways, scraping over the edge, and plunged into the water.

"That's one down," Hawke said, allowing himself a small measure of satisfaction. "Now, see if you can't find us a way back to the road."

She gaped at him, incredulous. “You’re daft.”

Hawke shrugged and kept the G-Class racing forward, its wheels kicking up divots as they charged over the lawn of the estate. The headlights picked out a row of meticulously trimmed topiary animals standing between them and the next barrier: a wrought iron fence backed by a thick hedgerow.

Hawke grimaced. “Hang on.”

Compared to the security gate at Bocharov Ruchey, the fence offered all the resistance of a sheet of tinfoil. The bars flew apart, scraping the exterior and bouncing off the hood. Then they were smashing through the hedge, branches scraping along the sides of the vehicle, before breaking out onto a narrow drive. Hawke yanked the wheel hard to the right, tires screeching as he fishtailed onto the pavement.

All of a sudden another vehicle—the second pursuing G-Class—roared into view directly ahead of them, charging toward them head-on. Its headlights blazed like twin spotlights.

Hawke slammed on the brakes, throwing Silk hard against the dash, and then he shoved the gear selector into reverse.

“Hang on,” he said again—he realized he was getting a bit repetitive, but what else could he say?—and jammed down on the accelerator. The G-Class shot backward, the engine climbing to a deafening wail as it redlined, then lurched with a guttural stutter as the rev limiter kicked in. Then the steering got twitchy, the rear tires skidding across the asphalt as he struggled to keep the SUV running on a true course. But reverse gear was no match for the speed of the oncoming vehicle. The headlights filled the interior of the G-Class.

“They’re closing!” Silk shouted.

“I noticed,” Hawke snapped.

Collision alerts began wailing like banshees as the gap between the vehicles narrowed alarmingly. Hawke waited until the last possible second, then spun the wheel hard to the left, kicking the rear of the G-Class into a sharp arc that sent it sliding off the pavement and into the hedgerow. Just as quickly, Hawke popped the transmission into drive and yanked the wheel the other way. The maneuver spun the vehicle around, tires shrieking, and just like that the SUV was going in the right direction again.

Unfortunately, the maneuver had cost them what little buffer zone remained, and an instant later the other SUV slammed into their rear bumper. The G-Class bucked under the impact but then they were moving again, accelerating away from their assailant.

Ahead, the narrow drive curved sharply to the right, flanked by another row of decorative hedges and a low stone retaining wall. Hawke leaned into the turn, the G-Class groaning under the strain as its bulk shifted precariously, but then it righted, and they were speeding out of the turn. The speedometer ticked past 70 kilometers per hour, far too fast for the tight quarters of the drive. Another bend loomed ahead, this one to the left, the hedges giving way to a steep drop-off that offered a harrowing view of the city lights below.

Silk gripped the door handle. "For God's sake, slow down!"

Hawke ignored her, sending them barreling into the curve. The tires screamed in protest as he expertly feathered the wheel, countersteering just enough to keep the rear end from breaking loose. The sheer drop to the right yawned beside them, creating the illusion of nothingness, but the SUV held on.

Behind them, their pursuer executed the same turn with equal expertise, charging out of the bend with a vengeance. It was abundantly clear that the other driver was every bit as capable as he, and, unfortunately for them, he had the home field advantage. If Hawke didn't find a way to change the game, things would end badly for them.

"Enough of this." He glanced around, looking ahead and then off into the darkness at the roadside, then at the GPS display. He couldn't make sense of the street names, but the map showed them moving along the winding drive, showed other roads running parallel to it, and showed the end of the road, now rapidly approaching.

Then inspiration dawned.

He glanced over at Silk. "You should buckle your seat belt."

"Oh, God," she groaned, eyes wide as she pulled the belt across her body and clicked it in place. "Do I even want to know what you're planning now?"

"Probably not," he said, not looking at her.

"Let me guess. Hang on?"

Hawke managed a grim nod, then yanked the wheel hard to the right. The Mercedes swung off the pavement, smashed through the stone wall, and plunged down the embankment.

The descent was pure chaos. The SUV pitched and bucked violently as it hurtled down the slope, its suspension groaning under the abuse. Hawke gripped the wheel tightly, his arms straining to maintain control as the tires fought for traction over loose dirt and uneven ground. Grass and debris flew up in wild sprays, the headlights lurching wildly. The sharp jolt of the wheels hitting a hidden dip jarred his spine, and for a sickening moment the SUV became airborne. Time seemed to stretch as the vehicle hung in space, the engine's roar the only sound in the void.

Then gravity slammed them back to earth with a bone-crunching thud. The impact sent a shock wave through the cabin, rattling his teeth and momentarily blinding him with the glare of the headlights bouncing off the dirt. He clenched his jaw, focusing on the narrow gap between two massive oaks ahead. Hawke barely had time to register the crash of branches against the windshield as the G-Class shot through the gap between the trees. The rear wheels skidded on loose earth, threatening to spin the vehicle sideways. He eased off the throttle just enough to regain control, and the tires dug in again, propelling them forward through the chaos of underbrush and shadows.

A flash in the mirror caught his eye: a pair of lights bouncing erratically down the slope behind him. Their pursuer had followed, just as he knew they would. But here, off-road, the other driver's skill deficit was evident. The other SUV was slewing wildly across the embankment, the driver trying to cut across the slope laterally like a skier attempting to slow his descent by carving back and forth across the run, but in this instance it was exactly the wrong thing to do. Hawke could practically feel the driver's panic as the vehicle turned sideways and then went into a roll, tumbling down the hill. One headlight was extinguished, then the other, and the SUV was lost to Hawke's sight.

There was no time to celebrate, though. Ahead, the slope steepened further, and the vehicle jolted violently as it careened over hidden roots and jagged rocks. Each impact sent shock waves through the cabin, but Hawke remained resolute, his knuckles white on the steering wheel. The tree line was thinning now, patches of open ground visible beyond the whipping branches. Then, mercifully, the incline leveled out and a few seconds later spat them out onto the narrow access road Hawke had spotted on the satnav. He eased off the accelerator and let the Mercedes roll onto the asphalt before tapping the brakes, bringing them to a stop.

Beside him, Silk let out a shaky breath, pushing her glasses back up her nose. "You're completely mad," she blurted. "You know that."

"It's been suggested a time or two," he replied tersely. "Now, be a good girl and find us a route back to the marina."

She blinked at him, clearly needing a moment to process the request. "You want me to . . . We just—" Silk cut herself off, shaking her head as she turned to the center console. "Fine."

She studied the screen for a moment, swiping with her fingers to zoom out. "All right, it looks like you need to go that way." She pointed to the left.

Hawke turned the steering wheel accordingly and eased down on the accelerator, rolling along the narrow lane at a considerably more sedate pace. Tall, shadowy pines lined both sides of the road, their interlaced branches hiding the outside world from view.

Hawke allowed himself a moment to breathe, his grip on the wheel relaxing ever so slightly. Purely out of habit, he glanced at the rearview mirror but saw only darkness. Beside him, Silk leaned back in the seat, gazing out the window.

"This is better," she said quietly, almost to herself.

Hawke was inclined to agree, but then they rounded a corner and saw the flashing blue lights of a pair of police cars blocking the road ahead.

THIRTY-EIGHT

Bollocks. How the bloody hell did they get here ahead of us?"

The police cars were parked in a herringbone formation, front ends nearly meeting and facing them to minimize the chances of being pushed out of the way by an onrushing vehicle. To either side of the road, the forest closed in, the undergrowth thick and unyielding. It was, by design, a perfect choke point.

But how had they known where we'd be?

Then it hit him. "They're tracking us. Bloody GPS." He shook his head. "Let's hope it's not one of those systems they can shut down remotely."

"I should say it hardly matters," replied Silk, pointing toward the roadblock. "We're not getting past them."

Hawke set his jaw. "Well, now. We'll just see about that, won't we?"

Without another word, he punched the accelerator again, and the G-Class surged forward. The distance to the roadblock closed rapidly, the police vehicles looming larger with every passing second. As they neared, Hawke could see more than half a dozen uniformed figures arrayed behind the line of cars, the reflective panels on their vests catching the glare of his headlights. Several of them had pistols drawn, and at least one was leveling an AK-pattern rifle across the hood of a cruiser. Over the roar of the engine, he thought he heard an electronically amplified voice, doubtless ordering him to halt.

Not going to happen, he thought grimly.

The policemen must have realized it because a moment later the bright yellow of muzzle flashes joined the blue strobes. Bullets sparked off the SUV's armored exterior and smacked against the ballistic glass, leaving white spiderweb fractures across the windshield. Silk ducked reflexively. Hawke didn't even flinch.

At the last possible instant he yanked the wheel hard to the right, veering away toward the roadside, then cut back left, swinging the vehicle's front end around and lining up on the rear quarter panel of the closest cruiser, striking it at an oblique angle. The policemen hiding behind it barely had time to dive out of the way before the impact sent the vehicle spinning amidst a storm of debris and noise.

Hawke kept the pedal down, steering through the gap he'd just created. The Mercedes fishtailed slightly as the rear tires transitioned from loose earth to macadam, but then they were past the roadblock. Unfortunately, there were two more police cars waiting just beyond it, parked nose to tail in the center of the narrow road.

"Of course," he muttered. "Why make it easy?"

But he did not slow down. Instead, he aimed for the narrowest point, easing the SUV onto the grassy verge to put two wheels off-road. The tires grabbed at the loose earth, sending up a spray of dirt and gravel and causing the Mercedes to torque slightly to the right, but the vehicle's smart 4MATIC all-wheel-drive system compensated before Hawke was even aware of the problem. With proximity warnings blaring, the SUV slipped past the first car with inches to spare, but then fate placed a new obstacle in their path: a massive tree loomed ahead on the verge, its trunk narrowing the gap through which they needed to pass. Hawke could tell that there wasn't going to be enough room to pass between the second police car and the tree. He was going to hit one or the other, or both—it was up to him to decide which.

He chose to take his chances with the police car, steering into it just as the front ends of the two vehicles passed each other. There was a torturous screech of metal on metal as the SUV scraped along the side of the police car, shoving it sideways and out of Hawke's way.

A volley of gunfire tore into the rear of the G-Class, thudding loudly against glass and armor, but none penetrated. Hawke ignored the tumult, focusing instead on the dark road ahead as the police roadblock receded behind them.

"Find us a route to the marina," he said without looking over at Silk.

For a few seconds she did not move. Just stared straight ahead as if in shock. Then she turned to him. "It's not possible. We're never going to make it through."

"Just get me to the bloody marina!" Hawke snapped.

She glowered at him a moment longer, then leaned forward and began manipulating the satnav. "When you reach the main road, take a right."

Without even meaning to, Hawke glanced at the screen, confirming what she had just said. Maybe it was her sudden episode of defeatism or lingering distrust about her true motives, but he suddenly felt like he couldn't take her at her word. But, based on what satnav was showing, her directions were correct, so when he reached the junction, he made the right turn.

Within half a mile they passed into the outskirts of the city. Sochi stretched out ahead of them, a mix of tree-lined boulevards and narrow streets. The buildings grew taller and closer together as they approached the urban center, their facades of modern glass and faded stucco, the kind of architecture that whispered of Sochi's dual identity as both a resort town and a remnant of Soviet ambition. Streetlights illuminated both the sidewalks and the battle scars and bullet marks that marred the exterior of the SUV.

Here and there, a solitary figure trudged along the sidewalk, casting long shadows under the overhead lights. Occasionally, a passing car would slow, its driver rubbernecking at the sight of the mud-splattered Mercedes hurtling past.

At Silk's direction, Hawke maneuvered through a sharp bend that funneled them into a narrower street. Parked cars crowded the curb to either side, their reflective surfaces shimmering like ghostly shapes in the dim light. Ahead, the road curved again, and farther out, the vast expanse of the Black Sea opened up before them.

Well, that's a hopeful sight, thought Hawke.

They descended into a neighborhood of seaside villas and boutique hotels, neon signs flickering against the dark backdrop of the sea. A pair of headlights emerged unexpectedly from a side street, forcing Hawke to swerve, which resulted in him narrowly missing a parked delivery van, the driver of which chastised him with a long horn blast.

Another turn brought them onto a busier thoroughfare. Hawke could see the signs of nightlife ahead: neon lights glowing faintly above cafés and restaurants, their terraces dotted with late-night patrons oblivious to the events that had just occurred uphill from them.

"Next right," said Silk.

He slowed and took the turn, putting them on a street that ran parallel to the coastline. Directly ahead, a swarm of flashing blue and red lights was headed right toward them. A moment later the distinctive two-tone wail of sirens reached them.

Hawke breathed a rare curse, then slammed on the brakes and cut the wheel to the left, throwing the G-Class into a spin. It would have been a nearly perfect one-eighty, but the street wasn't quite wide enough. The SUV struck and then mounted the curb with a violent jolt, barreling into the outdoor seating area of a café, sending chairs, tables, and a few unlucky late-night patrons scattering. Hawke swerved back onto the street, now heading away from the rapidly closing patrol cars. More sirens blared from a cross street they had just passed: a second wave of police vehicles racing to cut them off.

"Shortcut," Silk hissed, pointing to a narrow alley on their left.

The passage looked barely wide enough to accommodate the G-Class. Hawke hesitated for a fraction of a second, then spun the wheel, turning into the alley. The driver's-side mirror was torn away, the side panels scraping down the rough stucco walls in a shower of sparks.

Hawke resisted the impulse to steer away, instead enduring the torturous racket, and charged toward the distant end. Behind them, a patrol car attempted the same maneuver, but its driver misjudged his approach, grinding to a dead stop and momentarily blocking the way for the rest of the pursuers.

The alley spat them out onto another street, this one wider but crowded with parked cars and late-night revelers spilling from nightclubs. Hawke slalomed around the obstacles, sideswiping two of the cars, but somehow managed to reach the open traffic lanes. Within seconds, however, flashing blue lights appeared behind them.

"This isn't working," said Silk. "You said it yourself: they're tracking us. As long as we're in this car, they'll know exactly where we are. You aren't going to outrun them forever."

"You might as well give up."

She didn't say the last, but it was there in her tone.

Hawke remained resolute. "I don't need forever. Just get me to the marina."

Silk exhaled sharply, then relented. Leaning forward, she began manipulating the satnav display. "Next right, then follow the road along the promenade. It'll take you toward the marina."

Hawke took the turn and found himself on a road running parallel to the coast. Beyond the streetlights, the Black Sea shimmered faintly under the moonlight. Then the marina complex came into view. Sleek yachts and sturdy fishing trawlers were moored side by side, their silhouettes stark against the glow of the promenade's well-lit walkways.

A large modern structure with an angular glass facade sat like a watchtower overlooking the harbor beyond, its reflective panels mirroring the city lights and the sea. Beyond it, the pier stretched into the open water like a bridge to nowhere.

Behind them, the wail of sirens grew louder. More flashing lights emerged from the side streets, the patrol cars converging in a determined pursuit. Hawke made a sharp turn toward the pavilion, the tires screeching across the macadam.

"This is a dead end, Alex!" cried Silk. "You'll drive us straight into the sea."

Hawke didn't slow. The concrete promenade leading to the marina entrance stretched out ahead of them, leading directly onto the pier.

"Alex!" Silk shifted in her seat as if bracing for a collision. "What the hell are you doing?"

The pavilion fell behind them. There was nothing ahead now but the pier.

"Alex, stop!" Silk screamed, gripping the dashboard.

Finally, without looking at her, he spoke. "If you are what I think you are," he said calmly, "you'll know what to do."

And then, with the pedal pressed to the floor, Hawke drove the G-Class straight off the pier.

THIRTY-NINE

The G-Class soared off the end of the pier, arcing out over the water, and then hit with a tremendous splash. The initial impact jarred Hawke against his seat belt, a bone-rattling jolt that left the cabin briefly suspended in a surreal, weightless silence. Then, very quickly, the vehicle nosed forward and dove beneath the icy water, dragged down by the added weight of its armor package.

Water surged into the interior, flooding the footwells and climbing rapidly.

Anticipating all of this, Hawke moved quickly. He reached for the window controls and pressed the switch. Thankfully, the electrical system was still functioning, and both front windows began lowering. Shockingly cold water immediately rushed in like a torrent. Even though he had been expecting it, Hawke recoiled at the first touch. Beside him, Silk let out a strangled gasp as the water suddenly swirled all around her.

"Unbuckle and get ready to swim for it," Hawke shouted over the chaos, the cold almost snatching his breath away. "Wait until we're fully under before you try to get out—it'll be easier. Stay close and follow me."

He caught a momentary glimpse of Silk, her eyes wide behind her glasses, nodding, and then the water engulfed them both. The freezing black tide gripped Hawke's body, squeezing the breath from his chest.

The pressure was a vise around his head. How deep were they already? How much deeper would they sink before hitting bottom? His pulse thundered in his ears, mingling with the groans of the dying SUV and the chaotic hiss of escaping air. The world shrank to a murky haze of churning bubbles and darkness, the icy current numbing his limbs almost instantly.

Where was Ariadne?

He glanced over and, by the dim light of the still-illuminated screen of the satnav, saw her struggling with her seat belt. He reached over, pushing her hand out of the way, and worked the stiff release until it finally let go, then took her hand in his and used his other to pull himself through the open passenger window. As soon as he was through the opening, he braced his feet against the side of the sinking Mercedes and pulled Silk through, using the motion to propel them both away from the doomed vehicle. He kicked hard, doing a one-handed sidestroke as he drew Silk along behind him. After a moment of disorientation, she seemed to realize what he needed of her and began kicking as well.

The darkness swallowed them. No surface light penetrated the depths. Hawke couldn't even tell for certain which direction was up. He forced himself to stay calm.

Panic would kill them faster than the icy water.

He pressed his free hand against his chest, feeling the faint tug of buoyancy from his lungs. That was up. Or close enough to it. But rising to the surface would be a death sentence. They had to stay submerged until they could find cover from searching eyes onshore.

In the absolute darkness, Hawke had to rely on memory and intuition, recalling the layout of the marina from the brief seconds before they had plunged into the water. The boats had been to their left as they drove down the pier. If he judged their position correctly, swimming left and slightly upward should get them where they needed to be. He adjusted his angle and resumed kicking with powerful strokes, hoping the motion was carrying them in the right direction.

Silk's grip on his wrist tightened, and Hawke felt the occasional drag as her kicks faltered. She was slowing, the cold stealing her strength. Under ideal conditions, he could stay under, holding his breath, for well over two minutes. These were not ideal conditions. And there was no telling what Silk's lung capacity was. He squeezed her hand firmly, urging her to keep going. They didn't have the luxury of stopping to rest.

Then his hand brushed against something hard, rough, and vertical: a pier piling. The texture of algae and barnacles scraped against his frozen fingers as he latched onto it, relief flooding through him. They'd reached some sort of structure. Hopefully, it would provide the cover they needed, but whether it did or not, the carbon dioxide boiling in his veins told him that it was well past time to ascend.

With one hand in contact with the piling, he began kicking desperately for the surface, dragging Silk along behind him. The pressure gripping his skull immediately began to abate, but the distance to the surface stretched out interminably. His body screamed for the breath he couldn't yet take. Each kick felt agonizingly inadequate, the weight of Silk pulling against him as he tried to maintain his grip on her wrist. He could now see a faint light penetrating downward, but it remained maddeningly distant, taunting him with a promise of air. Every second felt like an eternity, the fire in his chest a raging inferno as his lungs burned with the effort of restraint. And then at last the water began to brighten around him. The surface rippled into view, and with one final, desperate kick he broke through.

The cold night air rushed into his lungs like fire. He stifled the urge to gasp too loudly, forcing himself to take shallow, controlled breaths. Around him, the world was a chaotic blend of dim lights, the distant wail of sirens, and the hollow slap of water against hulls.

Silk broke the surface beside him, gasping and coughing, her face pale and streaked with water. Her glasses were gone, and her hair clung to her face in dark strands.

"This was your plan?" she managed between gulps of air.

Hawke didn't answer. He was scanning their immediate vicinity, trying to assess their situation. Blue and red strobes lit up the waterfront, and bright spotlights stabbed out across the water, cutting wide arcs as they swept the surface, but for the moment they were hidden in the shadow of the pier.

"We can't stay here."

Silk glared at him. "Obviously," she said, her voice hitching a little as she forced the words past chattering teeth. "I suppose you have another brilliant plan to get us out of this fix?"

Hawke glanced up at the pier above them. The underside of the structure was a maze of crossbeams and barnacle-encrusted supports. It offered some cover, but it was far from ideal. He turned his attention to the marina beyond the pier. Rows of sleek boats and yachts bobbed gently in the water, their hulls reflecting faintly in the scattered light.

One of them would be their ticket to freedom.

Cautiously, he pulled himself up onto the pier, water dripping from his sodden clothes and pooling on the deck. He lay motionless for a moment to ensure that he was not being observed, then reached down and hauled Silk up out of the water. For nearly a minute they just lay there, shivering and exhausted. Then Hawke willed himself to move. He rolled over and came up in a crouch, scanning the immediate area once more, then turned to Silk.

"We need to find a boat."

Silk pushed herself to her knees, hugging her arms around her chest. "And then what? They're not going to let anyone leave."

"One problem at a time. We have to keep moving."

She looked like she wanted to argue but then pressed her lips together and gave him a terse nod.

Hawke returned the nod, then calmly stood up, straightened his sodden jacket, and extended a hand to her. "Up you go."

Silk stared at him, incredulous. "What the hell are you doing?"

"No skulking about. We need to look like we belong here."

"You're mad! They're looking for *us*."

"They're looking for two people sneaking about like criminals. The best way to stay invisible is to act normal."

"We're soaked through."

"No one will give us a second look. Now, come on."

Reluctantly, she accepted his hand and let him draw her up. She took a moment to arrange her hair so that it wasn't a stringy mess hanging about her face, then took his hand again. Hawke moved with measured but purposeful strides, his body language radiating the kind of quiet confidence that discouraged unnecessary questions. Silk did her best to follow suit, though her furtive glances betrayed her unease.

They passed several boats, ranging in size from sporty runabouts, their open cockpits empty and gleaming, to compact sailing yachts. More than a few showed illuminated cabins, and occasionally voices could be heard. Hawke moved past all of them without a second glance.

Then he saw what he was looking for: a forty-foot cabin cruiser tucked between two larger motor yachts. If the darkened windows were any indication, there was no one aboard.

"This one," he said, steering Silk down the slip. He paused one last time, scanning the surrounding boats for any signs that they were being observed, then hopped over the gunwale onto the cruiser's aft deck. Silk hesitated, glanced nervously over her shoulder at the faint blue glow of police lights in the distance, then joined him.

The boat was tidy, with no unsecured personal belongings lying about. Hawke quickly moved to the cabin door, found it unlocked, and peeked inside. The cabin was compact but comfortable. A small galley with polished countertops occupied one side, opposite a wraparound settee upholstered in cream-colored leather.

"All clear," he said. "Come on in. We'll hide here for the moment."

Silk didn't move. "And then what? We're trapped in a bloody marina surrounded by police."

Hawke looked past her, out at the harbor, where a few boats could be seen coming and going. "If I can get this beast running, we can slip out before they realize we're not trapped on the bottom. Now, come in here and warm yourself up. I'm going to head up to the helm."

Hawke didn't wait to see if she would comply but swung himself up the companionway to the raised cockpit. He quickly scanned the instrument panel, checked the ignition, and confirmed what he had already expected: no keys.

"Of course not," he muttered.

He knelt down to check under the console. Boaters often kept a hidden spare, just in case they lost their key over the side.

Behind him, the faint creak of someone ascending the companionway—Silk, no doubt, coming to check up on him.

"Nagging won't make this happen any quicker," he said without looking up.

Sudden pain exploded at the base of his skull, followed almost simultaneously by the clang of a heavy metal object hitting the helm controls. Stars exploded across his vision as he crumpled to the deck. Despite lying prone, he felt the world tilting unevenly, felt himself sliding away into oblivion, but through the fog he heard someone shouting. The words were in Russian, and while he didn't comprehend the language, he caught one familiar word: *politsiya* (police).

Yet, it wasn't the cry for help that wrenched at him but the identity of the person shouting it.

Silk.

The betrayal seared through his disoriented mind, sharper than the pain in his head.

She was working with Mulmuscovy.

The realization struck like another blow. The puzzle pieces aligned in a flash: the mission to bring Putin to Sochi, the assassination, her willingness to surrender, and her insistence that they could not escape. All of it part of a plan—the Warmonger's plan—to remove Putin from power and put the blame on Alex Hawke.

He tried to raise himself up, but his body refused to comply. His ears rang, the sound like rushing water drowning out everything but his racing pulse. Fighting through the blackness, he made his right hand move, groping until his finger found his sleeve and then the hard, cool surface of his cuff link, and with the last of his strength he pushed the panic button.

A moment later his world went completely dark.

INTERLUDE—PART EIGHT

TOBOLSK, SIBERIA, SOVIET RUSSIA
APRIL 1918

The four-day journey across Siberia had been long and exhausting, but for all the hardship, a sense of purpose or hope buoyed their spirits. And now, at last, the goal was in sight.

The former governor's mansion in Tobolsk was a relatively plain but solid two-story structure, its whitewashed walls standing out starkly against the frigid gray Siberian skies. Still, the seat of local authority, albeit now under new management, was the figurative gateway through which many a dissident passed on their way to exile. Now it also served as a de facto prison for the deposed Tsar and his family, confined there under house arrest first by the provisional government and now by the Bolsheviks, who were still deciding their fate.

A group of rough-looking men—attired in peasant garb with red armbands and holding rifles—loitering about the front of the mansion watched with naked suspicion as Alexander and Natalya climbed down from the cart that had brought them from the rail station.

"Red Guard," Natalya murmured with a faint trace of disgust. "They are . . . undisciplined."

As they approached the entrance, a wiry armed man with a patchy beard challenged them in Russian. Natalya, showing not the least sign of being intimidated, answered. Alexander understood almost none of it, but he did catch a few names. *Volkova. Avdeev.*

The Red Guard's response was curt, and his hand lingered on the rifle slung across his chest. Natalya turned to Alexander, speaking English in a low voice. "He says Comrade Avdeev is no longer in charge here. He's been removed."

Alexander felt a sudden chill that had nothing to do with the icy Siberian wind. "Removed?"

Natalya posed another question in Russian, and the guard muttered an answer, his tone tinged with irritation. She translated quickly, "The order came down from the Central Committee. A Comrade Medvedev has taken over the Tsar's security."

"Then I guess we need to talk to him."

Natalya addressed the guard again, leveling her authoritarian air and tone like a bludgeon against the Red Guard's obstinacy. After a terse exchange, she turned to Alexander again. "Medvedev left for Yekaterinburg several days ago."

"Brilliant." Alexander felt the hopefulness that had sustained them through the arduous journey beginning to waver. "Well, who do we bloody well need to talk to?"

Natalya fired off another machine-gun burst of Russian. Alexander heard Sverdlov's name, and at the mention, the Red Guard's eyes narrowed. Natalya then turned to Alexander. "I told him that we are here under orders from Comrade Sverdlov himself and demanded he take us to whomever is in charge."

Almost as she said it, the man was speaking again. He then turned and opened the door, gesturing for them to enter.

"He's going to take us to his commander, Comrade Malyshev," Natalya whispered.

"Well, that's progress," said Alexander, even though his apprehension was mounting.

They were shown into an office near the rear of the mansion, sparsely furnished with a battered desk and a mismatched pair of chairs. The Red Guard commander, his uniform a patchwork of military and civilian garb, sat behind the desk. His narrow eyes assessed them, lingering on Alexander a moment too long.

Natalya stepped forward, addressing him in Russian. She gestured briefly to Alexander and gave his full name. He also heard her mention *"Korolya Anglii,"* which he thought might be a reference to King George. The commander regarded her with an unsettling smile, then gave a short response in Russian. Alexander's anxiety continued to grow as the exchange grew sharper. Natalya's voice rose, becoming sterner, almost angry, but the commander remained indifferent.

After another terse exchange, the commander stood, gesturing for them to follow. Natalya turned to Alexander for the first time since they'd entered the room, her expression carefully neutral.

"He's taking us to meet with the Tsar," she said in English, though her tone carried none of the satisfaction he would have expected from such a concession.

"What's wrong?"

"Maybe nothing. He claims that he hasn't received any instructions from Moscow regarding the Romanovs."

"Maybe the telegraph lines are down?"

She shook her head uncertainly. "I've asked him to wire for confirmation. I think he will, but he's . . ."—she hesitated as if afraid of being overheard—". . . arrogant."

They followed the Red Guard commander through the central hall and out into the courtyard. Alexander immediately noted the presence of several more Red Guards occupying the fenced enclosure. Natalya, too, seemed to take note of the armed men. She halted abruptly and started to turn as if to flee back into the house, but before either of them could make such a move, two of the men stepped in front of the door, blocking access. That was when Alexander realized they were surrounded, the Red Guards' rifles no longer slung over their shoulders but in hand and held at the ready, pointed none too subtly at him and Natalya.

"What the bloody hell is this?" Alexander hissed.

Natalya whirled on the Red Guard commander, uttering a question with as much authority as she could muster. The commander said nothing, but someone else spoke up from behind the gunmen, the answer in halting but passable French. "Welcome, Comrade Volkova. It is so good to finally meet you."

Natalya turned toward the voice, her face blanching, eyes wide in sudden terror as a tall, gaunt figure emerged. The man had a narrow face, pronounced cheekbones under thin, sallow skin, and a short, neatly trimmed mustache.

"Comrade Dzerzhinsky?" Natalya said, the words almost a groan. "What are you doing here?"

Alexander's heart shuddered. Felix Dzerzhinsky. Iron Felix. The head of the Bolshevik secret police was here. For them.

Dzerzhinsky's thin lips curled into a smile that didn't reach his eyes. "Why, waiting for you, of course."

"Well," replied Natalya, trying to regain some of her earlier nerve. "You needn't have bothered. This is an affair of state and does not require the attention of the secret police. I am here at Comrade Sverdlov's behest. If you doubt it, I suggest you send a telegram to him. He will confirm it."

Dzerzhinsky's humorless smile widened. "Comrade Volkova, who do you think sent me when I told him of your . . . arrangement? With this British gentleman, he asked me to investigate. And when Viktor did not report back to me, I began to suspect some impropriety in your intentions. Your communiqué regarding your intention to escort the Tsar and his family out of Russia stank of a ruse."

"It's no ruse," interjected Alexander. "I am here on behalf of His Majesty King George V in answer to your comrade Sverdlov's invitation. The British Crown has offered asylum to the Romanov family."

Dzerzhinsky turned to him fully now, his sharp gaze dissecting him. "Lord Alexander Hawke," he said as though savoring the name. "Yes, I know who you are. An officer of the Royal Navy, an aristocrat, a man with many powerful friends. But let us dispense with the theatrics, shall we? You are no mere envoy. You are a spy, sent here by the wealthy aristocrats of Europe to liberate the Romanovs so they can rally the White forces and crush the Revolution."

"That's not true," Alexander countered, his tone firm. "My mission is exactly as I've stated. For God's sake, man, your government invited me here."

"Is that so?" Dzerzhinsky sounded almost amused. "Very well. If you won't tell the truth voluntarily, I'm sure we can find some way to compel you." He turned to the Red Guards flanking him and gave a terse order in Russian. Two of them slung their rifles and advanced on Alexander, seizing his arms and bracing him between them.

Natalya moved toward him, her voice rising in protest. "This is madness! Comrade Dzerzhinsky, you cannot—"

"Your plan has failed," Dzerzhinsky interrupted, still addressing Alexander. "The Tsar and his wife are no longer here. They were moved to Yekaterinburg two days ago. I have no doubt that they will soon stand trial for their crimes and receive the sentence they so richly deserve. You, *Lord Hawke*, will share their fate. I am taking you to Moscow, where I will wring the truth out of you."

Natalya stepped forward, locking eyes with Alexander. "I will speak to Comrade Sverdlov. He will get this sorted out."

"I'm afraid that won't be possible, Comrade Volkova." Dzerzhinsky's voice was ice. "You see, you won't be coming with us to Moscow."

Natalya's face betrayed a flicker of alarm, but she quickly masked it. "What do you mean?"

"You are a traitor to the Revolution."

Natalya's composure faltered for a moment, her lips parting as if to protest, but no words came. Dzerzhinsky pressed on, his tone cold and methodical. "By aiding this British agent, you have conspired to smuggle the Romanovs out of Russia—an act of treason not only against the Soviet government but against the people themselves."

"That's not true!" Natalya finally managed, her voice sharp with indignation. "I came here under orders from Comrade Sverdlov!"

Dzerzhinsky sneered. "Do not insult my intelligence, Volkova. Sverdlov anticipated your duplicity, which is why he sent me. Your death was already assured the moment you set foot in Tobolsk."

Natalya stepped back, her face pale but resolute. "If you believe that, then take me to Moscow. Let me face the Central Committee. I will explain everything."

Dzerzhinsky shook his head slowly, his expression almost pitying. "You know as well as I do that cannot happen. Your treason must not become public knowledge. The Revolution cannot afford the scandal of one of its own collaborating with an enemy of the state."

He reached into a pocket and took out a revolver.

"This is madness," Alexander shouted, struggling against the men holding him. "You can't just execute her without a trial."

Dzerzhinsky ignored him, raising the gun and aiming it at Natalya. "Your death will serve the Revolution. Officially, you were killed by the British assassin who infiltrated Tobolsk. And he, in turn, will be brought to Moscow to face justice for his crimes."

Natalya turned to Alexander, her eyes wide with urgency. "Sasha—"

The revolver barked once.

"No!" Alexander wrenched against his captors and managed to throw one of them off-balance before the butt of a rifle slammed into his kidney. Through a red flash of pain, he saw Natalya staggering back but still on her feet, her hands crossed over her breast, a dark stain spreading out from beneath her fingers. Her eyes met his, her lips forming a word that would never be uttered.

And then she was gone.

FORTY

SOCHI, RUSSIA
PRESENT DAY

Stokely Jones Jr. crouched at the corner of the old boathouse, slowly sweeping the city skyline with his night-vision spotter scope. From down here, everything looked quiet and peaceful. But that wasn't the message Fitz's commo expert—Dakota Mathers—was receiving.

Things had gone smoothly enough at first.

Exactly according to plan.

When Hawke had vetoed the idea of coming in hot and heavy in the helos, Fitz and Boomer opted for something more in keeping with their SEAL team roots. Under cover of darkness, the full team plus one—Stoke—covertly went ashore using diver propulsion vehicles. The sleek, torpedo-shaped devices allowed them to travel swiftly and silently beneath the surface. Each man was kitted out in a state-of-the-art wet suit designed to minimize his heat signature, his gear sealed in a watertight bag strapped to his DPV.

The shoreline where they had emerged was deserted, a private stretch of beach fronting an unoccupied dacha they had identified from an online vacation rental website. Stokely and Fitz quickly secured the property, ensuring there were no surprises waiting for them, while the rest of the team carried out their respective assignments: setting up the commo station, procuring vehicles, and generally getting ready to react if and when Hawke hit the panic button.

All of that had happened like clockwork.

Then, all of a sudden, things got very strange.

The first hint of trouble came when Mathers called in over the team commo frequency, sounding more than a little anxious. "Hawke is moving."

Mathers had come to T and L by way of the 75th Ranger Regiment, where he had excelled at long-range reconnaissance and calling in artillery strikes. He wasn't the type to cry wolf: if he was worried, there was probably a damn good reason.

Fitz's voice had cut in. "Moving?"

They had expected Hawke to spend at least a couple hours at Bocharov Ruchey. "Where's he going?" Fitz went on.

"Can't say where he's going," Mathers replied, "but he's booking. Definitely in a vehicle. He hasn't hit the panic button, though."

Fitz then passed the ball to Stoke. "Skipper? What say you?"

"Alex won't call for help unless he needs it," Stoke replied with more confidence than he felt. He felt his stomach twisting into a knot. "If he hasn't hit the panic button, then let's not panic."

Then Mathers broke in with another update. "Local police freqs just lit up like crazy."

The knot in Stoke's gut tightened. "What are they saying?"

"It's all in Russian," Mathers said. "Give me a second. I'll run it through a real-time translation app." There was a long silence; then Mathers came back. "It's a vehicle pursuit—high speed. Calling all cars."

Stoke couldn't tell if that was Mathers's idea of a joke. If so, it wasn't very damn funny.

"Could be unrelated," Mathers was saying, "but, based on the coordinates they're passing around, I'd say they're looking for our boy."

"But no panic button?"

"Not yet."

Stoke muttered a curse, glassing the skyline again. Whatever was happening up there, it was beyond the reach of his spotter scope.

He understood why Hawke would hold off on pushing the panic button, even if the shit was hitting the fan in great big bucketfuls. Thunder and Lightning were the nuclear option. A last resort to be used only in the most extreme circumstances. And, like nukes, even if they succeeded, the fallout would be considerable. Hawke would not summon them unless he had exhausted every alternative. That was just the sort of guy Alex Hawke was.

But that didn't mean Stoke had to just sit around with his thumb up his ass.

"Let's mount up," he said. "We'll start moving in his direction. That way, if he needs us, we'll already be on our way."

"We don't know where he's going," countered Fitz. "We could end up driving in circles."

"So we drive in circles. You got somewhere else to be, Fitz?" Stoke didn't wait for Fitz to reply. "Mathers, call up the birds on the *Fox*. Tell them to get in the air and start heading this way. If this turns sideways, I want them ready to extract or lay down support."

Stoke got up and gathered his equipment, then began trekking around to the front of the house where their vehicles were staged. Earlier that day, before leaving the *Flying Fox*, Fitz had used a throwaway phone number and bogus identity to rent four SUVs—late-model Land Cruisers that wouldn't look out of place on Sochi's streets—to be delivered to an innocuous address just a few blocks from their current location. Now those vehicles were standing by, ready to take them to the fight if the call came.

He was halfway there when Mather's voice came over the net again. "Skip, I can't raise the *Fox*. They're not answering."

Stoke froze mid-step, Mathers's words hitting him like a punch to the gut. "What do you mean they're not answering?"

"I mean there's no response. Primary comms, backup, emergency channels—nothing. Either their systems are down, or . . ." He didn't finish the thought, but Stoke knew what he was implying.

"Or something's happened to them," Stoke muttered under his breath. His mind raced. The *Flying Fox* was their lifeline, their escape route. If they had lost it . . .

"Keep trying. They've got to be out there."

"Roger."

Stoke pushed the dire possibilities out of his head and continued to the vehicles. Fitz and Boomer were already there, with most of the rest of their crew already occupying seats in the SUVs. From their dour expressions, it was apparent that the two SEAL veterans had caught Mathers's last transmission.

Fitz addressed the proverbial elephant in the proverbial room. "Skip, if we've lost the *Fox* . . ."

"Then we've lost her," Stoke said. "We drive on."

Stoke's voice was firm, but the weight of what he'd just said settled heavily in his chest. He climbed into the lead vehicle, sliding behind the wheel. "Mathers," he said, forcing his tone to remain calm and controlled, "what's Hawke's signal doing now?"

"Still moving," Mathers replied after a beat. "He's heading down toward the shore. Signal's steady, but no panic button."

Stoke inhaled deeply in order to make himself focus. "All right, let's roll. Move to contact. We don't stop until we know he's safe or we're out of options. Understood?"

"Understood," came Fitz's voice from the SUV behind him, echoed by Boomer and the others.

Stoke eased the Land Cruiser out onto the narrow road, his hands firmly holding the wheel. He wished he could say his thoughts were as steady as his grip, but they weren't. The implications of losing contact with the *Flying Fox* were staggering. Had it been compromised? Destroyed? Worst-case scenarios played in his mind, each one darker than the last.

If they didn't have the *Fox*, their extraction plan was dust. No air support, no escape route. And if Hawke was in trouble—and Stoke had no reason to believe he wasn't—how the hell were they supposed to help him now?

His obligation weighed heavily on him, but he shoved the doubts aside. Leadership wasn't about certainty; it was about making the best call you could with the information you had. Right now, that meant moving toward Hawke, even if it felt like wandering blindly into a minefield.

The minutes stretched into what felt like hours as they closed the distance to the marina. Mathers provided sporadic updates on Hawke's signal, his tone becoming more urgent as they got closer.

"He's stationary now," Mathers reported finally. "Signal stopped at the water's edge."

The marina came into view ahead, and Stoke's gut clenched as he took in the scene. Dozens of police cars were clustered near the docks, their flashing lights casting chaotic reflections across the dark water.

"Shit," Fitz murmured. "It's a damn circus."

Stoke clenched his jaw, his fingers tightening around the wheel as he guided the Land Cruiser past the marina's main approach. "We'll circle around to find a vantage point."

The police presence thinned as they left the epicenter of the commotion behind, and after a few more minutes Stoke spotted what he was looking for: a quiet overlook partially obscured by trees, offering a direct line of sight back to the marina. He pulled off the road, got out, and made his way to the edge of the viewing area, where he trained his spotter scope on the drama unfolding at the water's edge.

Just then he heard Mathers's frantic voice in his ear. "Skip! Hawke just pushed the button."

"Son of a bitch!" Stoke growled, feeling completely helpless. He shook his head, refocusing his scope on the activity below.

The marina was arranged with a main arterial promenade that extended from the central pierhead. Branching off this central pier were multiple finger piers, their narrower structures lined with slips where an assortment of vessels bobbed gently in the water. Each finger pier was separated by a narrow channel, the reflections of distant streetlights shimmering across the surface like fractured glass.

Several police officers, many of them kitted out in tactical gear, were now moving out along the network of piers.

"Now, what do you suppose they're up to?" muttered Fitz, who was now beside him, watching the scene through binoculars.

Stoke was pretty sure it was a rhetorical question. The answer was obvious. They were looking for Hawke.

He continued to watch as the policemen converged on a boat moored halfway down one of the finger piers. His view of the vessel was partially obstructed by the larger yachts to either side, but he kept the scope trained on the area, waiting for something to happen. For a long time, nothing did.

"Think they got him?" Fitz wondered.

Another rhetorical question? Probably. Fitz was one of those guys who couldn't stand long periods of silence.

Then something did happen. Not on the boat but rather on the pier. Another group of men—three hulking forms in ill-fitting suits—were making their way down the pier, moving purposefully, and clearly moving toward the boat at the center of the police activity. They didn't look like cops.

They looked like trouble.

"Now, who the hell are these guys?" Stoke murmured.

That was definitely a rhetorical question—two could play that game—but Fitz fielded it anyway. "Operators. Spetsnaz. You can tell just by looking at them."

Stoke was inclined to agree. The men both looked and moved like professionals, but that in itself didn't mean much. There was no shortage of employment opportunities for men with special operations experience. They might be FSB, GRU, or some other Russian government agency, or mob enforcers, or maybe private sector security contractors.

What kind of trouble have you gotten yourself in, Alex?

As expected, the trio made their way to the same boat the police had gone to and then disappeared from view. A moment later, however, they reappeared, and this time they had company. Braced between two of them—half carried, half dragged—was an all-too-recognizable form.

"Damn," Fitz groaned. "They got him."

The third thug stepped out right behind them, leading Ariadne Silk by the arm, then the rest of the police contingent emerged and moved to form a protective bubble around the big men and their prisoners as they made their way up the pier.

Fitz spoke up again. "Are we gonna do something about this, Skip?"

Stoke lowered his scope and glanced over at his friend. "Do something?" he echoed. "What exactly is it you want to do?"

Fitz jerked his head toward the marina. "Go get them out of there. We can do it. We've got the firepower. Shock and awe. Hit 'em hard. In and out, before they know what's going on."

Stoke looked down at the marina. At a glance, he estimated close to three dozen police officers, along with the three enforcers, whoever they were. In strictly mathematical terms, Thunder and Lightning were at a slight numerical disadvantage, but since any one of the mercenaries was easily equal to five ordinary men, it would be the police, not T and L, who would be facing long odds.

But there was more to the calculation than just who had the superior fighting force. There were lives to consider: Hawke's and Silk's, yes, but also those of the mercenary fighters and even the local cops. A rescue attempt would end in bloodshed on a massive scale, and while he did not doubt that the mercenary force would win the firefight, that didn't necessarily guarantee a successful rescue. And if by some miracle they did succeed . . . then what?

Down on the pier, Hawke and Silk were frog-marched to a waiting black SUV and loaded into the rear. Most of the policemen returned to their patrol vehicles and climbed in, clearly preparing to depart the scene.

"They're about to move them," observed Fitz. "We can hit them just as they start to move out. Disable that vehicle and create a bottleneck for the pursuit. We won't get a better chance."

Stoke had no difficulty visualizing what Fitz was suggesting. It was doable. High probability of success. And he wanted to do it. Wanted to act. Needed to do something. Anything.

Which was why what he said next was so hard.

"We can't," he said, barely choking the words out. "Even if we could pull it off, without air support we'd be so far up the creek that it wouldn't even matter if we had a paddle."

Fitz gaped at him. "So that's it? We just let them take him?"

Stoke put a hand on his old teammate's shoulder. "We're not giving up, Fitz. But if we're gonna help Alex, we have to be smart about this."

Below, the black SUV was moving, rolling out, with a dozen police cars providing escort. Whatever window of opportunity they might have had was now closed.

Fitz watched the procession depart, then turned back to Stoke. "'Be smart'?" he said, his voice low and edged with anger. "What the hell does that look like?"

Stoke let out a long breath, then shook his head. "I don't have a damn clue."

FORTY-ONE

LONDON

When he closed his eyes, he saw her.

Not as he had found her but as he chose to remember her. As she ought to have been.

Smiling. Full of light.

Alive.

Ambrose Congreve had never known grief like this. Not when his parents had died. Not when he had lost comrades in the line of duty. This . . . this hell on earth . . . was a pain he could not have believed possible.

He was a man who thrived on self-discipline, a logician who prided himself on compartmentalizing his emotions. But there was no compartment for this. His chest felt hollow yet suffocating. Breathing required an effort so monumental, it seemed absurd that it came naturally to others.

And in his mind's eye, he saw her again. Not the lifeless figure the police had quietly covered on the floor, but Diana as she was the first moment he'd seen her all those years ago.

He'd been captivated. Chief Inspector Congreve, the man with every step of his life mapped out, suddenly found himself adrift yet exhilarated. She was the light he hadn't known was missing from his life.

Now that light was extinguished. And the darkness that remained was sucking him in.

Heart's Ease Cottage was empty now, not just of her presence but of him as well. He couldn't bear to be there without her. It was a crime scene now, a place of pain and shadows. But even if it weren't, how could he ever return to it? He recalled her teasing him about how the cottage was lonely when he wasn't there. Now, without Diana, it would be forever lonely.

Instead, he found himself in a sterile hotel room arranged by Scotland Yard. It was functional, detached, and utterly devoid of anything personal.

Just like me.

It was all he could do not to break down sobbing.

How do I go on without you?

It was Diana herself who answered. Her voice that he heard in his head.

Silly. You just do.

"But how?" he wailed into the emptiness of the hotel room.

It is a problem, she admitted. *But you, my dear, excel at solving problems.*

Well, that was certainly true. But this wasn't a problem that could be solved with logic and deduction. There were no facts to weigh. No evidence to consider. This wasn't a . . .

Wasn't a murder investigation.

Except, of course, it was.

His breath hitched as the thought took shape.

Yes, it *was* a puzzle. A case.

A murder investigation.

But that was absurd. No, worse than that. The idea of reducing Diana—his Diana—to the status of *a case* . . . *an investigation* . . . felt grotesque.

And yet . . . wasn't that what she had become?

Ambrose Congreve had spent the better part of his life solving crimes. He had peered into the minds of killers, unearthing their secrets, following their trails, dismantling their logic until they had had nowhere left to hide. It was who he was. It was what he did. It was how he made sense out of a too-often senseless world.

I have to do this.

It's the only way I will ever be able to fix this.

The thought came to him out of the blue as if someone had thrown him a lifeline.

Of course, it wasn't true. Solving Diana's murder wouldn't bring her back. It wouldn't fill the gaping hole she'd left behind. But it was something. It was a task, a goal, a way to claw his way out of the abyss.

If I just do this . . .

His mind was already shifting gears, putting his grief aside, locking in on the facts of the crime. He already knew who had committed the crime. The villain had practically signed his name to it.

Silence.

But *who* was the man behind the nom de guerre?

That was one of the questions he would have to solve, but there was an even more important question, one that cut to the bone.

Why?

Why kill Diana?

The answer whispered itself almost immediately, unbidden, like the logic of a mathematical proof unfolding in his mind.

Because of me.

His investigation of Silence's murders had brought him to the killer's attention, and Diana along with him. It was the obvious conclusion, and it came with no small measure of guilt.

I got you killed. I'm the reason you're gone.

The thought struck like a knife to the heart, twisting with every beat.

I did this to you. Silence may have taken your life, but I'm the one who put you in his sights.

He sank onto the edge of the bed, his head in his hands, drowning in the enormity of it. The case, the puzzle, the need for answers—none of it mattered. Nothing mattered without her.

And then, like a candle flickering in the dark, he heard her voice again.

Silly. You didn't do this, and you know it.

He shook his head, gripping it tighter. "I did. You wouldn't have been in London if not for me."

You would still be here if you'd never met me.

I came because I wanted to be with you. Her voice was gentle, firm, cutting through his anguish. *I chose this life, Ambrose. I chose you. And I'd choose you again.*

He let out a shuddering breath, her words wrapping around him like a balm. He could almost believe she was there, sitting beside him, her hand resting on his, her eyes full of that quiet, unshakable belief in him.

This wasn't your fault, love. You couldn't have stopped it. But you can stop him. *You're the only one who can.*

The guilt didn't vanish—he doubted it ever would—but her voice steadied him, gave him something to hold on to in the storm. Slowly he sat up, letting his hands fall to his lap.

"I'm sorry," he whispered to the empty room.

Don't be sorry. Be brilliant.

And for the first time since her death, the corners of his mouth twitched upward, faint and fleeting but real. His mind circled back to the unanswered question—*Why?*—and this time he was able to approach it with cold logic.

You were afraid I was close. That's why you killed her.

Somewhere in his investigation, he had uncovered something crucial. If Silence had taken such drastic action, it meant he knew the police were closing in.

His thoughts shifted to the suspect list—the passengers who had traveled from Bermuda to London during the narrow window between the murders. That was the connection, the thread tying the crimes together. One of them *was* the killer.

He crossed to the small desk where Scotland Yard had left him the dossier. His hands trembled slightly as he opened the folder, spreading out the passport photographs.

One of them was Silence.

One of them had killed Diana.

Which one?

He studied the faces, searching for some hint of hidden evil, a psychopathic gleam in the eyes.

Wasn't there an old saying about the eyes being the window to the soul?

"Diana, darling, do you remember what you said on the plane—about the crime scene staging being a window into the killer's soul?"

The words left his mouth before he even realized he was saying them aloud, but for a brief, blissful heartbeat he waited expectantly for her answer.

Then the truth hit him all over again, a crashing wave of anguish that took his breath away. He reeled backward, collapsing onto the bed, and pressed his hands to his face, trying to stem the tide. It was no use. The grief poured out of him in heaving, racking sobs.

He might have stayed like that forever if not for the gentle but insistent knock at the door.

He tried to ignore it, hoping whoever it was would go away. The thought of facing anyone in his current state felt impossible.

The knock came again, firmer this time.

"Go away!" he shouted, his voice hoarse and ragged.

For a moment he thought the message had been received, but then a third knock came, patient but resolute.

With an anguished groan, Congreve forced himself to his feet. His limbs felt like lead, his body resisting every step as he shuffled to the door and yanked it open, ready to unleash a tirade. The words died in his throat as his eyes landed on the figure standing in the hallway.

"Your Majesty?"

There, standing in the hallway, dressed impeccably in a bespoke suit, was King Charles III. Two bodyguards lingered a few paces behind, watchful but unobtrusive.

"Ambrose. I came as soon as I heard. You have my deepest sympathies. Truly."

Congreve swallowed hard, his throat tightening. The King's words, so heartfelt and sincere, cracked something within him. He opened his mouth to reply but could only nod, the words refusing to come.

The King waited a moment, his gaze steady and kind. Then, as though sensing what Congreve needed most, he continued, "May I come in?"

Congreve blinked, momentarily stunned, then stepped aside to allow the King entry. "Of course, Your Majesty. Please, forgive the state of things."

As the King entered, his sharp eyes swept the room: the dossier spread across the desk, the chair pulled askew, the faint outline of grief lingering in the air. He gestured to the chair opposite the desk. "Shall we sit?"

Congreve nodded again, suddenly self-conscious. He moved to straighten the chair, but the King waved him off and sat down.

"Ambrose," Charles began, leaning slightly forward, "there's another reason I've come. As you'll recall, we were to meet to discuss Dr. Ariadne Silk's mission."

Congreve inhaled sharply, guilt flashing across his features. "I'm sorry, Your Majesty. With everything that happened, I—"

"There's no need to apologize," the King interrupted gently. "I know why you didn't come. But I also know the sort of man you are. A man of purpose. A man who finds his way through even the darkest hours by focusing on what he does best."

Congreve swallowed hard. His hands fidgeted briefly in his lap before he nodded. "You're right, of course."

The King gave a faint smile. "Then let's get to it, shall we? I believe you indicated that Dr. Silk may be in some sort of danger?"

Congreve sat straighter, his mind already shifting gears, setting his emotions aside, donning his professional demeanor like a suit of armor. He quickly recounted the facts of the case and the ultimate identification of the contract killer, Silence, as the perpetrator. "Dr. Ariadne Silk is the connection between the two victims," he concluded. "I believe she may be the killer's next target—" He faltered, realizing that his original assumption on that score had been tragically in error but then shook his head and went on. "And I think it may have to do with whatever it is that she is doing on your behalf. I believe she was engaged on business for the Crown?"

The King leaned back slightly, steepling his fingers. "I understand that you've spoken with Lord Hawke about this?"

"I have. He was reluctant to violate your confidentiality and suggested I approach you for more information."

The King nodded slowly. "What I am about to tell you is known only to a handful of people."

"You may depend upon my discretion, Majesty."

"Of course." The King smiled again but then seemed to hesitate as if unable to decide how to begin his tale. "You are aware, I take it, of Dr. Silk's position with the Royal Archivist."

"I have her file. She's a forensic document examiner."

"Yes, that's correct. Dr. Silk has gone to Russia in order to authenticate a letter purportedly written by my ancestor George V. A letter that concerns the fate of our cousins the Romanovs, and which might prove embarrassing to the Family if it were made public. President Putin has the letter and has offered to return it to us in exchange for certain . . . considerations relating to his adventure in Ukraine."

"He's blackmailing you."

"I believe that is his intention. Dr. Silk has gone to determine the letter's authenticity. Lord Hawke is escorting her at my request to ensure her safety." The King paused a beat and then continued in a low voice. "And to covertly exchange the document for a forgery."

Congreve absorbed the information, his mind racing to connect the pieces. The international implications of Silk's mission—and Hawke's, for that matter—went a long way toward explaining why someone might hire a killer of Silence's caliber to take her out.

"Who would stand to gain by preventing Dr. Silk from accomplishing her mission?"

The King was ready with an answer. "Anyone who might believe that I would go along with Putin's scheme."

Congreve gave a thoughtful hum. "Eliminating her would leave the letter's authenticity in doubt. But only until you send someone else to do the job." He narrowed his eyes, feeling as though he was missing something obvious and wanting very much to have a pipe of tobacco.

"But why kill her friends?" he went on. "Why target her former schoolmates—women with no connection to her current work? Why . . . *silence* them?"

The King spread his hands. "I'm afraid this is your area of expertise, old chap."

Congreve leaned back, his brow furrowing as he turned the question over in his mind. The King's revelations had brought Silence's motives into sharper focus, but he felt no closer to an answer.

"Have you made any progress identifying this killer?" asked the King.

Congreve gestured to the desk, where the dossier lay open, passport photos scattered across its surface. "We're working under the assumption that he traveled from Bermuda to London in the narrow window between the murders. These are all the people who meet that criteria and who have not been otherwise eliminated from the list of possible suspects. One of them is almost certainly Silence."

The King looked down at the array, studying them with what seemed like mere curiosity. Then he reached out and picked up two of the photographs. "These women. Who are they?"

Congreve saw that the King was holding the pictures of the identical twin sisters and smiled knowingly. “Rather fetching, aren’t they? Swimsuit models from Poland. A bit odd. Their stay in Bermuda was rather short, but I suppose that’s the life of a jet-setter for you.”

The King’s lips pressed into a thin line. “You said that you had Dr. Silk’s file? Do you have a photograph of her?”

Congreve shuffled through the larger case file until he found the requested document and then took out Silk’s personnel photograph and handed it over.

Charles studied the photo for a long moment, his expression unreadable, then looked up. “This is not the woman who met with Alex and myself at Clarence House,” he said quietly.

He set the photograph down and then took up the pictures of the two Polish sisters, scrutinizing them carefully and then choosing one, which he then displayed to Congreve with grave certainty. “This is her. This is the woman traveling with Alex.”

FORTY-TWO

OUTSIDE GYUMRI, ARMENIA

Savannah Stone crouched low on a ridge above the old airstrip, the rugged terrain and scruffy vegetation offering just enough concealment for her to observe her subject unnoticed. The outpost—one of dozens built by the Soviets during the Cold War and scattered across the region—had once served as a staging ground for reconnaissance flights and spy missions, but with the collapse of the Soviet Union, it had been left to decay, just like the empire that had created it. Now it was not even a ghost of its former self. Overgrown and forgotten, with cracked tarmac and the skeleton of a hangar looming at one end, it seemed an unlikely destination for General Osman Gul.

Nevertheless, here he was.

Following her meeting with Gul at Konya Air Base, Savannah had brought her concerns to Daniel Hughes. While it was the position of His Majesty's Government that Gul's comments to the NATO leadership represented nothing more than empty posturing, Hughes had agreed to put the technical expertise of the Secret Intelligence Service at her disposal. Gul's phone and emails would be monitored. Savannah wasn't sure what, if anything, they were looking for, but something about Gul's demeanor during that meeting had unsettled her enough to press her case.

For the first two days the surveillance yielded nothing. Gul's phone records showed no unusual activity, and his email communications were limited to routine military matters. If he was plotting something, he wasn't careless enough to leave a trail. Savannah had begun to doubt her earlier resolve. But on the second night, at 19:47 local time, Gul received a call. Despite its being routed through a VPN and several layers of encryption, MI6 managed to trace its origin to Russia. The call was brief, containing just two words, spoken in heavily accented English: "It's done."

The significance of this message would not become apparent until late the next afternoon when the news broke: *President Vladimir Putin was dead, the result of an audacious assassination.*

Moscow was in chaos. Prime Minister Mikhail Mishustin—a weak Putin loyalist with little real authority—was floundering in his attempt to hold the government together. Tanks now patrolled Red Square, their engines rumbling against a backdrop of protests and counterprotests. Crowds surged through the streets, some chanting for reform and an immediate withdrawal from Ukraine, others demanding vengeance and a show of strength to reaffirm Russia's dominance.

The identity and affiliation of the assassin had not yet been revealed, but the Kremlin had announced that a suspect was in custody. Conspicuously, Putin's assassination had been carried out at nearly the exact time Gul received his cryptic phone call.

Savannah didn't believe in coincidences.

At the time, however, Savannah knew only that Gul was indeed up to something. Early the next morning, Gul—dressed in civilian clothes and driving a personal vehicle—departed from Konya Air Base. His route took him northeast, through the stark landscapes of eastern Turkey. MI6 tracked his progress via satellite, feeding Savannah updates as she tailed him at a discreet distance. Now, as she lay hidden on the ridge overlooking the desolate airstrip, watching Gul and waiting to see who would meet with him, she felt vindicated. The only question was whether Putin's assassination was the culmination of Gul's scheme or merely the opening gambit.

Savannah now watched as Gul moved across the tarmac, his figure barely discernible in the moonlight. At first she thought he was pacing, restless. But when he stopped at regular intervals to kneel down, she realized his little jaunt served another purpose.

"It looks like he's marking the runway," she whispered into the microphone of the state-of-the-art satellite communication link connecting her to Daniel Hughes in the intelligence operations center at the embassy in Ankara. "Infrared torches. He's expecting a visitor."

"Checking Armenian and Turkish civil aviation logs," replied Hughes. The line was quiet for a few moments; then Hughes came back, an edge of disappointment in his voice. "Nothing in the system. No filed flight plans that would put a plane anywhere close to where you are."

"If they're running dark," Savannah replied, "I doubt you'll find any official record of the flight. They'll be staying below the radar."

Down on the runway, Gul had placed the last of his IR beacons and was making his way back to his car to wait for the arriving aircraft. A few minutes later Savannah heard the faint sound of an aircraft in the sky, a sound that quickly escalated in volume as the plane made its approach. She scanned the sky, looking for running lights, but saw nothing until the plane was nearly on top of her. Even then, it was just a silhouette against the terrain as it touched down, engines roaring as it decelerated on the uneven tarmac. Based on her best estimate of its length and engine configuration, she guessed that it was a small private jet—a Bombardier or a Gulfstream. The plane needed most of the runway to finish braking near the far end of the strip, almost three hundred yards from Savannah's vantage point, whereupon the pilot immediately began turning the plane around, lining it up for takeoff.

Down below, Gul got back in his car, started it, and drove down the tarmac to meet the arrival. Whatever security considerations had prompted the plane to fly in blackout mode, they did not seem to apply once on the ground. Gul drove with his headlights on, giving Savannah a glimpse of the plane as it approached.

As Gul made his way to meet the aircraft, the plane's main entry hatch opened, the jet's internal lights providing a second source of illumination. In its glow, she saw half a dozen men emerge, armed with carbines and wearing camouflage, and fan out to the edges of the runway to form a perimeter around the plane.

Gul brought his vehicle to a stop near the foot of the fold-down steps and got out, its headlights still blazing, though angled away from Savannah so that it offered her only an oblique view of what was happening there. As Gul approached, another man descended the jet's stairs. He wore a heavy black coat that hid his physique, but Savannah had the impression of great bulk. The face, though difficult to make out even with the magnification of her binoculars, looked very familiar.

She keyed her mic. "I'm going to try to get closer for a better look."

"Be careful, Savannah," cautioned Hughes. "You've no net to catch you if you fall."

She didn't bother to respond. Instead she scooted backward, dipping below the ridge, and then began moving in a low crouch, staying parallel to the runway until she was within about fifty meters of the jet.

Settling into position, she trained her binoculars on the fuselage of the plane, bringing the tail numbers into focus.

"I've got an ident on the plane," she whispered into her mic. "RA-731KP."

RA was the prefix for Russian civilian aircraft.

"Give me a second," Hughes replied, his tone all business. The line went silent for a moment; then he returned, his voice tight. "That aircraft is registered to the Perun Group."

Savannah felt her pulse quicken. With the revelation of the plane's ownership, she was able to put a name to the man who was now meeting with Gul: Sergei Mulmuscovy. The man believed responsible for the attack on the NATO summit, the attack in which Savannah herself had briefly been taken hostage.

The implications of this meeting churned in her gut. Had Gul played some part in the attack on the summit? She recalled that Amir al-Fulan, the Turkish defense minister and Gul's immediate superior, had also been among the captured. Had the assault been a power play on Gul's part, meant to advance him to the number two position in the Turkish government?

And what about Putin's assassination? Had that also been orchestrated by these two men? The timing of Gul's cryptic phone call and this meeting could not be ignored. But what did they hope to accomplish? Was this an alliance to destabilize NATO, or something even more audacious? She turned the pieces of the puzzle over in her head, trying in vain to make them fit. One thing felt certain: whatever was happening here, it was only just beginning.

The meeting concluded quickly. Gul and Mulmuscovy shook hands; then the former returned to his car, leaving the Russian alone on the runway.

"Gul's leaving," Savannah reported.

"A long way to come for a short talk," remarked Hughes.

Savannah was thinking exactly the same thing. Whatever the two men were scheming, it was nothing they wanted to risk discussing over the telephone. "What do you suppose they're up to?"

"Nothing good." There was a brief pause, and then Hughes went on. "I'll pass this on to Vauxhall. You were right to suspect him, Savannah. You've got good instincts."

Savannah appreciated the vindication, but her thoughts were already elsewhere. The threat posed by Gul and Mulmuscovy far outweighed any satisfaction she might feel. "I'm going to stay put until the jet leaves."

"Just be careful."

"I'll be fine, Mother," Savannah replied, with a hint of a smile. "I'll check in once they're gone."

The line went quiet, and Savannah settled back into her position. She adjusted her binoculars, scanning the scene below. Mulmuscovy had gone back into the plane; aside from that there was no sign of activity near the aircraft.

"All right," she murmured. "What are you lot waiting for?"

She shifted slightly, her muscles already growing stiff from holding the same position for so long. The air was cold, her breaths shallow and quiet, but she forced herself to stay still. Nothing in the scene below changed, but her unease grew.

Then, out of nowhere, she felt the sharp grip of hands on her shoulders, pinning her to the ground. Heart pounding, she struggled, trying to wriggle out from under her unseen assailant, but the man had already seized her arms, pinning them behind her back. He hauled her to her feet and then began dragging her from her overwatch position. Unable to break free, she tried crying out, even though there was no one but Mulmuscovy's men around to hear. The effort earned her a rough shake and a growled *"Zatknis'!"*

Savannah didn't need a translation.

Her captor hauled her down to the runway, dragging her up the fold-down stairs and into the brightly lit cabin, where she found Mulmuscovy waiting.

"Commander Stone," he said in heavily accented English. "It is good to finally meet you."

Savannah's stomach turned. How did he know who she was? She cursed herself for not having given some thought to a cover story. "I'm not . . . I don't know what you're—"

"Please," Mulmuscovy said, waving a dismissive hand. "Let us not insult each other's intelligence. We spotted you with our infrared scopes when we came in for a landing. When I told General Gul that we had an uninvited guest, he mentioned that you had been sniffing around him in Konya. It wasn't hard to put two and two together."

Mulmuscovy regarded her for a moment, his expression calm, almost pleasant, as if this were a casual conversation over tea. Then his smile faded, his voice turning cold. "The question, Commander, is not who you are—but who else knows you're here."

Savannah clamped her mouth shut. The man knew too much already. Any lie she attempted now would crumble under scrutiny, and the truth would just get her killed.

Mulmuscovy tilted his head slightly as though amused by her refusal to cooperate. "Your silence forces me to make assumptions. Those tend to have very unpleasant consequences."

Despite the fear coursing through her, Savannah maintained a mask of defiance and kept her voice steady. "You have my name and rank. I'm also authorized to give you my service number if you like."

The Russian returned a humorless smile. "Perhaps you will change your mind." He turned to her captor. "Commander Stone will be traveling with us. Make her . . . uncomfortable."

INTERLUDE—PART NINE

MOSCOW, SOVIET RUSSIA
APRIL 1918

The days—or was it weeks?—blurred together into a meaningless haze, a nightmare from which he could not awaken. The dark cell where they kept him when he was not being questioned was little more than a tomb, cold and unyielding. The walls, built from rough, damp stone, closed in on him, their oppressive weight seeping into his bones as he lay naked, battered, and aching on the cold concrete floor. Sleep eluded him.

His time in the interrogation room was much, much worse. They would come for him at irregular intervals, dragging him down a dimly lit corridor to the torture chamber—a stark, unforgiving room with a reclining chair bolted to the floor under a bare bulb that dangled like an executioner's noose. They would strap him into the chair, holding him fast with leather restraints, and then the guards would go to work on him. The questions came relentlessly, punctuated by blows, threats, and the occasional caress of a blade against his skin. "Tell us who sent you," the Cheka interrogator—the only one of them who spoke English—would demand. "What was your mission? Who else is involved?" Alternately, the man would tell him the answers and offer respite from the ceaseless torment if he would just admit to his crimes and sign a confession. He gave them nothing.

Nothing but his screams.

In the end, it wasn't the torture that broke him. It was the hopelessness.

Natalya was dead—executed by Dzerzhinsky without trial or mercy—and her loss had hollowed him out more effectively than any of their instruments ever could. Her death had extinguished the flame of purpose that had kept him going through the endless days of their journey. Now there was nothing left for him except more of this. More cold. More pain. More despair. And eventually death. What was the point of holding on? What good was resisting when there was no one left to save?

So he told them about the letter.

FORTY-THREE

THE GULF OF FINLAND
PRESENT DAY

Errant flakes of snow swirled about the *Blackhawke*'s powerful exterior, leaving a faint dusting on the deck where Anastasia Romanova stood, her hands buried deep in the pockets of her coat as she gazed out across the steel-gray expanse of water. Above, the sky hung heavy with clouds, a pale slate gray that seemed to absorb what little sunlight managed to filter through.

The yacht lay at anchor in the Gulf of Finland at the very edge of Russian territorial waters, as close to the line as one could get without crossing it. From her position, the low coastline of Estonia was a faint smudge on the southern horizon, while just twelve nautical miles to the east, tiny Kotlin Island guarded the entrance to Neva Bay and the approach to Russia's second-largest city, St. Petersburg.

The decision to position the *Blackhawke* here had been hers, made in anticipation of what she feared might go wrong. She had learned very little about Alex's secret mission. Vasily Markov had told her only that Alex was going to Russia and that he was walking into a trap. But Russia was a very big place, and she had no idea where the trap would be sprung, so she had elected to position the yacht within easy reach of St. Petersburg, a city she knew well and where she still maintained a few contacts.

If the need arose, she knew she could slip into the city unnoticed, leveraging those connections to gather intelligence or move about the country with relative ease, going wherever Alex might need her.

It was a decision born of desperation. If Alex did need saving, then any help she might provide would likely come too late. That had been her fear, and now it was her reality. For the trap had been sprung, and Alex was caught in its teeth.

The first hint of just how much trouble her beloved was in had come two nights earlier, in a call from Alex's close friend Stokely Jones Jr. He revealed that Alex had been arrested in Sochi, more than 1,300 miles away. But that was only the tip of the proverbial iceberg. The reason for his arrest—the trap in which he had been caught—was almost beyond belief.

Vladimir Putin was dead, assassinated in a brazen attack that had thrown Russia into chaos. Anastasia had first heard the news on international broadcasts, where the details were still murky. Reports conflicted about the how and the where—a sniper's bullet in Sochi, a bombing in Moscow, a poisoned chalice at the Winter Palace—but the nation was reeling. Tanks had rolled into Red Square. Moscow was engulfed in turmoil. Protesters filled the streets, some demanding reform, others calling for vengeance. And while there had been no mention of Alex's involvement, Anastasia knew in her heart that her lover was in the thick of it—and very likely directly responsible for ending the Russian president's life.

God only knew he had sufficient reason.

Stokely had not revealed any of this to her and in all probability had learned of it along with everyone else. What he was able to tell her was that Alex had been moved to Moscow shortly after his arrest but that his GPS tracker had gone dark soon after his arrival in the capital. It was Stoke's intention to mount a rescue attempt, but to do so, he needed resources that he hoped Asia could provide. Unfortunately, given the present chaos into which Putin's assassination had thrown the nation, she could no longer count on those resources to be there for her.

Then she'd gotten a call from a representative of His Majesty's Government.

The call was brief and vague, the representative—a woman with a rather haughty British accent—stating that she had urgent information relating to "Lord Hawke's situation" and "would like to meet, soonest."

When Asia had explained that she was presently in the middle of the Gulf of Finland, the woman replied, "I'm aware, and I'm currently on the way to your location now. I should be there within the hour."

The unnamed representative was as good as her word. Forty-eight minutes after the call, the *Blackhawke*'s radar operator reported an inbound aircraft, and shortly after that the radio officer received a call from the same, requesting permission to land.

Curious, Anastasia went out on deck to receive the visitor.

She easily located the Royal Navy Merlin HM2, a dark silhouette against the gray sky, growing larger and roaring louder as it approached. Once over the yacht's decks, it maneuvered into position above the helipad, its rotors whipping up the snow into stinging gusts, and then touched down.

Anastasia squared her shoulders, pulling her coat tighter, and waited as the aircraft disgorged a single passenger—a tall figure whose features were mostly hidden under a heavy parka. She then moved forward to greet the newcomer just beyond the still-spinning blades.

"Welcome aboard," she said, shouting over the din. "Come, let's go inside where we can hear ourselves think."

The newcomer inclined her head in silent agreement and followed down a short companionway and through a polished teak door into one of the yacht's luxurious salons, where Tommy Quick was waiting.

As soon as they were inside, the visitor removed her parka, unleashing a cascade of blond hair that fell about her shoulders and revealed a tall, willowy figure in a smart pantsuit and with a face that belonged on the cover of a fashion magazine. Her sharp blue eyes appraised Anastasia for a moment, then lit up when they fell upon the *Blackhawke*'s chief of security.

"Tommy," said the newcomer, greeting him with a dazzling smile. "It's been ages."

A grin split Tommy's face. "Pippa. I'll be damned," he said, taking her hand in a firm shake. "You're the last person I expected to see stepping off that chopper. What's it been—ten years?"

"Close enough," she replied, her tone warm. "You look exactly the same, Tommy. Haven't aged a day."

"I could say the same about you."

Anastasia watched the exchange with growing unease. *Ten years?* She could do the math.

And Alex had a type.

"I see you two know each other," she said, trying, without much success, to keep the ice out of her tone.

Tommy caught the edge in Asia's comment and turned toward her, clearing his throat as if to ease the shift in atmosphere. "Oh, uh, yes. Pippa worked with . . . ah, us, years ago when we were setting up Red Banner."

"Pippa?" Anastasia echoed, raising an eyebrow.

Before Tommy could elaborate, the blonde smoothly interjected. "An unfortunate nickname I haven't been able to shed," she said, her voice clipped but amused. She extended a hand to Anastasia. "Actually, it's Gwendolyn. Gwendolyn Guinness."

Anastasia accepted the handshake, her expression carefully neutral. But her thoughts were less composed.

Did Alex call you Pippa?

"A pleasure to make your acquaintance, Miss Guinness. I'm sure you didn't come all this way to reminisce about the good old days. You said that you had information about Alex?"

Pippa regarded her for a long moment as if trying to decide how much trust to extend. "Can we sit?"

Anastasia gestured to one of the chairs. Pippa took it, and then she and Tommy sat as well.

"As you are no doubt aware," Pippa began, "President Putin was assassinated two days ago. The situation in Moscow is . . . turbulent, to say the least. Protests, military presence in the streets, a nation in chaos."

Anastasia's jaw tightened, her tone sharpening. "I know all this. And I know that Alex has been arrested. He's in Moscow."

"He's in Lubyanka Prison," Pippa said bluntly.

The words hit Asia like a blow. Every Russian knew about Lubyanka. It was more than a prison; it was a monument to fear, oppression, and death.

The sprawling Lubyanka Building, constructed during the reign of the Tsars, stood just a few blocks from the Kremlin, its imposing yellow-brick neobaroque facade both stately and, perhaps because of its historic role, foreboding. Originally built in the late nineteenth century as the headquarters of an insurance company, the structure was repurposed after the Bolshevik Revolution to become not only the headquarters of the Cheka—the first iteration of the state secret police—but also the prison where countless dissidents, spies, and so-called enemies of the state were held, tortured, and in many cases executed. Though the Soviet Union had fallen, the Lubyanka Building continued to serve as headquarters of the FSB, the successor to the KGB, and remained an enduring symbol of authoritarian control, its very name synonymous with fear.

And if Alex has been taken there . . .

The very thought made her want to throw up.

She faced Pippa. "Did he do it? Did Alex kill Putin?"

This clearly was not the response Pippa had been expecting. She gazed back at Anastasia for a moment before answering. "I don't know."

"But you sent him there. To Russia. On some secret mission." She cut her eyes at Pippa. "I know who Alex works for," Anastasia snapped. "Who *you* work for. We can dispense with the cloak-and-dagger nonsense."

Pippa inclined her head. "Fair enough. But we did not send him there. Alex was doing a favor for His Majesty. A personal errand. He most definitely was not sent there to assassinate the President of Russia." Pippa paused a beat. "That said, we've uncovered information to indicate that the King may have unwittingly been duped into sending Alex to Russia by the conspirators who actually carried out the plot."

"Duped?"

"Alex believed that he was escorting a representative of the Royal Archivist to Sochi in order to authenticate a historical document. We've since learned that the representative was murdered by a notorious contract killer known as 'Silence,' who then assumed her identity and convinced the King to send her and Alex to Russia. Exactly what happened when they arrived is not clear at this time, but our best guess is that either Silence contrived to have Alex pull the trigger, or she did so herself and then framed Alex for the crime."

"*She?* Silence is a *woman?*"

Pippa pursed her lips. "If the information we've uncovered is correct, Silence is actually *two* women. Identical twin sisters. One of them accompanied Alex, while the other was busy eliminating anyone who might have been able to expose her sister as an imposter."

"But either way, the Russians are blaming Alex."

"They haven't done so publicly, but, yes, that is our assumption."

Asia nodded. "So, what are you going to do to get Alex out of there?"

"That's why I'm here. The situation is difficult, yes. But it's not hopeless."

"Then you have a plan?"

"Not as such," Pippa admitted. "We . . ." She hesitated, as if trying to decide whether to trust Anastasia. "We have some assets in Moscow. Our network is not as extensive as it once was—we've had to tread carefully in recent years—but there are still people we can call on. But for something like this? There's only so much they will be able to do."

"Then why are you here?"

"I was hoping that you might be able to bring something to the table."

"*Me?*" said Anastasia. "I'm not following you."

"I know who you are, Ms. Romanova. And I know that you know people."

Anastasia nodded slowly. "I have a few contacts in St. Petersburg who might be able to help, but Moscow is a different beast."

"Especially right now." Pippa crossed one leg over the other. "But the chaos in Moscow could work to our advantage. Putin's assassination has thrown everything into disarray. The power vacuum at the top has left the Kremlin scrambling to maintain control. Nobody is certain who's really in charge right now. The FSB is spread thin, trying to deal with the fallout: protests in the streets, factions vying for influence, and the very real threat of further attacks. They're prioritizing securing the Kremlin and keeping the streets from descending into full-blown anarchy. As a result, they don't have the luxury of concentrating their resources on a single prisoner, even one as high-profile as Alex."

Anastasia tilted her head, processing this. "And Lubyanka? You think it's vulnerable?"

"It's not *invulnerable.* Even the most secure facility has its weak points. Right now, with the FSB's attention divided, those weak points will be harder for them to shore up. And if the situation in Moscow worsens, their focus will shift even more toward crowd control and securing key government locations."

"'If the situation worsens,'" Anastasia mused. "Are you suggesting that perhaps we should find a way to make that happen?"

Pippa smiled. "I think you're starting to follow along just fine."

"I believe I may have the solution to that problem. Stokely Jones Jr. is already in Russia, on his way to Moscow."

Pippa's eyebrow went up. "Stokely Jones? Alex's American friend? Former SEAL, built like a bloody tank?"

"The same," Anastasia confirmed. "He's the one who alerted me that Alex was taken. He was there to provide support for Alex in the event that . . . well, something like this happened. Unfortunately, when it did, it happened too quickly for him to intervene. But he's not giving up on Alex. He wants to mount a rescue operation."

Pippa's lips pressed into a thin line. "Well, that's ambitious. But isn't he a bit"—she paused, clearly searching for a diplomatic term—"conspicuous?"

Asia allowed a faint smile to tug at her lips. "He's not exactly subtle, no. But maybe subtlety is not what we need right now. If anyone can stir up enough chaos to pull the FSB's attention away from Lubyanka, it's Stokely."

Pippa leaned forward, tapping her fingertips together thoughtfully. "You make a good point. All right. I think we have the start of a plan. Let's coordinate our assets. You reach out to Stokely and make sure he's ready to move. I'll contact our people in Moscow and see what resources we can bring to bear. If we're going to do this, it has to be soon."

Asia nodded, but Pippa wasn't finished. Her blue eyes softened just slightly, the calculating edge giving way to something warmer. "We'll save him. One way or another, we're getting Alex back."

For some reason, Pippa's assertion sent a chill through Asia.

"We'll save him."

As if this rescue was as much her mission as it was Asia's. As if she had some deeper connection to Alex that gave her the right to say *we.*

Am I reading too much into this?

"Tommy," she said without looking away from Pippa, "could you give us the room for a moment?"

Tommy glanced between the two women, his brows lifting slightly, but he didn't argue. "Sure thing," he said, rising and making his way to the door. "I'll be right outside if you need me."

Asia waited until Tommy had left the room before turning back to Pippa. "I need to know something."

Pippa raised an eyebrow, her cool demeanor unshaken. "All right."

"If we're going to work together, I need to know . . ." She faltered. "What exactly is your relationship with Alex?"

For the first time, Pippa's confident facade faltered. She leaned back in her chair, exhaling softly. "Ah. I see." She studied Asia's face for a moment before continuing. "We've worked together for some time. I suppose, technically, I'm his superior . . . but Alex doesn't really answer to anyone, does he?" She paused a beat. "But that's not what you meant, is it?"

"Are you lovers?" asked Asia flatly.

Pippa was quiet for a long moment, but she did not blink. "We were. Once. It was a long time ago. Just one night, if you must know. We were both much younger, and let's just say . . . circumstances conspired."

"Just once?" Asia asked, unable to hide her skepticism.

"It was a mistake. There was rum involved." She gave a half-hearted smile, as if the addition of that detail might somehow diminish the memory. Then her expression became serious again. "Since then, our relationship has been strictly professional. Whatever happened between us, it's ancient history. Water under the bridge."

Asia tilted her head slightly, scrutinizing Pippa's expression. "Does Alex know that?"

"Of course he does," Pippa replied, her tone edged with a hint of defensiveness. "If you're worried that I have some lingering claim on him, you can put that fear to rest. I'm not here to rescue Alex so that I can win him back from you. I'm here because he's in danger and because I can help."

Asia studied Pippa's face, her cool, composed beauty, her piercing blue eyes that seemed to look straight through people. There was no sign of guile, no hint of a lie. However, there was something in the way Pippa spoke about Alex—a note of finality that should have reassured her but instead twisted the knife.

The truth was Asia wasn't afraid that Pippa was trying to steal Alex. That wasn't what this was about. What she felt wasn't jealousy as a result of competition. It was rooted in something far worse.

It was the fear that Alex wasn't hers to lose in the first place.

Pippa had known him in another life long before Asia came into the picture. A time when Alex had been different, perhaps even freer, unburdened by the weight of all the battles he had fought and all the scars he carried. Pippa had known that version of Alex, the one who might have laughed more easily, who hadn't yet grown so adept at walling himself off from the people who loved him.

But even being with *that* Alex, Pippa had said, had been a mistake. A drunken, fleeting mistake.

What did that say about *her*? About the version of Alex she knew—the one she loved? She'd never deluded herself into thinking Alex could be tamed. But lately she had begun to wonder if there was even room in his life for her. Or anyone.

Was Alexei the only thing keeping them together?

The thought stung, even though she'd considered it before. Their son was everything to her—the light in her life. And she knew Alex loved their boy as fiercely as she did. But was that enough to keep them together?

"I don't think Alex will ever let anyone claim him," said Asia, more to herself than to Pippa.

Pippa's expression shifted. For the first time there was a flicker of something deeper behind her calm exterior—something that might have been pain. "Maybe so. But right now it's fallen to the women he's loved to save him."

FORTY-FOUR

MOSCOW

They had taken everything. His clothes. His watch. His dignity.

Alex Hawke sat naked on a freezing concrete floor with his back pressed against a damp concrete wall. The air reeked of mildew and fear. His hands, shackled behind his back, were raw from the bite of the metal cuffs. Somewhere above him, water dripped at maddeningly irregular intervals.

He wasn't sure what was worse, the cold or the waiting.

Thankfully, his captors hadn't hurt him. Much. Aside from a new crease in his skull and some bruised ribs, he was effectively uninjured. He wondered how long that would last.

How long had he been here? Twelve hours? Maybe more? Time was a slippery concept under such conditions.

It was not the first time he'd been imprisoned. In some ways, that made it worse, because now he knew what horrors awaited him. The first time? When he'd been shot down over Iraq, tortured for days by operatives of the Iranian Quds Force who were secretly supporting the insurgent fighters, he'd been naively unaware of the depths of depravity to which another human being might sink. It had been much, much worse than his worst nightmares. He had no doubt that the FSB's techniques would similarly exceed his worst expectations. But those prior experiences also gave him hope. Because every other time he'd been captured . . . imprisoned . . . tortured . . . he had endured. Survived.

He would survive this too.

He anchored himself to sanity by focusing on . . .

Her.

Ariadne Silk.

It wasn't her real name, of course. She had told him that much the last time he'd seen her, stuffed into the back of one of Mulmuscovy's armored SUVs on their way to the airport.

Right after she had betrayed him.

Even looking like a drowned rat, she was still beautiful.

"Was it something I said?" he had asked. "Or is this just because I wouldn't sleep with you?"

Her lips had turned down into a pout. "I feel sad for you, Alex. You'll never know what you missed. It was always going to end this way, but we could at least have had a little fun first."

"So you like playing with your food, is that it?"

She laughed. "It was nothing personal, darling. I needed you . . . preoccupied."

"Ah, yes. The magician's beautiful assistant distracting the audience while the magician stuffs the rabbit down his trousers."

"Only in this case you're the rabbit, dear Alex."

"Quite a trick. You did all of this . . . that phony letter . . . the story about my great-grandfather . . . all of it so that you could kill Volodya and then hang it on me?"

Silk tilted her head to the side. "The letter is real enough, at least as far as I know."

"That's your professional opinion, Dr. Silk?"

She laughed again. "As you've probably realized, I'm not Ariadne Silk."

"No, I don't suppose you are. Did you kill her?"

The woman gave an indifferent shrug. "It was necessary in order to take her place. Putin's blackmail attempt was the perfect opportunity to get close to him—and to involve you as well."

"You're working for Mulmuscovy, I take it."

She waggled her hand. "Him, or whomever he is working for. Politics don't interest me. This was just a job. Once I've delivered you to the FSB, my part in it will be finished."

Just a job.

The words stung afresh in Hawke's mind as he sat in the dank cell, the cold seeping into his bones. He seethed at how easily she had manipulated him. But anger was a waste of energy. He would deal with Ariadne Silk—or whatever her name was—in due course.

First, he had to survive.

The cell door creaked open, flooding the tiny space with light so harsh, it brought tears to his eyes. Through the blur, he saw two men looming in the doorway. They entered, yanked him to his feet, and unlocked his shackles, then dragged him out of the cell down a narrow corridor that smelled of blood and piss.

He didn't resist.

Not yet.

The room they brought him to was as cliché as it was horrifying: a bare bulb hung from the ceiling, casting sharp shadows across the cold tile floor. An ancient dentist's examination chair—equipped with leather restraint straps—was positioned in the center of the room, directly under the light and right beside a rusted, ominous floor drain. The men shoved him into the chair, one of them holding him down while the other fastened the straps tightly around his wrists, ankles, chest, and throat. Then they exited the room, leaving him alone with his imagination.

The torturer, when he finally arrived, looked like someone sent over from central casting. He was a short, wiry man with greasy black hair slicked back against his scalp and a pair of round glasses perched precariously on his sharp nose. He wore a white lab coat stained with something brownish red—blood, no doubt—and was pushing a decrepit trolley with squeaky wheels upon which rested a cracked leather Gladstone bag. He rolled the trolley forward until it was positioned to Hawke's immediate left and then regarded him with a grin that was as cold as a dull knife.

"Lord Alexander Hawke," the man said in accented English, clapping his hands together. "Such an honor! I must admit, I have admired you for many years."

"Always a pleasure to meet a fan. But look here, old chap, I want to be clear about something. This *is* part of the basic tour, right? I'm not shelling out extra for the deluxe package."

The torturer actually threw his head back and laughed, a sight so comical that Hawke couldn't help but join in. When at last the man's mirth ebbed, the dead grin returned to his face. "Are you enjoying your accommodations? This may interest you. I don't know if you are a student of history, but the cell where you will be staying was once occupied by your great-grandfather, who was, if I understand correctly, also named Alexander Hawke."

"You don't say."

"I do." The man opened his bag and began methodically removing its contents—medical instruments, forceps, needles, scalpels, and sundry tools Hawke didn't recognize but could easily imagine their purpose—setting each instrument down on the top of the trolley with deliberate care. "In fact," he went on. "The chair you're sitting in? Your great-grandfather sat in it as well. And these"—he gestured to the array of medical equipment—"these are the very tools my predecessor used when he interviewed your ancestor more than a century ago. Such wonderful symmetry, don't you think?"

"Symmetry? Well, if that's what you want to call it. Frankly, I'm a bit disappointed that the FSB can't afford to modernize after all these years. Next you'll be firing up a coal furnace to warm the irons."

The torturer's thin lips curled into a smirk. "You see, this is why I admire you. Always the clever quip, even facing"—he gestured to the tools—"this."

Alex allowed himself a faint smile, though inside, his mind was working furiously. The whole setup—the flickering light bulb, the archaic tools, the grotesque theater of it all—was designed to unnerve him. It was the classic interrogator's gambit—show the tools and let the victim's imagination do the rest. Make him anticipate horrors that might never come and, in doing so, break his spirit before you break his body.

Hawke knew how the game was played and wasn't going to cooperate.

"Well, you've certainly got the ambience nailed," Hawke said lightly, testing the straps securing his wrists. No give. Of course not. "Very retro. I almost feel like I should start humming the *Mission: Impossible* theme."

"It is curious, no?" said the torturer. "Your sense of humor. Does it comfort you? Or are you so arrogant as to believe that, in the end, you will be spared? I've read the reports of your great-grandfather's interview. He clung to hope just as you do now. In the end, it wasn't enough for him."

Hawke held the man's stare, his expression calm but his voice icy. "I've seen worse than this, old boy. Your little puppet show isn't going to have me quaking in my boots. Oh, wait—sorry, I forgot—you took those too."

The torturer picked up a scalpel and held it up to the light, turning it and gazing down its edge. As he did, Hawke saw the familiar stainless steel band of his own watch—the GMT Master that had once belonged to his father.

I'm going to get that back from you, you bloody bastard, if it's the last thing I do.

"These methods may seem quaint to you," the man was saying, "but I assure you, they will produce results. The only question is how much pain and mutilation you will endure before you break."

Hawke now looked away and leaned his head back against the chair's headrest, his smile undiminished. "Do your worst. But I'd appreciate if you sterilize those instruments first. Wouldn't want to get a nasty infection, now, would I?"

The torturer's grin returned, colder than ever. "I think you'll find that sanitation is the least of your worries."

He placed the scalpel back on the trolley, then picked up a pair of needle-nose pliers. "Who sent you?"

"Nobody sent me. I'm on holiday. I was thinking of seeing the ballet."

"Where shall we begin?" the man said, seemingly apropos of nothing. He brought the pliers close to Hawke's face, holding them so that the tip was just above his eye. With an effort, Hawke managed, just barely, not to blink. "Here?"

He held the pliers there for a long moment, then moved them away, touching the tip to Hawke's cheek, dragging it lightly across his skin, tracing the line of his jaw, across his throat, down the center of his chest. Then it went lower. "Or maybe . . . here?"

Hawke felt the cold metal slide through the dark thatch of his pubic hair, circling the base of his penis, tugging at the skin of his scrotum, finally coming to rest on one of his testes.

"Yes, I think you value this more than even your eyes. Who sent you to kill President Putin?"

"I didn't bloody kill him," Hawke rasped.

Answering the question directly, simply acknowledging it if only to refute it, violated every tenet of tradecraft, but Hawke knew that if he was going to survive this, he would have to throw out the rule book.

His response seemed to surprise the man. "You deny it?"

"Of course I bloody well deny it," Hawke snapped, letting some genuine anger bleed into his voice. "I was set up. You lot are barking up the wrong tree. But if you're interested in the right one, I'd suggest you start looking at Sergei Mulmuscovy."

The torturer paused, the name clearly striking a chord. He set the pliers back down on the trolley, folding his arms as he studied Hawke's face. "Mulmuscovy," he repeated, his tone carefully neutral.

"Yes," Hawke pressed. "Your very own warlord-cum-oligarch. You think I had the resources to pull off an operation like this under your noses? Think again. Mulmuscovy's the one with the motive and the means."

The torturer's lips pursed, his gaze sharp as his scalpel. "You expect me to believe that Sergei Mulmuscovy would assassinate his good friend, our president?"

"I don't expect you to believe anything," Hawke replied, his voice low and steady. "But I'm telling you this: you're wasting your time with me. While you're down here playing with your antiques, Mulmuscovy's already three steps ahead, consolidating power and preparing to carve up what's left of your country."

The torturer said nothing, but Hawke could see the gears turning behind his eyes. It wasn't this man's job to interpret the answers his subjects gave, merely to extract them, but Hawke knew he was weighing what to do with the information. If the FSB shifted even a fraction of their focus onto Mulmuscovy, it might be enough to loosen their grip on him.

The torturer straightened, his expression cold and unreadable. Without a word, he turned and strode toward the door, rapping twice before it swung open. Two guards entered, unlocking Hawke's restraints and hauling him roughly to his feet.

"Take him back to his cell," the torturer instructed, speaking in English, no doubt for Hawke's benefit. "Let him contemplate his cleverness for a while. We'll resume shortly."

As the guards dragged him out of the room, Hawke allowed himself a faint smile. He was still alive and still in possession of all his body parts. It wasn't much, but it was a start.

FORTY-FIVE

"Feels like we're driving straight into a Stephen King novel," muttered Stokely Jones Jr. from behind the wheel of the black Mercedes G-Wagon. Outside, Tverskaya Street had the look of a ghost town. Businesses were shuttered, their once-bright signage now dim and lifeless. What few pedestrians there were moved about furtively, scuttling from place to place as if fearful of being caught in the open. The wide boulevard, usually choked with traffic and the incessant honk of horns, was eerily quiet, save for the occasional rumble of military trucks trundling by in convoys.

When they had learned where Alex had been imprisoned, Stoke and the mercenaries of T and L were confronted with the challenge of making their way north to Moscow. Moving clandestinely through enemy territory was something they had all trained for during their time working in military special operations, and they received some assistance from Anastasia, who sent couriers to supply them with forged travel documents, cash for bribes, and low-profile transit routes through backwater towns and rural train stations, but it was nevertheless a grueling experience. For Stoke, the challenge was even greater. Blending in was impossible, so instead he stayed in the shadows, moving at night, and avoiding crowds altogether. By the time he reached the rendezvous at the safe house Anastasia had arranged on the city's outskirts,

Stoke felt like he'd gone through hell week all over again. But that was nothing to what they were now attempting.

The closer they got to Tverskaya Square, the more surreal the atmosphere became and the tighter the knot in Stoke's stomach grew. The square, dominated by the imposing Hotel National and just a stone's throw from the Kremlin, marked a subtle shift in atmosphere: less desolation, more tension. Armored personnel carriers were parked at intervals; soldiers loitered nearby with rifles slung across their chests, smoking or watching passersby with cold, predatory eyes. Barriers had been erected where the street fed into Mokhovaya Street, cutting off direct access to Red Square. Beyond them, the red spires of the State Historical Museum loomed against the overcast sky, dark and foreboding.

"Coming up on the checkpoint," Stoke announced. He flicked his eyes toward the rearview mirror, where Fitz, sporting gold chains, a chunky Rolex, and a gaudy red tracksuit, was slouched across the back seat, feigning drunken unconsciousness. It wasn't much of a stretch for the hard-drinking former SEAL. "You comfortable back there, big guy?"

"As a babe in his mother's arms," Fitz murmured, the faintest of grins tugging at his lips.

"Well, that makes one of us," Stoke muttered.

"Nervous, boyo?"

"I'm the only brother for a thousand miles, and we're rolling up on Red Square. What do you think?"

"Think of yourself as a unicorn," Fitz replied cheerfully. "A very large, very intimidating unicorn. Folks won't know whether to pet you or run for their lives."

Stoke's knuckles tightened around the wheel as he eased the G-Wagon toward the checkpoint. "I'll settle for them not shooting me on sight."

Fitz let out a chuckle, low and lazy. "You're the bodyguard, man. It's all about attitude. Keep scowling like that, and they'll believe you wrestle grizzly bears for a living."

"Not the vibe I'm going for," Stoke muttered. "I'm trying to not look like I'm about to snap someone's neck."

"You do have the tougher role," Fitz admitted. "The tracksuit's doing most of the heavy lifting here."

Stoke flicked his eyes toward the mirror again. Fitz, adorned in his ridiculous red outfit, gold chains gleaming in the dim light, looked like a third-rate party animal on the verge of alcohol poisoning.

Stoke shook his head and sighed. "We'd better hope the soldiers at that checkpoint buy it. Otherwise, you're going to have to wake up real quick, Mr. 'Vadim Petrovsky.'"

"Don't you worry about me. I'll be snoring my way through this like a pro."

"You'd better."

Stoke slowed as they approached the makeshift checkpoint that had been set up across Tverskaya Street. The soldiers behind the barricades looked as nervous as Stoke felt, despite the fact that they were equipped with Kalashnikov rifles. A sergeant—tall, broad-shouldered, and scowling—stepped out from behind the barrier, one hand raised, palm out.

"Here we go." Stoke eased the G-Wagon to a halt, dropped his window, and plastered a big smile across his face.

The sergeant did a wide-eyed double take when he saw Stoke, but then his face went hard again. He barked something in Russian—clipped and impatient.

"Sorry, my man," Stoke replied. "I don't speak tank commander. You speak English? *Nyet?* I didn't think so."

The soldier frowned and leaned closer, clearly irritated, repeating, *"Dokumenty!"*

Stoke understood that but decided to play dumb. "One second, big guy." He fished his phone from the cup holder in the center console, opened a translation app, touched a finger to the microphone button, and began speaking.

"Look, I'm just trying to get my boss . . . that's him passed out in the back. Big party. Big night. I'm just trying to get him back to his penthouse on Nikolskaya Street. You know how it is. Too much vodka, too many girls." He flashed an apologetic grin. "Played in the NFL. Now I work for this guy. Pays well, lets me drive nice cars. Life could be worse. Football star turned babysitter. That's me."

He let go of the button, and his phone immediately began a long recitation in Russian of what he hoped was an accurate translation of his words.

The sergeant's brow furrowed as he listened to the slightly robotic voice, then he leaned in, his gaze flicking suspiciously toward the back seat. Fitz, to his credit, let out a perfectly timed snore and muttered something incoherent.

The soldier narrowed his eyes and barked another order, louder this time.

Stoke, who had been ready with his thumb on the button, sighed dramatically and waited for the translation. The monotone voice, now speaking English, said: "Who is your boss? What's his name?"

"Name?" Stoke repeated, adopting his best big, dumb bodyguard persona. "That's Mr. Vadim Petrovsky back there. Maybe you've heard of him. Big money guy. Oil and gas." He leaned toward the soldier and stage-whispered conspiratorially, "The ladies love him. Or maybe they just love his money, but, hey, what else is all that money good for if not bringing in the chicks? You feel me?"

The officer's scowl deepened as the app provided the translation. Stoke could feel the sweat pricking at the back of his neck. For a long beat, the sergeant didn't move, didn't speak. He just stared. Then someone behind him shouted out in Russian: *"Pust' proydet! U nas yest' boleye vazhnyye problemy!"*

Stoke's app dutifully translated: "Let him pass. We've got bigger problems."

The sergeant hesitated, then gave an irritated wave, stepping back from the vehicle. "*Spasibo*, my friend," Stoke said with a grin, and then, under his breath, "And don't forget to tip your server."

He kept his eyes on the road, letting the G-Wagon roll forward at a deliberately casual pace. The tension in his shoulders eased just slightly as the soldiers and their barricades receded in the rearview mirror.

"Bigger problems," Fitz muttered, cracking both eyes open now, his smirk tempered with a glimmer of curiosity. "You think he meant us?"

"We can only hope," Stoke replied as he made the right turn onto Ulitsa Okhotnyy Ryad. "Pippa's puppets should be moving by now."

"Anti-war lefties and nationalist nutjobs," said Fitz. "How long do you think before they start throwing rocks—or worse—at each other?"

Four hundred miles away, aboard the *Blackhawke*, Pippa Guinness was coordinating with a team of MI6 cyber-operations specialists who had spent the better part of the last twenty-four hours flooding the most popular Russian social media platforms—VK and Telegram—with inflammatory posts and rumors designed to bring two very angry groups of protesters to Lubyanka Square. The first group, composed of anti-war activists, was already on edge after Putin's assassination and the subsequent military clampdown. The narrative being fed to them was simple: the Lubyanka Building, symbol of FSB oppression, was now the Kremlin's command center, where hard-liners were consolidating their grip on power. The second group was a more dangerous mob: ultranationalists stirred to a frenzy with whispers that Putin's assassin—a foreign agent—was being held inside the Lubyanka and that he needed to be dragged into the street to face mob justice. The unrest was already simmering, and with a little nudge from Pippa's white hats, it would boil over into something the FSB couldn't ignore. Once the protests turned violent, all attention would be diverted to dealing with the chaos.

"And then us, throwing sparks on that powder keg," Fitz added.

Stoke made a left turn onto Ulitsa Okhotnyy Ryad, keeping his pace steady and his posture relaxed as the G-Wagon rolled past darkened shop fronts and silent cafés. The grand facades of the street's prerevolutionary buildings loomed on either side, their ornate details muted in the gray, overcast light.

Ahead, the wide boulevard funneled toward Teatralnaya Square, where the iconic Bolshoi Theatre stood in austere elegance. Its grand columns and white facade, usually a beacon of culture and sophistication, now seemed cold and indifferent. Several military trucks were parked just off the square, their presence a silent warning to anyone considering gathering here. Soldiers lounged nearby, rifles slung over their shoulders, their breath visible in the frigid air. Stoke noted a pair of officers standing in conversation, their faces serious, one gesturing sharply toward the western edge of the square.

He veered right, onto Leninsky Prospect, following the curve of the road as it skirted the square. From here, the view toward Lubyanka was blocked by rows of low-slung administrative buildings.

At Neglinnaya Street, he made another turn, this time heading north. The road narrowed slightly as it curved along the western edge of the city's historic center, flanked by office buildings and the occasional boutique hotel. The G-Wagon passed another military truck parked at the curb, its driver seated in the cab with a cigarette dangling from his lips. The man barely spared them a glance. Protesters and malcontents usually didn't roll through town in style.

Stoke finally pulled the G-Wagon into an open parking spot near the entrance to the Hotel Savoy. "Time to stretch our legs," he said.

"Pity," Fitz grunted, sitting up. "I was just starting to get used to the chauffeur-driven lifestyle."

"Yeah, you and Miss Daisy." Stoke got out and joined Fitz on the sidewalk. The shops along the street front were shuttered, their iron grates drawn tight. It felt as though the entire area were holding its breath, sheltering in place until the unrest subsided. The faint sound of distant shouting and the occasional bark of a military vehicle's engine carried through the air.

Their destination lay about half a block to the north: a pair of arched passageways that led to the courtyard where the vestibule entrance to the Kuznetsky Most Metro station was located. On an ordinary day, the courtyard would have been a hive of activity, but today there was not a soul to be seen. The station wasn't closed, but the local population evidently had no interest in going anywhere.

Stoke paused just outside the entrance and pulled his phone out to make a call. Anastasia picked up on the second ring.

"Are you in position?" she said, her voice calm but laced with tension.

"We're heading into the station now. I don't know if we'll be able to get a signal once we go underground."

"Understood. The plan is still a go. My friend should be waiting for you at the south end of the platform."

"Got it. How are we gonna recognize the dude?"

"He won't have any trouble identifying you," she said, a trace of amusement creeping into her tone. "When he approaches you, he will say, 'The river flows south.' You will respond with, 'Only in the spring.'"

Stoke suppressed a chuckle at the old-fashioned cloak-and-dagger routine.

"'Only in the spring,'" Stoke repeated. "Got it."

There was a pause on the line. When Anastasia spoke again, her voice had softened. "Be careful, Stoke. And . . . bring him back."

"Bet on it," Stoke said, and then ended the call. He turned to Fitz.

Stoke pocketed the phone and looked at Fitz. "Ready to make some new friends?"

Fitz rolled his neck, his gold chains jingling faintly as he fell into step beside Stoke. "Into the belly of the beast," he muttered. "Just another day at the office, eh?"

"Something like that."

Moscow's metro system was more than just a transportation network; it was a marvel of engineering and artistry, often referred to as "the underground palace." Built during the Soviet era to symbolize the power and grandeur of the USSR, its stations featured opulent designs meant to inspire awe and reverence. Chandeliers hung from vaulted ceilings adorned with mosaics, bas-reliefs, and intricate tile work. Marble columns, polished to a gleaming shine, flanked corridors that felt more like the halls of a royal palace than a subway.

Kuznetsky Most, while not as ostentatious as some of the older stations on the system, maintained a quiet elegance that reflected its more modern construction. Opened in the late 1970s, the station was designed with functionality in mind but still bore the hallmark arches and clean lines of Soviet-era architecture. Its single island platform was framed by a series of smooth, white-tiled arches that curved gracefully overhead. Softly glowing light fixtures recessed into the arches bathed the platform in a warm, diffuse light, contrasting with the gleaming black granite flooring.

As Stoke and Fitz descended to the platform, their footsteps echoed against the tiles, adding to the sense of eerie stillness. The station, like the streets above, was mysteriously deserted, its usual hum of commuters replaced by silence. The arches stretched into the distance, framing their path as they made their way toward the southern end.

At first, the space seemed entirely empty, but as they drew closer, a figure came into view, standing just outside the soft pool of light cast by one of the recessed fixtures. The man was unremarkable in appearance, wearing scuffed leather boots, dark trousers, and a black leather jacket zipped up to his throat. His hands were shoved into his pockets, and he leaned casually against one of the tiled walls. He didn't glance around nervously or make any attempt to blend in; he simply waited, as though the deserted station was a perfectly normal place for him to be.

"Think that's our guy?" Fitz muttered under his breath, the faint jingle of his gold chains cutting through the silence.

"You see anyone else it could be?" replied Stoke, quickening his pace and taking the lead as they approached the man.

When they were a few steps away, the man pushed off the wall, straightening and fixing them with a sharp, appraising look.

“You’re late,” he chastised in heavily accented English.

“Now, just hold your horses a wee minute, comrade,” Fitz said. “We’re not late. We’re exactly on time. And aren’t you supposed to tell us something?”

The man gave Fitz an exasperated look, then turned to Stoke, clearly deciding to address him instead. “Do we really need to play these spy games? I know you are not FSB.” He gave Stoke a meaningful look. “That is obvious. And if I am FSB, then you are already fucked. But if it makes you feel better”—he waved his hand dismissively, his voice dripping with sarcasm—“‘The river . . .’ Shit. I don’t remember it.”

“Close enough, my man.”

“Good. Now, let’s get off this platform before somebody notices us.”

“I guess that’s him,” Fitz muttered.

Stoke turned back to the man—Markov, he presumed. “Lead on.”

Without another word, Markov turned sharply on his heel and began moving to the very end of the platform. With only the slightest hesitation, he dropped down into a sitting position, letting his legs dangle out over the edge, and then scooted forward, lowering himself down onto the track bed. He turned and looked up at Stoke and Fitz.

“Don’t touch third rail.” He jabbed a finger toward the electrified rail running parallel to the tracks, its insulated shield glinting faintly in the dim light. “Is mistake you only make once.”

Stoke exchanged a quick glance with Fitz, who indicated with a gesture that Stoke could go first. Stoke shook his head, then dropped down onto the track bed. He thought he could hear the third rail buzzing ominously with residual energy but knew that was just his imagination. Fitz followed, his gold chains jangling faintly as he hopped down.

Markov motioned for them to follow and set off at a brisk pace, his footsteps crunching lightly against the gravel scattered between the ties. The tunnel ahead was dimly lit by sparse maintenance bulbs mounted high on the walls, their weak, yellowish glow casting long, distorted shadows. Thick bundles of cables lined the walls, some neatly secured, others sagging or frayed, their insulation worn with time. As they continued into the tunnel, the air grew noticeably cooler, the faint metallic tang of the station replaced by the earthy scent of damp concrete and old steel. A light breeze, almost imperceptible, carried hints of oil and something faintly acrid.

"What do we do if there's a train?" Fitz asked, his voice low but edged with unease.

"I do not think they are running near Red Square right now," said Markov, unconcernedly. "But if one does"—he shrugged—"hug the wall."

"Hug the wall," Fitz repeated. "Real reassuring."

The farther they walked, the more oppressive the darkness became, swallowing up the sparse lights and amplifying every sound: the scrape of their boots, the faint hum of electricity, the distant drip of water echoing like a metronome.

Markov led them another hundred yards down the track bed before stopping in front of a nondescript steel door embedded in the tunnel wall. Without hesitation, Markov produced a set of keys from his jacket pocket, selected one, and inserted it into the heavy lock. It turned, and he pulled the door open, revealing a narrow shaft with a rather rickety-looking steel ladder bolted to the opposing wall.

"I'm guessing this isn't OSHA-approved," muttered Stoke.

Markov glanced back at him. "Is tight squeeze. Better suck in your gut."

"Hey, brother. Haven't you heard? We're all about body positivity now."

But their guide had already stepped out onto the ladder and begun descending.

"Gonna get your ass canceled saying shit like that," Stoke muttered. He gave Markov a few seconds' lead time before following him down.

The shaft was barely wide enough to accommodate Stoke's broad frame, his shoulders brushing the rough concrete walls as he climbed down. He counted twenty-five rungs before his boots hit solid ground, and he found himself in a faintly lit corridor lined with corroded pipes and adorned with graffiti and the grime of decades of neglect. The air smelled of damp concrete and faint mildew, cooler than the train tunnel but carrying an undercurrent of stagnant water and rust.

"Cozy," remarked Fitz as he stepped off the ladder.

Markov had moved a few yards down the corridor to their right, and Stoke now saw that he had been joined by another man, tall and wiry, wearing a pair of grease-streaked coveralls and a respirator slung around his neck. A large duffel bag rested on the concrete floor beside him.

"This is Dmitri," Markov said, gesturing to the man. "He knows these tunnels better than anyone alive. He will guide us the rest of the way."

Dmitri nodded curtly and said something in Russian, his voice low and gravelly. Stoke thought about activating the translation app, but Markov beat him to it.

"He says: 'Welcome to the other Moscow. The city beneath the city.'" He laughed. "Dmitri is hopeless romantic."

Dmitri laughed along and then knelt down and opened the duffel, taking out additional respirators, coveralls, and headlamps. As he began distributing the equipment, he launched into a monologue, which Markov dutifully translated. "This tunnel system was built during Stalin's time, originally for maintenance and military access. Over the decades, it expanded—sewer lines, ventilation shafts, electrical conduits, and escape routes. Some say it connects to Metro-2, the government's secret underground network, but you'll hear that from conspiracy theorists more than engineers. The truth is, no one knows how far it all goes."

Dmitri paused to let Markov catch up, then thumped his chest and added, "Except for me."

Stoke pulled on his coveralls, which were about two sizes too small, and then donned his respirator and headlamp. Dmitri then handed each of them a pistol—sturdy, old Soviet military-issue Tokarevs. Although they'd come into the country with an arsenal, Fitz and Stoke hadn't wanted to take the chance of being caught with weapons on the streets of Moscow. Underground was a different story.

"Not my first choice," Fitz groused, giving the weapon a quick inspection. "But I suppose it's better than walking around with my dick in my hand."

Markov translated this, eliciting a laugh and a comment from Dmitri. "He says if you have to use these, then you are probably already fucked."

When they were all thus equipped, Dmitri turned and headed down the corridor, his powerful flashlight showing them the way.

"This place has its own mythology," Markov said, still translating for Dmitri, who evidently felt compelled to play tour guide. "Explorers call it the 'Moscow Underground,' but it's more than just tunnels; it's layers of history. Basements of long-forgotten factories. Bunkers from the Cold War. Even prerevolutionary catacombs. Some levels are flooded. Some are sealed. And some"—another dramatic pause—"some have no explanation at all."

"Lovely spot for a stroll," muttered Fitz. "I'll have to pick me up a T-shirt in the gift shop."

Stoke checked his watch, noting the time with a frown. "As much as I enjoy seeing the sights, I have to remind you that we've got a schedule to keep."

Markov relayed this to Dmitri, who answered with a dismissive wave. "He says, 'Plenty of time,'" and then added with a shrug: "Don't worry. Following Dmitri is only way. Without him, we will never find our way into Lubyanka. Or back out again."

Thus chastened, Stoke withheld further comment as they moved deeper into the three-dimensional labyrinth, up and down ladders, crawling through passages so tight that Stoke feared he would get stuck, only to enter cavernous cathedral-like vaults. And all the while, the clock kept ticking down.

The tunnels eventually gave way to a narrow, disused train line, the tracks warped in places and coated with grit. Dmitri gestured with his flashlight toward the path ahead.

"This line," Markov translated, "was built in the 1930s. It was used to move prisoners in and out of Lubyanka's lower levels during the darkest days of Stalin's purges. They say no one who came through these tunnels ever saw daylight again."

The tunnel seemed barely wide enough to accommodate a train. Old light fixtures, long since burned out, hung from the ceiling, leaving the space in a state of oppressive gloom.

"So, when can we expect the Lubyanka Express to roll through?" asked Stoke with a chuckle.

Markov shared the joke with Dmitri and then translated his response. "Dmitri says we are lucky it is too forgotten for anyone to bother maintaining it. That means no patrols."

Stoke checked the time again. Less than a minute to go . . .

Thirty seconds.

He watched the second hand of his Omega Seamaster Planet Ocean 600M tick down.

Five . . .

Four . . .

Three . . .

Two . . .

One.

"Boom."

Up above, on the streets near Lubyanka Square, four strategically placed improvised explosive devices would be detonating in quick succession, courtesy of Fitz's mercenaries. The bombs were not designed to kill but rather to add to the chaos of the protests. Smoke would fill the air, glass would shatter, and the already escalated crowds would erupt into panicked confusion.

They didn't hear the explosions or feel the vibrations—too far underground for any of that—but the knowledge of what was happening above lent an unspoken urgency to their steps.

After another fifty yards, they reached the end of the line. Dmitri played his flashlight beam on a wall of brick and mortar stained dark with years of grime.

"This is it," Markov announced. "The entrance to Lubyanka's lowest levels."

Stoke regarded the featureless wall. "Shouldn't an entrance have more of a . . . well, an entrance?"

"Entrance was bricked up decades ago," Markov explained. "To keep people from doing exactly what we're doing."

Dmitri handed his flashlight to Stoke and pulled a heavy wrecking bar from his bag. Without a word, he jammed the flat edge into a seam between two bricks and gave it a sharp, practiced shove. The brittle mortar cracked and crumbled instantly, sending a cascade of brick dust to the ground. After a couple more taps, he was able to work one of the bricks loose, revealing a dark void beyond. With the first brick removed, Dmitri was able to make quick work of his task, creating a jagged opening wide enough for a person to slip through. He gave the final brick a shove, sending it tumbling to the floor with a dull thud.

Dmitri dusted off his hands, then shrugged out of his coveralls, revealing a plain black suit underneath. Markov also shed both his protective outer layer and his leather jacket, under which he wore a similar outfit. As a finishing touch, they clipped red plastic ID badges to their lapels.

"Red badges are for senior FSB officers," Markov explained. "Will give us full access to any part of the building. Nobody will stop us."

The badges, which had to be forgeries, looked authentic enough to Stoke's untrained eye. He hoped they would fool the people who were used to seeing the real ones. Fortunately, if all went according to plan, they wouldn't have to deal with too many security checks.

Markov had learned that Alex was being kept in the lowest subbasement of the building, on the same level they were about to enter, in a part of the old prison that had been long since decommissioned. In fact, most of the old prison had been mothballed, and while there was still a detention facility at FSB headquarters, it was little more than a temporary lockup and not a high-security penal institution.

Why Alex had been brought to Lubyanka and installed in a mothballed prison block was unclear. Pippa Guinness had theorized that the new Russian leadership wanted him kept out of the official penal system. Whatever the reason, that decision had presented Alex's rescuers with a unique opportunity.

The plan was for Markov and Dmitri to enter the Lubyanka prison levels posing as FSB agents with urgent orders to relocate the prisoner—Alex Hawke—in anticipation of the building being overrun by the protesters. The chaos outside would not only lend urgency to their fictional mission but hopefully leave the real FSB agents too confused to recognize the deception.

Stoke and Fitz, however, couldn't risk being seen inside the building. A pair of foreigners—especially one as conspicuous as Stoke—would draw immediate suspicion. Their role was to stay behind in standby mode, close enough to intervene if things went sideways but far enough to avoid compromising the mission. More importantly, if Hawke wasn't in any condition to walk out on his own, it would fall to Stoke and Fitz to carry him through the tunnels to safety.

With their disguises complete, Markov and Dmitri slipped through the opening, leaving Stoke and Fitz to guard the exit.

Without another word, the two men slipped through the jagged opening, their footsteps fading into the darkness as the beam of Dmitri's flashlight receded.

Stoke watched until the Russians were swallowed entirely by the gloom, then turned to Fitz. "Here's hoping they make this look easy."

FORTY-SIX

Hawke's muscles ached from a night spent on the hard floor of his cell. The damp chill had seeped into his bones, leaving him stiff and sluggish. His stomach churned with hunger—a gnawing, hollow ache that had become a constant companion. His wrists and ankles bore raw, angry marks from his manacles, and a deep bruise had blossomed along his ribs from an overzealous guard's boot. His mind, however, remained sharp, and that wasn't such a good thing. He knew what was coming, and the knowledge weighed on him like a millstone hung around his neck.

And now he was back in the chair.

The torturer stood over him, his tools once more laid out on the trolley. "Now that you've had some time to consider your position, Lord Hawke," he said, "I hope you've seen the futility of continued stubbornness. Things will go much easier for you if you simply tell us who sent you to kill the President."

"I already told you, you bloody idiot. I didn't kill him."

The torturer leaned down, bringing his face level with Alex's. His breath smelled faintly of tobacco and coffee. "You are known to have worked for the British intelligence service in the past. Did they send you? Confess, and all of this"—he waved a hand to indicate the torture room—"all of this ends. You will be given clothes and a hot meal."

"I'm not a spy. And I didn't kill Volodya."

The torturer straightened, his smile faint but condescending. He picked up the scalpel, turning it slowly in the light. "You persist in this lie, even when the testimony of an eyewitness identifies you as the man who pulled the trigger."

Hawke was about to explain, not for the first time, that it was the eyewitness—Sergei Mulmuscovy—who had arranged the assassination, but just then the door creaked open and one of the guards who had brought him to the torture room stepped inside. There was a brief exchange in Russian, none of which was intelligible to Alex, but he noted the agitation in the torturer's voice.

Then the door opened again and two men in plain suits entered and moved directly to Alex's side. One of them addressed the torturer. Alex didn't understand what he said, but there was no mistaking the haughtiness in his tone. The man was almost certainly a senior FSB officer, and Alex did not doubt that he was the subject of the discussion.

"What's going on?"

He wasn't really expecting an answer and so was surprised when the second newcomer spoke in English. "There is a threat to this building. You are being moved for your own safety."

The torturer rounded on him, switching to English as well, his voice rising. "This is most irregular. I will have to get confirmation of these orders before I release him."

He started for the door, but before he got two steps, the second FSB officer called out, "Wait. I have your confirmation right here."

Bound to the chair as he was, Hawke couldn't see what happened next, but he heard it: a muffled bang. He knew that sound: a suppressed pistol shot.

The guard gasped in surprise, but before he could do anything else, a second shot rang out, and he slumped to the floor.

Hawke twisted in his seat, his pulse quickening as the first FSB officer stepped forward, his pistol still drawn but now aimed at the ground. The other man holstered his weapon and turned his attention to Hawke, his expression unreadable.

"You are coming with us," he said in heavily accented English. "You have somewhere better to be."

Hawke was still processing what had just occurred. Was this some sort of rescue, or had he just been pulled from the frying pan only to be thrown into the fire?

Not that there's much I can do about it.

"Who the devil are you?" he demanded.

The man regarded Hawke with a gimlet eye as he began unbuckling Hawke's restraints. "I am Vasily Markov," he said. "Am friend of Anastasia Ivanova."

Hawke straightened at the mention of Anastasia, his mind racing. "Asia sent you? How the devil did she even know I was here?"

Markov finished undoing the last strap and stepped back, allowing Hawke to push himself unsteadily upright. "When Anastasia Ivanova wants something, she gets it. And what she wants is you—alive." He gestured toward the other man. "This is Dmitri. He has no English."

Dmitri stepped forward, reached into his bag, and pulled out a set of dark coveralls. He tossed them to Hawke, who caught them reflexively.

"Ah, yes," said Hawke, shaking out the garment and sliding his feet into the legs. "I was feeling a bit underdressed for the occasion. You wouldn't happen to have a pair of shoes in there too, would you?"

Markov grimaced. "Shoes? No, we did not think of that." He looked around the room. Then his gaze settled on the guard. "His might fit you. He won't be needing them ever again."

Hawke wasn't especially enthused at the thought of looting the dead, but beggars couldn't be choosers. He finished pulling on the coveralls, then knelt down and relieved the man of his footwear. The boots were unpleasantly hot and sweaty against the bare skin of his feet. They were also about half a size too small. Hawke hoped he wouldn't have to walk very far in them.

"Well, they're not my John Lobb oxfords, but I suppose they'll have to do." He shifted over to the body of the torturer and retrieved his wristwatch. "Thanks for taking care of this, old chap, but I'll just have it back now."

The band chafed the already raw skin of his wrist, but having the Rolex back was oddly comforting.

Markov's lips twitched into the faintest hint of a smile. "Good. Now is time to go."

"Are we going to be leaving out the front door?" Hawke asked. "Because if the plan is to shoot our way past everyone who questions us, I hope you brought along a gun for me."

Markov shook his head. "We came in through the old tunnels. Will leave same way."

He nodded to Dmitri, who took point, leading the way into the dim corridor beyond. The corridor was narrow, lined with crumbling plaster and peeling paint. Dim overhead lights flickered intermittently, casting long shadows that danced across the damp, cracked tiles. They passed rows of old cells, their iron bars rusty and their interiors littered with forgotten debris: discarded blankets, broken furniture . . .

"Lovely place for a holiday," he remarked, mostly to himself. "Pity I can't stay."

Markov glanced back over his shoulder but said nothing. After leaving the cell block behind, they came to an unmarked door, which Dmitri opened. Beyond was a dark storeroom, its walls lined with old shelving units stacked with moldered old boxes. Dmitri produced an electric torch, which he switched on to light their way.

At the far end of the room, two figures emerged from the shadows. "It's about damn time," said the larger of the pair.

Hawke's heart soared. "Stoke! Fitz!"

Stoke crossed the room in a few long strides, his towering frame filling the narrow aisle between the shelving units, and swept Hawke up in a bear hug. A stab of pain shot through Hawke's bruised ribs, and his involuntary wince prompted Stoke to let go. He held Hawke at arm's length and gave him a quick once-over.

"You don't look nearly as bad as I thought you would."

Hawke managed a weak grin. "My interrogator was just getting warmed up when your new friends here came in and broke up the party."

"Lucky you," Fitz quipped. "Lounging about while we've been doing all the hard work."

"Lounging," Hawke repeated dryly. "Yes, that's exactly how I'd describe the last few days. Now, what the devil's been going on? How did you find me? And Asia—how did she get mixed up in this?"

"It's a long story, boss. We'll catch up later, but right now we need to get moving before anyone realizes you're gone."

As if on cue, the muffled clangor of alarm bells reached them. The sound seemed to emanate from somewhere above them, filtered and distorted by layers of concrete and steel, but nevertheless ominous.

Hawke grimaced. "Too late for that."

FORTY-SEVEN

The distant clang of alarm bells receded as they moved down the old rail tunnel at a fast jog, hoping to put some distance between themselves and the secret entrance. While Hawke's escape had been discovered, it would take time for the FSB guards to discover his means of egress, but once they did, agents would flood the tunnels, searching for his trail.

Once out of the old train tunnel, they slowed to a cautious pace, their steps as quiet as possible against the uneven ground. Any sound beyond their immediate movement—the faint creak of a shifting pipe, the distant drip of water—set their nerves on edge. Each turn seemed to offer new shadows, new places where danger might lurk unseen. The glow of their headlamps—now switched to red light to reduce their visibility—barely illuminated the tunnel, casting everything in an eerie, blood-colored hue. Dmitri took point, his red-hooded flashlight bobbing in the darkness as he led them through a maze of tunnels. He seemed always to know exactly which way to go and which direction to go when presented with a choice.

They moved through a labyrinth of crumbling corridors and steep descents. The tunnels alternated between narrow passages, where the walls seemed to close in on them, and vast, echoing chambers with ceilings so high, their beams of light couldn't reach them. Rusted pipes and broken grates lined the walls, and in some sections their boots splashed through shallow pools of stagnant water that reeked faintly of mildew and decay.

Every now and then, Dmitri would pause at a junction, tilting his head to listen. Then, with a quick gesture, he would signal them onward, always choosing the path that descended deeper into the earth. The air grew colder and heavier the farther they went, the faint tang of rust giving way to an earthy dampness that clung to their skin.

As he followed along, Hawke wrestled with the uneasy realization that his survival now hinged entirely on Dmitri's expertise. He didn't know the man, couldn't read him, and had no choice but to trust that he knew what he was doing. Dmitri and Markov had gotten him out of Lubyanka, and that was nothing short of a miracle, but down here, in the oppressive darkness, with every turn, every descent, feeling like a blind leap of faith, he was painfully aware of how little agency he had in this situation. He had always prided himself on being in control, on having a plan or a contingency. Now he was following a stranger into the depths of the earth, relying on nothing more than torchlight and assurances.

A hiss from Stoke and a raised fist brought them all to a sudden halt. In the ensuing quiet, with even the soft shuffle of their own movements muted, he could make out the unmistakable murmur of voices. The sound was distant, distorted by the tunnels' acoustics, but it was unmistakable proof that the hunters had discovered their point of egress.

Markov sidled back to them, leaning in close, his voice barely above a whisper. "They will not just follow us here. They'll send agents into the underground from multiple access points . . . Metro stations, maintenance shafts, storm drains. Try to cut us off."

"So what you're saying," intoned Fitz, "is that our escape plan just went tits up."

"Dmitri knows these tunnels. He can lead us through. It will just take a little longer."

Hawke listened to the exchange, a flicker of irritation rising within him. An alternate route seemed like a contingency they should have considered when devising the escape plan. But he held his tongue. No point in saying it now; they were already committed.

Markov turned to Dmitri and whispered in Russian. Dmitri gave a short nod and motioned for the group to follow, but after only a few minutes they caught the sound of voices echoing faintly through the tunnels, distorted by the winding passages. They froze, listening as the voices grew louder. Dmitri turned and gestured for them to retreat back the way they'd come. They backtracked a couple hundred yards to a low, narrow passage barely wide enough to accommodate Stoke's bulk and emerged into what Hawke guessed was part of the city's stormwater system.

Dmitri continued moving confidently, but now he took longer pauses at each junction, muttering under his breath as he recalculated their route. Twice more, however, the sound of search parties moving in the tunnels ahead forced them to turn back. The second time they even saw the glow of distant lights.

The hunters were closing in.

Dmitri muttered something under his breath in Russian, his tone sharp. Markov shook his head. "They're moving fast," he whispered. "We must go deeper."

"Deeper?" Fitz retorted. "We go any deeper and we'll be looking up at the devil's arsehole."

Hawke silenced him with a raised hand. "Deeper it is. Let's be about it, shall we?"

Dmitri took the cue and led them back to the previous junction and took the tunnel he had earlier rejected. The sound of pursuit grew fainter, but Hawke knew that they were no longer moving toward an exit. They were completely at the mercy of the maze.

Dmitri took them down a narrow side tunnel but stopped to kneel over a corroded grate set low into the wall. Using his wrecking bar, he tested the edges until he found a crack to wedge it into and then pried it free to reveal a sloping passage that seemed more like a chute than a tunnel.

An infernal stench wafted out of the darkness.

"What fresh hell is this?" Fitz whispered.

Markov turned to the group, his expression grim. "This leads to the sewer system. Hopefully, they won't think to look for us there."

Hawke stared at the opening. "Charming. Is this where the oligarchs come to unwind?"

"No oligarchs," Markov replied with a faint chuckle. "Just rats. Big ones."

Fitz rolled his eyes. "Fucking rats. I hate 'em."

Stoke waved a dismissive hand. "I'm from Harlem. The rats there will mug you for a slice of pizza. I think I can handle a Moscow sewer rat."

Dmitri lowered himself headfirst into the chute and began crawling down it. One by one, the rest of them followed. Stoke, bringing up the rear, pulled the grate into place behind him.

The passage sloped sharply downward before leveling off into a brick-lined tunnel with a stream of fetid water running along its center. Dmitri led them along the narrow ledge to one side, avoiding the filth as best he could. Their boots squelched with every step, the sound loud in the otherwise oppressive silence. Their red lights lent a hellish cast to the infernal odyssey. Rats scurried along the edges of the water, their beady eyes looking demonic as they darted into crevices. Hawke found himself breathing shallowly through his mouth, but even that did little to keep the vile smell at bay. His coveralls clung to his skin, soaked with sweat and sewer humidity, while his ill-fitting boots pinched with every step. Dmitri paused frequently at intersections, his red-filtered light playing over rusted maintenance signs and crumbling brickwork, searching for anything that might confirm their location. Occasionally, he muttered something in Russian, more to himself than the others, before signaling which way to go.

Dmitri stopped at a junction where the sewer tunnel split into three. One branch climbed steeply upward, its opening partially blocked by a mass of twisted rebar and concrete rubble. The second tunnel led deeper into the labyrinth, its far end swallowed by shadow. The third veered sharply to the left, a foul torrent of water pouring from its mouth into a grated basin below. Dmitri shone his light against the wall near the downward tunnel and spoke quickly to Markov.

Markov turned to the group and explained in a low voice, "This branch connects with the stormwater overflow channels. It runs parallel to a sanitary line that should take us closer to an access point near the Moskva River."

"'Should'?" replied Hawke.

Markov gave a faint shrug. "Sewers are old. Maps aren't perfect. And . . ." He trailed off as Dmitri motioned for them to keep moving.

The narrow tunnel gave way to a broader chamber where several pipes converged, their contents spilling into a central drain with a steady roar. The sound masked their footsteps, but it also made it harder to hear anything approaching. Dmitri motioned for silence, gesturing toward a ladder bolted to the far wall.

Markov leaned closer and whispered, "This leads to a service hatch near Borovitskaya station."

Dmitri climbed the ladder and tried to open the hatch at the top. It didn't budge. Defeated, he descended. *"Nyet,"* he muttered, shaking his head.

"I knew we should have brought along some C-4," said Fitz. "Where's Boomer when I really need him?"

"Blasting our way up into a Metro station would announce us louder than church bells on Easter Sunday," Markov said dryly.

"Great," Stoke muttered. "Another door slams shut on us."

"Rather reminds me of a Russian novel," Hawke murmured. "'But yet it was still worse than before.'"

Markov regarded him with a bemused grin. "You read Dostoyevsky?"

"Not when I can help it."

They continued down the tunnel, eventually moving into a larger, vaulted chamber, its ceiling shrouded in gloom. Thick iron pipes crisscrossed the space like veins, dripping water onto the floor below. Dmitri raised his flashlight, revealing a network of ladders and maintenance walkways that disappeared into yet more darkness.

"What is this place?" Stoke whispered, his voice reverberating faintly in the cavernous space.

"Old pumping station," Markov said. "It hasn't been used in decades. Dmitri says we're close."

"Close to what?" Fitz asked. "A proper bath?"

Markov shrugged. "A way out."

But the way he said it made Hawke think that he too was beginning to lose faith in their guide.

Dmitri led them across a slippery metal walkway, his flashlight beam bouncing erratically as he navigated the treacherous footing. The group followed in single file, their movements cautious and deliberate. The sound of their footsteps seemed amplified in the vast space, each creak of the metal grating threatening to give them away.

At the far side of the chamber, Dmitri ducked through a low archway that led into yet another tunnel. This one was different—older, with walls that looked like they had been hewn from raw stone. The air was cooler here and, blessedly, fresher.

Ahead, Dmitri had come to an abrupt halt, his red light illuminating a steel-reinforced door. The door was streaked with rust and grime, but its design was unmistakably utilitarian: heavy-duty and built to last. Above it, faintly visible in the beam of light, a Cyrillic letter and a number:

Д-6

Markov stepped forward for a quick exchange with Dmitri, then turned back to the others. "This is it," he whispered, almost reverently. "We found it."

"Found what?" asked Hawke.

Dmitri gave the solemn answer. "Metro Dva."

Metro-2.

FORTY-EIGHT

According to a persistent urban legend, there was a second secret train system running under the streets of Moscow. Called Metro-2, it had allegedly been constructed during the early years of the Cold War for the purpose of providing secret transport for high-level government officials in order to ensure the survival of the Soviet leadership in the event of a nuclear attack. The underground network was believed to connect key government and military sites across Moscow, including the Kremlin, Lubyanka, and the Ministry of Defense. Some claimed it stretched as far as Vnukovo Airport or even to secure bunkers located in the countryside many miles from the city.

The tunnels of Metro-2 were said to be larger than those of the public Metro, capable of accommodating both trains and military vehicles. Stories of cavernous bunkers, secret command centers, and entire underground cities—complete with living quarters, supplies, and air filtration systems—added to the mythos. Urban explorers occasionally claimed to find hints of Metro-2's existence: sealed doors, abandoned tunnels with unusual architecture, or faint whispers of activity far beneath their feet. None had ever returned with definitive evidence of its existence, but as was often the case with urban legends, the absence of real proof only intensified the speculation.

Unlike most urban legends, however, Metro-2 was real.

Dmitri removed the red cover from his flashlight and swept the beam across the vast open space on the other side of the door. The light revealed walls of rough-hewn bedrock and partially reinforced concrete. Crystalline extrusions, where limestone had begun to leach out through the cracks in the concrete, glittered in the light like ghostly daggers. Massive steel support beams crisscrossed overhead, many of them rusted through, their jagged edges jutting out like skeletal remains. Running through the middle of the debris-strewn floor, half-buried in rubble, was what appeared to be a slightly raised track bed with evenly spaced railroad ties, but there were no rails.

"If the plan was to take the train," remarked Hawke, "I think we're in for a bit of a wait."

"This is the legendary Metro-2?" asked Fitz. "Color me unimpressed."

"Tracks must have been removed for scrap," said Markov. "But the tunnels remain. This is proof. We can follow them to another station."

"You sure about that?" asked Stoke. "I'm no daredevil explorer, but it seems to me that if there were other ways into this place, the folks who are would have found them by now."

"They did not know where to look. But finding a way out will be much easier than getting in."

Hawke did not share their guide's confidence but—absent any better alternatives—he kept his skepticism to himself.

Dmitri, who was continuing to probe the darkness with his electric torch, spoke, and Markov translated. "We are between stations here, but if we follow the tunnels, we should find an exit that connects to a station on the Metro line."

Dmitri set off down the tunnel, his flashlight beam bouncing off the damp walls, illuminating streaks where water had seeped down, carving pale rivulets into the concrete. The sound of dripping water was constant, echoing faintly in the cavernous space, and the air smelled of wet stone and rust.

Hawke stayed near the middle of the group, his eyes darting to every shadow, every faint movement of light that might hint at danger.

The floor beneath their boots turned slick, patches of moss growing in the constant dampness. A trickle of water running along the edge of the tunnel soon widened into a shallow stream, and within minutes the group found themselves wading through a sunken section of the passage.

The water came up quickly, rising to their knees, and then it was waist-high. Hawke sucked in a breath as the icy water seeped through the fabric of his borrowed coveralls. Behind him, Stoke let out a yelp and muttered something about "shrinkage."

Hawke didn't laugh. He was too focused on Dmitri, who was holding his torch low to the water's surface, checking the depth.

"Let's hope that station we're looking for isn't under a lake," Hawke said.

As they moved farther into the flooded section, the beam of Dmitri's flashlight illuminated a mass of debris up ahead. A section of the ceiling had collapsed, spilling jagged chunks of concrete and rebar into the tunnel. The rubble formed an uneven blockade rising out of the water, its surface slick with mildew and grime, but there was open space at the top of the rockfall.

Dmitri immediately began climbing, looking back when he reached the crest and calling down to them.

"He says the way is clear on the other side," said Markov. He cautiously began his own ascent, but his foot slipped on the slimy surface, forcing him to clutch at an exposed length of rebar. He muttered something in Russian that didn't require translation.

Hawke followed, gripping the slippery edges as he scrambled upward. The cold water running off the rubble made every step precarious, and his borrowed boots—already too tight—felt like vises clamping down on his toes when he pushed himself up. A jagged piece of rebar caught at his coveralls, nearly throwing him off-balance, but he carefully freed himself and managed to haul himself up and over the top.

Behind him, Stoke growled in frustration as he struggled to find purchase on the narrow, unstable footholds. "This is why I stay out of caves," he complained, his boots sending a small cascade of rubble tumbling into the water below.

On the other side of the blockage, the water was not even ankle-deep, and once they were clear of the collapse zone, the tunnel was mostly obstacle-free. Dmitri pressed forward with a renewed urgency, and Hawke soon saw why. Revealed in the light of their guide's torch was what appeared to be the platform of a train station.

Unlike the ornate public Metro stations, with their chandeliers, bronze statues, and marble floors, this platform was literally just that: a long, rectangular structure raised just above the flooded floor of the tunnel, just high enough to allow passengers to step aboard whatever trains were once meant to run along the tracks.

Rising up from one end of the platform was what appeared to be a badly corroded metal dogleg stairwell ascending upward to vanish into a vertical shaft cut through the ceiling. Affixed to the wall behind it was a rusted metal sign, the Cyrillic lettering just barely legible.

"Arbatskaya," Dmitri said, reading the sign. "Arbatsko-Pokrovskaya Liniya," he said, his tone thoughtful.

Hawke arched a brow. "And that means what, exactly?"

Markov turned back to him. "Arbatskaya is an important Metro station. Very close to Kremlin. If I were FSB and looking for us and knew that we were underground, I would watch the station."

Fitz glanced up at the skeletal stairwell. "The riots should be keeping them busy, yeah? How much manpower can they spare for the tunnels?"

"Riots?" wondered Hawke aloud.

"A little diversion to keep the FSB off our asses," Stoke explained.

"We are still too close to Red Square," said Markov. "They will be watching it."

"So, what are our options?" asked Hawke. "No matter where we try to come out, there's going to be risk."

Markov turned to Dmitri and asked him something. He nodded at the other man's reply, then addressed the others again. Markov spoke in a low, measured tone. "Dmitri thinks we should make for Kiyevskaya. There should be a way to reach the surface there, and is farther from Lubyanka. FSB may not be watching it. Not yet."

"How far away is it?" asked Hawke.

"Not far. Three kilometers, perhaps more. We should be able to reach it in less than hour, provided the tunnels are still intact."

Hawke grimaced at the prospect of two more miles in his toe-crushing boots, but he did not voice the complaint. Dmitri motioned toward the far end of the platform, where the track bed continued into darkness, and the group set off again.

They moved at a brisk pace through the tunnel, Dmitri's torch showing them the way. Despite the discomfort caused by his footwear, Hawke was starting to feel cautiously optimistic. The tunnel was mercifully straightforward, and they encountered no sudden drops, no flooded sections, and no collapsed ceilings to scramble over.

His positivity proved to be short-lived. They had been walking for about twenty minutes when he first noticed the sound, a low rumble, so faint at first that he thought it was a trick of the acoustics. It quickly grew louder, however, distinct and unmistakable: the sound of rushing water.

"What's that?" asked Fitz.

"Moskva River," said Markov. "We must be passing under it."

"*Under* it?" The nervous edge in Fitz's tone sharpened. "How far under?"

Markov shrugged. "If we are deeper than the Metro line? Fifty to a hundred meters."

"So there are fifty meters of solid rock between us and the river, but we can still hear it? Isn't that a little . . . concerning?"

"Metro trains cross under the river every day without problem."

"But that sound . . ." Fitz looked about the tunnel and gazed up at the ceiling as if looking for cracks.

"The acoustics make it seem louder than it is." But Hawke heard the uncertainty in Markov's voice.

The rumble soon became a roar, echoing off the tunnel walls with an almost tangible force. Dmitri slowed his pace, his flashlight sweeping the walls and ceiling with a new urgency. The tunnel began to noticeably slope downward, the damp air growing heavier, carrying with it the unmistakable scent of mildew and decay. Then, with hardly any warning, the source of the sound was revealed.

On one side of the tunnel, the ceiling had collapsed, creating a ragged hole from which spewed a torrent of water. Spray from the cascade filled the air, creating a fine mist that clung to their faces and clothes. Where the waterfall should have crashed down onto the track bed, there was only a dark chasm that seemed to swallow it entirely.

All that remained of the tunnel was a narrow ledge that seemed to cling precariously to the opposite wall. The ledge was barely wide enough to walk on, and the constant spray from the waterfall made the footing slick and unstable, but pieces of exposed rebar seemed to form a sort of handrail.

Hawke edged closer to the ledge, the roar of the waterfall filling his ears and setting his heart racing. The breach looked to be about twenty feet wide, and, judging by the ferocity, there were hundreds of cubic meters of water coming through every second, yet the tunnel to either side appeared mostly dry. He peered down into the swirling chaos below, trying to discern where the water was going, but the darkness swallowed everything beyond the frothy torrent.

Decades ago, perhaps when the tunnel was first bored out, small cracks in the bedrock had allowed water to seep through. Over time, and with no one maintaining the tunnel, those cracks had worn away stone and concrete, opening the path for still more water, widening the channels, and wearing away at the surrounding rock until the pressure built and the ceiling finally gave way.

The collapse wouldn't have been dramatic—not the sort of catastrophe that brought engineers scrambling. Likely, no one even realized it had happened—not here in these forgotten depths. The relentless pounding had subsequently eroded the tunnel floor away, creating a sinkhole or perhaps opening a new channel to an underground river.

"Bloody hell," Fitz shouted. "How the hell are we supposed to get past that?"

Dmitri and Markov conferred for a moment; then Markov faced the others. "We will have to cross over that," he said, indicating the ledge. His tone held no enthusiasm for the prospect.

Fitz barked a laugh. "Are you touched in the head?"

"I'm not sure we've got a choice, Fitz," said Stoke grimly. "Going back ain't an option."

"He's right. We would never make it out of Arbatskaya."

"I say we go back, lay low, wait them out."

"That's not a plan," Hawke interjected, his voice calm but firm. "That's stalling, and it assumes the FSB will get bored and leave. They won't. They'll keep searching the underground until they figure out where we went."

Fitz gestured toward the chasm. "So we're just supposed to tightrope across that thing? Hope the bloody rebar holds? What if it doesn't?" He rounded on Stoke. "You going to trust it to hold you, Skipper?"

Stoke appeared to consider this for a moment. "I guess maybe I better go first, then."

Dmitri stepped forward, shaking his head firmly. *"Nyet,"* he said, pointing at the ledge. Then he pointed at himself and spoke to Markov in rapid Russian.

Markov translated, his voice raised just enough to be heard over the roar of the waterfall. "Dmitri says he will go first. If the ledge does not hold, it is better he is the one to test it."

Stoke frowned. "What if he falls? What's the plan then?"

Markov relayed this to Dmitri, who simply shrugged and replied, "Then you will know not to cross."

Stoke shook his head. "That's not very comforting."

Dmitri stepped to the edge of the ledge and tested the first foothold. Then he grabbed the rebar with both hands and leaned his weight against it, giving it a solid tug. Satisfied, he began to move, one deliberate step at a time.

The group watched in tense silence as Dmitri edged forward. The spray soaked his clothes, making his movements appear even more precarious as water streamed off his shoulders and arms. The rebar, slick and rusted, looked as though it might snap at any moment, but Dmitri's grip was steady, his movements confident.

Hawke found himself holding his breath as Dmitri reached the midpoint, the point where the chasm below seemed deepest. He glanced down once and immediately looked away, focusing instead on the far end of the ledge. Step by careful step, Dmitri made it across, finally stepping onto the tunnel floor on the other side. He turned and gave a thumbs-up.

Markov exhaled sharply and nodded. "Good. Now I go."

Markov was less sure-footed than Dmitri, his grip on the rebar tighter, his steps less fluid. Twice his foot slipped on the slick surface and he clung to the rebar for balance. Hawke could see the tension in his shoulders, the strain in his grip, but Markov pressed on, ignoring the spray that drenched his face and the roar that seemed to press down on them from all sides.

When Markov reached the other side, he turned and motioned for the next person.

Fitz and Hawke exchanged a glance. "Shall we flip for it?"

Hawke, sensing the other man's reluctance, shook his head. "I'll go."

He stepped forward, feeling the cold spray on his face like a rain. The roar of the waterfall seemed to reverberate inside his skull as he reached for the rebar. His fingers curled around it, feeling the roughness of rust and the slickness of water. It felt solid enough, but the idea of trusting it with his life filled him with apprehension.

"One step at a time," he told himself. "And don't look down."

His boots slipped on the slimy concrete with his first step, but the rebar held firm as he caught himself.

The midpoint was the worst. The sound of the cascade was deafening, the chasm a hungry beast roaring in anticipation of its next meal. Ignoring his own advice, Hawke risked a glance down and immediately regretted it. The torrent below was a chaotic swirl of white water and pitch blackness, and it took all his willpower to loosen his grip on the rebar rail and move on. But then he was past the worst of it. He shuffled the last few steps and found Dmitri waiting with an outstretched hand to welcome him back onto terra firma.

"That," Hawke said, "was entirely too exciting."

On the other side of the breach, Stoke clapped his old swim buddy on the back. "You're up, Fitzy."

Fitz shot him a one-fingered salute but then squared his shoulders and reached for the rebar handrail. He gave it a tentative tug, then leaned his weight against it and stepped out onto the edge. His steps were cautious, his grip firm, and while his progress was more tentative than any of the others, he appeared to be managing. As he reached the midpoint, the place where the chasm below seemed to gape widest. He froze for a moment, glancing down despite himself. Hawke could see his lips moving, shouting curses into the void, but the roar of the waterfall drowned them out.

"You're doing fine!" Hawke called from the far side. "Just keep—"

Suddenly, the ledge crumbled beneath Fitz, dropping him into the abyss. His arms were jerked taut as the full burden of his weight fell against his death grip on the rebar rail, leaving him swinging like a pendulum. His legs kicked instinctively, scrabbling for a foothold that no longer existed.

Dmitri reacted before anyone else could, darting back out onto what remained of the ledge and stretching out with one hand to grasp Fitz by the wrist.

"Hold on!" Hawke shouted, moving to the edge and reaching out toward Dmitri in order to brace him.

Across the chasm, Stoke was also venturing out onto the ledge, but Dmitri frantically shouted, *"Nyet!"*

Hawke hesitated, catching the urgency in Dmitri's shout. His eyes flicked to the fractured ledge on which Dmitri stood and saw the cracks radiating through the concrete.

"Go back, Stoke!" he yelled, easing away from Dmitri. "The ledge won't hold!"

Stoke froze mid-step, his hands clenched into fists at his sides as he stared at Fitz's dangling form. For a moment his jaw worked soundlessly, his face a mask of frustration and helplessness. "Damn it, Fitz, hang on!" Stoke exhorted him.

Dmitri's face contorted with the strain of holding Fitz, but his assistance gave Fitz just enough support to begin probing what remained of the wall for a toehold.

"I've got it!" he yelled as he managed to get his foot onto a jutting chunk of concrete.

"You've got this, Fitz!" Hawke exclaimed.

Dmitri adjusted his hold, using every ounce of leverage to pull Fitz upward inch by inch.

Hawke thought he caught a faint laugh of relief from Fitz.

Then the ledge on which Dmitri stood shuddered violently. Cracks raced outward like lightning bolts through the concrete, and with a deafening crack the entire section of wall broke loose and fell away, taking Fitz and Dmitri down into oblivion.

FORTY-NINE

The roar of the waterfall had faded into the distance, but its echo lingered in Hawke's mind as he and his two remaining companions continued down the tunnel toward Kiyevskaya station. There were no jokes now. No quips to break the tension. Only the shared understanding that nothing could be done for the men they had lost.

In a cruel twist of fate, the collapse that had claimed Fitz and Dmitri had left behind a safer path across the void. The jagged edges of the scalloped depression formed a rough but stable route, almost as if the gods of the tunnel had demanded a sacrifice for the crossing, and with that grim toll paid, the tunnel had nothing left to throw at them. Beyond the chasm, the tunnel began rising, and ten minutes later they came to another platform almost identical to the one they had found underneath Arbatskaya. At the far end of the platform, a rickety metal staircase spiraled upward.

Markov approached the base of the staircase and tested the first step. A bitter groan echoed through the chamber, but the step held. "I can't promise this will hold us," he said warily.

Hawke gazed up to where the steps disappeared into the darkness of the shaft overhead. "Looks like quite the climb. But it's not as if we've got much of a choice. I'll go first—"

"I'll go," Stoke interrupted, his tone indicating that the matter wasn't open to debate.

Hawke felt for his friend. He knew a thing or two about survivor's guilt. Right now, Stoke was thinking that Fitz and Dmitri had died because he hadn't gone first. Losing Fitz would be an especially tough blow.

"All right," he said softly. "But take it slow."

Stoke grabbed the rail and began his ascent, his headlamp illuminating the flight immediately ahead. The staircase groaned and creaked under his weight, but the structure held together. At first he moved cautiously, testing each step before committing fully, but by the time he reached the first landing, he was moving more confidently. When he disappeared around the first turn, only the dim, diffuse glow of his headlamp was visible. The echoes of his footsteps grew faint and then faded entirely.

In the silence, Hawke's head filled with the memory of Fitz cursing like a sailor and laughing in the face of danger—sounds he would never hear again. He had not known Fitz nearly as well as Stoke did, but they had fought together on many occasions, and the rescue from Lubyanka was not the first debt Hawke owed the man. A debt that now could never be paid.

Fitz was gone, just like that.

And Dmitri . . . He knew nothing about the man who had sacrificed himself without a second thought. Two men. Two lives spent to save one. His.

He didn't allow himself to dwell on it. Not yet. There would be time to wrestle with those feelings later.

When Stoke completed his ascent, Hawke began his. The metal handrail was rough, the rusted surface scraping against his palm as he moved. The walls of the shaft seemed to close in on him, amplifying every sound: his breath, the soft scrape of his too-small boots, the faint creak of the stairs. But then it was behind him. On the top landing, he found Stoke standing before a metal-framed doorway. Instead of a closed door, however, there was a concrete block wall that presumably prevented access to the now-defunct Metro-2 station.

"Hell of a climb," Stoke said, his voice low, as if speaking too loudly might bring the staircase down behind them.

"Yes. Next time, I'll wait for the lift." Hawke nodded toward the doorway. "What do you make of that?"

Stoke ran his fingers over the uneven mortar. "It's solid enough. But old. I think we'll be able to chip our way through. The only problem is we don't know what's on the other side. If we smash through in the middle of a crowded subway station, we're bound to attract some unwanted attention."

"I don't think we've got much choice in the matter," replied Hawke.

Stoke just shrugged.

When Markov joined them, now carrying the duffel bag Dmitri had left behind before making his ill-fated attempt to save Fitz, Stoke retrieved the wrecking bar and commenced hacking at the old mortar.

Once the first brick was out of the way, Stoke's concerns about breaking through in a crowded area were put to rest. On the other side of the wall, there was only darkness. Stoke pried another brick loose and another and soon was able to simply shove the blocks out of the way. He poked his head through the opening and swept the beam of his headlamp back and forth.

"Definitely not a subway station," he said. "Looks like some kind of maintenance tunnel."

He pushed a couple more blocks out of the way, creating an opening large enough for him to pass through. Hawke and Markov quickly followed.

A short way down, the corridor opened into a cavernous vertical shaft. A massive metal grate spanned the floor and through it, barely visible, were two sets of train tracks. Above, the shaft stretched upward into darkness, the dim red glow of emergency lights marking its upper reaches.

"What the hell is this?" Stoke asked, but neither Hawke nor Markov had an answer.

They moved along the perimeter of the chamber and found a metal door, rusted but solid and secured with a locking wheel. Unlike much of their surroundings, the mechanism appeared to have been maintained, with faint traces of grease visible along its edges.

Stoke gripped the wheel and gave it a test turn. The mechanism resisted a little, but then the latch bars slid back from their latch bores. Stoke leaned into the door, pushing it open, and a gush of fresh air washed over them. Beyond the doorway lay an ordinary street in a residential neighborhood.

"I know what this is," said Markov. "This building is . . ." He paused, searching for the right word. "Like Potemkin village. A false front. Hiding a ventilation shaft for the Metro."

"We've got the same kind of setup in New York," said Stoke, nodding. "There are houses that look just like regular brownstones, but they're fake. Hollowed out inside to let air down into the subway."

"We are very lucky," said Markov, taking out his phone. "This is perfect place to hide."

Hawke considered pointing out that things hadn't turned out lucky for Fitz and Dmitri but decided to let it go. Instead he asked, "Hide? And just how long are we going to be doing that?"

"Not long," assured Markov, taking out a mobile phone. He brought up a satnav application and used it to fix their location: a few blocks from Kiyevskaya. He then placed a call and began speaking in Russian.

Hawke understood very little of the one-sided conversation, but two words stood out. Two names. Dmitri and Fitz. But for the most part Markov seemed upbeat, and when he ended the call, he was smiling. "A ride is on the way. Thirty minutes. I'll keep watch out here. You two stay out of sight."

Markov perched on the stoop just outside the door, his phone in hand, scanning the quiet street for any sign of their ride, while Hawke and Stoke retreated inside the dark structure to settle in for the wait. For a long time neither man spoke, the weight of their recent loss hanging over them like a dark cloud.

Finally, Stoke broke the silence. “You know,” he said, his voice low and gruff, “Fitz always said he didn’t plan on dying of old age.”

Hawke looked up, startled by the suddenness of the statement. “He did?”

“Yeah.” Stoke’s mouth quirked into a faint, wistful smile. “Said he’d rather go out with his boots on, doing what he loved, than rot away in a rocking chair. Guess he got his wish, in a way.”

Hawke let out a slow breath. “Still feels like a damn waste.”

“Maybe,” Stoke admitted, his gaze distant. “But you know Fitz. He didn’t see it that way. Man lived for the fight. He was a warrior through and through. Best damn fighter I ever had by my side.”

Stoke nodded, his gaze distant as he leaned back against the wall. “You know, there was this time in Afghanistan. We were pinned down outside Kandahar. Whole damn unit was caught in a kill box. Snipers in the hills, machine-gun nests dug in like ticks, and no cover worth a damn.”

Hawke said nothing, sensing this was one of those moments when silence meant more than words.

“Fitz . . .” Stoke’s voice softened, a faint reverence creeping in. “He didn’t even flinch. Took one look at the situation, grabbed the SAW, and charged the hill like he was goddamned bulletproof. He just . . . ran straight into it, bullets kicking up all around him.”

“What happened?”

Stoke’s mouth twitched into a small, bittersweet smile. “He got to the first nest and took it out with a grenade. Then he used their own position to lay down suppressive fire, gave the rest of us a chance to move. Guy probably saved half the unit that day. When we finally got to him, we saw that he’d caught a couple bullets. Probably would have bled out if we hadn’t got to him when we did. But I swear the bastard was grinning like a damn fool when we found him. Told me, ‘If I die, make sure they say I went out in style.’”

Hawke managed a faint smile, though his chest felt heavy. “He was one of a kind.”

"That was what got him his Medal of Honor."

Hawke knew that Fitz had earned the U.S. military's highest decoration but had never heard the story before.

"And another Purple Heart for his collection," Stoke added. He fell silent for a moment, his head bowed as though in prayer. When he looked up again, his jaw was set, his expression hard with resolve. "He wouldn't want us sitting around here crying over him. He'd tell us to get the hell moving. Charlie Mike."

Charlie Mike was military slang for *continue mission.*

"And the mission isn't over until we get you out of Russia," Stoke went on. "We may have busted you out of lockup, but we've still got a long ways to go until you're safe, so we need to keep our heads in the game."

Hawke let a moment pass before speaking. "I'm not ready to leave yet, Stoke. I've got some unfinished business."

Stoke narrowed his gaze. "Unfinished business? What the hell is that supposed to mean? You're public enemy number one around here."

"There's something bigger at play here. Framing me for killing Volodya wasn't the endgame. It's just the beginning."

"Are you fucking shitting me?" Stoke said through clenched teeth. "Fitz and Dmitri died getting you this far. Now you're telling me you're planning on sticking around and kicking the hornet's nest again?"

"Sergei Mulmuscovy—the man responsible for all of this—isn't done. He's planning something big . . . I don't know what it is, but I know we have to stop him. *I* have to stop him."

"Fitz didn't give his life so you could go off and get yourself killed anyway," Stoke shot back, his voice sharp with anger. "Don't you dare throw that away."

Stoke's words hit like a punch to the gut. Hawke swallowed. "I'm not throwing it away, Stoke. I owe Fitz everything. But that's exactly why I have to finish this. If I don't . . ." He sighed. "If I don't, then Fitz really will have died for nothing."

Stoke's expression softened, but the anger didn't fully leave his eyes. "You're serious about this?"

"Deadly serious," Hawke said quietly.

Stoke exhaled sharply, dragging a hand down his face. "Damn it, Alex. You better know what you're doing."

Before Hawke could answer, the door swung open and Markov appeared, silhouetted against the bright daylight spilling in. "Time to go. Our ride is here."

He took a step back, and as Hawke and Stoke stood up, a second figure appeared, backlit by the brilliance of midday. For a moment Hawke couldn't make out the features, but then she stepped inside, and the light seemed to follow her, framing her like an angel come to carry him away to heaven.

Anastasia.

In an instant she was in front of him, throwing her arms around his neck, pulling herself up to him, kissing him. He staggered back half a step, caught off guard, but then he was pulling her tightly against him, burying his face in her hair. For a heartbeat the world narrowed to just the two of them. All the uncertainty, all the doubts he'd carried about their relationship, melted away in an instant. He couldn't summon a single coherent thought, only the overwhelming realization that this woman—this radiant, fierce, impossible woman—had come for him. She had fought her way back into his arms, and at that moment nothing else mattered.

She pulled back from him just enough to murmur, "I thought I'd never see you again. When they told me you'd been taken to Lubyanka . . . Alex, I thought I'd lost you forever."

"Never," he whispered. "I'll always come back."

She pulled back slightly, her hands sliding down to rest on his shoulders, holding him at arm's length. Her eyes searched his face, her expression a mix of relief and something deeper, something unspoken, that made his chest tighten.

"Alex . . ." she began softly, her voice trembling with emotion.

"Yes, Anastasia?" he replied, a faint, almost dazed smile tugging at his lips.

"You need to take a shower," she said, wrinkling her nose. "You smell absolutely horrid."

Hawke blinked, then laughed, the sound bursting out of him like a dam breaking. It was raw and unguarded, startling even himself. He cupped her face with both hands, brushing his thumbs over her cheeks as he chuckled.

"I love you," he said, the words slipping out before he could think to stop them.

FIFTY

Hawke stayed under the shower far longer than was absolutely necessary. The nearly scalding water sluiced the stink of the sewers from his body, washing it down the drain, but it did little to erase the cumulative emotional residue of the past few days.

Volodya's assassination.

Silk's betrayal.

Imprisonment in Lubyanka.

Fitz's death.

It would take more than seeing Anastasia and taking a shower, no matter how bloody hot the water was, to scrub all of that away.

Anastasia had brought them to a dacha nestled in the woods far outside Moscow, away from prying eyes and electronic surveillance, and where the operators from Thunder and Lightning were waiting, having accomplished their mission to create chaos in the streets near Red Square to cover the rescue attempt.

The reunion, however, had been bittersweet.

Boomer, always reserved, had gone deathly silent when he heard the terrible news. Fitz was more than a comrade to him—he was a brother. The rest of the team had responded similarly, their grief subdued but palpable, hanging in the air like a storm cloud.

When Hawke stepped out of the bathroom, toweling his hair, the sight of Anastasia stopped him in his tracks. She was sitting cross-legged on the edge of the bed, lit up by the soft glow of the bedside lamp. The red silk nightgown clung to her curves, stimulating an immediate reaction from Hawke.

Her lips curved into a playful smile. "Are you happy to see me, Alex?"

"You can't imagine."

Anastasia lifted her arms to him invitingly. "Tomorrow morning we will drive to St. Petersburg. From there, one of my associates will get us to the *Blackhawke*, and then all of this will be over. But tonight"—her smile broadened—"tonight is for us."

Hawke resisted the urge to accept her embrace, and instead sat down next to her. "Asia . . . darling, uh, you see the thing is that . . . I'm not leaving."

Anastasia eyed him without blinking. "What do you mean you're *not leaving*? Of course you're leaving. If you're caught in Russia—"

"Something terrible is going to happen. Volodya's death is only the beginning. The man responsible, Sergei Mulmuscovy, is planning something even bigger. He's the bloody Warmonger, Asia. I can't just walk away from that."

Asia stared at him, her expression fluctuating between disbelief and anger. "You can't walk away? No, Alex. You mean you *won't*." She shook her head, anger winning out. "I didn't risk everything to get you out of Lubyanka just so you could throw your life away."

"A lot of people are going to die if I don't stop him," Hawke replied. "Mulmuscovy orchestrated Volodya's assassination and set me up to take the fall so that he could blame the West. I think he's going to use that to seize power and maybe even take us to the brink of nuclear war."

"You think you can fix this? Stop Mulmuscovy single-handedly? You're not a superhero, Alex. You're just a man—a man who was lucky to make it out alive." She paused a beat before adding, "Not everyone did."

The accusation was a slap in the face, and it cut Hawke to his core.

"Fitz and Dmitri gave their lives to get me out, Anastasia. But if I don't do this, then they will have died for nothing."

Anastasia's hands balled into fists at her sides. "Don't you dare use them to justify this madness. Fitz and Dmitri didn't die so you could go on some suicidal mission. They died because I—" Her voice broke and she turned away, pressing her hands to her face.

Hawke slid closer to her, cautiously putting an arm around her. "Darling . . . I know this isn't what you want to hear. But it's what I have to do."

A tear slipped defiantly from Anastasia's eye, running down her cheek. "You're going to get yourself killed," she said in a low voice. "You're going to leave Alexei without a father. Is that what you want, Alex? For Alexei to grow up without a father? Like you did?"

"Think of all the children that'll grow up without fathers if I don't. The senseless killing." Hawke took a deep breath, steadying himself. "I'm going after Mulmuscovy, Anastasia. End of story."

Her lips parted as if to argue, but he held up a hand, softening his tone. "But if it makes you feel any better, I won't be doing it alone. I need to contact Sir David and let him know what's going on. MI6—"

"They already know," Asia interrupted. "I've been working with them. With . . . your old girlfriend."

"Old girl . . . *Pippa?*" He shook his head. "She's not my—"

Asia waved away the denial. "I don't care about what happened in the past, Alex. Water under the bridge. She's aboard the *Blackhawke* right now, coordinating our efforts to get you out of Russia." She paused, narrowing her eyes at him. "Talk to her. Maybe she can convince you to see reason."

Hawke stared back at her for a long moment. "How do I contact her?"

Anastasia stood abruptly, the movement sudden enough to make Hawke flinch. Without a word, she walked to a nearby chair where a red silk robe lay draped. She slipped it on over her nightgown, cinching the sash tight around her waist. The subtext was unmistakable.

There would be no intimate reunion tonight.

Hawke scrubbed a hand over his face as Asia moved to a small table near the window and opened a laptop computer. The screen flickered to life, displaying the encrypted log-in of a secure communications platform. Anastasia typed in a password, selected a contact from the list, then turned the computer screen so that it was facing Alex. Hawke went over and sat in front of the computer as the call request went out into the ether.

Pippa Guinness's face appeared on the screen, looking tired but alert. Her expression softened with visible relief as soon as she saw Hawke. "Alex," she said, leaning closer to the camera. "Thank God."

"I'm alive," Hawke said, managing a faint smile, "but we've got a bigger problem. Sergei Mulmuscovy is the madman behind this. He set me up to take the fall for Volodya's assassination, and now I think he's going to try to seize power in Russia."

Pippa nodded grimly. "We already suspected as much. And there's more. One of our officers—a British Army liaison in Turkey—reported contact between Mulmuscovy and General Osman Gul of the Turkish Armed Forces just after Putin's assassination. That officer hasn't been heard from since."

Hawke's brow furrowed. "Gul? He was at the NATO summit in Istanbul."

"We're not sure how Gul fits into this, but they are clearly up to something. We do know that Mulmuscovy is now at a Perun Group training facility near St. Petersburg, and whatever he's planning, it's big." She paused a beat. "I know you've been through hell, Alex, but you're in the best position to do something about this."

"That's exactly what I was thinking," Hawke replied without hesitation. "I'll take Thunder and Lightning and—"

"Absolutely not!" Anastasia's voice cut through the room like a whip. She stepped forward, glaring at the screen. "He barely made it out alive, and now you're sending him right back into the fire?"

Pippa's expression hardened. "With all due respect, Anastasia, this is the job Alex signed up for."

Asia bristled, her hands clenching into fists. "You don't give a damn about Alex, do you? I thought maybe you still love him, but he's just another piece on the board to you. Someone to use and throw away when he's no longer useful."

"Anastasia—" Hawke began, but she wasn't finished.

"You know what? Fine. Do what you want. But don't expect me to stand here and watch you send him to his death." She turned on her heel and stormed out of the room.

Pippa watched her go, then turned back to Hawke, her expression carefully neutral. "She'll come around."

Hawke let out a weary sigh. "I'm not so sure you're there, Pip."

A brief silence followed, and when Pippa spoke again, her tone was somber. "Alex . . . there's something else. Something you need to know."

"What is it?"

"As I'm sure you're now aware, the woman you knew as Dr. Ariadne Silk was actually a contract killer."

"Well, I knew there was something off about her," replied Hawke with a rueful grin. "I started having rather serious doubts about her when she put a bullet in Volodya's head."

"She's part of a team, working with her twin sister. We don't know their real identities yet, but they go by the name 'Silence.'" Pippa took a deep breath before continuing. "While the one posing as Dr. Silk was accompanying you, her sister . . ." She hesitated, her voice breaking with emotion. She took another breath and then started again. "Ambrose Congreve was investigating a series of suspicious deaths linked to Dr. Silk."

"He told me all about it," Hawke said, recalling his phone call with Congreve.

"He was close to identifying Silence, so to throw him off the scent, the other sister killed . . ." The words caught in her throat again. "It's Lady Mars, Alex."

Hawke's gut twisted. "*Diana?* Pip, what about her?"

"She's dead, Alex. Murdered. By Silence."

If Hawke had not already been seated, he would have collapsed to the floor.

Diana, dead?

No, it's not possible.

He realized, with a sick feeling, how it had transpired. Congreve had told him everything during that call—told how he was closing in on the killer. And the phony Silk had been sitting right there, listening to every word. That conversation had put Congreve on Silence's radar.

And Diana had paid the ultimate price for their mistake.

His throat tightened and he struggled to speak. "Ambrose . . ."

Ambrose Congreve was his dearest friend. The thought of what he was going through . . . it was suddenly too much for Alex to bear.

Hawke thought back to his own loss: his wife, Victoria, stolen from him by a sniper's bullet on the steps of their wedding chapel. The ache that had dulled almost to the point of forgetfulness now flared white-hot in his soul.

He fought to contain his emotions and through clenched teeth asked, "How is Ambrose?"

Pippa hesitated. "Not well, I've heard. He's thrown himself into the hunt for Silence."

"I know what he's going through," Hawke said quietly, his eyes distant. "I've been there. And there's no road map out of that darkness."

Hawke felt torn in two.

Part of him wanted to be there for Congreve: not to shepherd him through the grieving process—he had no earthly idea how to console his friend—but to hunt down the bitch who'd taken Diana out of the world.

But another part of him knew he couldn't do that. Not yet. Not until he dealt with Sergei Mulmuscovy.

He clenched his fists, his resolve hardening, and faced Pippa again. "I'm leaving for St. Petersburg first thing in the morning."

Pippa looked back at him, her expression no longer quite as resolute as before. “Alex, what Anastasia said about . . . I *do* care about—”

“You shouldn’t, Pip. Nasty things tend to happen to the people who care about me.”

And before Pippa could respond, he slammed the laptop shut, severing the connection.

FIFTY-ONE

LUGA, LENINGRAD OBLAST, RUSSIA

Hawke lay prone at the edge of a stand of trees, gazing out across the football pitch–wide cleared zone that acted as a buffer between the forest and the walls of the ad hoc installation that now served as an operating base for Mulmuscovy's mercenary outfit, the Perun Group. Those walls—stacked wire-mesh gabions filled with coarse gravel—rose at least twenty feet high and were topped with loops of concertina wire that gleamed faintly in the silvery glow of moonlight. Guard towers sprouted at intervals along the wall, but none appeared to be presently occupied.

On the other side of the wall, a haze of light suffused the sky and a low hum of activity drifted up, carried on the breeze.

"Busy place," murmured Stokely from his vantage just a few feet away. "Sounds like they're throwing a party."

"It certainly does. What say we crash it?"

Stoke chuckled. "Won't be the craziest thing I've done this week."

The intel they'd gathered on Mulmuscovy's operation suggested the activity inside was anything but routine. The compound, situated near Luga, about ninety miles south of St. Petersburg, was enormous, sprawling across roughly five hundred acres. Satellite imagery provided by Pippa showed a patchwork of cleared fields, gravel-paved motor pools, and temporary structures the stretched-out size of circus tents. A single airstrip, capable of landing cargo transport planes. The satellite imagery showed Mulmuscovy's private jet sitting at one end of that runway alongside two Sukhoi Su-27 "Flanker" fighter jets. It also showed more than a hundred vehicles, mostly GAZ Tigrs—roughly the Russian equivalent of the U.S. military's venerable "Humvee"—but also armored personnel carriers, five-ton trucks, and even a squadron of T-72 battle tanks lined up on the roads inside the facility. It seemed clear that Mulmuscovy's troops were preparing for an operation on a massive scale, and it was imminent. Given the sheer size of the enemy force and their state of heightened readiness, Hawke's mission—locating Mulmuscovy, discerning the exact details of his plan, and eliminating the threat—was both urgent and extremely fluid.

An all-out assault by Thunder and Lightning was simply unthinkable. The installation's size and the overwhelming firepower housed within made any such attack tantamount to suicide. Even with a team as skilled as the men under Boomer's command, they would be no match for hundreds, perhaps even thousands, of mercenaries. This would have to be a stealth operation, with just Hawke and Stoke going in. Thunder and Lightning would hold back as a reserve element, ready to provide a diversion for Hawke and Stoke to escape if things went pear-shaped.

Fortunately, perimeter security didn't seem to be a high priority for Mulmuscovy's forces. The unmanned guard towers and the lack of visible patrols along the cleared zone suggested that the compound's defenders either had little concern about the possibility of intruders or were too consumed by the preparations going on inside to care. Either way, it gave Hawke and Stoke the sliver of opportunity they needed to slip in undetected.

The stakes were high, the margin for error virtually nonexistent, and Hawke, to his great chagrin, was having trouble keeping his mind on the mission.

Anastasia was gone.

There'd been no note, no goodbye, no further argument. She had simply driven off.

And he had let her go.

But try as he might to put the whole business out of his mind, he found that he could not. It was the cost of the life he'd chosen.

He told himself that it was for the best and that once the mission was done—once he'd made the Warmonger nothing but a rotting corpse and a footnote in history—he would do whatever it took to reconcile with her, but her departure and the uncertainty of their future together weighed heavily on him.

Get your head back in the game, old boy. Or you might not get the chance to fix this.

"Well, no time like the present." He glanced over at Stoke. "You ready?"

"Brother, I was born ready."

Well, that makes one of us, thought Hawke, rising from the prone position. "Cover me."

He set out across the cleared zone, moving in short bursts, in between which he provided cover for Stoke. The two men leapfrogged their way across the open ground, expecting at any moment the alarm to go up and a storm of bullets to come raining down on them, but they completed the crossing, reaching the wall without incident.

Hawke immediately began climbing, the rough gravel-filled gabions providing precarious but usable handholds. Stoke followed close behind, moving with surprising agility for someone so large. From the top of the wall, Hawke finally got a look inside Mulmuscovy's base.

The scene below was a hive of activity.

Soldiers hustled around the vehicles, hauling crates of ammunition, jerricans of fuel, and stacks of rations. Mechanics darted in and out of the crowd, making last-minute checks on engines and weapon mounts, while others barked orders over the din of idling engines and the clank of the metal treads of the T-72 tanks as they were being driven onto flatbed trailers.

"Looks like the whole damn circus is packing up," Stoke muttered as he crested the wall beside Hawke.

"They're not just getting ready—they're mobilizing. Damn it, Stoke. We're too late."

Even as he said it, the massive gates at the southern end of the installation began to grind open and the first vehicles in the column began rolling out, their headlights piercing the darkness outside. Half a dozen Tigrs led the way. Behind them were a dozen Kamaz trucks, their cargo beds covered with tarps, and then more Tigrs, vehicle after vehicle streaming out in an endless procession, a river of light disappearing into the forest.

Hawke pulled a satellite phone from his pack and dialed. It took only a moment for the connection to be established and Pippa's voice to sound in his ear. "Yes, Alex?"

"I'm afraid we're late to the party. Whatever Mulmuscovy's planning, it's happening right bloody now. They're rolling out as we speak."

"How many vehicles?" Pippa's voice was sharp, all business.

"All of them, by the look of it." Pippa had seen the same satellite imagery he had and knew what that meant. "If they're headed for Moscow, it's game over. He'll seize control before anyone can stop him."

There was a brief pause before her reply. "Alex, listen to me. If we can present undeniable evidence of what Mulmuscovy is planning, we can still stop this. Warn the Russian leadership. They may be fractured, but they'll act to protect their own survival. We've got time: the column still has to cover the distance to Moscow."

"And if they don't believe you?"

"They'll believe it if you find something concrete," Pippa pressed. "Maps, orders, communications—*anything* that proves what he's planning."

Hawke stared out at the compound below, a sprawling hive of activity. The vehicles may have been rolling out, but the facility itself was still buzzing with troops and logistics. For all he knew, Mulmuscovy might still be there, overseeing the operation from a command center rather than traveling in the vanguard.

Maybe there's still a chance to deal with him.

"Fine," he said at last. "We'll go in, get what we need, and get out."

"Be careful," Pippa said softly. "And, Alex? Don't be a hero. If you can't get in and out safely, then don't even try."

Hawke ended the call and stowed the satellite phone in his pack. He turned to Stoke, who had been watching the conversation with silent intensity.

"We're going in," Hawke said simply.

"Well, seeing as we're dressed for the occasion . . ." Stoke said, grinning. "Lead on, boss."

They traversed the top of the wall, staying low to avoid presenting a silhouette, and descended once they approached the nearest watchtower. The elevated overwatch position was itself empty, as they had suspected, its interior littered with discarded cigarette butts and empty water bottles. From there, it was a quick climb down into the installation.

They dropped behind a large festival tent at the outer edge of the installation. There was little chance of them being heard, given the din of the mobilization, but they crouched in the shadows, moving out carefully, darting from one patch of cover to the next, ever vigilant. Hawke peeked inside a few of the tents as they passed. Most were crowded with bunk beds and cots, everything neat and orderly and completely devoid of occupants. No one, it seemed, would be remaining behind.

As they moved deeper into the compound, closer to the lines of vehicles now fully loaded up and awaiting their turn, they had to move much more cautiously, hugging the shadows and timing their movements carefully. As Hawke crouched at the corner of a tent, observing the scene, he noticed something odd. The mercenaries manning the trucks and Tigrs were attired in standard-issue Russian Army fatigues with the distinctive EMR "Digital Flora" camouflage pattern.

"Mulmuscovy's men are wearing Russian Army kit," he whispered to Stoke.

"Maybe he wants the regulars to think he has the support of the Army when he rolls up on the Kremlin. Kind of like a Trojan horse."

It was as good an explanation as any, but something about it seemed off. With so much firepower at his disposal, Hawke wondered, what did Mulmuscovy gain from subterfuge?

"Check that out," whispered Stoke, pointing to a large tent on the other side of the lineup. It was smaller than the troop quarters, but it was the array of radio antennas and satellite dishes outside it that had caught Stoke's eye. "That's their TOC."

A TOC—tactical operations center—was what American operators like Stoke called a command post. It was Mulmuscovy's headquarters, and if the Moscow Mule wasn't leading his men into battle, that was where they would find him. And if he wasn't there, then at least they might be able to find the proof Pippa had asked for.

"That's where we need to go," said Hawke.

"We've got to get past those assholes first."

"We're going to have to take the long way round," agreed Hawke, drawing back from the corner of the tent.

The long way involved moving through the mostly abandoned maze of tents to find a route that would take them around the rear of the line of vehicles so they could approach the TOC from the other side. By the time they reached the back end of the procession, those vehicles were already moving, and in a matter of minutes they were rolling out.

Hawke felt a pang of disappointment as he watched them go. If Mulmuscovy was riding out with his men, then he was already out of reach.

As the last of the vehicles rolled away, an eerie silence fell over the installation. Without the din of activity, every sound seemed magnified: the soft crunch of gravel under their boots, the rustle of canvas as the breeze tugged at the tents . . .

"Feels like a damned ghost town," Stoke murmured.

"Doesn't it?" Hawke replied. "All the same, let's stay on our toes. We might not be completely alone here."

The TOC was smaller than the residential tents. Rectangular, with heavy canvas sides stretched taut over a rigid frame. There were no windows, and the only means of entrance or egress was through the vestibule at the front.

"Do we knock," Stoke asked, "or just walk our happy asses right on in?"

"With no idea what we might be walking into," replied Hawke, "I'm thinking maybe we should try the back door."

Stoke took another look. "What back door?"

Hawke tapped the hilt of the Ontario Mark 3 Navy knife, which hung inverted from Stoke's combat harness. "The one you're going to make."

"I like how you think, boss. I'm always up for a little B and E."

Giving the entrance a wide berth, they circled around to the rear of the tent. Stoke knelt and pressed his ear against the canvas, listening for any sound from within. Satisfied with what he heard—or rather didn't hear—he drew the knife and worked the point into the taut fabric, opening a small gash. He then withdrew the blade and used his finger to widen the opening just enough to create a small peephole. He bent low and peered through the opening for several seconds before pulling back.

"All clear," he whispered, and then reinserted the blade, cutting a C-shaped hole just wide enough for him to fit through. As the heavy fabric parted, it revealed only darkness beyond.

Stoke brought his rifle—an HK417 from Thunder and Lightning's arsenal—to his shoulder and aimed it into the opening. But rather than firing the weapon, he instead touched a small stud just above the trigger, activating the SureFire LED flashlight mounted to the rifle's side rail. A shaft of brilliant white light sliced through the gloom, revealing a small space—little larger than a broom closet—partitioned by canvas walls.

"Not quite what I was expecting," Stoke admitted. Cautiously, he stepped through the opening. "There's a cot in here. Must be where the boss goes for nap time . . ." He trailed off and then hissed, "What the hell?"

Hawke thrust himself through the opening, his rifle at the ready, but careful to avoid flagging Stokely. Once clear, he did a visual sweep of the little room. His mind took in the scene by degrees.

He saw the cot Stoke had described . . . saw the person stretched out upon it, and the cable ties cinched around wrists and ankles, and the strip of gaff tape across the mouth.

Her mouth.

Hawke saw the blond hair spread out around her head, glowing like a halo in the radiance of Stoke's SureFire.

Then he saw her face.

Hawke's breath caught. "Savannah?"

FIFTY-TWO

Savannah stirred, her head lolling to one side as her eyes fluttered open. She immediately winced, squeezing her eyes shut against the harsh glare of Stoke's light.

Hawke hurried over to her, kneeling beside the cot. "Easy," he murmured. "You're safe now."

Stoke moved the light off her. "You know this chick?"

"We met in Istanbul."

Stoke chuckled, shaking his head in disbelief. "Of course you did. Only my man Alex Hawke could run into an old girlfriend in a place like this."

"She's not—" Hawke broke off, shaking his head. "Just cut her loose, Stoke."

He returned his attention to the captive woman, touching the strip of tape over her mouth, using a fingernail to lift one corner. "This might sting," he said apologetically, then yanked it off in one swift motion.

"Bloody hell!" Savannah gasped, her voice hoarse as she glared at him. "You could've warned me properly . . ." Her words trailed off as recognition dawned, her eyes widening. "Alex? What the devil are you doing here?"

Before Hawke could answer, Stoke slid the tip of his knife under the cable tie holding Savannah's right wrist. "Don't worry, lady. I'll be gentle," he said, and, with a slight twist of the blade, sliced through the restraint. He then moved to the left wrist, glancing over at Hawke. "You going to introduce us?"

"Stoke, meet Commander Savannah Stone, Royal Navy. Savannah, this is Stokely Jones Jr., former Navy SEAL and the best man to have at your side in a place like this."

Savannah managed a faint smile. "Charmed."

"Likewise," Stoke replied. "You two want to explain how you know each other, or should I just make up something scandalous?"

Hawke waved him off. "That can wait. Right now, I'd rather hear what you're doing here."

Savannah sat up and began rubbing her wrists. "I was tailing our old friend General Osman Gul. He left Ankara suddenly after getting a call from someone in Moscow—Mulmuscovy, as it turns out. I tracked Gul to a meeting in Armenia, but Mulmuscovy's men spotted me. I've been enjoying his hospitality ever since."

Hawke nodded slowly. "Pippa told me that someone had reported in on a meeting between Gul and Mulmuscovy and then gone missing. Had no idea it was you."

Savannah tilted her head to the side. "You're not here for me, are you?"

Hawke shook his head. "I'm here for Mulmuscovy. Too late, it seems. He's already on his way to Moscow."

"Moscow? No, Alex. He's not going to Moscow."

Hawke's eyes narrowed. "What do you mean?"

She leaned forward, her voice low and urgent. "Mulmuscovy's not leading a mutiny. He's orchestrating a false flag operation to make it look like the Russian Army is attacking Estonia."

Stoke let out a low whistle. "Estonia? They're part of NATO, boss. He attacks them, and NATO will kick his ass."

Savannah shook her head. "No, unfortunately, right now, a swift, unified response from NATO isn't a certainty. Putin's little display with the Tsar bomb has a lot of them questioning whether it's really worth it to risk nuclear war by standing up to Russia."

"Mulmuscovy only has a couple thousand troops at best," said Hawke. "I suspect the Estonian military will be able to repel this invasion without any help from NATO."

"They won't need to," said Savannah, "because General Gul is going to swoop in and save the day."

"Gul?"

"*He* is the mastermind behind all of this. The puppet master holding Mulmuscovy's strings. The attack on the NATO summit in Istanbul? That was another false flag operation, engineered by Gul, not only to get rid of his boss, Defense Minister Amir al-Fulan, but to give Gul a chance to launch a reprisal against Russia, who would have taken the blame if you hadn't gotten in the way."

Realization dawned for Hawke. "Gul's the bloody Warmonger."

Savannah nodded. "He doesn't just want to be the defense minister or even the president of Turkey. Gul wants to resurrect the Ottoman Empire with himself as emperor. He wants to elevate Turkey to the status of a global superpower. By acting unilaterally to crush this phony Russian invasion of Estonia, he will make Turkey—and himself—the hero of NATO's failure."

"I get the part about him riding to the rescue," said Stoke. "But how does stopping a small invasion force in Estonia elevate him to global status? That's hardly empire-building material."

"Gul's not going to stop at Estonia's border. Crushing Mulmuscovy's false flag invasion is just the opening act. Once his troops are committed, he'll push deeper into Russian territory under the pretense of neutralizing a continued threat. He's counting on Russia's leadership being too fractured to coordinate an effective response and their conventional forces too gutted from years of war in Ukraine to hold the line. NATO will have no choice but to back Turkey's play."

"And what happens if Russia decides to use nukes?"

"It's a risk Gul is willing to take. I think he's betting on Russia's fractured government being too paralyzed to make that call."

Stoke shook his head. "There's no way Mulmuscovy doesn't see how this is going to play out."

Hawke nodded in agreement. "The plan's too transparent. Gul uses Mulmuscovy's forces as cannon fodder in Estonia, then paints a big target on Russia's back for NATO. Mulmuscovy has to know that he's being sacrificed, not that I feel at all sorry for the bastard."

"He does know," said Savannah. "Only he's not the one being sacrificed. Mulmuscovy doesn't care about his men—they're just pawns. Expendable assets to advance the game. He knows exactly what Gul is planning, and he's all in. Once Gul's forces dismantle the current regime in Moscow, there'll be a power vacuum. With NATO backing Gul's narrative, Russia's oligarchs and military leaders will be scrambling to find someone to stabilize the country."

Hawke frowned. "And Mulmuscovy plans to make himself that someone."

"Exactly," Savannah replied. "He positions himself as the strongman who can rebuild Russia after Gul's 'heroic' victory."

"What's the play?" asked Stoke. "How do we stop this?"

Savannah's expression remained grim. "I'm not sure we can. The dominoes are already falling. Even if we provide proof of what Gul's up to, bureaucratic inertia will give Gul all the time he needs to reach Moscow."

Stoke frowned. "So, what, we just give up?"

"No," Hawke said decisively. "We're going to stop Mulmuscovy's army from reaching Estonia. Nip this little power play in the bud."

"And how are we going to do that?" asked Savannah.

But before Hawke could answer, a voice, only slightly muffled by the canvas partition, interjected, "Yes, Lord Hawke, I would very much like to know how you intend to stop me."

FIFTY-THREE

Hawke and Stoke reacted instantly, bringing their rifles up, aiming at the partition, and sweeping back and forth in search of a target.

"I know that you're armed," said Mulmuscovy, his tone calm and measured. "You were observed entering the camp alone. Please put your weapons on the floor. I'd hate to have to shoot you before we've had a chance to talk, but trust me—keeping you alive isn't really that important to me."

Hawke glanced over at Stoke, who gave a barely perceptible shrug.

"All right, Sergei," said Hawke. "This round goes to you. We're putting our guns down."

He and Stoke both placed their rifles on the floor, along with the handguns they'd brought as secondary weapons.

Mulmuscovy waited a few seconds before speaking again. "One of my men is going to come in now. If you make a move against him, the rest of us will fill you so full of holes that even God won't recognize you."

A section of the canvas partition slid away, revealing one of Mulmuscovy's thugs, backlit by the dim glow of several overhead fluorescent light fixtures. The man held a pistol aimed at Hawke. His eyes flicked down to the guns on the floor of the tent, then came back up to Hawke and Stoke, who already had their hands raised in a show of surrender. He barked a few words in Russian, and then another section of the partition was removed, revealing Mulmuscovy and three more of his men, all attired not in camouflage, but in business suits.

"Gentlemen, I see that you're acquainted with my other guest."

"Yes," replied Hawke, refusing to show even a hint of concern to his captor. "She's been entertaining us with a wild fairy tale about a mad ogre who thinks he's going to take over all of Russia."

Mulmuscovy chuckled. "I'm in your debt, Lord Hawke. You've given the Russian people a second chance to see President Putin's assassin brought to justice. When I heard that you had escaped from Lubyanka, the last thing I expected was for you to hand yourself over to me again."

Hawke returned a smile. "I'm rather looking forward to having my day in court and telling your countrymen who really killed their beloved president." He paused a beat, then added, "Of course, they won't have the opportunity to put you on trial."

"Oh? What makes you say that?"

"Why? Because you'll already be dead. I'm going to kill you myself."

Mulmuscovy laughed again. "Such brave words. But, no, that's not what's going to happen. I will rule Russia, and you will die before a firing squad, executed as a spy and an assassin."

"I'll admit," Hawke went on, ignoring him, "I thought you would be leading your men into battle. Oh, but of course," he added with mock realization, "you're not sending them to fight. You're sending them to be massacred by your master, the Warmonger."

Mulmuscovy's look of amusement faltered, his smile tightening into a grim line. "You presume too much."

"Do I?" Hawke asked, stepping forward slightly, even as Mulmuscovy's men tensed, their pistols held nervously at the ready. Hawke looked into the eyes of the man guarding him. "How do you feel about your boss sending your comrades off to die?"

"He doesn't speak English," said Mulmuscovy dismissively. "And in any event, he doesn't care what happens to those men. They are all scum. Rapists and pedophiles. I take them out of prisons and pay them to put on a uniform and hold a gun. I am doing Mother Russia a favor by sending them off to die."

Hawke brought his attention back to Mulmuscovy. "And did it occur to you that Gul might feel exactly the same way about you? You think you're going to ride his coattails to the Kremlin, don't you? You're just another pawn in his game. And pawns, Sergei, are always expendable."

"Your insolence will not go unpunished, Lord Hawke," Mulmuscovy growled. He waved a hand, and one of his men stepped forward, his pistol swinging toward Stoke. Another aimed his weapon at Savannah, who stiffened visibly but kept her chin high.

"Hostages," Mulmuscovy went on, "are immensely useful. They open doors, secure negotiations, and, most importantly, serve as leverage. You, Lord Hawke, are useful to me. A symbol. A trophy, even. But these others?" He made a disdainful gesture. "I don't really need them. Certainly not *both* of them."

"Touch a hair on their heads," Hawke said, his voice low and deadly, "and you'll regret it."

Mulmuscovy raised an eyebrow, feigning surprise. "Regret? Oh, I regret nothing, Lord Hawke. Not my ambitions. Not my alliances. And certainly not the lessons I teach to those who stand in my way."

He stepped closer to Savannah, his gaze locking with hers as she glared back defiantly. "Tell me," he said almost conversationally, "which of them do you value more? I will let you decide who stays and who"—his lips curled into a malicious smile—"goes."

When Hawke did not reply, Mulmuscovy's cruel smile broadened. "Come now, Lord Hawke. If you do not choose, I will kill them both."

Hawke met Mulmuscovy's gaze, calm and unflinching. "Sorry, old chap, but I'm not going to play your sadistic little game. And you're not going to be killing anyone. You see, there's something I haven't told you."

Mulmuscovy's brow furrowed slightly, curiosity flickering across his visage.

"You got one little thing wrong."

"Oh? And what might that be."

Hawke leaned forward as if imparting a secret. "We didn't come alone." And before Mulmuscovy could respond, Hawke pitched his voice to a shout. "Now, Boomer!"

FIFTY-FOUR

When Mulmuscovy had first revealed his presence, Hawke had clicked on his radio mic, transmitting everything that followed to Boomer, letting him know that things had taken an unfortunate turn and that it was time to implement the emergency plan. He hadn't known exactly what shape the diversion would take; he had only told Boomer to be ready to act if and when he gave the signal.

Boomer, in characteristic fashion, had brought the thunder.

A fraction of a second after Hawke's shout, the world seemed to come apart. A series of tremendous explosions shook the night. The tent walls snapped and bulged as if buffeted by hurricane-force winds. Each detonation felt like a gut punch, but unlike Mulmuscovy and his men, Hawke and Stoke had known what was coming, and so, instead of reeling from the explosive power, they immediately sprang into action.

Hawke sidestepped the gunman guarding him, clamping his hand down over the pistol he held, twisting the weapon out of his grasp. Then he deftly pivoted, swinging the man in front of him, using the man's bulk to absorb a volley of panicked shots from one of Mulmuscovy's other thugs. The reports were deafening in the confined space, setting Hawke's ears ringing, but that was the extent of the harm he suffered. His human shield, however, did not fare as well. The man shook with the impacts of the rounds and fell back, taking Hawke down to the floor with him.

Stoke, meanwhile, had used the distraction of the explosions to charge the man warding him. Stoke plowed into him, knocking his gun hand aside and spoiling his aim. The guy was of comparable size to Stoke, but Stoke hit him high enough to knock him off-balance. The sheer momentum of the collision sent both of them reeling into the command center, where they slammed into a line of folding tables.

Papers flew into the air. Computer monitors and radio equipment crashed to the floor. In the midst of the tumult, the thug managed to heave Stoke off him, hurling him through the air to slam down amidst the rubble of the command center. The impact drove the wind from Stoke's lungs, leaving him momentarily stunned, and his opponent was quick to capitalize on it, pouncing on Stoke, straddling him, and pinning him down. One massive hand clamped around Stoke's throat while the other drew back in a fist like a sledgehammer.

On the floor and partially pinned under the lifeless weight of his human shield, Hawke saw Savannah diving for one of the HKs. He also saw the gunman who had just unsuccessfully fired at him now attempting to track her.

"Savannah, down!"

Hawke could barely hear his own voice over the ringing in his ears, and it seemed unlikely that Savannah would have heard the warning, but his shout caught the gunman's attention, distracting him just enough to buy Savannah a split second. Hawke used that moment of indecision to grasp the pistol still clutched in the lifeless hand of the man atop him. Rather than try to wrestle it free, he covered the dead man's hand with his own, raising gun, hand, and arm together, and squeezing the man's trigger finger.

His first shot caught the man in the shoulder, spinning him sideways.

The second struck him in the chest, dropping him in his tracks.

"Got it!" shouted Savannah, coming up in a crouch, holding an HK, and looking for a target.

Hawke shoved the dead man off him and was trying to wrest the pistol from his death grip when a flicker of movement at the edge of his vision snapped his attention sideways. The fourth of Mulmuscovy's thugs, who had been momentarily distracted by the chaos of Stokely's struggle, was now turning his attention back to Hawke.

Abandoning his attempt to extricate the dead finger from the trigger guard, Hawke instead rolled away even as rounds seared the air where he had been only a moment before, punching into the back wall of the tent.

Then the louder report of the HK thundered in the close quarters, and the gunman staggered and went down. Hawke glanced over at Savannah, who still held the smoking assault rifle at the high ready, her cheek welded to the stock. She caught his eye and winked.

Hawke nodded in gratitude but then spied a flash of movement from the corner of his eye: Mulmuscovy, slipping through the front entrance of the tent.

He also saw Stoke, still locked in a brutal brawl with the enormous thug. The man had Stoke pinned to the floor, one hand gripping his throat while the other drove hammer-like punches into his ribs.

His face red from the pressure on his neck, Stoke growled deep in his throat and shot a hand up, grabbing the thug's wrist and wrenching it to the side, momentarily breaking the choke hold. With a sudden burst of strength, he twisted his entire body, forcing his attacker to lose his balance. Both men went down in a heap, crashing into a pile of scattered equipment.

The thug was quick, rolling atop Stoke and pressing his massive forearm against Stoke's throat. Stoke's legs thrashed, boots kicking against the floor in a desperate bid to create space.

Hawke scrambled to his feet and grabbed the other HK417. He swung the rifle toward the grappling pair, but the two were moving too frantically, twisting and turning in close quarters. He couldn't get a clean shot.

"Come on, Stoke," Hawke muttered, the rifle following the chaotic struggle. "Give me a shot."

With a burst of feral energy, Stoke bucked his hips, forcing his attacker forward, then drove his elbow into the man's temple, stunning him just long enough to twist free. Dazed but still dangerous, the man struggled to rise. But Stoke was faster. Before the man could get his feet under him, Stoke bounded up, grabbed a folding chair off the floor, and swung it like a club.

The chair was of lightweight construction, made of plastic and aluminum, and consequently didn't have a lot of mass, but the edge of it struck the thug in the side of the head with a resounding thwack. The man's head snapped to the side, and he went down.

Stoke, still holding the chair, which had developed a curious bend in one of the upright posts, looked over at Hawke. His face was swollen from the battering he'd received, and blood was streaming into his eyes from multiple cuts, but his grin remained fierce. "Well, are we gonna go after that asshole or what?" he growled.

Hawke didn't need to be told twice. Shouldering his HK, he bolted for the exit. Shoving through the vestibule, he burst into the cool night air just in time to see a lone GAZ Tigr pulling away from the compound, its tires kicking up a spray of gravel that peppered the nearby tents.

"Bloody hell," Hawke muttered, breathless. He considered giving chase on foot but quickly dismissed the idea: the Tigr was already accelerating faster than he could sprint. Instead, he shouldered the HK417, flicked the selector to full auto, and pulled the trigger.

Rounds hammered the rear of the vehicle, sparking off its armored plating in bright flashes, but the Tigr did not slow. Stoke and Savannah emerged from the tent just in time to see the vehicle vanish into the distance.

"Well, now what?" Stoke asked, still wiping blood from his battered face.

Growling in frustration, Hawke lowered his rifle and grabbed his radio handset. He slipped off the elastic band that was holding the push-to-talk button down, then clicked it again. "Boomer, do you copy?"

Boomer's deep voice sounded muffled, as if the mic were wrapped in a pillow due to the lingering effects of the gunfire on Hawke's hearing. "Boomer here. Heard everything. What's your status?"

"Mulmuscovy just bolted. I need you to get to the front gate and cut him off."

There was a beat of silence before Boomer replied, calm as ever. "Already ahead of you. We moved up as soon as his army rolled out. We've got the gate locked down."

Hawke allowed himself a sigh of relief, but Stoke quickly quashed his mood. "If he's trying to get to the gate, he's going the wrong way."

Hawke blinked at him, trying to grasp the importance of this observation. Savannah provided the missing piece of the puzzle. "He's not heading for the gate. He's going to the airstrip. His jet's parked there; that's how we got here."

"Bugger," snarled Hawke, staring into the shadowy road Mulmuscovy had taken. He tried to envision the satellite map of the installation and the general location of the airstrip. From the center of the camp, it was about half a mile in a straight line. Mulmuscovy was probably already there. He turned to the others, his voice decisive. "We can get there before he takes off. It's only about half a mile."

Stoke nodded. "All right, then. Let's go."

Savannah, however, balked. "You're serious? You want to chase down a jet . . . on *foot*?"

"It will take a few minutes to get ready for takeoff, even if the pilots have a gun to their heads. If we move, we can get there first."

Savannah gave a weary sigh, then handed her rifle to Stoke. "Something tells me your mile time is better than mine."

Stoke laughed as he accepted the rifle, then took off running. Hawke was right behind him.

At a fairly relaxed pace on flat terrain, Hawke knew he could cover half a mile in about four minutes. Two and a half at a full sprint. But this wasn't a straight line. The base was a maze of unfamiliar roads, and they would be navigating them in the dark. Nevertheless, the urgency of their plight drove him onward.

A sudden roar cut through the darkness—the unmistakable harsh whine of jet engines winding up. Hawke's head snapped toward the sound. "Bloody hell," he muttered, digging deep for an untapped reserve of speed. It would still take a couple more minutes to get the plane aloft. Maybe, just maybe, he could get to the runway first and stop it.

Thirty seconds passed.

A minute.

The noise of the jet engines grew steadily louder, and not just because he was getting closer to the source.

Almost without warning, the airstrip materialized ahead of him, the runway marker lights casting just enough illumination for him to make out the shape of the aircraft now rolling into position for takeoff.

Hawke skidded to a halt on the gravel runway, breathing hard as he grappled with the problem of what to do next. Forcing his way aboard wasn't an option. Even if he could close the remaining distance, the doors would be locked from inside. No, the only way to stop the aircraft from taking off was to disable it before it could reach takeoff speed.

He swung his HK417 up to his shoulder and took aim at the jet's starboard engine nacelle. With the fire selector on full auto, he curled his finger around the trigger and—

"Get down!" Stoke's urgent shout preceded the crack of rifle rounds creasing the air mere inches from Hawke's head by only a millisecond. Hawke threw himself flat even as the reports reached his ears and then rolled sideways across the packed earth surface as more rounds stitched the ground, chasing after him.

Lying prone at the edge of the airstrip, he began searching for the source of the incoming fire. Bright flames—muzzle flashes—were erupting from right behind the landing gear of one of the Sukhoi fighter jets parked just off the runway, a hundred yards from where he lay.

Hawke rolled again as another burst of fire chewed into the spot he'd just vacated. Dirt and gravel kicked up by the impacts pelted him like hailstones. He bounded up and then dived into a shallow drainage ditch paralleling the landing strip.

The ditch wasn't much—barely deep enough to let him keep his head down—but it was enough to remove him from the line of fire. When the shooting stopped, he waited a moment longer before risking a quick peek.

The wink of more muzzle flashes cut short his observation, forcing him to duck down again, but what he saw in those brief seconds nearly dashed his hopes of stopping Mulmuscovy. There were at least two shooters, maybe more, firing from the general direction of the two Sukhoi fighter jets. Even worse, Mulmuscovy's plane was now lined up on the runway, its engine roaring louder as the pilot brought the turbines to full power in preparation for a static takeoff. Time was running out, and the shooters weren't giving him an inch.

The jet's engines were screaming now, the vibrations thrumming through the ground under him. Hawke weighed his options. Staying pinned down in the ditch would only guarantee failure. But if he left its scant cover, his odds of staying alive long enough to do something to stop it were slim. If that plane made it off the runway . . .

He gritted his teeth. Damn the odds. He had to do something.

Hawke took a breath to calm his nerves, brought his HK to his shoulder, and sprang up from the ditch.

The jet was moving now, just beginning to roll as the pilot released the brakes, spoiling Hawke's hopes of a quick reflex shot. He tracked the starboard engine nacelle, trying to lead his target, and squeezed the trigger. The HK417 barked several times, the sharp reports punctuating the roar of the engines.

His shots had no visible effect.

"Bloody hell!" Hawke hissed through clenched teeth, diving back into the ditch in response to a fresh round of reports from the shooters. But he did not duck down. Instead, he brought the rifle up again, sighting on the plane (which was now racing down the airstrip), and resumed firing. The rush of jet exhaust blasted him with grit, but he kept his finger on the trigger, throwing rounds after the receding aircraft until the magazine was empty. The engine noise reached a bone-shaking crescendo and then, as the plane lofted skyward, began to diminish.

Hawke flattened himself in the ditch, slamming a fist into the ground. Frustration surged through him. He'd taken the chance, and it hadn't been enough.

But this wasn't the time to wallow in despair. Mulmuscovy might have slipped through his fingers, but the fight wasn't over. The shooters were still out there, and they wouldn't stop until he—or they—were dead.

Better them, he thought, ejecting the spent magazine from his HK417 and slamming a fresh one into place with more force than necessary.

He began low crawling forward down the ditch, using the scant cover to find a better position from which to engage the enemy. With the departure of the jet, an unsettling quiet had fallen over the base. Hawke imagined the hostiles also moving, looking for him. He stopped moving, cocking his head and straining to hear any sound that might give away the enemy position, but there was only silence.

He popped up, rifle at the ready, sweeping back and forth, ready to fire at the first sign of movement, ready to drop at the first muzzle flash. He saw neither. No motion, no shooting.

Where the hell did they go?

He knew he'd been exposed too long, that an enemy marksman

might even now be drawing a bead on him, so he dropped flat again and resumed crawling.

Then he did hear something. A shout.

"All clear! Alex! All clear!"

It was Stoke.

He rose cautiously, still gripping the HK but keeping the business end pointed down.

"Over here!"

Hawke turned toward the source of the sound and spotted Stoke and Savannah standing near the closest Su-27. Stoke had his HK, and Savannah was holding a Kalashnikov, which she had evidently appropriated from one of the motionless forms that lay at their feet.

"Thanks for drawing their fire," Stoke remarked. "Made it a lot easier for us to come up on their flank."

"For all the good it does us," replied Hawke acidly. "Mulmuscovy got away."

"Yeah, well, even you can't outrun a jet, Alex. We did what we could."

"And it bloody well wasn't enough."

"We'll call it in," said Savannah, though her tone betrayed her hopelessness. "Let everyone know what's really going on. Maybe it's not too late for a diplomatic solution."

"Diplomacy," scoffed Hawke. "By the time anyone in London or Washington gets around to doing something, Mulmuscovy will be measuring the curtains in the Kremlin."

"And I suppose you've got a better idea?" snapped Savannah, and then, not waiting for an answer, added, "I didn't think so."

Hawke opened his mouth to reply but stopped, his gaze drifting past her.

Savannah must have sensed the change in his demeanor, for her tone softened. "Alex?"

"I know that look, boss," intoned Stoke. "You're about to do something I'm going to regret."

Hawke smiled. “I’m going after him, Stoke.”

“And just how do you propose to do that?” asked Savannah. “Are you going to sprout wings and fly?”

Hawke nodded at the Sukhoi Su-27 parked right behind her. “Something like that.”

FIFTY-FIVE

Before he was a spy on His Majesty's Secret Service, Alex Hawke had been a flyer. He had cut his aviation teeth in the cockpit of a Harrier jump jet. Over the years, his skill and nerve had carried him into the skies aboard an extraordinary array of aircraft. He had flown American jets, including the F-14 Tomcat and the state-of-the-art F-35 Lightning, as well as the aircraft of foreign powers, including a Russian-made MiG-29, of which the Sukhoi was something of a spiritual successor. He was still occasionally called upon to test-fly experimental prototypes, pushing the limits of engineering and his own nerve in equal measure. For Hawke, the cockpit had always been a second home, a place where instinct and training fused into something close to perfection.

So, when Stoke, his brow furrowed, observed, "You sure about this, Alex? That's a damn Russian fighter jet. This ain't like borrowing somebody's car and finding out it's a stick shift," Hawke had been able to confidently reply, "As a matter of fact, Stoke, it's very nearly exactly like that."

Emerging from the Cold War arms race, the Sukhoi Su-27, known by its NATO reporting name, "Flanker," had been designed to rival the American F-15 Eagle in range, speed, and agility. With its twin AL-31F turbofan engines, each capable of producing 27,560 pounds of thrust, the Su-27 could reach speeds of up to Mach 2.35—more than 1,500 miles per hour at altitude. It boasted a combat radius of nearly eight hundred miles, allowing it to patrol vast territories or engage targets deep behind enemy lines. For its era, it was a powerhouse, and even decades later it remained a capable aircraft, respected by allies and adversaries alike.

One of the Su-27's standout features was its agility. Its advanced aerodynamics, aided by its massive wing surface area and the use of relaxed static stability, allowed it to perform sharp turns and complex maneuvers, outpacing many of its contemporaries in a dogfight. The addition of the fly-by-wire control system provided pilots with precise handling, making it deceptively nimble for its size. The Flanker's airframe was robust and designed to carry a substantial weapon load, including air-to-air missiles, unguided bombs, and even a GSh-30-1 30mm autocannon, giving it versatility in both air superiority and ground attack roles.

A quick walk-around of the aircraft confirmed that both were combat-ready—fully armed with an array of air-to-air missiles, the transport safety pins already removed. It was a safe bet that the autocannons were also fully loaded and the fuel tanks topped off.

"These planes are combat-ready," he said when he was done with his inspection. "Mulmuscovy must have been planning to use them to provide air support once his ground forces crossed the border."

"Makes sense," said Stoke. "So, where are the pilots?"

Hawke gestured toward the crumpled bodies littering the ground nearby. Unlike Mulmuscovy's thugs in their cheap suits or the mercenaries in their Russian Army uniforms, these men were attired in coveralls. "Right there, I imagine. Along with the ground crew." He looked around, spotting a small shipping container near a parked refueling truck. "I need to find a flight suit."

"You're serious about this, aren't you?"

"It's the only way to stop him, Stoke." He hastened over to the container, opening it to reveal what appeared to be an ad hoc aviators' ready room, with gear cubbies containing flight suits, helmets, and oxygen masks. Shedding his combat harness and jacket, he grabbed the nearest flight suit. The olive-green flame-retardant coverall looked to be about the right size, so he pulled it on, securing the front zipper before adjusting the Velcro straps at the cuffs and waist for a snug fit. It was a little tight in the shoulders but otherwise manageable.

He decided to pass on the G suit—a heavy overgarment with inflatable bladders designed to counteract the effects of high g-forces during combat maneuvers. Donning and adjusting the G suit would take time that he didn't have, and he wasn't anticipating getting into any dogfights. He put on the helmet, which was a better fit than the flight suit, then grabbed an oxygen mask and a pair of gloves and headed out.

Emerging from the container, feeling the cool night air on his face, he got another look at the sleek, twin-tailed fighter jet. That was when the enormity of what he was about to do finally sank in.

There was always risk involved in flying an unfamiliar aircraft, and Hawke wasn't blasé about the dangers. The Su-27 was, by all accounts, a reliable machine, but it wasn't his machine, and a moment's hesitation or a misstep in an unfamiliar cockpit could prove fatal.

And yet, the thought didn't fill him with dread. Instead, there was a thrill building inside him, electric and undeniable, like the rush before skydiving. This was what he loved most: the challenge, the raw, visceral experience of mastering a machine built to defy gravity and push the limits of human capability.

He found Stoke and Savannah waiting near the closest jet, their conversation trailing off as they noticed his approach.

"You're really going through with this," Savannah said, her tone sharp but tinged with concern.

"It's the only way to stop Mulmuscovy." He grabbed ahold of the metal ladder affixed to the fuselage of the Sukhoi, then turned to face

Stoke. "Link up with Thunder and Lightning and get out of Russia. Head west and cross the border any way you can."

"What about you?"

"Once I splash Mulmuscovy's plane, I'll have a few minutes at best before the Russian military scrambles fighters to intercept me. They won't ask questions, and they won't care that Mulmuscovy is the real enemy. I'll fly like the devil to reach Estonian airspace. Hopefully, they'll let me land. If not . . ." He gave a small shrug. "Either way, I'm not coming back here."

Savannah was incredulous. "You mean to tell me you're going up there knowing you've got no way out?"

"I've got a way out," Hawke said evenly. "It's just not guaranteed. Nothing in life ever is. But right now, stopping Mulmuscovy is all that matters. I'll worry about my own escape once he's dead."

Stoke clapped a hand on Hawke's shoulder. "Keep it simple up there. No showing off, okay?"

"Wouldn't dream of it, old boy." Hawke mounted the ladder and climbed up to the open cockpit. When he reached the top, he glanced down at Stoke. "Get the ladder clear and remove the chocks, then move back a bit. This is going to get loud."

"Got it, boss."

Settling into the seat, Hawke pulled the harness straps tight across his chest and thighs and secured the multipoint buckle. He then donned the helmet and plugged the mask's supply into the aircraft's oxygen system.

"All clear!" shouted Stoke from below. "Give him hell."

Hawke raised a hand in acknowledgment, then turned his attention to controls. Cyrillic labels stared back at him, unreadable but not incomprehensible. Years of experience had taught him to recognize the universal language of instrumentation: dials and switches, gauges, and readouts. His hands moved instinctively, toggling switches and watching for the expected responses.

The HUD flickered to life, casting a green glow over the cockpit.

Fuel levels—good.

Hydraulic pressure—steady.

Weapons systems—armed.

Finally, his fingers hovered over the engine ignition. He leaned out of the cockpit, shouting toward Stoke and Savannah, who stood just beyond the jet's reach.

"Clear the area! I'm starting the engines."

As they moved farther away, Hawke flipped the switch to lower the canopy, the dull hiss of hydraulics giving way to a solid click as the polycarbonate bubble locked into place. After another check to ensure that his companions were safely out of range, he flipped the final switch.

The AL-31F engines roared to life, the sound a thunderous crescendo that vibrated through the cockpit. He checked the HUD, confirming stable RPMs and fuel flow, then released the brakes and eased the throttles forward. There was a faint lurch as the Su-27 began to roll forward on the packed-earth airstrip. With a combination of gentle pressure on the rudder pedals and a deft touch on the tiller, he quickly guided the fighter to the centerline of the runway, aligning perfectly for takeoff.

"All right, let's see what you can do."

He pushed the throttles forward, unleashing the Flanker's full power. The engines thundered, and the Sukhoi surged ahead. Acceleration pressed him back into the seat, the sheer thrust of the twin AL-31Fs turning the uneven airstrip into a blur beneath him.

The airspeed indicator climbed rapidly—50 knots, 100 knots, 150 knots. As the jet gained speed, the lift generated by the movement of air across the wings partially unloaded the weight from the wheels, and the rough jolts smoothed into a steady hum.

By the time the airspeed needle hit 180 knots, the sensation was almost one of weightlessness, the Su-27 skimming over the ground with barely a shudder. Hawke felt the control stick come alive in his hands, the jet eager to leave the earth behind. He eased back on the stick, and the nosewheel lifted smoothly.

Moments later the main gear followed, the packed earth vanishing beneath him as the Flanker climbed into the night sky.

FIFTY-SIX

The roar of the engines faded as Hawke throttled back a little, leveling off at five hundred feet. The radar altimeter's readout on the HUD was blinking insistently with a none-too-subtle reminder that he was barely skimming above the treetops. At five hundred feet, there was little room for error, but flying low was a necessary and calculated risk. The last thing he needed was to show up on Russian long-range military radar. At this altitude the terrain would provide some cover, masking his presence from long-range military systems while he searched the skies for his quarry.

Mulmuscovy had about a ten-minute lead. Hawke had only caught a glimpse of a jet on the runway, but he thought it looked like a Gulfstream V. If so, it could conceivably have covered about seventy-five nautical miles in that time. For the Flanker, 75 NM was nothing. If Hawke lit the afterburners, the Flanker could close that gap in five minutes.

Distance wasn't the problem. Direction was.

Mulmuscovy could be heading anywhere: west toward the Estonian border, north for the short hop to St. Petersburg, east toward Moscow, or south into the heart of Russia. Without knowing the Gulfstream's heading, it didn't matter how fast the Flanker could fly.

He banked the plane into a wide, sweeping turn around the airstrip. The Su-27's radar was good, but its range wasn't unlimited—about 80

NM give or take. That meant Mulmuscovy was likely at or just outside detection range. Hawke's best chance of spotting him was to expand his search area without straying too far from his starting point.

The glow of St. Petersburg loomed faintly to the north, a sprawling constellation of lights that seemed deceptively calm, given the chaos unfolding in the region. Below him, the countryside stretched out like a shadowy quilt. Then, as the Flanker turned toward the west, he spied what looked like a river of light flowing across the darkened landscape.

Mulmuscovy's invasion force.

He watched the procession slide across his field of view, seeming to move from left to right as Hawke continued his turn.

They'd barely started their journey—ten, maybe fifteen miles out. At their current pace, it would be hours before they reached the Estonian border.

Hours before the chaos began.

The invasion force fell behind him, and he returned his attention to the monochrome glow of the radar display. The central grid remained empty, save for faint static from ground clutter. Beyond that, a vast expanse of empty airspace stretched out in every direction.

Then, at the very edge of the screen, a dot appeared.

Hawke leaned forward, adjusting the radar's focus. The contact grew clearer with each pass of the sweep line—a faint blip moving south at altitude. The radar resolved its position and speed: seventy-five miles out, bearing south-southeast, cruising steadily at 35,000 feet. No transponder code flashed to identify it, but Hawke didn't need confirmation.

Mulmuscovy.

The Gulfstream was heading deeper into Russian territory, perhaps toward Moscow or some other destination known only to its pilot.

Hawke adjusted his heading, matching the target's trajectory, and pushed the throttles forward. With a throaty roar, the Flanker surged ahead. Mulmuscovy was seventy-five miles away—a gap he could close in minutes if he pushed the Su-27 to its limits.

His hand hovered over the afterburner controls, hesitating, but only for a fraction of a second. Once he kicked them in, the Flanker's fuel consumption would spike dramatically. He'd have just enough, maybe, to accomplish his mission and then make it across the Estonian border. And the sonic boom would likely not go unnoticed by observers on the ground.

On the other hand, if he flew conservatively, just below Mach 1, it would take him at least half an hour to overtake the other plane, and he'd be that much deeper in enemy territory, that much farther from safer skies.

"Damn the torpedoes," he muttered, and shoved the throttles into the afterburner detent.

The effect was immediate.

As a stream of pressurized fuel poured into the engine exhaust, the Sukhoi shot forward like a rocket. The roar was deafening, a physical force that vibrated through the cockpit, shaking the very air around him, the thrust slamming Hawke back into his seat.

At low altitudes, every sensation was amplified. The denser air magnified the pressure wave, creating a shock cone that rippled outward, leaving a stripe of bent and broken treetops in the jet's wake. Climbing would have smoothed the ride considerably, but he stayed on the deck to reduce the likelihood of popping up on Russian long-range radar.

Hawke watched the airspeed indicator as it rapidly ticked upward—500 knots, 600, 650—the pressure outside the jet increasing as he neared the sound barrier. The world around him seemed to compress, the dense air at low altitude buffeting the jet with raw force. At this altitude, the transition to supersonic wasn't subtle. A shudder passed through the airframe as the plane broke through Mach 1, creating a thunderous sonic boom that rolled across the countryside.

The airspeed indicator continued climbing—700 knots . . . 800 . . . 900 . . .

Supersonic, the jet smoothed out slightly as the pressure wave shifted behind him, the worst of the buffeting subsiding. The Gulfstream's blip remained steady on the radar, creeping toward the center of the screen, its bearing and distance updating with each sweep.

Sixty nautical miles.

Fifty-five.

Fifty.

Forty nautical miles.

That was within the range of the Flanker's R-27ER air-to-air missiles, but not without complications. The missile relied on the plane's radar to guide it to the target, meaning Hawke would have to maintain a steady lock until impact. At this distance, the missile would need nearly a full minute to reach the Gulfstream—sixty seconds of holding a stable trajectory.

Too long.

If he closed the gap to ten miles, the missile's time to target would drop to about fifteen seconds.

He would also need to climb. The Flanker's missiles were designed to operate at altitude. Even as low as 20,000 feet, the drag from the atmosphere would slow them down, increasing time to target. Unfortunately, once he got above 10,000 feet, Russian military radar would light him up like a bonfire. And that was when the clock would start ticking.

He'd have time to lock on, fire a couple of missiles, and watch them destroy their target, but after that . . . well, there was no telling how long it would be before the hunter became the hunted.

The Gulfstream's blip crept closer, edging toward the sweet spot for a missile launch.

Thirty nautical miles.

Twenty-five.

Twenty.

Almost there.

He throttled back slightly, preparing for the climb. The roar of the Flanker's engines softened as the jet slowed, the turbulence returning as it dropped below the Mach threshold. His fingers hovered over the controls, his mind running through the sequence.

Climb, lock, fire. A textbook intercept.

And then run like hell.

He took a deep breath, knowing that he was about to go all in. He was about to show up on every radar screen in western Russia. But the payoff was worth it.

Wasn't it?

His hand hesitated on the stick as a heavy and unwelcome thought settled upon him.

Killing Mulmuscovy—delivering justice for all the chaos he had caused—would be satisfying, but that was about all it would accomplish. It wouldn't derail the Warmonger's plot. The invasion of Estonia would proceed. Gul would launch his counterinvasion and find some other puppet to rule in the Kremlin.

Maybe someone worse than Mulmuscovy.

It occurred to Hawke that Gul and Mulmuscovy had staked their very lives on Gul's scheme. If they succeeded, Gul would solidify his grip on power, and Mulmuscovy would be the face of a new Russian order. But if they failed—if Hawke could find a way to stop the invasion—when word of their conspiracy got out, they would be arrested, tried as traitors, and likely executed.

"Cut off the snake and the heads die," he murmured.

The blip on the radar moved steadily toward the edge of the screen, but Hawke had already let it go. His focus shifted west, back to where he'd seen the column crawling across the countryside.

He banked the Su-27, coming around on a new heading, and throttled forward.

FIFTY-SEVEN

Hawke kept the Flanker subsonic for the return trip to conserve fuel. He'd burned through nearly two-thirds of his supply racing after Mulmuscovy, leaving him with just slightly more than 8,000 pounds. At full burn, the engines devoured 1,800 pounds per minute, but as long as he kept the plane at a sedate 400 knots, he'd have more than enough fuel to find the invasion force, make a few strafing runs, and then head for safer skies, provided he didn't have to do any fancy flying.

About ten minutes after turning back, he spotted the column, still about twenty miles away, a glowing serpent slowly winding through the dark countryside.

He adjusted his heading slightly, swinging wide to the east to position himself for a pass from the rear of the column, then leveled off again, slowing to just under 350 knots to give himself more time to assess the situation. The road below was a black ribbon separating the forest through which it passed, upon which Mulmuscovy's army moved relentlessly forward—a train more than a hundred vehicles long.

Hawke toggled the infrared search-and-track system, and a faint grid overlay appeared on the HUD. The system's sensors scanned the ground below, detecting heat signatures from the engines of the convoy.

The larger targets near the rear of the column—fuel tankers and cargo haulers—glowed the brightest because of the heat radiating from their engine exhaust. Hawke decided that was where he would strike the first blow. Without fuel, food, or an ammunition resupply, the invasion wouldn't last long.

Ahead of the cargo trucks were the flatbeds carrying the battle tanks. Targeting them would be a waste of his own limited supply of ammunition. The 30mm rounds from the cannon likely wouldn't penetrate the tanks' armor. Besides, without fuel, the tanks would be effectively useless to the invasion force anyway.

Ahead of the flatbeds were the five-tonners, which were likely being used to transport infantry, and ahead of them, comprising the bulk of the column, were the Tigrs. Equipped with turret-mounted heavy weapons—Kord 12.7mm machine guns and AGS-30 grenade launchers—they alone possessed the ability to sting him. Normally, a fighter jet would have little to fear from such weapons, but he would be flying low and slow when he made his attack run, and that would leave him a little more vulnerable. Hitting a target moving at 300 knots was no mean feat, but luck was always a factor.

For the moment, their turrets weren't tracking him. Hawke imagined the gunners and their commanders craning their necks, trying to get a better look at the jet roaring overhead. Their curiosity was understandable; his overflight was unexpected to be sure, but they had no reason to believe he posed a threat.

That was about to change.

As he completed his first pass, he began a sweeping turn to the left, bringing the Flanker into a wide arc to line himself up for another run. At the furthest point in the turn, the column was once more just a string of lights winding toward the horizon on his right. He continued banking right, coming back around until he was lined up on the highway, still almost ten nautical miles out, and activated the Flanker's targeting system. The reticle on his HUD lit up as he toggled to the cannon. The ammunition counter showed a full combat load of 180 rounds—likely high-explosive incendiary rounds, interspersed with armor-piercing tracers—enough for three strafing runs if he kept his bursts short and precise.

Hawke nudged the stick forward slightly, tilting the Flanker's nose into a shallow dive. His thumb hovered over the cannon trigger as the targeting reticle on his HUD shifted downward and the lead Tigr came into view.

Hawke began a mental countdown. Timing was everything. Fire too early, and he would waste precious rounds on less desirable targets; too late, and he'd miss the opportunity entirely.

The column rushed beneath him, the headlights converging into a streak as the Flanker's speed compressed the distance. The reticle flashed green as each vehicle passed briefly into and out of range—the Tigrs, the five-tons, the flatbed with the T-72s.

"Tallyho," Hawke said, and depressed the trigger.

The GSh-30-1 barked to life, a thunderous burst of cannon fire that rocked the aircraft slightly. Tracer rounds streaked through the night like fiery comets, their glowing trails lancing into the trucks below. From the cockpit, it looked almost as though the tracers were lazily drifting forward, but in reality the rounds were moving six times faster than the jet. He counted the tracers.

Three . . .

Four . . .

A flash lit up the night behind him. The heat bloom radiated against the canopy as one of the tankers went up in a fireball.

Six . . .

At seven he released the trigger. If the Su-27's ground crew had followed standard procedure, every sixth round would be a tracer, and so his burst would have expended about fifty rounds, give or take. A glance at the ammo counter confirmed his estimate—122 rounds remaining.

He pulled back on the stick, banking sharply to the left, and then nudged it to the side, rolling the Flanker into a smooth corkscrew. The horizon spun around him in a blur of forest, highway, and fire. Bright flames licked skyward from one of the tankers, casting a fiery glow over the surrounding vehicles. The blazing wreckage fell to the rear of the formation, flames already spreading into the surrounding forest. The trucks and transports that had been following it had already veered around it, swerving wildly to avoid burning debris. A second tanker sat unmoving just ahead of it, possibly disabled.

Two trucks down.

He had hoped for better.

The rest of the invasion force was continuing down the highway, the drivers of the larger trucks and Tigrs following the most basic rule of convoy safety when under attack: keep moving. But they were no longer a disciplined line. Instead, the column had broken apart, the individual vehicles breaking to either side of the road.

Streaks of light appeared outside the Flanker's canopy—tracers from the turret guns of the Tigrs, lancing into the sky. The storm of fire was erratic, the gunners firing blind in the darkness, but it was nevertheless a wake-up call for Hawke.

He carved another turn and then lined up for a second pass.

A patchwork of headlights lay spread out before him. Muzzle flashes twinkled like earthbound stars, and bright tracers filled the sky ahead of him like a swarm of angry red fireflies. And then, the storm was all around him. The air seemed to crackle with lethal energy.

Hawke had faced death more times than he cared to count, but this felt different. There was no plan B. Just him, a dwindling supply of ammunition, and ironclad resolve.

Angling into a shallow dive, he began his second run.

Tigrs and five-tons passed beneath him, and then a big cargo hauler came into view. He squeezed the trigger and the cannon roared again, the thud of each round sending vibrations up through the stick. Tracer fire from his own gun streaked toward the vehicle, missing it but slamming into a second truck right behind it. Sparks erupted as the rounds tore through the vehicle's frame, and then a secondary explosion lit up the highway as its contents—likely ammunition—detonated in a violent flash.

The shock wave hit the Flanker an instant later, slamming into the airframe like a slap from God, rattling Hawke's teeth. The stick bucked in his grip as turbulence buffeted the jet, but he kept it steady, swerving away as the fireball mushroomed into the sky. The Flanker's warning systems chirped with proximity alerts, and then a sharp metallic thud reverberated through the cockpit. A yellow alert flashed on the HUD, indicating minor damage to the port wing, either from a bullet or shrapnel from the explosion.

He flexed the stick experimentally, peeling off and heading out over the forest, away from the heaviest concentration of machine-gun fire. The Flanker was still responsive but felt slightly off. Keeping an eye on the damage indicator, he waggled the wings, trying to determine the extent of the damage. Probably nothing more than a bent flap. The plane was still airworthy. But Hawke knew he couldn't take many more hits like that.

He checked the ammo counter—eighty-eight rounds remaining.

His breath hitched as the realization hit him. He'd damaged a handful of vehicles, destroyed some fuel and ammo, but it wasn't nearly enough to stop the invasion force.

He could theoretically make another pass, provided he didn't get shot down in the process. But unless he could do substantially more damage, the odds of stopping Mulmuscovy's army from reaching its goal were now vanishingly small.

For the first time since Fitz's death, he felt the weight of futility bearing down on him.

He recalled what Stoke had said about their absent friend.

"*Fitz always said he didn't plan on dying of old age.* Looks like I won't either."

But Fitz *had* died, swept away deep beneath a foreign city, without even a body left to bury. *And for what?*

For you, old boy. He died saving you, Hawke told himself.

He shook his head slowly.

This can't be for nothing.

Think, Alex.

He scanned the HUD, looking for inspiration. Saw the blinking yellow damage alert, the fuel gauge—ironically, he still had over 4,000 pounds, more than enough to get him out of Russia—then the weapons menu caught his eye.

The 30mm cannon wasn't his only offensive weapon.

The Flanker carried six missiles—four medium-range radar-guided R-27ERs and two heat-seeking short-range R-73s. The missiles were designed to intercept fast-moving aircraft at altitude, not strike stationary or slow-moving ground targets. The targeting system wouldn't even lock onto the vehicles below.

But they didn't need to. A missile was still a missile, and with their warheads and speed, they could cause devastation even without a lock. The targeting system might not understand what he was doing, but physics didn't care.

Not perfect, he thought, *but it'll have to do.*

He brought the Flanker into another wide turn, lining up on the highway once more. Directly ahead, the column was in disarray. Many of the vehicles had switched off their headlights, their outlines barely visible against the faint glow of fires scattered along the road. They had learned from his previous passes, trading visibility for a chance at concealment. Farther back, the wreckage of several vehicles burned like a runway beacon, guiding him in.

He toggled to missile controls and armed an R-27ER. The HUD flashed a red warning in Cyrillic. Hawke didn't need a translation.

No lock.

Keeping the reticle centered on the highway, he murmured, "Fox one," purely out of habit, and then pressed the release.

The missile streaked away, its exhaust flare briefly illuminating the cockpit. Even as it flew free, he had toggled to the next weapon and fired again.

And again.

One after another, the Flanker's radar-guided missiles tore from their pylons, arcing downward toward the highway below.

The first explosion blossomed in a blinding flash as a five-tonner erupted in a ball of fire and shrapnel. The second missile struck a moment later, blasting a crater in the middle of the highway and flipping a pair of Tigrs that were passing to either side.

The rest of the missiles struck in quick succession, ripping apart vehicles and scattering men like leaves in a storm. The highway below was transformed into a nightmare of fire and twisted metal.

Yet, even as Hawke unleashed hell, the ground force returned it. Rounds were hammering into the aircraft. One burst through the deck between his legs and perforated the canopy above. The cockpit filled with alarms; the HUD flashed red messages of impending doom. Smoke was filling the cabin.

All of that would have been tolerable, but when the stick went slack in his hands, Hawke knew that the game was up.

He reached for the ejection handle between his knees and gave it a sharp tug. The canopy blew away with an explosive crack, the sudden decompression wrenching at his body as air howled into the cockpit. Hawke gripped the side rails instinctively, bracing for what he knew would come next.

The rocket motors in the ejection seat ignited with a thunderous bang, driving him down into the seat, compressing his spine, momentarily crushing his vision into a narrowing tunnel. His chest felt like it had been hit by a wrecking ball, and his head snapped back despite the helmet's snug fit.

As the seat cleared the canopy, Hawke managed to reach up and grab the bar mounted above his chest—an automatic reaction drilled into every aviator to stabilize the body during the ejection sequence.

Below him, the Flanker continued its doomed flight for only a few seconds more before crashing into the forest canopy in a fiery explosion.

The seat continued its upward arc, carried by momentum and the force of the rocket motor. A millisecond that felt like an eternity later, the drogue chute deployed, slowing the rising trajectory and stabilizing the seat as it reached apogee and began heeling over. Hawke remembered, barely, to unclench his grip on the bar, letting go just as the main parachute deployed with a sharp crack. The sudden deceleration jerked him free of the seat, and he was left dangling beneath the canopy.

He seemed to hang there, suspended beneath the parachute, but he was in fact plummeting toward the ground and would be there in mere seconds. The harness bit into his shoulders and thighs as he dangled in the cold night air, his ears still ringing from the ejection. Every muscle in his body felt bruised, but he was alive, and there was no better feeling than that.

The wind was carrying him laterally—he judged he had drifted nearly a quarter mile from the ejection site—but the highway and the remnants of Mulmuscovy's army were still disturbingly close.

His gloved hands found the risers, and he flared the chute to slow his descent while he began looking for a safe spot to land. Below and behind him, the invasion force was in chaos—burning wreckage, scattered vehicles—but he did not fail to notice a line of headlights breaking away from the main element and leaving the road behind, moving slowly but purposefully through the trees.

Moving toward him.

FIFTY-EIGHT

The parachute snapped and popped above as Hawke descended toward the dark forest. A small clearing caught his eye—a patch of open ground surrounded by dense foliage—and he tugged at the risers, guiding the canopy toward it.

Nevertheless, the ground was coming up fast, and the last few feet came too quickly.

Hawke hit the ground hard, the impact jarring every bone in his body, driving the air from his lungs. He managed, just barely, to pitch himself sideways as he'd been trained, rolling twice before coming to rest on his back, momentarily stunned.

The parachute tugged insistently at his harness, a light breeze filling the canopy like a sail. Gritting his teeth through the pain, Hawke fumbled with the quick-release catches, working blind in the darkness, but he found the clasp and gave it a pull. The harness popped loose, the tension on his chest easing as the chute came free and was carried away by the breeze. He rolled over, got to his hands and knees, then tore off his helmet, casting it aside. Without its protective insulation, the growl of approaching engines filled his ears.

Hawke wrestled out of his parachute pack, feeling the standard survival kit tethered to it. He opened it and reached in, searching the contents—knife, medical kit, torch—until his hand finally closed over the familiar shape of a pistol grip. He drew it out and then slung the pack over one shoulder and got to his feet.

The engine noise was growing louder now, and he could see the diffuse glow of headlights filtering through the surrounding forest. Ignoring the protest of his bruised body, he broke into a sprint, running away from the approaching lights.

The darkness was both ally and enemy, shielding him from the view of his pursuers but making every step a gamble. Low-hanging tree branches broke against him. The uneven ground threatened to trip him up. But then even the cover of darkness was taken from him as headlights penetrated the tree line, casting shadows across his path.

The Tigrs were closing in. He could hear the growling of their engines and the sound of tires grinding over roots and uneven ground. The noise seemed to be coming from everywhere—not just behind him but to either side—encircling him, corralling him like a wolf pack herding its prey to the kill.

Hawke ducked down behind the rotting trunk of a falling tree. His breath misted in the cold air, hanging about him like a fog, catching the light.

Fifty feet away, a Tigr emerged from the trees, moving cautiously through the understory, weaving around the boughs. The beam of a high-intensity torch lanced out from the turret, sweeping the surrounding terrain.

A second set of headlights crept into view from the other direction, their pale glow intensifying as the vehicle drew close and then roared into view, practically right on top of him.

He clenched his fists, every instinct screaming at him to run. But where? Every direction seemed blocked, every step taking him closer to being cornered.

A sudden movement caught Hawke's eye—a shadow darting through the periphery of his vision. His hand tightened around the pistol as a deer, spooked by the oncoming vehicles, burst from the underbrush, leaping into the air with an effortless grace that startled him.

Then, the deep throaty roar of a Kord 12.7mm machine gun filled the air as the gunner on the nearest Tigr opened up, evidently targeting the movement. Bark and splinters exploded as the rounds tore into trunks, filling the air with a pall of woodsmoke. The deer was lost from view, its fate uncertain, but Hawke doubted it could have survived the barrage.

He seized the opportunity provided by the distraction, bounding up and sprinting at a perpendicular angle to the vehicle's direction of travel. Adrenaline coursed through his veins, numbing the aches and pains from his earlier bruises. It lent him wings as he leapt over roots and crashed through undergrowth, the darkness his only shield.

Another eruption of machine-gun fire shattered the night, this time chasing after him. The bullets tore through the air—not the wasplike buzz of smaller rounds but a heavier, deeper crack, like little thunderclaps, as the massive projectiles split the atmosphere. The rounds, each nearly the diameter of a man's finger, slammed into tree trunks like sledgehammer blows. Wood splinters sprayed like shrapnel, cutting into his face and hands. The sharp tang of woodsmoke intensified, mingling with the scent of disturbed earth.

Something slapped his upper arm, nearly knocking him flat, and he felt a bloom of heat against his skin. A miss, he knew, but a close one. Had the bullet struck even half an inch closer, it would have ripped through muscle and bone, taking his arm—and perhaps his life—with it. The mere proximity of the 12.7mm round passing close—the heat and friction generated by the projectile, left his arm throbbing. He stumbled but kept going, reaching the cover of the tree line.

The growl of the Tigrs' engines filled the forest behind him. Hawke's lungs were burning, his legs screamed for rest, but he didn't slow. He knew the moment he stopped running, he was finished.

Sporadic bursts of heavy machine-gun fire continued to rip into the forest, the gunners either shooting at shadows or trying to flush him out. Then a new sound joined the cacophony, the slower, deeper hollow thump of an automatic grenade launcher.

The first volley came as a series of quick, muted bursts. A few seconds later, a section of forest, maybe a hundred yards away, erupted in chaos as a cluster of 30mm grenades detonated in rapid succession. The blasts lit up the darkness with rapid orange flashes, like firecrackers exploding in rapid sequence.

Another burst followed this one much closer. Multiple pressure waves struck him like hammerblows, the explosions lighting up the night. A tree not ten yards to his right exploded, its trunk sheared in half, sending its upper section crashing to the ground.

Hawke threw himself flat, shielding his face as debris rained down around him. His ears rang from the concussive force, and the heat of the blasts lingered in the air like an invisible shroud. The air was thick with smoke and the acrid stench of explosives. Fires sprang to life where the grenades had ignited dry foliage, their flames licking hungrily at the undergrowth. The men hunting him were setting the forest ablaze to flush him out.

He bound up and began running again, seeking only the darkness of the deep woods. Another burst of grenades arced into the forest ahead of him, their detonations lighting up the night like a chain of firecrackers. He veered to the left, only to stumble into a patch of open ground where the light from the fires left him completely exposed. He pressed on, his mind racing for options, but his momentum faltered as a Tigr rolled into view directly ahead, its headlights cutting through the smoky haze like twin lances. The vehicle came to a stop, its turret gun slowly swiveling toward him.

Before Hawke could even think about turning and fleeing back into the forest, he heard the sound of more engines grinding and growling from behind him. More Tigrs closing in, their beams sweeping across the clearing like searchlights.

He was surrounded.

The clearing offered no cover, no refuge. The surrounding woods were quickly becoming an inferno.

This was the end. There was no escape, no miracle to save him this time. Yet, as the realization crystallized in his mind, he found himself strangely calm.

He wouldn't cower. He wouldn't let them have the satisfaction.

Squaring his shoulders, he faced the enemy vehicle to the front, daring its occupants to come for him. Even though it was little more than a symbolic show of defiance, he brought his pistol up and took aim at the dim silhouette of the turret gunner behind his shield.

If this was the end, he would meet it on his feet.

But the next thing Hawke knew, he was on his back, staring up into nothingness. The world was a blur of firelight, smoke, and shadows. The acrid tang of burning fuel filled his nostrils, sharp and sickening, as he struggled to catch his breath. His ears were ringing—again—but through it he could just hear the muffled sound of explosions and gunfire.

And the ground beneath him was shaking.

His fingers dug into the dirt, searching for some anchor to reality. He rolled onto his side, his vision swimming, and tried to make sense of it all. The only thing he knew for sure was that he was still alive, but whether that was a good thing or not, it was still too early to tell.

He gradually realized that the Tigr he had been facing down was gone now—or, rather, it had been transformed into a sculpture of twisted metal and flame.

He blinked, trying to clear the haze from his vision. The heat of the nearby flames licked at his face, casting flickering shadows over the devastation around him. His body ached, his limbs felt leaden, but he forced himself to sit up. Slowly, shapes began to resolve out of the chaos.

Behind him, two more Tigrs were burning. Their hulking silhouettes twisted grotesquely in the inferno, black smoke curling into the night sky.

Above the din of battle, a new sound emerged—a rhythmic thrum that vibrated through the air and set his teeth on edge. Hawke tilted his head back, squinted through the stinging smoke, and finally saw them.

A pair of helicopters were hovering above the clearing, just high enough to be out of ground effect. They were running dark, barely distinguishable against the night sky, but he could tell from their profiles that they were attack aircraft—gunships.

Farther away, the whoosh of rockets launching and the distant crump of explosions carried through the smoke-filled air. The invasion force was under attack, their vehicles and troops scattering like ants beneath the relentless assault. Someone, it seemed, had come to finish what he had begun.

But who? And why?

He was still pondering this when the attack helicopters began moving off, leaving him alone amid the wreckage. A moment of eerie calm settled over the clearing, but then the rhythmic beat of rotor blades returned, growing steadily louder.

A helicopter appeared above him—not a wasp-shaped gunship but a wide-bodied transport. A troop carrier. And it was coming down practically on top of him.

His instincts screamed at him to move. He began looking around for his pistol, but before he could locate it, the helicopter was settling onto the ground a short distance away and camouflaged figures were spilling out of its cabin—Russian troops. These were not mercenaries in disguise but the real deal.

In seconds they had surrounded him, weapons trained on him and eyes sharp behind their goggles. Hawke froze, his hands instinctively going up, palms outward, a gesture of caution and surrender.

Well, that answers the "Who?" Hawke thought.

Another figure emerged from the helicopter. He was outfitted in full combat kit, but unlike the men surrounding Hawke, he wasn't carrying a rifle. His only weapon, a pistol, was holstered at his thigh.

When he reached the circle of soldiers guarding Hawke, he gestured for them to lower their weapons. Somewhat reluctantly, they complied.

The man then knelt down beside him, leaning close to be heard over the din of the helicopter.

"Lord Hawke," he said, his English surprisingly clear. "I'm pleased to find you still among the living."

Hawke regarded the man coolly for a moment before replying. "I'm afraid you have me at a disadvantage."

"Major General Ivan Grigorov, 76th Guards Air Assault Division."

"I'd like to say it's a pleasure to meet you, General, but that will depend on what your intentions are for me."

The faintest hint of a smile flickered across Grigorov's face. "Lord Hawke, I assure you, we have only the best of intentions. But, please, let's discuss this somewhere more comfortable. Are you injured?"

Hawke ignored the question. "Am I your prisoner?"

Grigorov looked aghast. "Prisoner? You are a hero of the Russian people."

"Hero?" Hawke remained wary. "How did you know where to find me?"

Grigorov shrugged. "I am a soldier. I follow orders. I don't question them. And the order to save you came from Prime Minister Mishustin. We were told where to begin looking for you. You did the rest when you attacked this rogue army."

Hawke's breath caught. "The Prime Minister? How did he know about any of this?"

Grigorov gave him a sly grin. "As I said, I don't question my orders, but from what I've heard, it seems that your woman was very persuasive."

"Anastasia?" Hawke's mind raced to keep up with this revelation.

When she had left him, he'd thought that was the end of it. Evidently, however, she had decided to take a different approach to solving the problem of Sergei Mulmuscovy—and saving her beloved—and had used her contacts to reach the Russian leadership—and not just reach them but convince them to intervene.

For the first time in what felt like hours, Hawke allowed himself to believe he might survive the night.

"Now," Grigorov said, his tone softening slightly, "shall we go?"

Hawke hesitated only a fraction of a second before nodding. "Lead on, old chap."

FIFTY-NINE

PARIS, FRANCE

Located on the ground floor of a Haussmannian building on the rue Bonaparte, just a short stroll from the Église Saint-Sulpice, tucked between a gourmet chocolatier and a designer draper, La Cave Élégante appeared unremarkable from the outside. The establishment was, in fact, one of the finest wine salons in Paris, catering exclusively to discerning connoisseurs and collectors who sought not merely to purchase bottles but to experience them. Aside from the gilt letters painted on the glass of the entry door—the establishment's name in elegant script, and below in smaller block face, the words *"Uniquement sur rendez-vous"*—there was little to distinguish it, or even offer a hint to what sort of business was conducted inside.

It was wine that had brought Ambrose Congreve to Paris, but while he once might have considered himself something of an oenophile, on this day his interest in the product of the vine had nothing at all to do with appreciating its gourmet attributes.

As he was reaching for the doorbell button, he caught a glimpse of his reflection in the glass and did not recognize the face that looked back at him. Although scarcely a week had passed since losing Diana, he seemed diminished, hollowed out. His normally plump and rosy cheeks were gaunt, the shadows under his eyes more pronounced, and the usual spark in his bright blue eyes seemed to have been snuffed out entirely. Only the grim certainty of purpose kept him going.

He could not bring Diana back, but he could see her avenged.

Officially, Congreve had been prohibited from active participation in the investigation, but no force on earth could have stopped him from finding her murderer. He had thrown himself into the hunt with all the determination of a man who had nothing left to lose, for indeed that was the case.

Identifying the twin sisters in the photograph had given Diana's killer a face but not a name. The passports they had used were expert forgeries, the names mere aliases, and efforts to trace their origins had come to naught. He did not know which one of them had adopted the nom de guerre "Silence" or if they used the name collectively. What he did know was that one sister had been masquerading as Dr. Ariadne Silk, accompanying Alex Hawke on a mission to Russia in order to frame Hawke for the assassination of the Russian president, while her twin had remained behind to kill Ariadne Silk and the few close acquaintances who might have revealed the substitution. When Congreve's investigation had gotten too close, Silence had come after Diana, thinking that killing her might put Congreve off the scent. In that, she had badly miscalculated. Nevertheless, by the time Congreve, with help from King Charles, had identified them, Diana's murderer had already slipped off the radar. The trail had gone cold, and Congreve had been left with just one clue—the killer's penchant for Château Pichon Baron, 2015.

That clue had brought him here.

He took a breath and then pressed the doorbell. The soft chime echoed faintly beyond the glass. A moment later the door opened, and Congreve found himself face-to-face with an elegant young brunette. Her hair was cut stylishly short, framing a face that was expertly made up to sharpen her cheekbones and accentuate her lips. She wore a tailored suit, impeccably pressed, to accentuate her lithe frame.

"Mademoiselle Durand?" asked Congreve, though he already knew to whom he was speaking.

"Oui," she replied, continuing in French. "And you must be Monsieur Sayers? Welcome to La Cave Élégante."

"Not exactly," he said, in the same language. "There is no Monsieur Sayers. I used the name to secure the appointment for reasons which I will explain presently. My name is Congreve. Chief Inspector Congreve of Scotland Yard."

The woman, with the delightful name of Élodie Durand, regarded him with a look of faint annoyance. "Scotland Yard? This is most irregular. And inappropriate. Coming here under false pretenses . . ." She tsked. "If you wanted to talk to me, you should have simply asked. And what does a police officer want with me anyway?"

Congreve gave her a measured look. "In my experience, most people tend to have difficulty finding the time to meet with police officials." He paused a beat before adding, "Even those with nothing to hide."

Her frown deepened. "I, of course, have nothing to hide. It's just that this is my livelihood. While I am talking to you, I could be seeing other customers. Paying customers. And I don't appreciate being lied to."

"Be that as it may, I do have some questions for you. I assure you, I require only a few moments of your time. And, of course, your expertise."

"Expertise?" She eyed him suspiciously. "I sell wine. What sort of expertise do I possess that could be of use to a policeman?"

"Your reputation precedes you, Mademoiselle Durand. You are one of the foremost authorities on fine wine in Paris."

She gave an exasperated sigh. "Very well," she said, switching smoothly to English, which she spoke with just a trace of an accent. "A few moments. Please, won't you come in."

The air inside La Cave Élégante was cool and faintly perfumed with the rich bouquet of aged oak and cork. The space was elegant, understated, and immaculately arranged. Floor-to-ceiling racks displayed an impressive array of bottles and wooden crates. In the center of the room, a sleek marble counter gleamed under pendant lights, flanked by high-backed stools upholstered in leather.

Élodie pulled one of the stools around to the other side of the counter and gestured for Congreve to take the seat across from her. "Now, Chief Inspector. What is it that brings you to my door under such . . . unconventional circumstances?"

Congreve made a show of looking around the salon before bringing his attention back to her. "I am interested in learning more about a particular vintage. Château Pichon Baron, Grand Vin, 2015."

Élodie arched a delicate brow, a faint smile playing at the corners of her lips. "Château Pichon Baron?" she repeated, her tone both amused and faintly condescending. "The 2015 is an excellent vintage, to be sure. Well-balanced, with impeccable structure. I'd say it's a fine introduction to Bordeaux—approachable, reliable." Her smile widened, though it did not quite reach her eyes. "But if you're interested in the Pichon Baron, I'm afraid you've come to the wrong place, Chief Inspector. My clientele tends to prefer selections that are a little more . . . unique. A bottle of Pichon Baron might fetch a few hundred euros, which is perfectly respectable for what it is, but I specialize in vintages that sell for thousands."

Congreve gave a small nod as though absorbing this with interest. "I see. So you wouldn't typically stock it here?"

"I do not," she replied smoothly. "It does not align with the expectations of my patrons. They come to me for the exceptional, not the . . . pedestrian." She leaned forward slightly, her hands resting lightly on the counter. "But now you have made me curious, Chief Inspector. Why are you interested in the Pichon Baron?"

"As it happens, it's associated with a series of rather gruesome murders."

Élodie's eyes widened in a look of horror. "My God. How terrible."

"Quite. A bottle of the 2015 was left at the scene in each case. Rather like a calling card, you might say."

Comprehension dawned in Élodie's eyes. "Ah, now I understand. You are thinking that if you can trace the sales of this wine, you might find the person responsible for these murders."

Congreve tilted his head slightly. "I imagine such a task is easier said than done."

"Indeed it is, Chief Inspector. Château Pichon Baron winery produces . . . I would say somewhere in the neighborhood of two hundred thousand bottles a year. The Grand Vin would make up roughly a third or more of that, so . . . eighty or ninety thousand bottles, distributed across multiple markets worldwide—to wholesalers, retailers, restaurants, and private collectors. Tracing the path of an individual bottle, or even a case, would be a monumental undertaking, even for Scotland Yard."

"A fair point." Congreve hummed thoughtfully. "Still, I believe that these bottles of wine are a thread that will lead us to the killer."

"Well, I wish you good luck," said Élodie, sliding off her stool.

Congreve remained seated. "Why do you suppose the killer chose that vintage?"

"I can't begin to imagine."

Congreve gave a patient smile. "Indulge me."

Élodie hesitated, tilting her head slightly as if weighing how much to humor him. "Well," she began, her tone cautious, "if I were to speculate—and, mind you, this is pure conjecture—I might suggest that the vintage holds some personal significance for the killer. Wine is a deeply personal matter for many, Chief Inspector. People project onto it their desires, their aspirations, their history. Perhaps it's tied to a memory, a milestone." She shrugged. "Or perhaps they just like that particular wine. It could be as simple as that."

"Interesting," Congreve mused, his voice steady and nonchalant. "And what about a family connection? Do you think a killer might choose something that ties back to their upbringing?"

"Of course. But, as I have said, this is just speculation. I don't know why killers do the things they do."

"Don't you, though?"

Something flashed in Élodie's eyes. "What are you saying, Chief Inspector?"

"I'm saying," Congreve continued, his voice cool and measured, "that you're no stranger to the workings of a killer's mind. After all, your father, Émille Durand, was suspected of being one of the most prolific contract killers in recent memory."

"That's an outrageous claim. My father was a businessman."

"A businessman," Congreve echoed with faint amusement. "Yes, that's one way to describe him. A businessman whose fortunes always seemed to rise in the wake of convenient accidents or untimely deaths. A businessman whose movements coincided far too often with the premature ends of certain high-profile individuals."

Her eyes narrowed. "That's a preposterous claim. If there were any truth to it, surely he would have been arrested, tried, and convicted."

"Scotland Yard pursued him for years, but there was never enough evidence to make the charges stick. Your father was clever. No smoking gun, so to speak. No fingerprints on the knife. Every death attributed to him could just as easily have been an accident or natural causes. A slip on the stairs, a car crash, a heart attack—each meticulously staged. We might not have even realized there was foul play involved—to say nothing of the deaths being the work of a single individual—until someone noticed a curious detail. An item found in the personal effects of each victim. A pressed flower—a rose, if memory serves—tucked into a pocket or placed somewhere near the body. At first, it seemed a coincidence, but over time it became clear that it was a message. Not to the authorities, of course, but to his clients. Proof of a job well done. Your father's little flourish, his signature."

"I don't believe any of this," Élodie said with a contemptuous flick of her hand. "Even so, if my father was guilty of these alleged crimes, why are you here speaking to me? He's been dead for years."

"That's right," Congreve said, leaning forward slightly. "I believe he shuffled off this mortal coil in . . . when was it? Oh, yes: 2015." He paused a beat. "But he set you up well enough. You . . . and your twin sister, Isaline."

Élodie said nothing.

"You were mistaken about one thing. Tracing the sales of 2015 was difficult but not impossible. And I was . . . quite motivated, you see. That's how I came across your name. You might not sell Château Pichon Baron but you did buy several cases of it a few years ago. When I saw the name Durand, I remembered our investigation of Émille Durand and decided to dig a little deeper. When I learned that Émille Durand had twin daughters, I knew I was on the right track. Identical twin daughters, carrying on the family tradition of murder for hire.

"You knew, of course, that we were looking at the passport photos of everyone who had traveled from Bermuda. Knew that we would see the picture of you and your sister and that, eventually, we would realize that your sister was impersonating Dr. Silk. You knew the net was tightening, so you decided to send a message."

He paused, the words catching in his throat, almost a groan. "That's why you killed Diana. You thought you could scare me off. You thought you could break me."

For the first time, Élodie's confident expression faltered. A flicker of something—regret?—crossed her face but vanished just as quickly.

"You almost succeeded," Congreve went on. "But Diana's death didn't break me—it gave me clarity. It gave me purpose. And now, Élodie, we're here. The end of your little charade."

Élodie's lips slowly curved into a sardonic smile. "You're very clever, Chief Inspector. And yet, you came here alone." Her hand came up from below the countertop, and in it was a small pistol aimed squarely at Congreve's chest. "How very brave . . . or very foolish."

Congreve remained perfectly still, his gaze steady, the steel returning to his voice. "And there it is. The mask slips."

"Tell me, Chief Inspector, how did you imagine this ending? Did you think I would simply allow you to put me under arrest?"

"Whether you come along or not, you must know that it's over for you. Silence is finished."

She laughed. "Finished? Hardly. I will miss this life, yes. Paris has been . . . comfortable. But this . . ." She gestured to the shop. "It's just a hobby. Most of our money is in offshore accounts. And with the payment for this last job, my sister and I will be able to start over. Anywhere in the world. New names, new faces, new lives. Silence isn't finished, Chief Inspector. But I'm afraid I can't say the same for you."

Congreve's eyes dropped briefly to the barrel of the gun, then came back to her face. "You'd be doing me a favor, you know. Reuniting me with my Diana."

He thought . . . hoped, even, that she would oblige him, but the game, it seemed, was not over yet.

"If you do," he went on, his voice harder now, the desperation slipping away, "you should know that, before I came here, I told a very good friend of mine about this. He was quite interested to hear it. Lord Alexander Hawke. I believe you've heard of him. He's quite keen to find both of you for reasons of his own."

He paused to let that sink in, then continued. "He actually wanted me to postpone this visit until his return from Russia so that he could accompany me here. He was rather fond of Diana."

He sighed. "Know this. If you pull that trigger, Alex will come after you. No matter where you go in the world, he will find you. And when he does, he won't bother arresting you or turning you over to the authorities."

Élodie's confident smile slipped. Her grip on the pistol faltered just slightly, and her gaze darted to Congreve's unwavering eyes, searching for any trace of bluff. She found none.

"I see," she said finally, her tone quieter now. "It seems you've thought this through, Chief Inspector."

Her lips pressed into a tight line, and then, with a heavy sigh, she set the pistol down on the counter and raised her hands in mock surrender. "Well, Chief Inspector," she said, her voice laced with bitterness. "It seems you've won this round."

Fast as a striking serpent, Congreve snatched the pistol off the counter and pointed it at her. For a fleeting moment he considered pulling the trigger—justice for Diana—but the thought passed quickly. That wasn't what he had come here for. With his free hand, he reached into his pocket, producing a pair of handcuffs.

"One question," he said when the cuffs were finally on. "Why the wine? Surely you must have realized that a clue like that would eventually be your undoing."

Élodie tilted her head, the faintest hint of a smile tugging at her lips. "Every artist has a signature. Just like Father with his roses. Proof of the job. And, like I said, I like that particular wine." She looked down at the steel bracelets binding her wrists. "You do realize that all you have are speculations and circumstantial evidence? Nothing that will hold up in court. My lawyers will tear your case apart."

"There won't be any lawyers," replied Congreve. "I think you'll find that MI6 has a slightly different procedure for their . . . I believe the term they use is 'detainees.'"

Her eyebrows furrowed. "MI6?"

Congreve's voice was steady, almost calm. "I'm afraid I told you another little lie, Élodie. I am a former Chief Inspector with the Yard, but I didn't come here as a copper, and I'm not turning you over to the 'proper authorities.' You'll be going somewhere far more interesting."

For the first time, genuine fear flickered across her face. The facade of cool confidence she had worn so masterfully began to crack. "You're bluffing."

By way of an answer, Congreve took out his mobile phone. When he heard the voice at the other end, he said simply, "You can bring the car around."

SIXTY

MARGARITA ISLAND, VENEZUELA

For the second time in half as many weeks, Alex Hawke flew through the sky under a parachute canopy. But unlike the short, sharp shock of ejecting from the doomed Flanker, this flight had more in common with Hawke's namesake.

Silent. Patient. Predatory.

Gliding high above the sea, not even a shadow in the vast, star-speckled expanse above the Caribbean. This time, however, he was not alone in the sky. All around him, a dozen drifting fireflies—infrared beacons, visible only in the display of his L3Harris BNVD dual-tube night vision goggles—marked the location of Stoke and a select team of operators from Thunder and Lightning. They, like him, were invisible against the night sky.

Five minutes earlier, the team had stepped out of a perfectly good airplane—a C-130 Hercules that was Thunder and Lightning's trusted warhorse—at 30,000 feet, deploying their RA-1 parachutes immediately to begin a forty-mile-long glide to their destination. This technique—a high-altitude, high-opening parachute jump, or HAHO—was not for the faint of heart. Unlike the rapid descents of HALO jumps—high-altitude, low-opening—where speed was the priority, a HAHO insertion was a slow, controlled journey, with jumpers navigating by GPS and wind patterns to glide across vast distances. Born from the need for stealthy insertions into hostile territory, HAHO jumps began with a leap from an aircraft that, to all appearances on the ground, was traveling at normal cruising altitude and speed, well clear of the restricted airspace over enemy territory. At such altitudes—higher than the summit of Mount Everest—the air was too thin to breathe, so jumpers had to use oxygen masks as well as insulated coveralls—worn over their full tactical kit—to counter the freezing temperatures. It was a grueling ordeal and not without significant risk, but it was the best way to reach their destination on Margarita Island, twenty-three miles off the coast of Venezuela, where Osman Gul and Sergei Mulmuscovy had taken up residence.

Tracking Mulmuscovy's movements had not been difficult, though by the time anyone in the Russian government realized they ought to scramble fighter planes to intercept his private jet, he was already well outside Russian airspace. He touched down first in Yerevan, Armenia, where he spent just enough time to change aircraft and rendezvous with General Gul. From there, the trail became murkier, but MI6 operatives managed to pick up the trail using a combination of satellite imagery, electronic surveillance, and good old-fashioned bribes. After a stopover in Algeria, they had boarded yet another private jet, this one taking them across the Atlantic. Their final destination was Venezuela, a country with a government more than willing to turn a blind eye to international fugitives for the right price. On Margarita Island, they found refuge in a sprawling villa nestled in the hills outside the small town of Los Robles in the island's interior. Part resort and part fortress, the compound was shielded by high walls and patrolled by hired local muscle and the last of Mulmuscovy's elite paramilitary unit, the Bastards. It was a luxurious exile, but as Hawke intended to demonstrate, not an impenetrable one.

The plan called for a twelve-man assault element, led by Hawke and Stoke, to infiltrate the island in the hills near Los Robles under the cover of darkness, breach the compound, neutralize the security force, and then eliminate or apprehend Gul and Mulmuscovy. Officially, it was a "kill or capture" mission, but Hawke was under no illusions. The powers that be, both in the West and in Russia, had little interest in seeing the two traitors have their day in court. Quiet eradication suited everyone involved. Once the mission was complete, the team would acquire vehicles and move to the coast, where the rest of Thunder and Lightning, who were even now making a covert landing on a deserted section of the island's north shore, were waiting with a pair of inflatable boats to ferry the team out to the *Blackhawke*, anchored in international waters. It was a sound plan, but as was true with all such endeavors, the enemy would get a vote.

So high up and so far from the designated landing zone, it was easy to forget that he was moving at nearly forty miles per hour and descending at a constant rate of about ten feet per second. A minor miscalculation might prove disastrous, sending him off course or dropping him short of the target. He kept a close eye on both his altimeter and his satnav, making minute adjustments to his glide path, working the toggles to counter shifting winds or correct subtle deviations to ensure that he would be over the LZ when he ran out of sky.

The faint outline of the island gradually came into view. In the display of his night vision goggles, the island stood out from the dark sea, even though most of the island remained shrouded in darkness due to the widespread and endemic power outages that plagued Venezuela's cities. There were, however, a few faint points of light on the island, likely the homes of wealthier residents who produced their own electricity with generators.

As he passed over the island's coastline, Hawke checked his altimeter again: 5,000 feet. The margin for error was narrowing with every second, but he was still within that margin. At 2,000 feet, the ground features became clearer in the display of his goggles: dirt roads, patches of scrub, and the jagged silhouettes of low trees. His muscles tensed as he prepared for the landing, angling his descent to ensure a smooth touchdown in the clearing. Stoke's calm voice sounded in his earpiece. "Two minutes to the LZ. Let's watch our spacing."

Hawke did not reply. There was no need, and this close to the ground, a lot of unnecessary radio chatter was a distraction none of them needed.

In those last few moments in the sky, he could just make out the compound, a dark rectangle about a quarter mile from their designated LZ. They'd all pored over the satellite images, committing every inch of the terrain to memory, but there was a stark difference between the lifeless, grainy shots and seeing it firsthand. Hawke scanned the walls and noted the gatehouse, which appeared unmanned, and the flat-topped roofs of the structures inside. Everything was still, no lights shone, and there were no telltale flickers of patrols moving about or shifting shadows along the perimeter.

Too bloody quiet, he thought.

One by one, the assault team came down on the LZ, shedding their parachutes and getting clear as quickly as they could before calling in that they were on the ground and battle-ready. Then it was Hawke's turn.

As the altimeter ticked down to nothing, Hawke finessed the toggles, adjusting his trajectory to align with the narrow stretch of hillside they had identified as the landing zone. The terrain rushed up to meet him, details snapping into focus through his night vision goggles. Rocks. Shrubs. A cluster of thorny trees off to the left. No room for error now. He braced for impact, legs bent, body leaning slightly forward, and pulled hard on the toggles, flaring the canopy for maximum breaking just before his boots hit the ground. Compared to his ejection from the Flanker, the landing felt featherlight.

The parachute canopy, still full of air, caught the breeze, threatening to drag him across the landscape, so he yanked the release toggles, collapsing the canopy and allowing him to haul it in and jam it into a stuff sack even as he moved clear of the LZ. When he had the chute stowed, along with his oxygen rig, he took a knee and brought his suppressed HK417 to low ready.

"Buccaneer is set," he whispered into his comms, utilizing the call sign Stoke had tagged him with. He generally disliked such foolishness—it was too much like something from a Tom Clancy novel—but in this instance it felt oddly appropriate. His pirate ancestor had once raided along the Venezuelan coast. Now, four hundred–odd years later, another Hawke hunted here. The wheel of time had come around again.

He listened intently as the last few remaining jumpers sounded off and allowed himself a moment of satisfaction when the final man was down. No mishaps, no injuries. So far, so good.

He stripped off his thermal coveralls and added them to the stuff bag, then picked up and moved back to the center of the LZ where Boomer and Stoke were waiting. Like him, they were outfitted in Crye Precision G4 combat uniforms with Adaptive Vest System (AVS) plate carriers and Ops-Core FAST SF helmets to which their night vision goggles were affixed.

"What do you think?" he asked.

"Too quiet," murmured Boomer.

"Like a goddamned ghost town," added Stoke.

Hawke nodded. "I was thinking rather the same thing."

"You think they've already bugged out?"

Hawke had considered this possibility. "They've got nowhere else to go."

"Could be they're sitting tight," suggested Boomer. "Practicing light discipline. Keeping a low profile."

"You think they might be expecting visitors?" asked Stoke.

"I'd be surprised if they weren't. Gul and Mulmuscovy are the most wanted men on earth right now." Hawke sighed. "I suppose we'll find out when we find out."

"Stick to the plan?"

Hawke nodded. "Boomer, you take Red Team and get up on that wall. You'll be our eyes and ears on the approach. See if you can't get a better look. But carefully. We can't afford to lose the element of surprise."

Boomer nodded once, already shifting his stance to lead his team.

"Stoke, you and I will take Blue Team in through the gate. Once we're inside, we regroup at the courtyard."

"Easy peasy," said Stoke.

"Let's hope so." Hawke paused a beat, giving the other men a chance to offer some last-second input, then said, "Let's move."

The teams coalesced behind their leaders and then flowed into the woods. Hawke took point with Stoke, moving with a stealthy, heel-to-toe, rolling gait. Even so, they covered the ground quickly, halting their advance just two hundred yards from the main gate. The gravel road, the only way to access the compound by vehicle, was about fifty yards to the right. The gate was a sturdy structure of steel bars. High concrete walls, their tops lined with jagged shards of broken glass mortared in place, extended outward in both directions, hemming in the perimeter. Just outside the gate, slightly off the road, stood the gatehouse, a low, square building of concrete and steel.

From this vantage, Hawke raised his rifle and studied the gatehouse through the attached optics. The Trijicon 4x32-power Advanced Combat Optical Gunsight (ACOG) sharpened his view of the little shack but revealed little else of interest. The interior was dark, and there was no sign of activity inside. Yet, as he crouched there, watching, he caught the faint, familiar scent of tobacco smoke in the air. There was someone inside, and they were smoking a cigarette. A sudden faint glow—eerily white in the infrared display of his night vision device—confirmed it. The guard had just taken another drag.

"Those things will bloody kill you, mate," murmured Hawke.

The mere fact of the guard's presence removed any doubt as to whether the compound was occupied but raised some new concerns.

The blackout conditions spoke to a heightened state of readiness. The men inside were expecting trouble.

Hawke broke squelch on his commo mic twice—a silent check-in. Boomer's voice came through a moment later. "Two on the perimeter, patrolling clockwise. Another one on the front porch, main entrance. No movement aside from that."

Hawke replied in a whisper. "We've got least one in the gatehouse, having a fag. No visible activity otherwise."

"Perimeter team is set on the west side. Clear sight lines to the porch and the patrols. Sharpshooters are in place. We can drop them on your signal."

"The signal is two clicks. Buccaneer out." Hawke turned back to his team and made a circling gesture—a signal to sweep wide and come up on the back side of the gatehouse.

They moved in a stealthy single file, pushing deeper into the woods before hooking back in the direction of the wall and approaching the gatehouse from its rear corner. Hawke moved with his weapon at the high ready, prepared to engage at the first sign of movement from inside the little shack.

Hawke gestured for the bulk of the team to hang back and cover him; then he and Stoke crept up to the corner of the building, stacking for a dynamic entry. Then he broke squelch twice again.

After a few seconds of total quiet, Boomer's voice sounded in his ear. "Tangos down."

Hawke raised three fingers and rocked back against Stoke once, twice, and on the third bump he moved forward, hooking around the far corner and through the open door. He immediately saw the guard seated in a chair in one corner of the structure, cigarette held to his lips with one hand, eyes shining like bright silver dimes in the display of Hawke's night vision device. His weapon—an old AK-47—was tilted up against the wall.

Hawke squeezed his trigger twice. Even with the suppressor, the shots came as loud bangs in the little enclosure. The man slumped forward, the cigarette falling from his lips onto the floor.

"Told you," whispered Hawke.

Stoke had entered right behind him, covering the opposite corner, just in case, but there was no need. The guard had been alone.

Hawke keyed his mic again. "Gatehouse is clear. Move in and sweep toward the main residence. We'll meet you there."

He gave the interior a quick once-over. That was all it took. Aside from the chair, there was a small side table on which sat an overflowing ashtray, an empty coffee cup, and a Baofeng handheld radio. Stoke knelt beside the fallen guard and turned out his pockets.

"Cancer sticks," Stoke muttered. "Cell phone. No keys."

"All right, let's have a look at the gate."

They slipped out of the gatehouse, stepping cautiously onto the gravel path that led to the main gate. The gate was of the sliding variety, mounted on heavy rollers embedded in a steel track set into the ground. There was no obvious latch. Hawke gave it a gentle push to see if that was all it would take to open it, but the frame did not budge.

"Must be motor-operated," he remarked. "See a control panel anywhere?"

"Nope."

Hawke frowned at the delay. Boomer's team was likely already moving through the compound and was counting on them to bring up their end. "Must be controlled from somewhere inside. A security office. The gate guard probably radios when he needs to open it."

"We ain't got time to mess around with it," said Stoke. "Maybe we can muscle this thing open."

Before Hawke could weigh in on this course of action, Stoke braced himself, grabbed the upright steel bars, and leaned into it like he was hitting a tackling dummy. Somewhere on the other side, there was a scraping noise as the gears and rotors of a mechanism were forced to move, and then the gate slid open a few inches.

"Got it!" Stoke said, panting.

Then an earsplitting wail erupted from somewhere within the compound. Floodlights flared to life, casting harsh white beams over the courtyard, illuminating the gate.

"Bollocks," muttered Hawke. "So much for the element of surprise."

SIXTY-ONE

Sergei Yevgenyevich Mulmuscovy woke with a start to the piercing wail of the alarm. For one disoriented moment he didn't know where he was. When the moment passed, the nightmare began.

He had known what it was like to be afraid. Growing up under the Soviet regime, dealing with black marketeers and organized crime figures, and later, navigating the uncertain political landscape of Putin's Russia, he had spent more than a few sleepless nights worried about an old vendetta resurfacing or the sudden reckoning for a deal gone wrong. But this was different. This was an existential crisis. The SVR would come for him. It was only a matter of time.

He had orchestrated Putin's assassination with the certainty that his schemes would leave him untouchable. But now, with the failed false flag operation in Estonia, his crimes were laid bare for all to see. No one would care that he had done it all for the glory of Mother Russia. He had already been branded a traitor; his death warrant had been signed. The SVR would not rest until the blood debt was paid. No corner of the earth was safe from their operatives, their poisons, their assassins who made death look like chance. And if they didn't get to him, there was no shortage of Western nations eager to see him hang for his crimes. The fortress on Margarita Island, the armed guards, the Bastards—they were only temporary measures to stave off the inevitable reckoning.

He blamed Osman Gul.

I never should have gotten in bed with him, he thought bitterly. *Never should have let him draw me into his crazy schemes.*

He sat up, sweat already slicking his chest despite the cool air of the villa's air-conditioning, dressed quickly, and reached for the GSh-18 on the nightstand. The pistol felt reassuringly solid in his hand for all the good it would do him.

As he reached for the door, it swung open to reveal Yuri, the chief of his Bastards—his face still black-and-blue from an injury sustained during Hawke's escape attempt in Sochi—standing there with rifle in hand.

"Sir," the man said, his voice clipped and urgent. "There has been an incursion."

Mulmuscovy's stomach churned. "Who?"

Yuri shook his head. "We don't know. They took out perimeter guards and breached the gate. It's not clear yet how many, but they're professionals."

Of course they are, he thought. *Nothing but the best for Sergei Yevgenyevich.*

Yuri gestured toward the hallway. "We must get you to the bunker."

Mulmuscovy hesitated for only a second before nodding and following Yuri down the villa's hallways. Over the wail of the alarm, he could hear the crackle of gunfire outside.

Yuri led him to a long staircase tucked behind a false panel in the wall. They descended quickly, the narrow concrete steps lit by a harsh fluorescent glow, and came to a heavy steel vault door nearly three feet thick, standing open. This was the reason he had chosen the property for his refuge: an underground bunker designed to withstand nearly anything short of a direct missile strike, with reinforced walls, an independent air filtration system, and enough supplies to last for weeks.

Not that it would matter in the long run.

As he stepped into the bunker, he immediately noticed Osman Gul, dressed in an elegant silk robe over matching pajamas, sitting in a chair near the surveillance monitors. Mulmuscovy felt an immediate surge of contempt at seeing the would-be Ottoman emperor. *My God*, he thought. *The only thing missing is a fez.*

He turned to Yuri. "Hold them off as long as you can," he told him. "I will contact my friend in the government. Reinforcements will be here soon."

Yuri gave a terse nod. If he had any reservations about being sent off to face death while his employer hid in a concrete panic room, it did not show on his face. He stepped back out onto the landing and started up the stairs. Mulmuscovy hit a button on the wall, and the door began to move, swinging ponderously into its frame. Once it was seated, there was a pneumatic hiss and the clank of a dozen steel locking bolts, each as thick as a man's thumb, sliding into place.

Mulmuscovy exhaled sharply. He knew he should take comfort in the security afforded by the blast door, but it felt more like being sealed in a tomb, buried alive.

He turned back to the security station, taking a seat beside Gul and placing his pistol on the countertop in front of him, then studied the moving images on the monitors. The villa's security cameras provided an incomplete view of the assault, with grainy feeds jumping between different angles of the compound. He caught glimpses of shadows moving through the trees, flashes of gunfire, and the limp forms of his men crumpling into the dirt.

They were losing. Badly.

"Who are they?" Gul asked, his voice composed but edged with unease.

Mulmuscovy grunted. "Does it matter? They're winning."

He cycled through the feeds, searching for anything that might give them an advantage. One camera showed a team stacking against the main entrance. Another revealed a pair of figures slipping around the perimeter, weapons raised, moving with the kind of coordinated precision that only came from years of specialized military training.

One of them stepped into full view, just long enough for Mulmuscovy to get a good look at him. Tall. Powerfully built. A Black man whose face was half hidden by night vision goggles.

A chill crawled down his spine.

He knew this man. Had seen him before.

In Russia.

Right before everything turned to shit.

"Hawke is here," he said in a low voice.

Gul glanced over at him. "How do you know?"

Mulmuscovy rewound one of the feeds and froze the frame on Hawke's big companion. "That Black *obez'yana* works with him. If he's here, Hawke is here."

Gul's thin lips curled into a sneer. "Twice now this man has interfered with my plans. If you had dealt with him when you had the chance, perhaps we would not be in this situation." He lowered his voice to a barely audible murmur. "Perhaps I should go up there and handle him myself."

Mulmuscovy stared at him, incredulous. "You?" He let out a harsh bark of laughter. "You're going to waltz up there in your silk pajamas and handle Alex Hawke? Be my guest." He gestured toward the door. "By all means, go. I'll even unlock it for you."

Gul glowered at him a moment but then made a dismissive gesture. "It doesn't matter. They can't get in here. Call your contact in the government. Have them deploy the military. They will handle this incursion."

Mulmuscovy stared at him. "You still don't understand what we're up against, do you?" he growled. "We're dead men. Even if we survive this, even if they leave, the SVR will come for us. The West will come for us. You think Venezuela will keep sheltering us after this? The moment we become more trouble than we're worth, they'll sell us out. Or kill us themselves. This"—he gestured toward the monitors—"is the cost of your madness. Your pipe dream of restoring the Ottoman Empire . . . You've made us targets for every intelligence agency on the planet. If they don't kill us tonight, it'll be tomorrow or the day after."

Gul's eyes narrowed. "*My* madness? You were more than happy to embrace my madness when it suited you."

"I didn't sign up for this," Mulmuscovy snapped, pointing at the screen.

"This is just a temporary setback. I have supporters in Ankara, men in high places, who are ready to move. Erdoğan's grip is slipping, and when the time comes, they will welcome me as their rightful leader."

Mulmuscovy shook his head, half in disbelief, half in bitter amusement. He had known Gul was ambitious, but until this moment he hadn't truly understood the depths of his self-deception. The man was talking about a grand return to power while the walls were closing in around them.

This is the man I staked my future on?

His gaze came back to the scenes displayed on the security monitors and then drifted to the pistol resting on the counter.

Maybe it's not too late to change my bet.

SIXTY-TWO

Sporadic gunfire from an upper-story balcony of the main house raked the courtyard as Hawke and his team advanced methodically using a bounding overwatch technique, taking turns covering one another with suppressive fire. While Hawke and two of his shooters hosed the balcony with short bursts, Stoke and the others sprinted forward, skidding behind a decorative fountain as stray rounds shattered the stonework around them. As soon as they were set, they took up the suppressive fire, allowing Hawke's half of the team to come up and join them.

As he slid down beside Stoke, Hawke saw a shape tumble from the balcony railing, hitting the ground below. One of the shooters accompanying Stoke had scored a hit on one of the hostiles. The intensity of the incoming fire decreased by half. A moment later another well-placed shot found its mark, and the shooting stopped altogether, leaving only the wail of the alarm echoing across the compound.

"Balcony's clear," Stoke said over the comms. "Move up."

Hawke cautiously rose from cover, keeping his HK at the high ready, and surged forward, closing the final stretch to the villa's main entrance. Boomer and two of his team, who had come in from the opposite side, were already stacked at the entrance. He gave a tight nod as Hawke and his team slid into position behind them.

"Took your sweet time," Boomer muttered.

"You know how the boss man is," replied Stoke, grinning. "Easily distracted. Saw something shiny, had to stop and pick it up."

"What's our situation?" asked Hawke.

"Light resistance," said Boomer. Stoke stifled a laugh, which prompted Boomer to add, "Nothing we couldn't handle. No friendly casualties. I've got Cookie, Bumper, and Modo watching the back of the house. Found a garage on the west side of the property. Six vehicles inside. Two nice SUVs. We'll be riding in style when it's time to roll."

"Mulmuscovy and Gul?"

Boomer shook his head. "Haven't seen them yet. They're either in the house or they were never here to begin with."

"They're inside," said Hawke. "These chaps wouldn't have put up this much of a fight to protect an empty house."

"Then what are we doing out here?" asked Stoke.

"The guys we took down looked like local muscle," said Boomer. "If Mulmuscovy has his Bastards in there with him, we're going to have our work cut out for us."

"If we wanted easy, we'd be playing golf right now," said Stoke.

"Stoke's right," added Hawke. "We need to get this done. I'm sure they'll already have sent out a distress call. We'll go in hard and fast. Overwhelm them."

"Shock and awe, baby," crooned Stoke.

"Stack up," Hawke said as he reached into a pouch on his rig and pulled out a fragmentation grenade.

Stoke smirked. "Not going to use a flash-bang?"

"Not really feeling that charitable."

They moved into position, lining up in two groups on either side of the heavy wooden double doors. Hawke took the front position on the right with the rest of Red Team, while Boomer and the two remaining men from Blue Team took the left. Hawke stripped the safety band from the grenade and then, with his fingers clamped over the spook, pulled the pin.

"Now, Stoke."

Stoke unslung the Mossberg 500 shotgun he'd been lugging along, took aim at the door's lower hinge, and fired. The report was stunningly loud, especially after the barely audible claps of the suppressed HK417s, even to the men who were expecting it, and through a haze of smoke Hawke saw a dinner plate–sized hole in the door. Stoke calmly racked the pump, advancing another shell, and then blasted the upper hinge.

Remarkably, the door remained upright, held in place by the frame and the lock bolt, but when Stoke reared back and drove a boot into it, it went crashing inward.

Hawke opened his hand, letting the spoon fly, counted to three, and then lobbed the grenade into the foyer.

"Frag out!"

No sooner were the words out when an eruption of smoke and debris shot out the open doorway like a blast from a cannon. Simultaneously, several of the front windows burst out of their frames in a shower of glittering fragments. Because the sturdy walls of the house were between them and the explosion, the noise of the blast wasn't even as loud as the shotgun, but Hawke felt the resulting pressure wave like a punch to the gut. Nevertheless, he swung his rifle up and shouted, "Go, go, go," hooked around the doorframe, and entered the smoke-filled interior.

Splinters and shards of glass crunched underfoot as Hawke advanced, moving quickly to clear the doorway and let the rest of the team enter behind him. The foyer was a wreck. The grenade had done its job spectacularly. Smoke still hung thick in the air, swirling with the dust knocked loose from the ceiling. The walls near the blast point were shredded, wood paneling stripped down to raw beams, and plaster blown out in jagged craters. A chandelier that had once hung in the center of the vaulted room now dangled at a sharp angle, most of its crystal ornaments blown loose by the concussive force. But it was what he didn't see that concerned Hawke the most.

No bodies.

The grenade had blown out all the lights in the foyer, but the corridors leading deeper into the house were glowing brightly in his goggles—so brightly that he had to switch them off and swivel them up and out of the way. The monochrome display was replaced by a deep gloom, the artificial light ahead now merely a diffuse, hazy glow.

Suddenly a burst of gunfire ripped through the smoke. Rounds struck the far wall, chipping away plaster and sending splinters flying.

"Contact front!" Boomer shouted, dropping to a knee and returning fire.

The team moved in tactical precision, peeling off to take cover behind whatever remained standing. Stoke ducked behind an overturned side table, his rifle already swinging toward the source of the incoming fire.

Hawke spotted movement beyond the wreckage—shadows shifting behind the remains of an archway that led deeper into the house. The Bastards had picked their ground well. They were dug in, using the inner rooms as a natural choke point.

"Wanna try another frag?" suggested Stoke.

"Bad idea," countered Boomer. "You'll bring the place down on top of us."

"Well, we're not getting through that doorway without catching lead."

Hawke's mind raced. Charging headlong into a bottleneck would be suicide. The Bastards had set up a solid defensive position, and with the house still standing, they had the advantage. He needed to disrupt them.

He keyed his mic. "Bumper, light up the back of the house. Shoot high. Cans off. Make it loud."

A double click of the mic signaled acknowledgment.

A moment later a burst of unsuppressed gunfire erupted from the rear of the house. The sharp bark of suppressed rounds was followed by the crack of glass shattering and the thump of bullets striking wood and plaster. The hostile shooters reacted just as Hawke hoped: shifting their attention, their fire faltering as some of them pivoted to address the new threat.

"Go! Go!" Hawke ordered.

He surged forward, Stoke and Boomer right on his heels, the rest of the team fanning out in pairs to clear their sectors. Stoke reached the edge of the archway first, snapping off a pair of quick shots as he stormed through and hooked to the left. Hawke was right behind him, turning right, sweeping his sector. He saw one of Mulmuscovy's Bastards ducking down behind an overturned table, his weapon—a pistol—aimed in Hawke's direction. Hawke snapped off a shot at the same instant the Bastard pulled his trigger.

Hawke felt an impact like a sledgehammer to the chest as the Bastard's bullet slammed into the ESAPI plate over his heart. Pain flared across his ribs, a deep, spreading ache that made every breath feel like he'd been kicked by a horse, but he stayed on his feet, gritting his teeth against the bruising throb settling into his sternum, kept his weapon trained on the enemy, and snapped off a second shot. There was no need for it, however; his first round had neatly divided the Bastard's eyes.

Gunfire erupted from a doorway, bullets stitching the wall behind Hawke. He turned toward the source and glimpsed the familiar if somewhat disfigured face of the man he'd dubbed Scar-Jaw ducking back behind the doorframe. Hawke shifted his aim about six inches behind the jamb and fired a burst on full auto. Half a dozen rounds punched through the wall in a grouping about the diameter of a poker chip. A moment later Scar-Jaw pitched forward, falling face down in the doorway, where he lay unmoving, a significant portion of his skull missing.

An ominous silence fell over the house. Even the alarms had gone quiet.

"Search the house," ordered Hawke. "Mulmuscovy and Gul are here somewhere. But stay sharp. This might not be the last of them."

The team split up, weapons at the ready, sweeping the house from top to bottom, clearing every room. They encountered no further resistance; nor did they find their quarry among the dead.

"Got something," Boomer called out from the great room on the ground floor. Hawke and Stoke joined him in front of a cleverly concealed doorway that now stood open, revealing a descending staircase beyond.

"Hidden passage," said Hawke. "Clever bastards."

"If this leads to an escape tunnel, then they're long gone," said Stoke.

"Well, let's just find out." Hawke took point, rifle at the ready, moving cautiously onto the stairs, half expecting to walk into an ambush. Instead, the steps brought him to a heavy vault door that looked like it might have been designed to secure a nuclear missile command center.

"Well, that complicates things," said Stoke, coming up behind Hawke with Boomer in tow.

"Boomer, did we bring enough C-4 to blow through that?"

Boomer shook his head. "Not enough C-4 in the world to crack this open. You'd have better luck with a nuke."

Stoke made a tsking sound. "I knew we should have packed one. Guess we could try knocking?"

Before Hawke could answer, a voice crackled through an unseen speaker, smooth and smug, with a faint accent. "No need, gentlemen. We won't be opening for you."

Hawke looked around for the source of the voice and spotted an intercom speaker mounted to the wall nearby next to a video screen displaying a live feed. "General Gul, I presume."

"Lord Hawke. I wish I could say it's a pleasure, but that would be a lie. You are annoyingly persistent. However, this is as far as you will get. You will not get through that door, but please feel free to try."

Hawke shot a glance at Boomer. "You're sure there's nothing we can do?"

The big Comanche shrugged. "We could drop the house on them. Wouldn't hurt 'em, but digging them out would be a son of a bitch."

"He's stalling," said Stoke. "Trying to run out the clock."

"Very perceptive," said Gul, sounding a little irritated. "In fact, the Venezuelan military is already en route. I don't think even you are formidable enough to survive an encounter with them."

"Figured as much," said Stoke. "We'd better get moving, boss."

"You may have played to a stalemate, Gul," said Hawke, "but you won't be able to hide here forever."

"I won't need to. This is only a temporary reversal of fortune. I have plans and contingencies which you cannot fathom. Soon . . . very soon, I will make my triumphant return. And when I do, I will make dealing with you my first priority."

"Boss . . ." Stoke urged.

Hawke raised a hand to forestall his friend. "Is Sergei in there with you?"

There was a faint rustling sound and then Mulmuscovy's voice issued from the speaker a heartbeat before his face appeared on the live feed. "What do you want, Hawke?"

"Does your friend in there really think he's going to come out of this alive?"

Mulmuscovy took a long moment to answer. "He's very resourceful."

"You're hedging, Sergei. You know better." He paused a beat, then went on. "Let's make a deal."

There was another long pause. Hawke thought he could hear Gul snorting derisively, but then Mulmuscovy spoke. "I'm listening."

"Open the door," Hawke said. "Let us have Gul and you walk. Free as a bird. Your plane's still at the airport. You can go anywhere you like. Anywhere that'll have you, at least. I won't come after you."

A sharp bark of laughter came over the speaker. "And why in God's name would he trust you?" said Gul.

"Because I give my word."

"Your word," scoffed Gul. "What is that worth?"

Mulmuscovy, however, said nothing.

"We both know Gul is the real prize here," Hawke continued. "The big fish." He shrugged. "Some would even say you did the world a favor by getting rid of Volodya."

Gul spoke again, an oily sheen to his words. "This desperate ploy is really very flattering, Hawke. It tells me that you *do* fear my—"

Mulmuscovy, his eyes suddenly cold as ice as he looked into the camera, interrupted. "Do you give your word as an English gentleman?"

"I do," Hawke said without hesitation.

"Sergei, you can't trust—" Gul started to say, but Mulmuscovy cut him off again.

"I'll make a counterproposal. Leave now, while you still can. I will take care of Osman Gul."

The man's face and hands were pleading. "Sergei—"

"Deal," said Hawke.

"What?" Gul's voice was sharp now, desperate. "Sergei, put that down!"

The video feed was dark and grainy, but even so, Hawke's eyes were glued to the screen. There was a single flash of light. Then a tortured burst of static erupted from the intercom, the report of the pistol so loud that it overloaded the microphone. The speaker crackled for a moment, and then Mulmuscovy's face filled the screen. His voice came through, now sounding tinny. "It's done."

Hawke inclined his head. "So it is." He glanced over at Stoke. "I think we'll call it a win."

"Good. Then let's get the hell out of here."

SIXTY-THREE

THE CARIBBEAN SEA

Three hours after making his bargain with Sergei Mulmuscovy, Alex Hawke, aboard one of a trio of heavy inflatable boats, made a triumphant rendezvous with the *Blackhawke* a little more than fifty miles northeast of Margarita Island. The sea had been rough on the ride out, the chop hammering the hulls of the RIBs, sending cold spray over the operators huddled low in their seats and generally pummeling their internal organs, but none of that could dispel the generally good mood shared by one and all. They were returning from a successful mission—*mostly* successful, anyway—with all hands and no injuries, and that was nothing to be taken lightly in their line of work.

Tommy Quick stood on the swim platform at the *Blackhawke*'s stern along with two of the crew, waiting to receive them. As Hawke's boat nosed up to the platform, Quick gripped the grab rope, which ran along the top of the inflated gunwale, steadying the boat so that its half dozen occupants could off-load.

"About time," he said as Hawke clambered over. "You had us worried. Thought maybe you'd stopped for drinks."

"Almost wish I had," replied Hawke, stepping onto the platform. The trip, which should have taken only about an hour—not including the overland journey from Mulmuscovy's refuge to the shore where the boats were waiting—had taken considerably longer due not so much to the rough seas as to the need to chart an erratic course in order to avoid detection by Venezuelan coast guard patrols.

His chest still ached from the bullet impact to his body armor, but he remained sanguine about the experience. A bruise, after all, was preferable to a body bag.

He turned and lent his assistance to Quick, holding the boat steady as Stoke climbed over the RIB's gunwale, followed by the other operators from T and L. When the last man was out, one of the crewmates clipped a four-point yoke that dangled from the davit mounted on the aft main deck high above to lifting points affixed to the boat. With a signal to the operator, the davit's hydraulic winch engaged, taking up the slack before slowly hoisting the RIB out of the water. The boat rose smoothly, swinging away as it was lifted up onto the stern deck, positioned to make room for the next.

Hawke clapped Quick on the shoulder. "I think I'll go find that drink now."

"Miss Guinness is waiting for you in the salon."

"Of course she is," said Hawke, laughing. "Mustn't keep Mother waiting." He turned to Stoke, who was just starting up the companionway to the stern deck. "Join me for a Diet Coke in the salon? Celebrate a job well done?"

Stoke glanced at him sidelong. "You drinking Diet Coke now?"

"I didn't say *I* was going to have one," replied Hawke with a wink.

Stoke laughed. "Think I'll pass. Been a long night and I need my beauty sleep. Besides, I don't think you and Pippa need a chaperone."

Hawke started to fire back a retort but hesitated. He hadn't thought of Pippa that way in years—hadn't allowed himself to. Whatever fire they'd once shared had long since cooled, especially since Asia came back into his life. His relationship with Pippa was professional. Friendly . . . comfortable.

But then again, he and Asia were now charting uncertain waters, weren't they?

As he watched Stoke climb the companionway, he wondered if his friend was just teasing or if maybe he was picking up on something Hawke wasn't even aware of.

He shook it off and climbed the steps, making his way to the salon, where he found Pippa seated at the table, studying the display of an iPad. A fine china teapot sat steaming on a tray beside two delicate cups, along with a small plate of biscuits.

She looked up to meet his gaze as he entered, then nodded toward the service. "Tea's hot."

"If it's all the same, I think I'd rather have something a bit stronger." He went to the teak bar in one corner of the salon and fetched a bottle of Goslings Black Seal. He poured a generous measure into a tumbler, then looked to Pippa. "Care for a shot?"

"Thanks but I'll pass."

Hawke shrugged, raising the glass in a mock toast before taking a slow, savoring sip. The dark rum burned pleasantly as it went down.

No better way to end the day, he thought.

Pippa watched him for a moment before speaking. "You'll be interested to know that Mulmuscovy's plane took off from Margarita Island ninety minutes ago."

Hawke eyed the bottle, contemplating another tot. Pippa was aware of the deal he'd made with the Russian oligarch; he'd radioed her with the news before leaving the compound. It pained him a little to know that the man who had framed him for murder and gotten him thrown into Lubyanka Prison would live to see another sunset, but Gul was the bigger prize, and a deal was a deal. He just didn't know how Pippa felt about it.

"His plane broke up over the Atlantic," she went on, a hint of a smile raising the corner of her mouth.

"Ah. A happy ending after all, then." Hawke splashed three fingers of rum into the tumbler, then went over to the table and sank wearily into a chair across from her. "Your doing?"

She spread her hands in a show of innocence.

Hawke gave a thoughtful hum. "No. Not your style. I expect one of Volodya's friends called in the butcher's bill."

"The SVR have used that method of assassination before," agreed Pippa.

Hawke took another sip of rum, letting the warmth settle in his chest as he turned the glass in his fingers. With Mulmuscovy's death, he could close the book on his mission—both his missions, really. The Warmonger, Osman Gul, was dead. And the mission for the King, whether a fool's errand or something of real historical significance, was complete. The alleged letter from King George V condemning the Romanovs to their fate was gone, turned to pulp during his immersion in the Black Sea. In the end, it didn't matter whether it had been authentic or not.

"So that's it, then," he said. "Crisis averted. Mission accomplished."

She shrugged. "Your part of it, at least. Things in Russia are going to be . . ."

Hawke laughed. "It's Russia. No need to say any more."

"You're not wrong. But for the time being, I think it will be a problem for the diplomats. We've done our bit." She took a sip of tea. "So, what's next for you? Rest and recover, I should hope. Shall I tell Tommy to set course for Bermuda?"

Hawke shook his head. "Not just yet. There's something else I need to see to."

She set her tea down. "Silence?"

Hawke nodded. "She's still out there. This won't really be over until I've dealt with her. For myself and for Ambrose."

Pippa studied him for a long moment. "Alex . . . you almost died."

"Believe me, I haven't forgotten. I intend to bring that up when I find Ariadne Silk . . . or Isaline Durand, or whatever the hell she's calling herself."

"That's not what I mean."

He cocked his head to the side. "Well, Pip, what the hell *do* you mean?"

She pursed her lips. "Forgive me if I'm stepping out of line here, but don't you think it might be a good idea to patch things up with Anastasia?"

Hawke felt his jaw go tight. His first impulse was to dismiss the question outright, wave it off with some deflection about how Anastasia knew what she had signed up for. Hadn't she told him as much?

But the truth was he didn't know how to answer her. The last time he'd seen Asia, there had been nothing but cold fury in her eyes. She had saved him, and he had repaid her by diving right back into the fray. Could he blame her if she had finally had enough?

He narrowed his gaze at Pippa. "You're right. You *are* stepping out of line. It's none of your concern."

"You're not just living for yourself, Alex," she pressed. "There are people in your life who care about you and, if nothing else, you owe them an explanation before you run off and gamble with your life again. If you had died, or if we hadn't been able to get you out of Lubyanka, you would have left Alexei without a father. Do you ever stop and think about that?"

Hawke exhaled sharply and set his glass down.

More than you'll ever know, he wanted to say.

But what was he supposed to do? Walk away from the fight? Live out his days at Teakettle Cottage, playing catch with the boy and pretending the world wasn't full of men like Mulmuscovy and Gul? He had seen what happened when they weren't brought to heel. If he didn't do it, then who would?

"Of course I think about it," he said, not meeting her gaze. "I lost my father . . . both my parents, when I was just a little younger than Alexei. But I do what I do *because* of Alexei. Because of the world he's going to inherit."

"Do you really? Or is that just an excuse you use to avoid dealing with what really matters?"

Hawke's jaw tightened. "Meaning?"

"Family is important, Alex. You can't keep running away from it. You need to nurture it."

Family.

The word felt heavier than it should. He had spent his life *moving*, never putting down roots, running from one fight to the next. He told himself that it was for the greater good, God and country, duty and honor, a future for Alexei and all the world's children. But the truth—the one he never let himself look at for too long—was far less noble.

The idea of standing still terrified him. Settling down wasn't just about taking his boots off and calling a place home. It meant accountability. It meant permanence. And permanence meant accepting the possibility of failure.

What if I'm not any good at it?

But while he ran from that fear, Alexei got older. And his feelings for Asia got colder. How long before there was nothing left to go back to? How long before he had traded the only thing that truly mattered for a lifetime of war?

He exhaled slowly, staring down into his glass, debating whether to go back to the bar and pour another. He let his head hang for a moment, then gave a slow nod.

"You're right," he admitted, the words tasting bitter. "You're right. I just . . . bloody well don't know *how*."

She regarded him quietly. "Nobody really does, Alex. You just do it. And you figure out how along the way."

He raised his eyes to her. "No offense, Pip, but you're hardly the one to be giving advice on the subject." He could see that the words cut her, deeper than he'd intended. But, really, who was she to lecture him on family?

For a moment he thought she might burst into tears, sweep herself out of the room, out of his toxic presence.

But she didn't. She just stared at him, wheels turning behind her eyes. Then, holding his gaze, she folded her hands on the tabletop.

"Alex, there's something I need to tell you. Something I . . . I should have told you years ago. I promised myself I never would, but I think it's time for you to know."

"What is it?"

Even as he said it, some instinct told Hawke that he didn't want to know the answer, but she told him anyway.

INTERLUDE—PART TEN

MOSCOW, SOVIET RUSSIA
APRIL 1918

I can prove that what I've told you is true," Alexander said one day before the bigger of his two regular tormentors commenced with the customary "softening up."

The interrogator raised a hand to postpone the beating. "And just how do you propose to do that?"

"Let me talk to Dzerzhinsky." He knew better than to trust this information to an underling. "I'll tell him everything."

The interrogator appeared to consider this while the big guard began administering blows. When the beating stopped, the guards stepped back to reveal Iron Felix himself.

"What is this proof you claim to have?" asked the head of the Cheka.

Alexander told his story with difficulty. His tormentors had largely avoided striking him in the face, so his mouth was uninjured, but the blows to his torso made breathing painful; he spoke in short gasps. "I told you that I was sent by the King . . . King George. Responding to a letter from Yakob Sverdlov . . . Natalya brought it to him."

"Comrade Sverdlov has categorically denied sending such a letter."

Alexander pressed on. "What I didn't tell you is that he . . . King

George . . . gave me a letter . . . a reply in his own hand. I was to deliver it to . . . Sverdlov."

Alexander felt no sense of betrayal at revealing the existence of the King's letter. It would eventually be found anyway, unearthed by a gardener tasked with planting flowers in the big planter.

Dzerzhinsky stroked his chin thoughtfully. "My agents told me that you carried a letter. It was not in your possession when you were arrested, so I assumed its existence was just part of the deception. Now you say it exists?"

"It does."

"Where is it?"

"I hid it."

"Where?"

"Alexander Station."

"Where, precisely?"

Alexander shook his head. "I don't know how to describe it, but I can show you if you take me there."

This was a small but calculated lie, but the possibility that he might not die in a dungeon under the Cheka headquarters building gave him a sliver of hope in his darkest hour. It was what kept him going when Dzerzhinsky showed his disdain for this offer by having the interrogator change the focus of the questions. He swore to himself that he would die before simply giving up that last bit of himself. He was going to die anyway, so what did he have to lose?

The nightmare resumed.

But then two or three days later, the cycle of torture and imprisonment was interrupted. The guards did not enter the cell as they normally did to drag him out but instead tossed something at him, and his interrogator, who had never visited the cell, called out, "Put them on."

In the dim light filtering through the door, he saw that they had given him back his clothes. He pulled them on and was aghast at how loosely they hung on his gaunt frame. Once dressed, he quickly thrust his hands into his pockets, checking to see if his captors had emptied them. They had. His counterfeit traveling credentials were gone, as was his wallet, pen, and notebook. But then his fingers closed on a small square of folded paper—an object so commonplace that the Bolsheviks had not even bothered to take it—and his heart soared.

The big guard entered and grabbed him by the upper arm, but instead of forcibly pulling him along, the man merely supplied just enough pressure to compel Alexander to walk under his own power. He was led down the all-too-familiar corridor, but instead of turning into the interrogation room, they led him into parts of the dungeon he had not previously seen—he'd been blindfolded when brought to this prison—eventually coming to a heavy iron door. The interrogator rapped sharply on it, the metal ringing like a gong in the dank stillness, and then a bolt slid back. The door groaned open, and the journey continued up two flights of stairs. Days of privation had left Alexander with barely enough energy to make the ascent, but his captors did not allow him the luxury of a rest break. A maze of hallways followed, and then the party emerged into a lobby with a glass-paned door, where for the first time in days—or perhaps weeks—Alexander Hawke saw daylight. He shielded his eyes with a trembling hand as the guards urged him forward.

They emerged onto a busy street, the noise and activity jarring after the suffocating silence of the prison. Crowds bustled along the sidewalks, faces weary and pale beneath heavy coats and scarves. Horse-drawn carts clattered over the uneven cobblestones, mingling with the occasional rumble of an automobile. A tram rattled by, its bell clanging as it threaded its way through the throng.

Alexander had just a moment to look back at the enormous yellow brick building in which he had been all but entombed before the guard compelled him into motion, steering him toward a waiting motorcar parked at the curb. Long and elegant, with custom coachwork, the automobile was distinctly bourgeois. No doubt, it had once belonged to a wealthy aristocrat, perhaps even the Tsar himself. Seated in the cabin behind the driver was none other than "Iron" Felix Dzerzhinsky himself.

One guard opened the coach door, and the other thrust Alexander forward into the open compartment. Somewhat awkwardly, he got himself onto the seat beside Dzerzhinsky. The head of the Cheka sat rigidly upright, his expression unreadable. He gave Alexander a brief sidelong glance but said nothing. Alexander thought it best not to break the silence. One guard slid into the driver's seat while his counterpart went to the front to crank-start the engine, and then they were off, rolling through the unfamiliar streets of Moscow.

The journey felt both interminable and strangely fleeting. Alexander's mind raced, running through every possible outcome of what lay ahead. He had only a vague idea of what he was going to do, and much of it would depend on luck, but he was certain of one thing: he would not let them take him back to the Cheka dungeon.

When they arrived at the train station, the bigger guard opened the rear door and pulled Alexander out, keeping a firm grip on his biceps. Neither the guards nor Dzerzhinsky displayed weapons, but Alexander felt certain they were armed.

"Now, Lord Hawke," said Dzerzhinsky, "where is this letter from your king?"

"It's inside near the . . ." He faltered as if suddenly unsure of his memory. "Near the . . . ticketing hall, I think it was."

Dzerzhinsky studied him for a moment, his gaze piercing. Finally, he gave a curt nod to the guards and said something in Russian. The guard tightened his grip on Alexander's arm and propelled him toward the station entrance. Dzerzhinsky followed.

Alexander's thoughts churned as they passed into the station. He had bought himself a little more time, but not much. Every step brought them closer to the moment when he would have to reveal the letter's hiding place, and he still didn't know exactly how he was going to turn this to his advantage.

The ticketing hall was a cavernous space, its vaulted ceilings stretching high above the bustling crowd. The counters along one wall were manned by harried clerks, each window marked with hand-lettered signs denoting destinations. Travelers queued with luggage in tow, a chaotic mix of weary refugees, uniformed soldiers, and ordinary citizens clutching worn leather satchels.

Alexander paused at the edge of the hall, his gaze darting around. He feigned uncertainty, letting his expression shift from confusion to strained recollection. “No,” he muttered, shaking his head. “This doesn’t look right.”

Dzerzhinsky stepped up beside him, his dark eyes narrowing. “What doesn’t look right?”

Alexander gestured vaguely toward the counters. “I thought it was near here, but now I’m not sure. It’s been . . . weeks. Where else did we go?”

Dzerzhinsky’s lip curled into a sneer, but he said nothing, watching as Alexander pressed a hand to his forehead as though trying to force the memory back.

“Oh, I remember now. It was near the telegraph office.” He turned to Dzerzhinsky and managed a relieved smile. “That’s where I hid it. You’ll see. The letter will clear everything up.”

Dzerzhinsky’s gaze bored into him, then he nodded for them to proceed. They moved through the hall and found the corridor that led to the telegraph office. Alexander’s pulse quickened as he laid eyes on the little garden courtyard. Everything was exactly as he had left it. His mouth was suddenly very dry.

“It’s there,” he said, pointing to the courtyard. “That’s where I hid it.” He pointed to the corner near the planter. “Behind there.”

One of the guards moved to the spot and crouched down, patting around the base of the planter. He came up empty-handed, looking back at Dzerzhinsky with a shake of his head.

“It has to be there,” Alexander insisted, feigning agitation. He stepped toward the planter, only to have the second guard block his path. He looked to Dzerzhinsky, who gave a terse nod.

Alexander moved over to the planter, looking where the guard had looked, then moved to another planter—the one where he had concealed the letter. He started to kneel but then caught himself. "I remember now," he said quickly. "I buried it."

Without waiting, he dug his fingers into the dry soil, scooping out clumps of dirt. His pulse thundered in his ears when his fingertips at last brushed the oilcloth pouch. With a deliberate motion, he pulled it free, holding it aloft as if to present it to Dzerzhinsky.

And then, fueled by a burst of adrenaline, he bolted.

Dzerzhinsky's voice rang out behind him, sharp and commanding, but Alexander didn't look back. He didn't dare. Clutching the oilcloth pouch to his chest, he sprinted toward the main hall of the station, weaving through travelers stunned into paralysis by the commotion. His energy reserves were quickly dissipating—hunger and torture had left him depleted—but desperation was a cruelly effective motivator.

He made it back to the ticket hall, hoping to lose himself among the masses, but the shouts of his pursuers cut through the clamor, turning heads and parting the crowds that Alexander had hoped would give him cover. He risked a glance over his shoulder and saw them closing the gap.

He veered down a corridor leading to one of the platforms, weaving around arriving travelers laden down with luggage. A moment later he burst onto the platform and looked about wildly for any avenue of escape. Directly ahead, a recently arrived train sat hissing and rumbling, steam still wafting from beneath its massive wheels while its disembarking passengers made their way toward the exit.

He plunged into their midst, no longer trying to move around them but plowing straight ahead, shoving people out of his way. The commotion intensified as Dzerzhinsky's men reached the platform, shouting in Russian.

His lungs were burning as he reached the end of the platform, but he didn't slow. Instead, he vaulted off the edge and landed heavily on the gravel-strewn tracks. Pain jolted up his legs, but he ignored it and kept going. The rails stretched out before him, joining with other tracks in a web of steel converging and curving gently out of sight.

A sharp crack split the air behind him, followed by another and another. Gunshots. He ducked instinctively, the terror of prey overtaking reason. Dzerzhinsky's men hadn't dared shoot at him inside the crowded station, but out here, on the tracks, with no one else in the line of fire, they felt no cause for restraint. But in order to take aim, they were obliged to halt their pursuit. Alexander felt a faint surge of hope as his lead widened.

Then it happened.

Something struck him in the back, just below his shoulder blade, with a force that felt like a hammerblow. It drove the air from his lungs, sending him stumbling forward but not falling. Not yet. There was no pain—only a horrible, chilling sensation.

He didn't need to look to know. He'd been shot.

His body continued moving on instinct alone, legs pumping even as his mind screamed at him to stop, to fall, to rest. But there was no time. He knew now, with the clarity of a wounded animal, that this run would be his last. Every step was borrowed time, a few precious moments stolen from the void that loomed ahead. The edges of his vision darkened, a creeping fog that threatened to swallow him whole.

Another step. Another.

He had known, from the moment he told Dzerzhinsky about the letter, that this would be his fate. He could not hope to escape the train station, much less all of Russia. He was resigned . . . no, not resigned: *resolved* to face death on his own terms. There was just one last duty to perform.

Without stopping, he tore open the oilcloth pouch, reached into it with trembling fingers, and took out the King's letter. He clutched the parchment, let the pouch fall away, and then reached into his pocket for the tiny square of folded paper his captors hadn't bothered to remove.

The matchbook.

He dropped to his knees, the gravel cold and unyielding beneath him. His strength was failing, his breaths shallow and ragged. He could feel the life draining out of him.

His fingers fumbled with the matchbook. He struggled to tear out one of the paper matches, and when he tried to strike it, the sulfur head crumbled uselessly.

But the second match caught, and as it flared to life, he held it to the parchment, watching as the flame began to spread, consuming the letter's elegant script, curling the edges into blackened ruin. The firelight danced in his fading vision, the only warmth in a world now utterly cold. The darkness surged forward to claim him, but his lips curved faintly into the barest hint of a smile.

In his own way, he had done his duty.

EPILOGUE

TEAKETTLE COTTAGE, BERMUDA
PRESENT DAY

Alex Hawke stood still as stone, his heart thumping in his chest, gazing out toward the horizon. He took a breath to calm his nerves—but calm his nerves it did not.

He had felt this way once before, a moment he remembered all too well.

All around him, the wind was picking up, ruffling the palms that lined the narrow pathway leading to the edge of the cliffs. The sky, already heavy with clouds, draped itself in a muted palette of grays and silvers as if drained of all vibrancy. Out beyond the shoreline, the ocean stretched wide and endless, a dark, rolling expanse reflecting the brooding mood of the heavens.

Bloody hell, thought Hawke. *Why am I so bloody anxious?*

But he knew the answer to his own question. In a word: *family*.

The situation with Anastasia remained unresolved. Their last exchange had been brief—polite but distant, a conversation between people who shared a common interest, namely their son, but no longer knew how to bridge the gulf that separated them. She was presently in the South of France with Alexei, waiting for him to decide if he was going to be part of their lives or merely an occasional shadow passing through.

Hawke still didn't know which it would be, but had promised himself that they would soon have the conversation he had been avoiding for too long.

After this.

Checking his watch, more out of nervous habit than a need to know the time, he remained at the edge of the overlook, watching the slowly approaching front. It had begun as a distant smudge on the horizon, a ripple in the clouds, but now it was a formidable presence—a hulking mass of dark thunderheads, thick and ominous, flashing with jagged bolts of lightning, lumbering forward like some ancient god.

Behind him a door opened and Pelham spoke. "Sir, they've just arrived. Would you like to come to greet them out front?"

Hawke swallowed hard. "No, no, old chap. Kindly show them inside, won't you? I'll be along presently."

"Are you sure, sir?"

He was not sure. Not thinking clearly at all. In truth, Hawke merely wanted a few more moments to process what was about to take place. He was stalling, to be sure, but maybe a few more seconds was what he needed to gather his wits.

"I'm sure. Invite them in, please."

"As you wish, m'lord."

A moment later the door shut and Hawke was alone again.

Below him the sea churned, already restless in anticipation of the coming fury. Whitecaps smashed against the jagged rocks, sending up sprays of mist that hung in the air like specters, dissolving into the salty breeze. The front hadn't reached the island yet, but the air felt alive with anticipation, charged with the electric hum of what was to come.

"A new storm," Hawke murmured, but he wasn't talking about the weather.

He breathed in deeply, the scent of rain now undeniable, and felt the first cool drops begin to pepper his face, beading up on his shirt-front. He knew he should go indoors and greet his guests in the warm shelter of the cottage's interior. It was, after all, a bit mad to greet them out here in the midst of the storm, wasn't it?

I should think so, yes.

Reluctantly, he turned and headed for the balcony door, but before he got there, it opened. He stopped, frozen, his breath caught in his chest. Pippa Guinness stood in the doorway regarding him furtively, clearly as apprehensive as he was.

"Hello, Alex."

"Hullo, Pip," said Hawke. Though he fought to appear calm, the pitch of his voice betrayed him. He cleared his throat, then added, "I hope the flight over was pleasant."

She gave a tense nod but said nothing. This wasn't the time for small talk.

He glanced past Pippa, looking for . . . *her*, but Pippa appeared to be alone. "Where is she?" asked Hawke, barely able to get the words past the lump in his throat.

Pippa hesitated, then turned slightly and gestured toward the doorway behind her. "She's just outside. I think she's just as nervous as we are."

"I very much doubt that." He followed Pippa through the house to the open front door where Pelham had stationed himself as if standing guard.

At the threshold, Pippa turned to him. "Before you meet her, I want you to understand . . . This wasn't easy for me. I made a choice. Maybe it was the wrong choice, but at the time I truly thought I was doing what was best."

"And now?"

It took Pippa a moment to answer. "She deserves the chance to know you."

Hawke swallowed hard but said nothing.

Pippa turned toward the doorway again. "Amelia?"

A pause. Then, slowly, a figure stepped into view.

Hawke's breath caught.

The girl—no, *young woman*—stood hesitantly on the threshold. She was tall and slender, with long blond hair, every bit her mother's daughter, attired in a pink cashmere sweater and faded jeans. Droplets of rain were already gathering in her hair and on her brow, running down her face like tears. She stood slightly askance, her weight balanced on one foot as if preparing to turn and flee if the moment demanded it. Her ice-blue eyes stared deeply into his own.

"Alex," Pippa said slowly, turning back to him, "this is Amelia. And, Amelia . . ."

Hawke could barely hear her over the sound of his heart hammering in his chest and the crash of waves on the shore.

". . . this," Pippa finished, "is Lord Alex Hawke. Your father."

She was, thought Hawke, the most beautiful thing he had ever seen. And for the first time in his life, Hawke understood what it meant to experience love at first sight.

His eyes moved slowly to Pippa, then back to her daughter.

Our daughter, he thought. Another Hawke.

But of course she wasn't. He had not given her his name or much of anything else. She was Amelia Guinness.

"Hullo, Amelia," said Hawke, managing a smile. "It's so very good to meet you. How old are you?"

A flicker of hesitation crossed her face. "Thirteen."

Thirteen years.

It seemed like an eternity.

"Thirteen," he said. "My goodness. You might not believe this, but when I was thirteen, I was exactly the same age you are now."

For a long moment she just stared at him as if he'd sprouted a second head.

Then she smiled—a small, careful smile, like the first hint of sunlight breaking through the clouds.

The wind picked up again, the weather nearly upon them.

Pippa turned to Amelia. "Let's get inside before the rain gets worse."

Amelia tore her gaze away from Hawke and turned to Pippa. "Please, Mum, can't I stay out just a bit longer?"

Pippa turned to Hawke as if looking for his approval . . . or forgiveness. "Sorry," she said with a little shake of her head. "She's just always loved storms. I don't know why. It never made any sense to me, if I'm honest, but I can never seem to pull her away from them."

Hawke let out a breath he didn't realize he had been holding.

Of course, she loves storms. She is my daughter, after all. Another Hawke indeed, regardless of name. Hmm, yes. A little Hawke . . . my little birdy.

And suddenly Alex's world slowed, his anxiety vanishing in an instant. A smile formed on his face, which drew a question from Pippa.

"Something funny, Alex?"

Hawke nodded. "Well, not funny in the ha-ha sense, no. It's just that . . . well, I've always loved storms too." He went on, turning to Amelia: "In fact, when I was a young boy, I used to pray that they would never stop." He paused, then added, "We can stay outside as long as you'd like."

His daughter smiled at him, and once again Hawke felt his heart melt.

There were questions that needed answers, to be sure. Not the least of which involved Anastasia. And then there was Ambrose Congreve, a broken soul who needed his best, most dearest friend. Hawke wasn't at all sure what was next or what the future would hold, but even so, looking at Amelia, her face turned to the heavens as she marveled at the storm clouds around them, for the first time in his life, Alexander Hawke knew that somehow . . . some way . . . everything was going to be all right.

ACKNOWLEDGMENTS

First, I would like to thank Ted Bell, my dear friend and mentor, for believing in me many years ago and for helping me gain a foothold in the publishing world. Never did I ever imagine, even in my wildest of dreams, that I would one day take over his series and get to write his characters.

Ted, I love you, my friend. Thank you . . . for everything.

I would also like to thank the talented team at Berkley for all their hard work. Tom Colgan is a legend, and working with him on these two books has been a dream come true for me. Tom, thank you for giving me the opportunity to continue Alex Hawke's legacy.

To my dear friend Byrdie Bell, thank you for trusting me with the awesome responsibility of carrying forward your dad's legacy. Getting to know you over the last two years has been like talking with your dad all over again, and as I've mentioned many times, I firmly believe he is looking down, laughing right along with us every time we talk. I have so much love for your family, Byrdie. Thank you. (And to baby Teddy, I hope you love discovering your grandpa's books one day, and that you take comfort in knowing what a special name you carry.)

John Talbot, it's crazy to think about now, but *Warmonger* is our seventh book together. I owe you so much, John, and I appreciate you far more than you know. Thank you for always being my biggest, fiercest champion. Your friendship means a great deal to me, as does your advice, feedback, and reassurance. I sure wouldn't be where I am today without you, so from the bottom of my heart, thank you.

To my wife, Melissa, and our precious children—Brynn, Ryan, Rylee, and Mitchell—I love you all more than life. Every hour I'm locked away in my office, writing and working, it's for you all. But that doesn't mean I always *want* to be pounding away on my keyboard, and sometimes it's hard not to look back and feel like life is moving far too fast. Like I've missed too many memorable, special moments. And yet, I am so thankful that God has blessed us beyond anything I've ever deserved. I love you all endlessly. And now that this book is done, here's to having a ton of fun and making lots of new memories.

My father, James Steck, is a huge Alex Hawke fan, and has sat patiently listening to me work out character and plot issues more times than I can count. But beyond that, it's regularly my parents, including my beautiful mother, Rhonda Steck, who step in to help when I'm locked away on deadline. From taking kids to gymnastics to Saturday morning breakfast dates and *so* much more, Mom and Dad, thank you so much for all that you do for me and my family.

Along with my parents, my inner circle includes my two best friends, Mikey and Emily Derhammer (names that readers of my Matthew Redd series may recognize), and I sincerely don't know what we would do without them. Guys, what more can I say? I love and appreciate both of you (and Lainey and forthcoming baby boy) more than I could ever express in the back of a book. I am so thankful to have you guys in our lives, and for how much you love my children. There're no BFFs I'd rather do life with than you.

To our brilliant narrator John Shea, the voice of Alex Hawke himself, thank you for your vote of confidence, friendship, and support. I hope you love this one, my friend. And to Cynthia Hornblower, thank you for everything you do to keep Ted's website up to date, along with all the other behind-the-scenes roles that you fill.

Lastly, to Ted's readers, thank you for taking the time to read *Ted Bell's Warmonger.* This book challenged me in ways I never expected, but it was a blast to write. As you likely picked up on, there are still some threads to pull on in Hawke's world, and I promise not to leave you hanging. There's a STORM coming, and I'm thrilled to announce that Alex Hawke will indeed return in 2027. We've got another fun announcement coming, too, one that will expand Hawke's universe in a way that die-hard fans will no doubt love.

So, stay tuned . . . because we're just getting started.